ANAMNESIS

TIMELESSNESS

BOOK 4

SUSANA IMAGINÁRIO

ISBN: 978-1-7398202-3-7 (hardback)
ISBN: 978-1-7398202-2-0 (paperback)
ISBN: 978-1-7398202-1-3 (ebook)

To all who made it this far.

I've made a huge mistake.

…

All right, fine. I've made many mistakes, of all shapes and sizes. This one is worse than most because I could have avoided it. I shouldn't have taken Zeus' soul as a trophy; I should have sent it to the Underworld, or better yet, destroyed it when I had the chance.

I should have acted as the monster everyone believes me to be.

But I wanted to prove them wrong. I wanted to be better, to be *good*. I was too proud to be a monster. And now my pride might have ruined everything: life, death, eternity itself. Because goodness, much like fairness, was not what they needed. They needed a monster able to stand up to other monsters, a monster willing to annihilate them.

They needed me.

While I thought I needed no one.

I was wrong, of course. And now none of us will get what we need. However, we might still get what we want.

ANAMNESIS 1

The Deal

Psyche stood on the balustrade of her prison overlooking the clouds.

There were always clouds below the gilded palace. She had no idea what lay beneath them, never mind how the palace remained in the sky in the first place. Such oddities no longer concerned her, for she knew well how easily the gods were able to subvert the immutable laws of reality that mortals had to abide by.

The sun was about to set. There would be no moon tonight, and Psyche could already see a few stars, the only company she had in the moments caught between light and darkness. She knew every constellation like the back of her hand and often fantasised if she were a goddess, she would visit every single one of those stars. Not just out of curiosity but because they were very, very far away – exactly where she wanted to be.

It'd been almost five years – one thousand eight hundred and one days to be exact – since the beginning of her captivity. No, that wasn't true. It'd been almost five years since her family left her to die on a mountaintop as an offering to a monster, and Zephyrus, the west wind, had carried her here. But she'd been a captive long before that happened. Psyche reckoned she'd been a captive since birth, restrained by circumstances, geography, culture, anatomy and gender. All humans were to some extent, but unlike most, she did not take her captivity easily. She had something many lacked: a mind of her own, and along with it, a will that would not allow itself to be restrained by anything. Or so she thought. The truth was, after years of isolation and torment at the hands of spiteful humans and capricious gods, her will was not what it used to be.

She'd tried to escape, of course, many times and in many desperate ways. She'd jumped out of windows and balconies, but the wind would always carry her back. She'd tried to starve herself, to open her veins, she'd even tried to set herself on fire once, but no amount of starvation would kill her, no blade would cut her, and no flame would catch on her inside the palace. It seemed the greatest restriction all mortals faced, their own mortality, was precisely the one she lacked. She'd laugh at the irony, except it wasn't that she couldn't die. She'd died many times – just not by her own hand. No, Psyche didn't laugh, nor did she dread or wish for death; she only feared the wait.

Get it over with, she said to the sun sinking slowly on the horizon.

Eros came mostly at night. He preferred to torment her in the dark. Not because he was shy or ugly, quite the contrary. The god of love was gorgeous, and he craved being looked at. He'd sculpted his features after Adonis, the most beautiful of mortals and a favourite of his mother, Aphrodite. But while Adonis' beauty, tempered with innocence and humility, shone beyond aesthetics, viciousness had tainted Eros' good looks, giving him a cruel sort of beauty. It suited him, since the reason he preferred the dark was because he saw perfectly in it, and Psyche didn't. He loved to keep her guessing about what he'd do next, dreading and sometimes wishing for his next move. He'd play with her senses in every way a malicious god could until she couldn't trust them anymore.

He didn't visit every night, though. Lately he rarely even showed up, in fact. And because he'd come the previous night, there was a good chance he'd leave her alone on this one. Then again, he also liked to break his patterns, change his behaviour, so she had no choice but to always expect his arrival, to be on guard for it.

To always be waiting.

She touched a burn on her breast and wondered, *What will it be tonight?* The belt, the chains, the rope…? Maybe the razors or maybe just his words. It could be anything, really, or any combination of things. The god of love never ran out of ways to hurt her. He'd been particularly vicious the previous night. She hoped that he would leave her alone for a few days, at least until her skin was fully healed. Eros never healed her completely. It was the only agency he'd left her: to heal alone so she would remember him during his absence. Every day she'd convince herself she would survive another night – and she did, for what choice did she have? – but sometimes in the moments right before dark, her resolution faltered, and the longer she waited, the harder it became to endure the wait.

Memories of the indignities he'd put her through

and all the ways he'd mistreated her ran through her mind while she waited, making her angry enough to scream. Psyche held on to the anger so she wouldn't break. But she was tired… She was so tired of holding on to anything.

In a moment of weakness, she jumped from the parapet onto the balcony and ran into the room, snatching up a candle from the candelabra along the way. She held the candle firmly in both hands as she knelt by the absurdly enormous four-poster bed that marked the centre of her perverted universe and began to cry. Psyche didn't cry often, for she knew how much Eros would relish those tears, but right then she didn't care. She had no one to talk to, nowhere to go. She didn't even dream anymore. She used to dream every night when she was a child, but Morpheus had no foothold in Eros' realm. Or perhaps he'd just abandoned her, like everyone else had. Her sobs turned to curses; curses turned to prayers. She knew she shouldn't pray, just like she knew she shouldn't cry. Prayers never helped, and worse, he could be listening. But she just had to say something, to express the unarticulated pain stuck in her throat before it suffocated her.

Psyche kept praying until after the last ray of sunlight had long vanished from the sky, and still she waited, gripping that waning candle as if it alone could keep the darkness at bay.

He probably won't come tonight, she finally allowed herself to believe. But as she was about to release a deep exhale of relief, she felt a presence. The anger flared again, this time at herself. She should have known better. Eros would never give her peace. Not while she breathed. And certainly not while she still hoped for a better life than the one chosen for her by the oracle at Delphi.

Psyche spared another glance at the dying flame in her hands and braced herself for whatever was to come next.

"I heard your prayers," a warm voice whispered behind her ear.

Psyche spun on her knees, tried to stand, lost her balance and half fell, half sat on the bed, bewildered. The man standing before her was tall and slim, dressed in black, with sleek hair to match, pointed ears, bluish skin, bright eyes and sharp canines displayed in a wicked smile. Not a mortal; that was obvious. But all gods she'd met preferred to look human – or at least nonthreatening to humans – while pretty much everything about this creature looked predatory.

"Who the fuck are you?" she asked, more than a bit disconcerted, for he certainly wasn't Eros. The god of love would never pick such an untrustworthy disguise to play with her.

"I am Loki." He spoke as if she should recognise the name.

"Loki what?"

He blinked, taken aback by the question. "Just Loki," he said slightly less haughtily.

"Never heard of you."

He seemed disappointed. "Oh, well… I don't suppose you hear much of anything in this place." He scowled at the walls, then gave her a roguish grin. "I have heard of you, and that's what matters."

In Psyche's experience, what mattered to a god differed greatly from what mattered to her.

She pointed the candle at him as if it were a dagger. "Why are you here?" She'd also very much like to know *how* he got there, for if he'd found a way in, perhaps she could use it as a way out, but chances were, she would not have the opportunity to use that knowledge depending on the why.

"I'm here to help you." His eyes burned blue as he spoke.

She almost laughed. *Help, indeed.* "You are a god." She uttered the word with loathing. "And gods don't *help*. At most, they facilitate our lives in order to promote their own agendas."

He tilted his head a fraction, pondering her assessment. "That's one way to put it. Another would be to appreciate the offer and take what you can from it."

"What do you want?" she insisted, too tired to argue semantics.

The god obviously didn't like being addressed in such a fashion. His nonchalant stance and tone shifted to one of defensive impatience. "My motives should be of no concern to you when you are the one benefiting from my actions, mortal."

"A god's actions are always selfish, their benefits short lived, and they always have too high a price," she said.

He pressed his lips in annoyance and leaned forward with narrowed eyes, inspecting her as her mother would a piece of embroidery for mistakes. "Such cynicism. Can't a god do something nice?"

"For a mortal? Tsk. That would be a first."

He blew out the candle. She cursed and rolled over the covers to the other side of the bed. When she looked back, he was nowhere to be seen. She could still smell him, though: an aroma of wet ash and lemongrass mixed with the lingering scent of beeswax and burned-out wick from the candle.

"You'll find I'm not like the other gods," his voice purred all around her.

No, she thought. That he wasn't. This god had to be a lot more powerful than most to be there uninvited and unchallenged.

Psyche ran to the balcony and the starlight, hoping Zephyrus was around to witness her predicament. Not that he'd ever done anything about it, mind. She reckoned he, too, enjoyed seeing her suffer.

Moments later Loki came strolling from the room, still smirking, head shaking, long coat billowing in the summer breeze. It was always summer in Eros' palace, the only thing she liked about the place. But right then, even that was of little comfort, for she knew well what gods like Loki did to mortals like her.

He stopped a few inches away, confident and amused. She had nowhere to go, so she didn't move. Her heart fluttered painfully inside her chest, but her breathing and posture remained steady. She could control that much at least.

"Don't be afraid. I won't hurt you," he said with a smile that almost looked sincere.

"You said you want to help me. How are you going to do that, exactly? And what's in it for you?" She kept her eyes on his when she spoke, her voice steadier than she felt, the questions a desperate attempt to buy more time to think of an escape.

"Your lover caused me a great deal of nuisance. I intend to return the favour," he said, leaning in for a kiss – or a bite. She really couldn't tell which.

"Right…" Psyche lowered her head, looking away. For a moment, swayed by the vertigo caused by his gaze, she'd almost considered the possibility that perhaps this dark deity could actually help her somehow. Now she saw her fate unfolding, and it wasn't a pretty sight. "You want to fuck me to get back at him."

Loki cupped her chin, forcing her to face him again. "Precisely."

"It's pointless. I have no power over Eros. I'm just his pet."

"A very special pet."

"When he finds out, do you think he's going to be mad at you?"

His lips brushed hers. "I certainly hope so."

"You say you want to help me, but you'll be punishing me for his actions instead, and then he'll punish me for yours!" It was impossible to keep the desolation from her tone.

Loki frowned. "I'm offering you the best night of your life. And after I'm done with you, he won't want you anymore. You'll be free." He pondered his statement. "Likely dead in your pantheon's Underworld, but still: free. That's what you want, isn't it? That's what you prayed for."

It was one of the many things she'd prayed for in her despair. It shouldn't count.

Anger welled up in her again. "Have you no mercy or compassion in your soul?" she asked without thinking. The answer was obvious.

"My soul" – he grinned as if the idea amused him – "is geared towards survival and self-interest."

"And vengeance, apparently."

"Yes," he hissed.

She slapped him. "And arrogance, ignorance, and narrow-minded spitefulness! The best night of my life? Do you realise what an arsehole you sound like? How offensive that is to me? Do you honestly believe mortals are so easily pleased? That *I* am so easily pleased? You gods are all so self-centred and clueless. You'll never understand the human heart. Had I an ounce of your power, I would make you understand."

Stars, it felt good to hit him, to shout in his face and just let it all out. But of course, there would be consequences. Psyche bit her cheek but kept her head high, prepared to face them.

His demeanour changed from menacing to bemused. The momentary affront giving way to a spark of delight. He squinted at her, as if actually seeing her for the first time. "Would you now?" he asked with a mischievous glint in his eyes.

"Yes!" she spat, still furious.

He moved to her side, massaging his cheek absently. "I'll amend my offer, then. *You* will carry out my vengeance for me."

"Huh?"

"You want control, mortal, but all you do is cry, curse, and complain. That will get you nowhere. Gods don't think like mortals, you see. And they really don't care that much for them, either. There's nothing you can do to us but annoy us with prayers, and by doing so, you give us the key to your heart's greatest desires. Foolish mortal." He spoke slowly, threateningly, and she almost jumped when he poked her on the forehead and said, "*You* don't understand how pathetic you are to us or how hard we restrain ourselves from making your short, wretched lives even more miserable."

Psyche swallowed the lump of dread and outrage stuck in her throat. He was right. So was she, but he had all the power, which meant his rightness prevailed over hers. Arguing with gods, she realised, was like fighting the wind. Utterly pointless.

"And how am I to carry out your vengeance, then?" Psyche asked, curious despite herself.

There was that mischievous glint again. "First, you need to take control of your situation."

"I'm listening."

"In order to do that, you need to use Eros' talent against him."

She guffawed mirthlessly. "Love? You want me to *love* him?"

"No, I want you to make him fall in love with you."

"According to his definition of love, he already is," she scoffed. No, Psyche decided, gods clearly didn't understand the hearts of mortals, nor those of their own kind either.

Loki sighed ostentatiously. "There are as many definitions of love as there are gods and goddesses of love in the Universe. Don't look so surprised. Yes, there are many others. I'm not lying."

It didn't sound like it. Then again, it was always hard to tell with his kind.

"Eros' definition of love is based on lust and possession because he knows no other. Show him something different. Seduce him. Make him care for you, and he'll be at your mercy."

"All right," she said for the sake of argument. "How do I do that?"

Loki moved a lock of her hair away from her face. "You're lovely, but you're not lovable. There's too much anger, too much wilfulness and defiance in you. You need to learn to be meek and endearing; otherwise, all you'll ever get from him is pain."

The god talked as if both tasks were easy. Psyche, meek? Loki might as well try to convince Zeus to be chaste!

"Once you learn that," he continued, "I'll teach you how to break a god's heart. Then I'll help you escape your cage."

"And in exchange?" Psyche asked, keeping her affront to herself.

"I'll have my revenge."

"And…?" She saw the way he still looked at her. She'd seen it in the eyes of many men, mortal and immortal alike.

He smiled flirtatiously. "The pleasure of your company while you learn."

She really did not trust this rakish god. There were too many contradictions in his speech and manner, too much wickedness and derision, yet she couldn't help but be captivated by him. This troubled her more than anything else. Perhaps he was one of those other gods of love he mentioned. A rival of Eros. And she wanted nothing to do with those. "What is your talent?"

"Mischief," he replied proudly.

"Ah… of course it is." She shook her head ruefully. All gods were prone to mischief. If that was really his actual talent, perhaps she was better off with another Eros. There would be no favourable resolution for her out of this.

"Well, god of mischief, you won't take offence if I don't believe you'll be content with just my company."

The smile turned into a grin. "I know I'll get my reward eventually. When you're ready."

She turned to face him, arms spread out. "I'm ready now, and I don't like having debts or company. Meekness is beyond any of my abilities, so have your revenge. Come on, take what you want. But I warn you, there's not much left to take. My breath, virtue, free will, even my skin has already been taken many times," she said in a hopeless attempt to discourage him.

His eyes and lips narrowed to slits. "How about I promise I'll take you only when you ask me to."

Psyche raised an eyebrow, surprised and unsure of how to respond. Gods were bound by their promises – Olympian ones, at least. This stranger was indeed a much more dangerous and cunning deity than Eros, or maybe even Zeus, and she knew she shouldn't indulge him in his game. Except, after so long of being desperate for an intelligent conversation, this uncanny exchange already counted as one of the best nights of her life, and the idea of seeing him again excited her. Still, she would never allow herself to be a god's pet again, let alone ask for it.

"Very well," she said, crossing her arms defiantly. "Teach me how to bend gods to my will so I won't have to ask."

The god of mischief grinned. "Deal."

CHAPTER 1

Aftermath Part I

"Psyche, Psyche, are you all right?" Aedan shouts at me.

Do I look all right, you idiot? I curse to myself, unable to move. My back, neck and ribcage are still mending, so breathing and therefore speaking is not yet feasible.

He rolls me on my back. Searing pain shoots through my spine.

You're not helping! I want to say but just moan instead.

Pan, fortunately, seems to understand my plight and pushes the Dharkan back. "She'll sort herself out." His tone is that of a predator protecting his prey, not one friend helping another. Even overwhelmed with agony, I can Reach his animosity and disapproval of how I handled Zeus. He'd rather I'd crushed his soul. Now, so do I. Regardless, I have more pressing concerns than regret for that choice. Explanations and amends will have to wait.

I focus on healing, and as soon as I can move my arms, I punch Aedan's scarred face, now looming above mine with an expression of quizzical concern. The impact knocks me back to the ground. More pain.

"What did you do that for?" he asks, holding his nose. It didn't break. Shame, I hoped it would.

"For… Loki," I mutter strenuously.

"I saved you!" Aedan protests in a voice not his own.

Stars, I want to hit him again, but it just hurts too much to bother. "I would have put Chronos' soul back in the fucking stone had you not stabbed him with the horn!" My voice breaks at every other word with the effort to speak.

"No, you wouldn't. He would have crushed you," Aedan says defensively in his own voice.

"He did crush me! It's only flesh," I hiss as I push myself to a sitting position. I feel as if a tree has fallen on me, which, to be fair, is not too far off the mark. Xylo's unnatural strength could rival a Titan's. There's something to be said about how well the Nephilim tailor their constructs to fit a god's needs. Flesh and bone can be such a hindrance sometimes. We are a lot freer without bodies: free from pain and gravity and cold… Sadly, also free from pleasure or any perceived agency in reality. That's why Chronos needed Xylo. The God of Time influences matter just by existing, but time itself is ethereal. Or was…

Aedan's jaw tenses, and he's about to give me a piece of his mind – or Loki's mind – when suddenly the air around us shimmers and the second barrier collapses.

"The hex is broken," Hecate declares with the gravitas of someone who just put down a heavy burden.

Daylight returns to its insipid normal under Niflheim's weak sun, and we're no longer in a realm trapped in a time bubble adrift from existence. There's a tremor, a barely perceived vibration from the world's core.

It seems the hex is not the only thing that's broken. Ideth screams. "Chiron! Oh, no, no, no. Chiron!"

She casts some sort of healing spell; her palms glow, pressed tight against the centaur's chest. It's a wasted effort. His body is lifeless, his soul already in Tartarus.

Forgive me, I pray to him.

'There is nothing to forgive,' replies an unfamiliar voice.

Aedan stands up, hands closed into fists at his side, sparking with rage, so furious he's almost flustered. "What do you mean you're trying? We had a deal. You heard what the witch said; the hex is broken. Get out of me now! You promised." He holds his head as if to pull it off his neck. "Out, I said!"

"Oh, burn it," Hel murmurs. She whispers something to Medusa, who is still glaring at Xylo.

"He doesn't petrify properly." She sounds offended rather than worried.

"It's good enough for now," Hel says. Unlike Medusa, she sounds extremely worried.

The gorgon reluctantly adjusts her goggles back into place. Hel leaves her to walk up to the Wraith, a suspicious frown on her face.

"Father? Is that you in there?"

"Goddess, make him leave," Aedan pleads exasperatedly.

I can tell something's exceptionally wrong by her expression.

"Aedan, did you… take Ambrosia by any chance?"

"Yes, I fed on Ileana after being stabbed in Relicum. I needed to heal."

Hel mutters a string of imprecations.

Aedan stops struggling with himself. "What's wrong, goddess?"

"Ambrosia has a peculiar effect on Dharkan, Aedan," Hel explains reluctantly.

"What effect?"

"It traps the soul inside the host."

Aedan blinks introspectively. "You *knew* this would happen?!"

Of course he did, I think, cracking my neck into place.

The Dharkan turns to me. "Psyche. Get him *out*. Loki says you can do it."

I am about to, then take a moment to reassess the situation with a clear head. Now that the pain has faded enough to allow me to think properly, I decide to teach both men a lesson for getting in my way again. There are several advantages to leaving them as they are. I only have to deal with one at a time, which is far less aggravating. The chances of Loki doing any mischief are drastically diminished by his host's stern influence. And, more importantly, Zeus won't be able to touch Aedan, or claim his talent back either.

"I'm too tired, Aedan. I need to recover my strength first," I say.

"The flame you do! You said it yourself; your talent requires no effort. If you can purge Odin from his host while inside the Stump, you can free me from Loki now."

I look at myself. "Can't I at least get dressed first?"

I conjure a new dress, identical to the one in shreds at Xylo's feet. It's the only one I know how to make, and

I hate it because it's the one I had on at my apotheosis, but it's still better than being naked. After all, I'm a goddess, not a nymph, for fuck's sake.

I get to my feet slowly and straighten my back. The vertebrae pop in quick succession under Aedan's impatient scrutiny.

"There. You're healed, dressed, and stretched. Now get him out of my head while I'm still sane!"

"How many times did I ask you to free me when I was inside the vault, Aedan?" I say, leisurely combing grass and dry leaves from my hair with my fingers.

Aedan grips my wrists, eyes flaring with rage. He opens his mouth to speak, then shakes his head ruefully. "Very well. You've made your point, Psyche. Now free me."

I step closer to him. My neck cracks again as I tilt my head back to stare the tall Dharkan in the eyes. "No. You both could use the company."

He tenses his jaw a few times before he jerks my wrists free with a deliberate jolt of energy, eyes burning with unspoken protests. All things considered, Loki might end up being a wonderful influence on the Dharkan.

The world rumbles again. The tremor is almost imperceptible without Reach. Its cause is clear, though. Hel unconsciously wraps Hades' cloak around her as if seeking protection or warmth from it, a fleeting worry on her icy features. Inside her mind, however, she's screaming.

How much time do we have? I ask her telepathically.

She looks at the god in question with undisguised loathing. *'I honestly don't know.'*

I Reach for Hades' soul, surprised not to find the Underworld Lord by her side the moment the barrier collapsed and find him already at work, trying to contain the situation.

"I'll do what I can," I assure her before I join Pan, Medusa, and Hecate next to the lump of rock that used to be Xylo. A petrified tree for all intents and purposes, seemingly lifeless to anyone but a god. Even through Hecate's net, Hel's layers of ice and Medusa's cursed stare, I can sense Chronos' soul. There's a lot more to it than I initially thought. And something else... I should have seen it sooner. I mean, I did. I just didn't understand what I was seeing. No one told me; no one taught me. And I was too ignorant to ask.

Probably too headstrong to learn as well...

Gaea stands a few paces to our side, breathing hard. She looks old and thoroughly exhausted. Her powerful soul is diminished, showing only wisps of its usual power. It can't all have gone to Zeus or Chronos' host, but even one of them was already too many in her depleted state. Her mind is a tempest, trying desperately to figure out how to save what's beyond her control.

I place a hand on her shoulder. "I didn't realise. I'm sorry."

She puts her hand on top of mine and nods silently. We share our regrets. She regrets handling me as part of an experiment instead of as a proper goddess. I regret how I reacted to the treatment. I wish she had confided in me sooner. But why would she? I never gave her a reason to trust me, either. Oh, what a mess we've made...

I glance back at Hecate, who avoids my gaze, and

then at Medusa, who seems unable to peel hers away. Two women who suffered at the whims of the gods, probably even more than I did. One would think this would make us friendly towards each other, if not friends, and yet they both despise me. It's funny how often I have that effect on women.

"What now?" Pan asks no one in particular. As a Wyrd, he's not fully aware of what's happening, only that he's missing something important. His feral gaze is on me. He wants me to free him so he can use his talent on Zeus, perhaps on all of us. This means whatever deal he made with Hades must include a free pass from the Underworld. I can't blame Hades. Giving souls a second chance is pretty much the only leverage he has. And after the way I abused my own talent, I know Pan won't let me get away with sensible arguments against revenge.

"Psyche!" Ideth shouts. "What are you waiting for? Get Chiron's soul back, for frost's sake!"

Stars, is the taking and giving of souls the only thing I'm good for? No wonder gods are so bitter if all everyone sees in them are their talents and how to exploit them. Yes, I understand it now, and I hate it.

I bite my cheek, hesitant to give her an answer. There's nothing I or anyone else can do for the centaur now.

"He's gone, Ideth."

"No, he's not! You can bring him back. I know you can."

"There would be no point. His body is ruined."

"Gaea can create a new one."

We both stare at the Goddess of Life. She shakes her head sullenly.

"She lies," Aedan says. "She claimed she couldn't bring Ileana back to life either, and yet she gave life to Xylo."

"That was different," Gaea protests.

"Yes, the difference is Ileana was not a goddess, and therefore she wasn't worth the trouble."

"You're damned right she wasn't worth it!" Gaea's composure cracks when she addresses him. She feels nothing but contempt for the Nephilim and their life-imitating constructs. I suspect she's not particularly fond of Dharkan, either, and I'm sure her vitriol is aimed as much at Aedan as it is at Loki.

"Can't you see how much pouring life into Xylo has cost her?" I say in Gaea's defence.

"I only see what she wants me to see," Ideth says resentfully. The nymph has indeed gained more knowledge than is good for her.

"Even if she was willing to create a new body for Chiron, it would make no difference, Ideth. His soul is now held in the Underworld by another god's curse. I can't break it," I say truthfully.

"Liar! You sent him there; you can bring him back!" she insists. Damnation. Knowledge without wisdom is like a tune hummed by someone who's tone-deaf.

"I cannot." I turn towards the king of Olympus, who's still pretending to be asleep at our feet, eavesdropping on our conversation. "But *he* can. Get up." I kick him.

"Careful, this body is not like his old one. He's

mortal. It will take time for him to adjust. It was the best I could do under the circumstances," Gaea clarifies almost apologetically.

"He's well adjusted," I say, then kick him again – harder this time. "Get. Up!"

CHAPTER 2

Aftermath Part II

The king of Olympus stands up slowly, deliberately and defiantly as if to prove it was his choice, not Psyche's kicks, that ended his deception.

"You kick like a mortal, *goddess* of the soul. If your intent is to command a god's attention, I suggest you wear boots fitted with spikes. And even then, you'd just be a nuisance, as you've always been: a thorny weed beneath the soles of our feet."

"I see you've adopted some of the Suzerain's expressions – appropriate for a disposable replica wearing only skin. I reckon you'll soon find out just how much of a nuisance thorny weeds can be," Psyche replies with a sadistic grin. There's something disturbingly different about her. She was rude and selfish before, but never cruel.

"You should never leave your enemies alive," he says.

"Rest assured, I won't make that mistake again."

Zeus turns to me with a scowl, his gaze loaded with disgust. "Dharkan. You have something of mine. Give it back so I can teach this cunt a lesson."

Loki takes over. "Haven't you been paying attention, former king of Olympus? Everyone here wants something they can't have. Besides, I like this talent." He shows him my hand and makes sparks dance between my fingers. I hate being a spectator in this interaction. Still, the expression on Zeus' face is worth it.

"It's not your talent," he snarls with indignation.

"It is now," I reply with satisfaction.

Zeus takes a step closer, and ice spreads at our feet. He immediately retreats.

"I don't need your talents to ice you, Olympian," I sneer.

Zeus transfers his scowl to Psyche again. "How dare you insult me like this? It wasn't enough to trap my soul and destroy my body. You had to give my talent to this *thing*!"

"I never touched your body, and stealing talents is his talent, not mine. You'll have to ask Hel how that works."

"Flaming sun! Would you stop the nonsense already, or have you forgotten why we're here? The real problem is standing right there." Hel steers our attention away from her and towards Xylo. "We need to do something about this piece of ash. Curses won't hold him forever."

"Chiron's body is growing cold," Ideth sobs, clearly not giving a cinder about our little strife or Hel's valid concern.

"And I'm growing annoyed," Pan warns.

I roll my eyes, or Loki does. Goddess, maybe we both do. I can't tell anymore.

"Can one of you free me so I can go back to being wild, please?" he asks politely; his tone is anything but. I expected Pan to be hostile towards Zeus. After all, wasn't he the one who made him a Wyrd? Instead, his hostility seems aimed at everyone except Zeus. I don't understand gods sometimes.

'*Sadly, I do,*' Loki says. I worry about the direction his thoughts are going.

Psyche, Zeus and Hecate exchange challenging glances.

"I need the moon," Hecate says stoically.

"I need my talent," Zeus says grudgingly.

Psyche bites her cheek, then turns to the satyr. If she frees Pan and not me, we're going to have issues.

"Promise me something," she says.

"No promises; no apologies; no regrets. Do what you have to do, Butterfly."

She bites her cheek again. "Very well."

"Don't you dare set that creature free in my world. People are terrified as it is!" Hel's apoplectic.

"They are not terrified enough," Psyche replies matter-of-factly.

"Psyche. Free me. Now."

"Wait!" I yell involuntarily. "How long have you been a Wyrd, god of the wild?"

Loki, this had better be good.

The satyr's jovial veneer is gone. He scowls at me, exposing the crude nature of his character. "Too long."

"So why the hurry? I reckon you're a lot safer as a Wyrd than you would be free in my daughter's world – against her wishes." The way Loki speaks these words does not intimidate Pan. Quite the contrary. I regret giving him Prana earlier and want to take it back. Loki is against it. *'He's mine,'* he informs me greedily.

"Is that a threat?" Pan asks, his attention split between Loki and Hel.

"Only an observation. Tell me, have you ever tried to free yourself before the blue sun vanished?"

"Of course I did. What are you getting at, Trickster?"

"What was the curse's condition, Wyrd?"

"Repentance."

"Is that so? The god of the wild, trapped in a mortal for millennia and never once felt regret for his actions? Fuck, even I felt genuinely repentant for my crimes thousands of times over while I was being tortured in the Underworld."

"Maybe I'm tougher than you."

"Or you're lying."

"Why would I lie? I have nothing to lose in this state."

"Exactly. You have everything to gain. If she frees you out of guilt, you won't have to submit to Zeus. You see, I think the condition was allegiance, not repentance, and no respectable god would ever submit himself to another, especially a wild deity such as yourself.

"I'm no ordinary god, Trickster," Zeus says. "I don't need curses to compel allegiances."

"Maybe not. But you don't like loose ends or others constantly interfering with your plans either." Loki turns to Pan again. "I believe Zeus sent you here to spy on Hades while he supposedly controlled the Suzerain. Great job, by the way. Oh, don't feel bad about it. Alek

Dveer fooled even Chronos. Hey, Pan, perhaps you should ask them to free you," – Loki uses my finger to point at the Stump – "wasn't that your initial plan? They tend to be the best ones."

Pan walks up to me. Even trapped inside a mortal host, the god's soul radiates with terrific power. I feel an overwhelming terror, and if not for Loki I'd be running to the shadow, screaming like a Narrum child after a nightmare. He's fear incarnate. "One day, you and I are going to have a problem, Trickster."

"We already have."

"So stop hiding inside that corpse and let Psyche free me so we can solve this like gods."

"Soon," Loki purrs.

The satyr headbutts me in the face. I lunge, determined to pull the horns from his skull. Loki holds me back. *'Calm,'* he says.

Calm?! You're not the one he hit!

'Technically, I am. I have it under control, don't worry.'

Everyone stares at us expectantly except Ideth, who's still trying to revive the centaur. Loki lifts my hands to call a truce. "Let the goddess of the soul decide."

That's a bad idea.

"Psyche, you owe me," Pan insists without taking his eyes off me.

She considers our behaviour with a bundle of mixed emotions. Her expression hardens when she reaches a conclusion.

"I think both of you are safer the way you are."

"Agree," Hel says.

Pan storms away from the group, heading in the

Stump's direction. Psyche follows him with her gaze, her countenance stuck somewhere between suspicion and concern.

Hecate blows out a mouthful of air and walks to the cabin.

"And where do you think you're going, witch?" Hel demands to know.

"I'm leaving!" Hecate's pupils narrow to vertical slits, and I could swear she stares straight at me as well as Hel and Zeus as she speaks. "My penance here is done. Chronos is your problem now."

"Not so fast. What about the hex you put on him?"

"Do you want me to undo it?"

"No! I want you to make sure it stays on."

"It will. Otherwise, Ideth can handle it."

"Me?!" Ideth lifts her head from the centaur's mane long enough to sniff the word out. How petty our quarrels must seem to her.

"Yes, you. Your affinity with magic is stronger than in any goddess. And you have none of our limitations. Use it."

"You've created a monster," Gaea says to Hecate almost appreciatively.

"Haven't we all, Mother of Life?" Hecate replies. The eyes of her spectral heads slit first at Gaea, then Hel, Psyche and finally on all of us. "I've spent an eternity in the Underworld. I'm done. Don't try to stop me."

"You're done when I say you're done," Hel says.

They glare at each other in a silent contest of stubbornness. I can't tell what else Hel says to her, but Hecate definitely has three faces now and none of them looks pleased as they seem to confer with each other.

Olympians are stranger than trees. Speaking of strange, the one they call Medusa and the snakes on her head all stare at me with ill intent. I suspect she, like most Olympians and snakes, doesn't like the cold.

'No, it's not the cold. She doesn't like you,' Loki says, amused at the idea.

Me? I've done her no harm. I've never even met the creature before!

'It's not because of the harm you can inflict on her but because she can't inflict any harm on you, and she resents you for it,' Loki says.

Resents me?! *That's nonsense.*

'No. That's human reasoning.'

Such lovely creatures, humans, I think sarcastically, then turn my attention back to Psyche, by far the loveliest of them all. Judging by her expression, she resents Zeus a lot more than Medusa does me, and still not half as much as he does either of us or Hel or even Hecate. I really can't see an amicable solution out of this.

"I need to fetch a few ingredients from the cabin, and I need privacy for a spell. And no, you can't ask what it is. It doesn't concern you. It's personal," Hecate says in a surprisingly reasonable tone. "I'll do what you ask, Hel. Then I'll leave this realm with or without your permission."

"Fine," Hel says. She waves the witch away and turns to the nymph. "Ideth, make sure the curse stays in place." Ideth is about to protest, but Hel just talks over her. "Psyche, can you Reach his soul? Take it, change it, or" – she takes a deliberate breath – "I don't know. Do whatever you do best."

"Yes," I say. "By all means, finish what you started.

I won't get in your way this time, nor will I stop him if he tries to crush you."

Psyche shoots daggers at me. "You don't think I've tried already?" She holds the butterfly pendant in front of my face as if I've never seen it before. "I can't even get to it now. The curse keeping his host contained also prevents me from Reaching his soul. It's all I can do to dampen his will. And that's not the worst of it. It…" She purses her lips. "I know this is going to sound absurd, but his soul is *tainted*. It's like there's more than one in constant flux, repelling itself like oil and water, and it's just as slippery." She squirms. "I swear I can still feel some of that *oil* on me from the first attempt."

"Oh no," Ideth says. "How much did you take?"

Psyche inspects the pendant dubiously. "Hard to tell… This doesn't exactly have a scale."

"No. How much did you take within yourself? That oil… it's not Chronos. It's…"

Psyche blinks at her; something like realisation crosses her face. I don't understand it, and Loki refuses to explain. I think he doesn't understand it either.

Psyche bends to pick up a handful of brown dust: Cornus' horn. There's nothing left of it except a tiny splinter no longer than my little finger and twice as thin. She punctures her thumb with it, and it immediately disintegrates.

"Shit."

I ask Loki for an explanation again and get the same mental shrug in reply. Gaea parts her lips as if to speak but says nothing. Zeus forgets to breathe. Hel buries her face in her palm.

Sometimes I hate gods.

Psyche casts about herself and up at the sky as if looking for something, then sets her jaw in that self-willing determination I've come to recognise as a prelude for trouble. "Medusa, be ready to petrify Xylo again if needs be. Ideth, we could use some of that magic. Aedan, give me the dagger."

"Why would you need –"

"Give me the fucking dagger!"

She clutches the butterfly pendant firmly in one hand, and the other then plunges the dagger deep into Xylo's ruined eye, the only part of him not completely solid.

"What is she doing now?" I ask aloud to no one in particular.

'I'm not sure,' Loki says. Whatever he thinks it is, it scares him more than Pan did me.

"If I can't take Chronos' soul, perhaps I can take hers," Psyche tells us.

Whose? I ask Loki. His emotional reaction makes me want to scream.

Zeus guffaws. "Godhood has clearly gone to your head, girl."

"No one asked your opinion!"

"And do what with it?" Gaea asks, more alarmed than curious.

"I don't know yet." Psyche buries her hand deeper into Xylo's skull. The sound of squelchy gravel makes me queasy. Within moments, the pendant glows a deep amber. She's not breathing. She's hardly breathed this whole time in fact, looking cold and proud like the other deities in the clearing. Maybe it's Loki's influence on me, or maybe it's this freezing light dancing through the trees, but for the first time, I think I see Psyche as a true goddess. And by the shadow, there's something about her that terrifies me.

'She's stopped caring,' Loki says darkly.

About what?

'Doing the right thing.'

Psyche begins to shake as if straining to lift a great weight. Her face reddens, her lips pull back in a snarl to reveal gritted teeth, and beads of sweat glisten on her forehead. "Fuck!" She pulls her hand out of his eye and throws the Soulstone to the ground in frustration. "It's like wrestling with a singularity. I can't do it."

"Only the best of us can," Zeus says.

"Shut up," Psyche snaps. "Or I swear I'll put your soul back into the stone. I assure you, *yours* takes no effort at all."

I bend to pick up the discarded pendant. The butterfly is still black as onyx apart from very faint swirls of amber at the centre. "Why don't you?" I ask. "Actually, why did you keep Zeus' soul in the first place?" The question is mine as much as Loki's.

"Yes, Psyche. Why did you?" Gaea asks. All eyes fall on the goddess of the soul. Even Ideth forgets her grief as she waits for an answer.

Psyche narrows her eyes at Zeus. "Because I could." It's the truth, and her tone is cold enough to rival Hel's temper.

"Well, well. It seems no god is above vengeance," Ideth scoffs, her grief channelled into something far more destructive.

"No being with power is," Psyche replies meaningfully.

Power radiates from the nymph. Her huge blue eyes turn completely black. "You know what? I might have to agree with you on that one."

"I'm not your enemy, Ideth."

"You're not my friend, either. You took Chiron's soul! But I have no soul, and you can't take away my power." Her hands turn incandescent. She looks... burn me. Now that I pay close attention to the nymph, she looks much older and, I have to admit, scarier. Is this me seeing the world through Loki's eyes, or have I missed something? Loki promptly lets me know that yes, I missed quite a lot, apparently.

A ball of green fire shimmers into being between her hands. I can feel its heat from here. Flaming sun, she'll burn us all.

Hel douses the flames with a flick of her fingers. "Seriously? One more flaming spell from you, witchling, and I'll send you to the Underworld to cool down."

Medusa nods approval.

Ideth stares at her hands, dumbfounded. "How did you –?"

I sympathise with the nymph. Powerful or not, no one's scarier than the goddess of the dead when she runs out of patience.

'Here it comes,' Loki says with a mixture of dread and pride.

"Gods can't undo other gods' designs. You can because you're not a god. But just because you can do something, it doesn't mean you should, Ideth. You harm us; we harm you. It is not about how much power you have, but how you use it. Piss off the wrong gods and, well" – Hel spreads her arms dramatically – "look around you for the results. How many years of your life have you spent on a lost cause, huh? Do you actually think a few spells are going to change anything now?" It's a rhetorical question, and Hel doesn't wait for an answer before turning her tirade on the others. "Gaea! By the fates, you're the Mother of Life and you look less alive than I am. Was cheating time that important to you? I sure hope it was worth it – for both of you." She scowls at Chronos, then changes targets again. "You, Medusa, was your virtue really that precious to warrant such a fate? Don't answer that! I really don't care. Zeus!" She shakes her head in deep disapproval. "I wish the Allfather could see you now. Tsk. And Psyche, when will you accept your power and use it for more than personal gain? By the way, the only prison you're in is the one you made for yourself. Believe me, I know." Hel leaves everyone ruminating on her words and stares the nymph down again. "Do not piss me off, Ideth. The same goes for you, Hecate – yes, I know you're listening! Just like Chronos." She leans closer to Xylo. "We're not done yet, O mighty God of Time. Not by a long shot." Hel looks at her audience again, then raises her voice. "All of you here! Listen very carefully: I've had enough of your bickering, your meddling and ploys. This is *my* world, in case you've forgotten. You'll do well to follow *my* rules. Do not try anything stupid until I say so."

Everyone's shocked into silence for a moment. Then, as if on cue, they start shouting their pent-up grievances at each other like starving Narrum after a failed hunt.

"Burn me..." I gape in disbelief. I'm the one who shouldn't be here. I should be on my way to the Stump to save Ileana, not putting up with… Seriously, I don't even know what to call this nonsense. Loki's laughter inside my mind is more manic than mocking, but utterly aggravating just the same.

Unnoticed by anyone else, the swirls inside the butterfly pendant turn brighter. I give it back to Psyche.

ANAMNESIS 2

Happiness

Psyche picked the lily from Loki's hand, tucked it behind her ear, then batted her eyelashes at him. "Is this lovable enough?" she asked meekly, nibbling on her bottom lip with a coy smile.

Loki cleared his throat. "A bit too much, I'd say. He'll know you're up to something."

She clicked her tongue, the coquettish loveliness replaced by her usual down-to-earth demeanour. "Eros doesn't think the way you do. He believes I'm finally tamed, and it's all due to him and his *talent*."

"That's good."

"No, it is not. He doesn't beat me or degrade me anymore. Instead, he wants me to dance for him or hold him to my bosom and pet him like I would a kitten while I whisper compliments to his beauty and prowess in his ear. And he wants it every fucking night! It's sickening. Yesterday, I almost begged him for the whip out of boredom."

Loki chuckled. "You are a hard woman to please, indeed."

"Don't jest, Loki. It's been months and my situation

has not changed in any way I'd consider an improvement. I'm still his prisoner, still a slave to his whims. At least before, I didn't have to pretend to enjoy it."

Loki reclined on the bed with a bemused smile. He was taking a risk visiting her in broad daylight. Actually, he was taking a risk visiting her at all. This was Olympian territory. Eros' own realm, no less. Just because the god of love was too arrogant to warden his palace against gods from other pantheons and Loki's illusions confused the simple-minded creatures employed to run the place, it didn't make it safe. But the truth was, Loki just couldn't resist the risk, nor the prisoner.

"Before, you had no one to keep you company during the day," he pointed out with a mocking sulk. "Isn't that an improvement?"

She began pacing the room, annoyed. "The company is fine, I just…" She glanced about herself and sighed. "I spent most of my life surrounded by walls. I don't want company; I want freedom."

"Freedom is as relative as time," he said absent-mindedly.

"Time… right. There's another thing I don't have," she grumbled to herself.

Psyche learnt fast. Like most women, she was a natural at manipulation, and her royal upbringing had refined that trait long before Loki's final touches. Sadly, she was also too clever, too proud and ambitious. All excellent qualities in a goddess, but tragic in a mortal. They were so powerless, their lives fleeting and pointless. Was he being cruel by enlightening her? After all, the only thing Psyche could do with her knowledge was to take it to an early grave.

"This revenge is turning into the realisation of all his dreams," she said bitterly.

"Excellent."

"Excellent?! He's happy. How is that good thing? What about your revenge?"

Loki waved a dismissive hand. "Making someone miserable is easy. Most creatures are unhappy without even realising. Sure, they know something's wrong or missing, a purpose lacking from their lives. It keeps them awake at night, makes them drink, start fights, go to war, steal and cry when they think no one's watching. They are the lucky ones. Their ignorance protects them from any actual pain. True unhappiness only happens once you've been happy. To feel perfect happiness and then lose it, knowing you'll never feel that way again, now *that* is pain. And *never* lasts a lot longer for a god than a mortal. It's the perfect revenge."

Psyche frowned, chewing on her cheek, arms akimbo. "Are you implying I'm lucky because I've never been happy?"

He pondered the question. "It does sound harsh when you put it like that, but yes, I guess I am."

"Go fuck yourself."

He smirked mischievously. "Maybe I will, since you won't."

"What is true happiness, anyway?" she asked, pointedly not rising to his bait.

He had to consider this for a moment. Every god had their own definition, surely. Odin would probably say happiness was victory in battle over his enemies, Loki in particular. Baldur would claim happiness could only be found through peace and meditation, while Thor was happy just throwing his hammer around. The simpler the mind, the easier for it to find happiness. (Loki made a mental note to steal Mjölnir as a prank next time he was in Asgard.) But what was true happiness to him? When was the last time he felt happy? Had he ever been?

"Hello?" she said impatiently.

Loki fought a flare of frustration. Words were the bane of thought. Every one of them an interruption, disrupting and diminishing what would otherwise be pure eloquence. Still, it wasn't her fault that she couldn't Reach his mind.

He sighed before he spoke. "To me, the best way to describe happiness is a feeling of belonging to either a time, a place or another being – ideally all three. It's the realisation that you are where you were supposed to be." He trailed off when he realised how comfortable he felt with this mortal woman, in an enemy's stronghold, far away from his realm. He stared at her in surprise as she adjusted the lily in her hair with one hand, the other still resting on her hip, completely unaware or indifferent to his scrutiny.

"No, I definitely don't know what that feels like," she murmured dolefully. "I suppose misery is easier to endure when you've always been miserable, but I fear I'm getting too good at enduring it, and that doesn't solve my problem."

"Patience is a virtue," he said.

"Tsk. To gods and their endless existences, perhaps. Besides, virtue isn't one of my virtues, either."

Loki laughed, definitely more amused and carefree than he should have been under the circumstances. He kept telling himself that Psyche was a means to an end. That using her – however he could – was the best revenge against Eros. That there was nothing wrong with enjoying himself in the process. Of course not, he was a god. The god of mischief, no less. This sort of thing was exactly what he was meant to do. However, what he felt went beyond vengeful enjoyment or prideful dedication to his craft. He came to visit Psyche every day, not because he had to or because she wanted him to, but because *he* needed to. She made him calm, and that, he realised, made him happy.

Fuck...

Had Eros caught them together and shot him again without him noticing? *No...* He desired her, for sure, but nothing like the angst-driven, blood-boiling madness he'd experienced with Angrboda. This was something else, something different, more complex, and far more dangerous.

"You never told me why you hate Eros so much. Did he make you fall in love with a horse or something?" Psyche asked, lying on the bed next to him.

"No, the horse was my idea," he replied absently.

"Huh?"

"Never mind. No, not a horse, an ice giantess."

Psyche blinked a few times as if trying – and failing – to conjure the image without grimacing. "Was she too cold or too big for you?"

He sneered at her. "Neither. She was all flame, with a soul almost as old and twisted as mine. Our love affair was epic – as love affairs go – and so were its consequences..."

"I don't understand."

"We had three children together."

"Oh… that many, huh?" She winced at the idea.

"Yes… And it's all I can do to keep them alive, even if that means the end of entire worlds."

She rolled closer, propping her head on her elbow, dark brown eyes alight with curiosity. "How so?"

There was no harm in telling her, he supposed. It was not like she could do anything about it or tell anyone. "Two of my children are imprisoned; the other rules the world of their prison. I don't mind when gods attack me or use me as a scapegoat for their petty struggles, but my children were innocent, born into this mess. Eros had no right. Neither did Odin."

"You're doing it again," she said tiredly.

"Apologies." Loki often forgot Psyche wasn't a goddess and therefore had no actual telepathic abilities. Words only revealed part of what he communicated – a very small part. He reckoned the biggest misunderstandings between gods and mortals came not from what the gods told them but from what they thought they had and was, in fact, left unsaid.

"It's not important," he said.

"Yes, it is. I want to know. Why are they imprisoned?"

He frowned, unsure of how to answer. His offspring barely fit into the minds of gods, let alone mortals. "Well, Jorma is too, er… big, and he just keeps growing. Fenrir is also big and, much like his brother, has an appetite for things no creature should be able to eat. More troublesome than that, we have been implicated in an apocalyptic prophecy."

Psyche kept silent, waiting for more. She looked

genuinely interested in his family's issues, so he kept talking.

"The prophecy was of Olympian origin and claimed he – or a creature matching his description – would kill the Aesir king and eat the sun. Odin is no fool. He suspected the prophecy had been ordained by Zeus. Still, he took no chances. He couldn't kill Fenrir or me, so with the help of Tyr, he deceived him into captivity instead."

"Who's Tyr?"

"Another god of war. The Aesir have many of those in the pantheon. This one fancies himself more of a champion of justice than a bloodthirsty warrior, but deep down, he's just as bad as the others. Worse, actually, since he's much smarter than Thor and more cool-headed than Odin." Loki's fists clenched whenever he thought about what they'd done to Fenrir. But there was no point telling her about that. His son was no longer bound in chains, just chained to his sister's world. He took a deep breath and continued. "And Hela, my daughter, she's just… Well, let's just say she doesn't fit into any of the conventional worlds. So much so, Odin allowed her to have her own world just so he wouldn't have to look at her face. The fact is, none of them belong anywhere, to be honest, but I still want them to. Does that make sense?" Now that Loki heard himself, he wasn't sure it did. Words tend to have that effect on the most straightforward and incontrovertible of thoughts.

"Of course. You want them to be happy," she said, and he realised she was right. Survival wasn't enough. They deserved to be happy as well.

Psyche nodded slowly, then jerked her head up as if she'd just remembered something left cooking over the fire. "Was the prophecy uttered before or after Eros shot you?"

"Before. Why?"

"Hmm, sounds like someone else had a stake in your affair with the giantess."

"Why do you say that?"

"Eros doesn't use his talents for the pleasure of his victims. I bet someone instructed him to shoot you, hoping the prophecy would come to pass."

"You're right. Aphrodite ordered him to do it after I scorned her," Loki admitted.

"You scorned Aphrodite?" Psyche burst out laughing. She almost sounded happy when she laughed.

"What's so funny?"

"No one scorns Aphrodite, Loki. If she wanted you, she'd have had you. But I doubt she ever did. You're not her type."

He lifted his head from the pillow in indignation. "I beg your pardon?"

"She likes pretty boys and big brutes. You're neither," she cooed playfully at him.

"I can be," he said, taken aback by her observation. "I can be anything!"

"And you choose to be cute."

"Cute?!" He nearly choked on the word.

"Yes, cute. With your slim physique, cheeky smile, and pointy ears." She tickled one of them as she spoke, adding a thrill to his indignity. "And if she really was offended," Psyche continued in the same tone, ignoring his protests, "Eros would definitely make you fall in love with a horse."

Loki sat upright. He'd never really thought about it that way. But Psyche might be right. His affair with Angrboda didn't feel like a punishment. Quite the contrary. And as soon as their offspring were born, the lust was gone, replaced by total indifference – on his part, anyway. His devotion to his children, however, never dwindled.

An idea occurred to him. "Would you like to meet them?"

"Who? Your children?"

"Yes."

"How?"

"I can take you to them."

"You –" Psyche closed her eyes and forced herself to breathe slowly. "You can take me away from here?"

"Of course I can. I can take you anywhere."

"Then why haven't you done so already?!" she shouted with such anger he nearly translocated across the room.

"I can only replace you with an illusion for a short time. It's risky and not a permanent solution. Not to mention, Hel's world is not kind to mortals."

"You know how much I long to get out of here, to see the world – any world! You could have taken me away any time, and you didn't. You're a monster!"

"It never occurred to me," he began before good sense intervened.

"Fucking gods!"

"I'm giving you the option now. Do you want to come or not?"

She gnawed on her lip, furious, but it didn't take her long to reply. "Yes!"

"Niflheim is an underworld," he warned.

"I don't care if it's under water! Even a brief break from this place is better than nothing."

"Very well. As you will."

CHAPTER 3

Discussions & Revelations

I entertain myself by thinking about Ileana while the gods shout at each other like the unwanted children of the Universe that they are, fighting for the attention of their disgruntled parents. How did I let myself get involved in this? It has nothing to do with me or the Dharkan. I left the Shadow to fight the Suzerain – a tangible enemy with a purpose at odds with our survival. He made sense; they do not. Now I'm here, a jaded, unwilling spectator forced to listen to their ash. Meanwhile, Ileana is probably waiting for me inside the Stump. Wondering where I've gone. Or worse, thinking I've abandoned her. What if she's in danger? What if she needs me? Oh, goddess, this is maddening.

"All right. That's enough!" Loki shouts louder than I knew my voice could.

Several sets of indignant eyes blink in my direction. Even Hecate pokes out from behind the cabin with raised eyebrows.

"Watching you bicker is very entertaining. Truly. Under different circumstances, I'd say, by all means, carry on. I've a few things to get off my chest myself.

But that's not why we are gathered here." He uses my hand to point at the creature they're all too willing to avoid dealing with. "Gather your fucking wits and use them to come up with a solution for this mess."

"This was Loki speaking, by the way," I explain quickly before they transfer their vitriol at me.

A moment of silent embarrassment follows.

"We can destroy it – Xylo, I mean," Ideth suggests.

"Chronos would just find another vessel," Gaea says wearily.

"And roam free in the meantime," Hel puts in. "No, we can't risk that. I want him out of my world permanently."

"What about the Underworld?" Medusa suggests.

Zeus' laughter inserts itself into the conversation, to everyone's chagrin. "It's one way to break the Universe."

A second silence falls over the clearing, heavier this time, as silences tend to get as more people engage in them.

"Give him to the Nephilim," Psyche says coldly.

I almost gape.

"I bet they would trade Fenrir for him," she elaborates.

"They might, but I don't want Chronos in their custody," Hel says adamantly.

"Sure you do," Psyche says. "If anyone can control time, it's the Nephilim. Let them. A god like him would keep them busy for centuries."

"Wasn't he already with them?" I ask.

"He was with the Suzerain," Gaea says, considering the option. "But neither the Suzerain nor Chronos were actually with the Nephilim. They just used them. Perhaps we should do the same."

"Psyche is right. We should let them take him," Hel says.

"Flaming sun…" I rub my forehead, trying to make sense of the goddess' sudden change of mind. "And how are we going to take Xylo, the frozen rock, to them?" I ask.

"With the glider," Psyche replies, as if it's obvious.

"He can't drive himself," I point out.

"Of course not. I'll take him," she says. She's far too enthusiastic about the treacherous things. My head still hurts from our 'accident'. Then again, that might be because of Loki's burning soul inside me, or all the shouting, or the daylight, or… never mind. Oh, how I miss the Shadow and the silence of death.

Loki chuckles at my exasperation.

Get out of my head!

'I would if I could. Hey, this is as much your fault as it is mine, and yet you don't hear me complaining.'

I have to take a breath. *Goddess, give me strength.*

"You'll take Xylo to the Nephilim out of duty and the kindness of your heart?" Hel asks sardonically. I don't know why I still call on her for strength. She's never actually given me any to carry her burdens.

"No," Psyche says. "Out of the selfish desire to leave this place through the roots of Yggdrasil, back to Midgard before it's too late."

Zeus bursts out laughing again. He laughs far too much for a god dispossessed of his powers and dignity.

"What's so amusing?" Psyche asks waspishly.

Hel looks dead serious. Loki is humming inside my

head, and Gaea's wincing at the sky like she's desperate to find shade.

"I know the World Tree isn't actually dead," Psyche says. "Gaea would die herself before she let that happen. No, please, no more lies. Its roots are still entwined with Yggdrasil's, are they not? From Asgard, we can go anywhere." She pauses as if suddenly self-conscious. "Odin told me so."

'Did he?' Loki's tone implies several layers of displeasure.

Gaea nods. "Yes, I have kept it alive – at significant cost. Still, Psyche, even if you reach Asgard, Yggdrasil won't take you to Midgard."

"Why not?" Psyche's tone discourages an answer.

"Because Midgard's World Tree *is* dead. You see –"

"There is no Midgard," Zeus interjects, still laughing.

Psyche's face slackens. "What?"

"You really don't know?" He dabs a mock tear with his thumb. "Humans destroyed it long ago."

Interlude 1

Seshat

"The future is about to happen," Seshat stated gravely, as if it already had.

A smothering silence followed. Ulla pressed both hands to her stomach, and Ulcan was about to push the goddess for an explanation when a naked Isko ran onto the temple's balcony.

"I'm leaving!" he declared gleefully.

Ulla's brows rose at the sight in surprise; Ulcan lowered his in disapproval. Nudity was frowned upon amongst the Narrum, and Hermes' host was pretty hard on the eyes, even with clothes on.

"Oh, I didn't realise you had company," he said, not embarrassed in the slightest.

"We are all leaving, apparently," Ulla said, further inspecting the man. "What's happened to your speech impairment, Isko?"

"Ah, that… it comes and goes. It's the weirdest thing." He winked at the dryad, then spared an apologetic glance at Seshat, who returned it with tired resignation before she spoke.

"Leaving where?"

"The forest." A partial answer, Seshat was sure.

"That's where we came from," Ulcan supplied unhelpfully, still dazed with drink and wishing he had more of it, no doubt.

Seshat glared at both men. "You'd leave me alone here, now. After everything I've done for you?"

Hermes feigned offence, casting his gaze around the group. "You're hardly alone. The temple is filled with people."

"Hilarious. And how are you going to feed yourself in the forest?"

He crouched next to her, eyes alight with excitement. "Hecate."

Seshat chuckled. "The witch?"

"*My* witch." He grinned. "She's free."

That couldn't be a good sign. Seshat took a breath to collect herself. "… The Underworld. Hades… Is he?" She glanced at the Nephilim's ship still clamped atop the Stump, her mind stringing together all sorts of bad plot twists.

Hermes shook his head. "I don't know, and I don't care. Hecate is here, and this might be our last chance to be together. I will not waste it."

That hurt her feelings, but in the grand scheme of things, not too much. Their relationship had always been one of convenience: he needed light, she needed an ally. Like most relationships between gods, it was destined to end as soon as something better came along. Why now, though?

"These two mortals just informed me that the –" She paused to make sure Toman wasn't eavesdropping behind the wall. The temple's new attendant was too curious and too stealthy for his own good. "That the *clock* is ticking in the forest, inside some sort of magic realm. I don't believe in coincidences."

"It's not a coincidence," he said enthusiastically.

"Cats, Hermes! Why didn't you tell me?"

He turned very serious. "Because you are not part of this story."

Seshat repressed the urge to scratch his face. "What is that supposed to mean?"

"I told you I was cursed because I crossed time to deliver a message. I never told you why or to whom because I wanted to spare you the same fate. Your role is to record these events so they won't happen again."

"My fate is not your responsibility. And how can I record what I don't know?"

"You know more than you think. The rest you'll soon find out." He winked.

"You have a visitor, lady sire," Toman announced from the archway.

"More visitors?!" she snapped. What an awful time to be popular. She had half a mind to summon Quetish and just vanish from everyone's sight before she inadvertently burned them all to a crisp.

"See, I told you you're not alone. Now can I bask, please? I'm famished. This last group was hard work," Hermes said eagerly.

She hissed at him in reply.

A familiar presence pierced her Reach. Seshat motioned everyone to keep quiet. Moments later, Anubis strode past Toman onto the balcony, the tail of his long robe dragging across the marble floor for added gravitas.

Cats! Cats! Cats!

"It's good to see you too, Seshat," he said, not bothering to reply to her expletives telepathically.

Anubis always made an entrance, even without wearing his true form – which he didn't, thank the stars. That would have caused more panic than a Wyvern landing on the roof of the temple. A few years back – even just a few days! – she'd have been delighted to see him again. Now his presence might as well be the very definition of a harbinger of death.

"Leave us," she said to the others. It was not a request.

"But, Seshat, I'm hungry," Hermes mewed.

"I don't give a clowder about your hunger, your witch or your plots. Let her feed you, you ungrateful puss." She turned to Ulla and Ulcan, their eyes darting from Hermes and back to her, then to Anubis and each other, confused. "You two, get as far away from here as you can; take as many people with you as you can. But don't force them. We don't want to alarm anyone. And don't waste time trying to convince those too stupid to be saved. Go!"

Hermes stood there a moment, muscles tight with outrage, then he stormed back inside without another word.

Seshat exhaled.

"Can I have my sunstone back?" Ulcan asked, about to pick it up.

"No!" She picked it up before he had a chance to.

"Bitch! I deserve to at least be compensated for it."

"You deserve to be immolated for it!" The audacity of the hunter to even dare hold a sliver of Ra, let alone claim to own it. Of course, she doubted Ulcan was even aware of what he'd had in his possession. To him, the sunstone was just a light source. Hephaestus was the real culprit of that insult. To craft such an artifact, then give it to a mortal, just showed how deep his contempt for the gods went.

"Let's go." Ulla grabbed Ulcan by the sleeve of his coat and all but dragged him with her towards the stairs. "Come. We'll pick something from the pantry for you to drink. That should make up for the loss. Toman won't mind. Will you?"

The temple's new attendant didn't seem to hear her at first, so focused was he on the gods. Then he nodded. "Yes, of course. Take whatever you want. Come!"

"What strange company you keep in this world, Seshat," Anubis said diplomatically once they were alone. "You were always more patient with mortals than I am, but I never expected you'd associate yourself with Wyrds."

"Free gods are rare these days. Not to mention, Wyrds are far less perfidious," she replied pointedly.

He chuckled. "If you say so."

"At least when a Wyrd betrays you, the most he can do is annoy you, not leave you stranded on a foreign world, trying to survive as it falls apart, questioning your every thought, word and deed, wondering what in the name of Ra you have done to deserve it!" She felt the urge to massage the dull ache building at her temples. "Anubis, I'd rather deal with a wet cat than you right now. Why have you returned?"

He grinned. "I missed you, sunshine."

"Tsk. Spare me." Seshat put down the sunstone.

She would go centuries without even being in the same quadrant of the universe as her ex-lovers. What were the odds she would have to deal with two of them in the same place, the same day? Coincidence or a consequence of Chronos' presence in the world? She decided it really didn't matter at this point.

Anubis picked up the discarded sunstone. "You accuse me of betrayal," he mused, tracing its contours with reverence, "and yet I'm not the one who let Ra's death go unrecorded. What would Thoth say?"

"Do not bring my father into this!" She snatched the sunstone from his fingers. The god of reckoning wouldn't say anything precisely because there were no records of it. "You were there, weren't you? On the *other side* of the battle."

"I was…"

"So why didn't you record it?"

"Not my talent," he said casually, crossing his hands behind his back.

"Tzzz. You're an embarrassment to our pantheon."

"That seems to be the consensus. It is why I left. At least I'm honest in my *deceit*," he said meaningfully.

"I deceived no one." Not exactly and not on paper, anyway, she could have added.

"You deceived me. Oh, come on, don't look so offended. Save it for those who don't know you like I do. You can play any character, Seshat. Your true talent is deception, not writing."

"And your talent is to assist the dead, not lifeless constructs."

"Touché." He spread his hands in a helpless gesture. "In my defence, I was tired of being unappreciated and overworked. My job was to tend to the bodies and souls of gods, not hordes of humans pretending to be gods. It was insulting and counterproductive. Their lives are too short, their souls and bodies too weak for rebirth. How would you feel if you could only write short stories and then have them thrown on a fire or, worse, locked in a tomb for thousands of years only to be put on display and read completely out of context?"

They glared at each other defiantly like two angry cats with bristled hair and raised hackles.

Anubis was the first to concede with a heavy sigh. "You're right. There's no point bringing any of that to the conversation. Let's make this brief."

"I appreciate it."

He took a deep breath, then began pacing the balcony with his hands clasped behind his back, as was his manner. Gods may change their appearance, their allegiance, their speech, even their mind. But they rarely change their demeanour.

"It's a good thing you weren't there, Seshat. The battle really wasn't worth recording." He stopped beside her and took her hand. "I'm glad you're safe," he said as he showed her what she'd missed and what he'd been doing with the Nephilim.

"How come they have kept you alive and free for this long?" she asked, curious despite herself.

He shrugged. "They needed someone to advise them on the Underworlds."

"I thought they had conquered death."

"Precisely. And because they did, they know nothing about it. They keep me around as an advisor since none dares to try my talents," he said proudly.

"They are clever."

"Very. Unfortunately," he added with annoyance.

"They had Zeus, and I suspect they have Seth, Ares and Aphrodite. Who else do they have?" she asked.

"Many," he admitted.

"Isis?"

"Yes."

"Shiva?"

"No. He figured he would be safer on the other side." Anubis sighed. "He ended up destroying himself and a whole solar system along with him. Now *that*, you should have been there to record."

"Is Bastet still with you?" She was almost afraid to ask.

He winced. "Not exactly. She's in a much better position than I am. She's linked. And as far as I can tell, getting along splendidly with her Nephilim."

"Cats…"

"Exactly. The things they've done to their world." He shuddered in remembrance.

"She has a world now?"

"Oh yes. It's run by cats. Their worship is mandatory." The gods shared a horrified expression. "Cats everywhere. You should read what the mortals write about them, the movies they make."

"Movies?" That was an unknown word to Seshat.

Anubis chuckled ruefully. "You've been away a long time, sunshine."

"I've been here. And not that long."

"Ah, but things have changed out there. Chronos altered the flow of time to suit his plans for this world and has disrupted many others in the process."

Seshat had figured as much long ago and was not too worried about it. One thousand or ten thousand years makes little difference to a god. And despite what Anubis said, things never changed that much amongst mortals during such a small time frame. Between their quarrels, short life spans and environmental disasters, they have to constantly rebuild their civilisations. Innovations are few and far between under those conditions and therefore easy to keep track of. Or were. The Nephilim played by different rules, apparently.

"Enough talk, Anubis. You can see I'm busy, and time is of the essence. Why have you come back?" she asked again.

"To warn you." However, in his mind he said, '*to save you.*' Seshat pretended not to have noticed.

"The world is ending, yes, I gathered as much, thank you. You lost your trip."

A commotion erupted from the forum, and soon the whole settlement was in an uproar.

"Cats! I told Ulla to not cause alarm!"

Anubis walked to the balustrade. "It's not the mortal's fault. The Stump is smoking."

"What?" Seshat joined him for a better view. "What have you done?!"

"I might have provided the spark. But I bet Apollo is the one controlling the flames."

"Apollo's in there?"

"You felt his presence, surely."

"I did, but I figured he'd taken Artemis and left – without even saying hello or offering me a ride, the cat. How did he end up inside the Stump?"

"You need to ask Hel that question."

"Oh, for cat's sake."

Seshat never quite understood how the mighty Stump vanished from the landscape in Judoc's and Agnar's accounts. The structure the Nephilim built inside the World Tree trunk was pretty much indestructible from the outside, and thanks to Hephaestus' craft, the gods were pretty powerless inside it. *Powerless, not talentless*, she reminded herself. If a god whose talent allowed him to ignite stars was trapped inside it, well… *that* – as Loki would say – would do the trick.

"I hoped it wouldn't happen so soon. Namrive will not take it kindly," Anubis mused to himself, still pondering at the ever-thickening smoke plumes coming from the remains of the World Tree.

"Who's Namrive?" Seshat asked on reflex. Her mind was focused on getting out of there. The question was: to the forest and help deal with Chronos – even if she could not fathom how, she would at least like to meet him – or to the Stump, so she could record its destruction in detail. For what purpose, though?

"Namrive's a pawn," Anubis replied airily. "She doesn't know it, of course, so" – he pressed a finger to his lips – "better to keep it off the record."

"I'm starting to doubt this madness is worth recording."

"You better record it. It would be bad if we were left with only the enemy's side of the story."

The Anubis she'd known didn't care about stories, only deeds and how much they weighed down souls. "What is *your* side of the story? Why have you betrayed us, Anubis?"

He clucked his tongue. "I didn't."

"You joined them!"

"I infiltrated them. There's a difference. I'm not a cat!"

There was something in the way he spoke that raised the hairs on Seshat's nape. He truly believed he'd done the right thing.

Anubis collected himself again. "I didn't come here to stir old grievances, Seshat. Let's just say we made our choices, and we were both right."

"How were you right?"

"I figured the Nephilim would become powerful enough to threaten our existence, and I told you this world and Chronos' experiment didn't fit into their agenda," he pointed out smugly.

She flared at him. "*I* told you that! It's the reason I'm here."

"So maybe you can tell me what Chronos' connection to the Suzerain is and what he's doing in Niflheim."

That doused the flame from her. "You… knew about him too?"

"I only just found out. I suspected it from the records at the Stump, but you just confirmed it." He grinned. She'd forgotten how clever he was and how much she hated him for it. Except she was now too curious for hate.

"There are records?! Where?" She'd searched every accessible room in the cursed place and had not found a single piece of written parchment.

"They are digital."

"What?" Another unfamiliar word to her vocabulary. This was unacceptable. Seshat had always prided herself on knowing every word in every language.

"You still store your manuscripts in your private little realm, yes?"

Seshat tutted. If there was one thing she had no talent for, it was realms. Her private slice of reality was barely large enough to keep her records safe and Quetish comfortable. "Hardly a realm… more a trans-dimensional library, but yes, go on."

"Digital, or virtual – I honestly can't tell the difference – it's what they call the information stored in their private realms."

"The Nephilim have their own realms?" That certainly changed things. "I thought they were grounded to this one, like mortals."

"Sort of… They use crystals, kinda like witches do. Hmm, what are they called again…? Ah yes: chips."

"Spaceships?"

"No. Microchips: Tiny little things with integrated circuitry. They can connect with each other and exchange information, like we do telepathically. Yeah, I don't really understand it either. It's like magic. But they do it. Their technology, machines, even most of their brains, are made of the stuff. They've stored information about the entire Universe in those virtual spaces. Out of our Reach."

"That's horrible!"

"Exactly, so you better keep your own records, just in case."

Seshat nodded, her mind already working on the record of how badly gods have underestimated magic.

"Is Chronos really here?" Anubis insisted.

"Yes, he's in the forest, apparently," she said.

"Doing what?"

"I don't know. I was going to find out when you arrived."

"So now we can both go find out."

The roar from the mob outside the temple increased.

"Lady sire," Toman said, rushing in, eyes wide.

"Let me guess: The people are scared. They want answers and reassurances, etcetera."

"Yes. Actually, what they really want is your permission to leave the settlement."

"They have it already!"

"They want to hear it from you. Er… no, not *you* you. The Suzerain would be ideal, but Iosh will probably do. Do you, by any chance, know when he'll return?"

"The gifted one? I wouldn't count on it," Anubis said, keeping his eyes on the Stump.

Seshat groaned. She disliked Iosh intensely, but he had his uses; charming mobs was one of them. She could make herself look like him; acting like him, though, was beyond her abilities.

"I'm not playing those characters again, Toman. They don't need mine, theirs, or anyone's permission to leave. Have them take the initiative for once. Help Ulla and that irksome man encourage them to go to the Gharb if possible. And… Toman, you should go too."

"But, Lady Seshat, they'll never listen to them. When too many people want the same thing, they refuse to even consider anything else."

"Then they'll die!" she said blatantly.

"They're mortals. That's what they do," Anubis supplied with a chuckle.

She gave him an exasperated look.

"I'm sorry, Toman. You're on your own."

The expression on the temple assistant's face was one she hadn't seen before. Just a brief spark of intellect and resentment, and something else, something almost familiar. "I thought so. Goodbye, Seshat," he said before he left. The way he spoke felt a bit too final for her taste, but she quickly shrugged it off. He was just another mortal, after all.

Anubis held out his hand to her. "Come with me, Seshat. There's nothing left for you here."

"Wait." Seshat fetched the box Eros gave her earlier. "Can you see what's inside this?"

He bored his gaze into it. "No. Is it one of Persephone's?"

"Yes."

"Why do you have it?"

"Eros gave it to me."

"Oh. You two are still –"

She glared at him. "No. I wasn't even aware he was in this world. He came here wearing a Dharkan and told me that inside this box is a sample of the blood of the Hydra."

Anubis raised his eyebrows. Even the hair on his crest seemed to have spiked at the revelation.

"Obviously, I did not open it to confirm he was telling the truth."

He handed her back the box and wiped his hands on his robe. "What does he want?"

"That's the thing. He only asked I keep it safe until he comes back for it."

"He wants you to remain here. That's another reason for us to go."

She wasn't so sure. "At first, I thought it was a threat.

Or a sick joke. He likes to torment others, you see. Now, I'm more inclined to think it was a warning, a clue telling me to open my mind to a possibility I have never allowed myself to consider." *A life-changing, likely fatal possibility…*

She waited for Anubis to say something. He didn't. She looked deep into his mismatched eyes in an attempt to Reach the god she once knew.

"Have you ever met Kali?" she asked, studying his reaction.

"I've talked to her. But I never met her. Not in person. No one has. Why?"

"Why do you think that is?" she asked back.

"The Three are eccentric deities. The Goddess of Death most of all. You know this." He was a lot more anxious than usual, she noticed.

Because he was lying to her face.

"The Suzerain once told me one only fears what one doesn't know." She chuckled bitterly. "He was wrong."

Anubis imitated her chuckle. "You really need to find better company than mortals, Seshat. Come on."

She remained still. "Kali is Chronos' character, isn't she?" It was more an affirmation to herself than an actual question.

"What do you mean?" he asked, overly surprised. Anubis was clever, yes, but he was a terrible liar. Likely part of the reason the Nephilim kept him around for so long.

"Aeons dealing with death, and you expect me to believe you never met its goddess?"

"We… talked. Through Reach. I've told you –"

"Stop lying! I wasn't actually sure about it until

now." She had to take a few breaths to collect herself. "Is that why you're here, Anubis? To take me away to safety because you think Chronos will unleash Kali into this world? Will we finally be allowed to kill each other, is that it?"

Anubis dropped the pretence. "He's insane, Seshat. Kali made him insane. If he's here, if he went to the trouble of gaining a foothold into Niflheim, it can't be good for us. No matter what he does, or who's in charge of his mind. We're not safe. The box only proves that."

She began to turn away.

He spun her back around. "Seshat. Listen to me. Few things can kill us. Kali is one of them. Unless you want to spend eternity writing about the Underworld, I urge you to come with me. I, for one, don't want to ever go back there."

"Where do you want to take me?"

"To them." He pointed at the Stump.

"You are the one insane."

Seshat tried to translocate away from him and failed again. Chronos' presence had really messed up the transdimensionality of this world, or more likely, Hel did. She didn't trust Hel. That's why she'd blocked her from her Reach. The goddess of the dead may not be able to prevent others from entering Niflheim, but she could prevent them from leaving if she so wished, making sure they ended up in her Underworld, under her control. It would not surprise Seshat if she had orchestrated this whole mess. Well, one way or the other, she would see the end of this story even if it did kill her.

She summoned Quetish. The giant sphinx appeared atop the dome. Chaos ensued.

"A wyvern!" someone shouted.

"A manticore!" Another voice cried.

"It's a daemon!"

For cat's sake. How can these mortals live in a world such as this and not recognise a sphinx? They can't even tell the difference between a gryphon and a manticore, apparently. They were so ignorant, she realised. Not the spoiled ignorance of safety and peace, just plain ignorance. They were livestock. Pieces left in a game long abandoned by their players. Nothing more.

"Seshat, listen to me!" Anubis shouted over the roar of the population. "You'll be safe there. I promise they won't bind you. They have no need for your talents. They perfected recording to a level even you can't comprehend. It's far more efficient and better than yours!"

"How dare you!" It was one thing to insult her, another to insult her work. She burst into flames. Sensing her mistress's distress, Quetish swung her tail at Anubis, missing and knocking down a wall in the process. Seshat jumped over the rubble, agile as a cat.

"It's true! Whatever you want to learn about the Nephilim is there," he said, dodging another attack from Quetish. "And memory!"

This gave Seshat pause. "What do they know about Mnemosyne?" His expression was as good as an answer. "They have her, don't they…? I think she tried to tell me about Kali right before she disappeared. I looked everywhere. They got to her first. Have they killed her yet?"

Anubis hesitated, torn between an answer and avoiding Quetish's attacks. "I don't know. She… the world they took her to suffered some sort of misfortune. It must have been horrific or extremely embarrassing.

The Nephilim won't talk about it. Believe me, I brought up the subject often enough. The whole affair has been declared an Oublié – of which knowledge has been lost."

"You mean forgotten."

He finally got close enough to force her to face him again. "I know how important she was to you, and I would never use that knowledge to deceive you. I tried to find her. I swear, I did. But I don't understand their technology. I don't understand their minds. You might, though. They've had Mnemosyne for a long time. Everything she recalled, they recorded. I bet she left you a message. That and all else she might have learnt from them can be yours." Anubis stretched out his hand. "Come with me, please. You won't find any answers here, only more questions."

Quetish knocked down another wall. The dome was about to collapse. Seshat made her choice.

"There's something I need to do first."

CHAPTER 4

Deceit

"That's not possible," I say. Stars, I've been saying that a lot lately. No matter how far I stretch the limits of possibility, something else comes along to challenge its definition. "Humans don't have the power to destroy worlds." If this is Zeus' idea of a jest, he's way out of line. This time, I will destroy his soul, and fuck the consequences.

"Oh, the world is still there, a lifeless rock in space. Depleted, wrecked, abandoned," Zeus says. "Humans were the plague that swept over it, consuming everything, like locusts, themselves included."

"As if you'd let them destroy Midgard. Olympus is linked to it," I say.

"Linked, yes. Not dependent on its well-being. Much like the Underworld is not subject to the world it is technically *under*," he adds with a hint of resentment. "I'm sorry to break it to you, Psyche. Humanity, like *Midgard,* is no more." He doesn't sound sorry at all. Quite the contrary. He does, however, hate the Aesir appellation for my home world. He'd tried to change it to Earth when he'd first taken over, but the dull name never quite stuck with its inhabitants. I bet this was one of the many grievances he had with Odin. But I digress. I always digress when I'm anxious. And it's not just because of Midgard.

Kali's soul is unlike any other. Separating it from Chronos' was easy enough; transferring it to the Soul-stone is not. Kali is not an entity in herself but the remnant of another, much larger and powerful soul combined with the mind of the God of Time. Free of his control, it reverted to its original form: the purest of souls. I can feel it blending with mine, altering it – no, repairing it – like thread darning a ragged cloth. The problem is, I'm so used to being ragged, I don't recognise myself whole. I'm not even sure I want to be. Would I still be me? I have to fight it. But the effort is draining so much of my energy, I can hardly stand.

I glance at each of the blank faces around us, expecting a reaction. No one's contradicting Zeus, so I guess he's telling the truth. I pretend to be greatly affected by the news while trying to contain the effects of the transfer.

"No! That cannot be true. Oh, stars!"

"You've been away too long, goddess of the soul," Gaea continues morosely.

"It was barely a millennium!" I say as I grip the butterfly pendant harder, both for effect and to cover its glow, then stare at Xylo, unsure. "Wasn't it?"

The gods exchange compromised glances again. I can almost hear them arguing about whose turn it is to speak. The very fact that they are speaking says volumes about what they're afraid to reveal with their thoughts. Myself included.

Gaea takes the lead again in a patronising tone. "Honestly, we don't know. A millennium for some is only moments for others these days. The Merge affected a lot more than just two Underworlds."

I shake my head. "Time is relative. I get it. But it doesn't matter if one thousand or one million years have passed. I wasn't always asleep. Their prayers kept me grounded in reality. If everyone in Midgard had died, I'd have known. I'd have felt it. And what I feel are the souls of trillions of humans. Their numbers keep increasing."

I remember Ideth saying humans had spread all over the Universe. This surprised me then. But once I was free again, I could confirm it was true. Gods have been moving people around like pawns for their games since long before I was born. But moved is not the same as gone. They are probably just hidden somewhere in some obscure world like this one, out of everyone's Reach.

"Oh, there are more souls now than ever," Gaea says. "The descendants of humanity spread over many tribes, many races. None remains from Midgard, though. Except you. And well, I guess you too, Medusa. If you still consider yourself human."

Her hair hisses again. "Of course I don't!" Judging by her tone, this is not news to the cursed creature. Even the souls in the Underworlds are better informed than I am, apparently.

"Spread how, exactly?" I ask, too tired and distracted to pretend to be anything but resigned to this new information.

"Evolved," Gaea replies tiredly.

"What?!" I say. It's more a sound than a word. Stars!

How didn't I see it before? This actually explains the Narrum: squat and almost exclusively carnivorous. The product of a punishing world with stronger gravity than Midgard and not much sustenance. Odin urged me to think like a goddess. He wasn't just talking about faith, but also perspective. Time doesn't affect gods, only mortals – all mortals. And humans are as susceptible to selective breeding as any other livestock.

Zeus sighs dramatically. "Congratulations, Psyche. You are the last true human alive."

I'm no longer human. And I was never a good example of one to begin with! I want to say. But what is the point? I was never at home amongst my people or my home world, and I never really intended to go back either. So why does it feel like I've lost something? Like I'm suddenly... alone? I clutch the pendant in my hand again, letting the effects of the soul slowly draining through me into it show. Let them think it's because of my humanity and the shock of learning this news, for what else am I supposed to do with this information?

INTERLUDE 2

Ulla

"Can you believe that shit?" Ulcan asked as he was being escorted – more like shoved – down the stairs to the pantry. "She stole my sunstone! Gods and their entitlement. They think they can just do anything they want, take anything they want."

"Because they can," Ulla said wearily.

"First, they barge into my home uninvited, have an argument, destroy my property, have another argument, taunt us, make us listen to their shit, then throw us across the land to this cesspit of humanity to deliver messages in a language we don't understand, and as a reward that bitch not only takes away the rest of my stuff, she expects us to be responsible for the survival of the idiots in this settlement?" He made a falsetto impression of Seshat. *"Take as many people with you as you can. But don't force them. We don't want to alarm anyone."* Seriously?! Fuck that! Fuck them! Gods, what a bunch of lazy, hypocrite bastards. Alarm… listen to the uproar outside. The people are already alarmed. That's the sound of insanity. We'll have a better chance of reasoning with a herd of basilisks! If we go outside and dare to even suggest they do anything, they'll crush us like a ratton in a snake's embrace. You'll see. Probably eat us alive too! If the goddess wants to save these people so badly, she can do it herself! Let the future come soon, I say. The world does need a purge. I'm tired of this shit! Haven't even had a good night's sleep or a good meal in days."

"Me neither…" Ulla rubbed her tired eyes. She hated being back at the temple. The memory of Fabrian's death was still raw in her mind. As was his life. She kept seeing him in every room, every corner, hearing him laugh. An echo of a reality that no longer existed.

They had arrived at the pantry, and Ulcan went straight to the wine rack, helping himself to the largest bottle on display.

"The gods have no shame, no respect for us. And did you see that bloke?" He kept going.

"Yes. I've never seen him before. Have you?"

"Often, always lurking around the Blacksmith's place. Wish I didn't see so much of him this time." Ulcan shook his head and spat. "No shame, absolutely no shame."

Ulla clicked her tongue. "Not Isko. The other one. He looked… odd."

Ulcan pulled the cork out of a bottle with his teeth. "No, haven't seen that one before. Didn't like him either."

"You like no one."

"Cheers to that!" He drank half the bottle in one go.

"If this is the end, I intend to die so drunk that I'll remain so in the afterlife."

Ulla released a long-suffering sigh. "Thank you,

Toman," she said to the temple's assistant, who was in fact not assisting much. He stood very still, homely face scrunched in thought. She felt sorry for him, having to deal not only with hordes of people each day but with gods as well. Not to mention Iosh, of course. The vain Shrine was high maintenance. She never understood what Arianh saw in the man. Then again, Fabrian had loved him too. When she'd asked him why, he simply said his flaws were not his fault. Sounded more like an excuse than a reason to her. And where was Iosh now when he was most needed? Probably with Arianh, both already safe and far away from this madness. The idea made Ulla jealous; jealousy made her angry. She was too tired for anger.

"Are you all right, boy?" she asked sympathetically. Focusing on someone else's misery always helped forget your own.

Toman shifted his gaze to her. "I'm insulted," he said in a rasping tone.

Ulla recoiled slightly. Narrum were vicious creatures, prone to violence when offended. Fabrian had been an exception in that regard, as in so many others. This boy was not. If anything, he seemed more violent than most.

"The louder they talk, the stupider they are. It's the quiet ones you need to worry about," the old queen used to say. She could almost hear her now.

"Stay here. I'll be right back," Toman said.

"We should go," Ulla said to Ulcan as soon as they were alone.

She had no intention of taking anyone with them, either. She only cared about saving herself and the life inside her. How dare Seshat dump such a burden on them? Did she actually expect them to go outside and say, "Hey, the world is about to end, follow us if you want to live"? Ulcan was right. By the sound of things, the mob would probably swallow them whole. And follow them where? *Far away from the Stump* is not exactly a destination. The farthest she could take them was the Gharb, but the Aossi would never take Narrum in. Slush, come to think of it, they probably wouldn't take Anann in either. And what is the point of gods if they can't even inspire people to follow them? If they can't provide for their safety. All they seem to do is turn them on each other.

"Ulcan, let's go!" she urged.

"Wait. I need to at least take something for the road," Ulcan said as he collected more bottles into a sack.

"Fucking mobs. They are like waves. Just keep coming," Toman grumbled, suddenly standing at Ulla's side again. She did not hear him return.

"This one sounds like a tsunami," Ulcan replied casually.

Toman smiled – a puzzling, ill-omened sort of smile. "Such an unusual word in a snake hunter's vocabulary."

Ulcan spat. "I wasn't always a hunter. I was a fisherman in my home world. '*There's nothing more dangerous than the sea,*' my mother used to say. Before she came here, that is." He took another swig.

"It's not the sea that's dangerous, but the creatures in it," Ulla said, referring to the horrors living beyond the Gharb's shore.

Ulcan snorted. "I doubt even your imaginary sea monsters will be enough to protect the Aossi this time."

Ulla bristled at this. "The sea serpent is not imaginary. I know what I saw. Scared me more than the freezing mob outside."

"Tsk. Scared you enough to run to the forest, just not enough to make you stay."

There was the resentment again. Ulcan would never forgive her for leaving, for breaking up their little family of outcasts. It wasn't her fault, though. Oric and Jonas would have left eventually, even if she hadn't. Not because of the Suzerain or each other, but because they were misfits, and misfits by definition don't fit anywhere. The best they can do is find a purpose and serve it to the best of their ability. Hephaestus gave them that purpose. He gave her a blade so she could protect the Aossi from their predators. He'd said nothing about protecting them from their queen, though… Still, what the frost was she doing trying to save everyone?

I'm such a fool.

"The only reason the Aossi lasted this long is because neither Narrum nor Dharkan can build a decent boat," Ulcan continued, taking another bottle from the shelf. "Ahhh!" he shouted as he dropped it.

"What?" Ulla shouted back, one hand on her sword, the other on her stomach.

Ulcan looked sheepish. "A spider."

"Spiders don't exist, you idiot," she said. "Not in this world, anyway. You're so drunk, you're seeing things. And you have the nerve to lecture me on imaginary creatures."

"I know what I saw!" he said. "We had plenty of spiders back in… Fuck, I don't even remember the name of the world I was born in." He stared at his thumb quizzically. "I think it bit me."

For frost's sake! If he drinks any more, I'll have to carry him, Ulla thought. "That's it," she said. "We can't hide here forever. We need to go. Toman, could you open the back door, please?"

The walls shook, then cracked. A huge chunk of marble stone fell from the ceiling directly onto Ulcan's head. Ulla could only stare as the blood spread from his crushed skull until it met with the still-twitching fingers of his hand. The thumb showed two barely visible red dots. *It does look like a spider bite,* she thought absently. Her mind would rather entertain the impossible than accept the reality at her feet.

The once sturdy stone walls of the temple shook like leaves in a storm. She heard glass shattering, wood splitting, people screaming. The world was crumbling around her – literally – and for once Ulla felt no sickness, no anger, no despair. She was simply too numb, too tired to fight. She cradled her stomach again and embraced the darkness.

ANAMNESIS 3

Niflheim

"It's fucking cold!" Psyche cursed through chattering teeth.

"I warned you," Loki said, not one bit affected by the temperature. A godly perk, she reckoned.

Psyche hugged herself for warmth while waiting for her eyes to adjust to the dim light so she could make sense of the dense mist rolling down and around the icy mountain ahead of them as if it had a will of its own. "What is this place?"

"Niflheim. One of the Nine Worlds linked by the roots of Yggdrasil." He grinned. "Beautiful, isn't it?"

He has to be joking, she thought. Psyche had never seen such a bleak and bleary sight, not even in night-mares, and she couldn't help but feel somewhat disappointed with the excursion. They were standing on ice, surrounded by it, and if they remained there much longer, she feared she would actually freeze. She'd imagined the worlds of gods to all look similar to Olympus: warm and sunny, filled with splendour and wondrous creatures. She'd been unimaginative, of course. It made sense there were all sorts of worlds depending on the tastes and personalities of the gods who abide in them. These clearly didn't want visitors, especially warm-blooded ones.

"Put these on." Loki handed her a fur cloak and long leather boots.

"Thank you." She didn't ask where he'd gotten them or how they were exactly her size. Nor did she hope to understand how they'd gotten there in the first place: one moment she was warm in her room, sitting on her bed; the next she was standing knee deep in snow, shivering. Instead of trying to figure out what'd happened between those two moments, her attention kept being drawn to the strange mist as it thinned slightly to reveal a pitch-black gash on the mountainside.

Loki pointed straight at it. "That's the entrance to Helheim, the City of the Dead."

Psyche blinked at him.

"Yes, didn't I tell you? Hela is the goddess of the dead. What's wrong?"

"When you said Niflheim was an Underworld, I assumed you meant it was underground."

Loki laughed mockingly. "Psyche, Psyche. How many times do I need to warn you about assumptions? When you assume something, you make an ass of you and –"

"Me. Yes, yes." Psyche ground her still-chattering teeth, fastened the cloak tight around her shoulders, then covered her head in embarrassment with the hood.

"I" – she paused to revise her next word – "*thought* one had to be dead to enter an Underworld."

"Not necessarily. Or not necessarily for every Underworld, I should say. Some have... how to put it – layers.

That's how gods are able to access them without being, well… dead. Some, like this one, even have a few areas that are, if not suitable, at least bearable for the living."

"Bearable, indeed," she grumbled, wrapping herself tighter.

The ice rocked under her feet. She'd barely steadied herself when it happened again. And again. Impact tremors. Each stronger – as in, closer – than the previous, all accompanied by a thunderous boom at odds with the softness of the snow-covered surface.

"What a –" Two yellow eyes appeared in the gloomy mist. At first, Psyche thought her own eyes were playing tricks on her, then she wished they had been.

"Stars!" she cried out, hiding behind Loki.

Psyche had stopped invoking the gods whenever she was in trouble, partly because they weren't very helpful, and lately because they were the cause of most of her troubles. The stars wouldn't be helpful either, she knew, but at least she didn't feel foolish calling out to them.

"This is Fenrir, my son," Loki announced proudly.

Psyche gaped at the monstrous creature standing in front of them. It looked like a wolf – a young wolf, at that – except it was almost as large as the mountain. *Or perhaps I'm just very small…*

Loki chuckled at her reaction, then left her with nothing to hold on to or hide behind to greet his son. "Tone it down, pup. You'll scare the poor mortal to death. She's just visiting."

To her bafflement, the gigantic wolf shrank to an easier-to-perceive size. Still larger than any wolf, at least now Psyche didn't need to worry about him crushing her under his paw.

"You brought a living mortal to visit Niflheim?" the wolf said without actually speaking; the words – more an accusation than a question – seemed to just emanate from him. "Hela will not be pleased."

"When is she ever?" Loki sighed, then beckoned at Psyche. "Come closer and say hello. He won't bite."

Psyche wasn't so sure about that, but now that she had her wits back, she would not pass on the opportunity to touch the creature. She knew gods could assume many aspects, and their offspring rarely resembled the parents. Still, this was something else! Tentatively, she stepped closer to the wolf. His large ears perked up, and he tilted his head inquisitively. Once she was close enough, she reached out with her hand and stroked his muzzle.

"Hello."

"I'm not a dog to be petted," the wolf growled.

"No, you're amazing," she said, entranced by the sheer magnificence of him and more than a bit past being sensible (something she would later blame on the cold and having been terrified to death moments earlier).

Fenrir pulled his ears back and whined softly, then leaped away into the mist.

"Oh… I didn't mean to offend," she said, despondent.

Loki shook his head. "You didn't. Come. Let's hope Hela is in a better mood."

∞

Psyche instinctively took several steps back when she met the goddess of the dead. Hela was not a giant wolf like her brother, but she was quite the surreal sight nonetheless: easily seven feet tall – perhaps more – with long white hair, even whiter skin, silver eyes and a face that defied description. Half was a flawless marble beauty, the other half…

"You're being rude," Loki pointed out.

Psyche couldn't take her eyes off it, so she closed them instead. When she opened them again, Hela's face was flawless on both sides, her lips pressed to bloodless slits. She stood a few strides away, arms folded beneath her breasts, her icy gaze fixed on Psyche with revulsion.

"What is *this*, Father?"

"A human."

"I can see that. It's not her time yet. Why bring her here?"

"I wanted her to meet you," he said cheerfully.

Hela blew out a breath. "Give me a break. I'm too busy to indulge your projects, Father."

She unfolded her arms and turned her attention back to the ice sculpture she'd been working on before they'd entered the cavern. It looked like a male version of herself.

"I see you have your own project now, Daughter."

Hela glared at him over her shoulder. "You suggested a hobby."

"That is a dangerous hobby."

"Don't worry. I won't give them souls. I'm trying something entirely different," she said coolly, then began running her hands all over the ice statue.

Psyche was very confused.

"How did you convince Freya to help you with this?" Loki asked, moving closer to inspect her work.

"I didn't," Hela replied emphatically. "You know how much that woman exasperates me. I'd never ask her for anything. Besides, she only works well with living flesh. This is my creation. Life has nothing to do with it."

Loki touched the statue with his eyes closed. "Impressive."

"Mm-hmm."

"Will it have free will without a soul?"

"Of course."

"Show me."

Father and daughter appeared to have entered some sort of trance. Psyche went from confused to bored. She began exploring her surroundings, looking for something of interest. Her assumptions had been only half-wrong. They were underground, after all, inside a colossal cavern, and there was nothing to do there, nothing to see apart from the icy walls, more incomplete or broken statues in one corner, a steaming pool at its centre and roots – massive roots, thicker than tree trunks – jutting from everywhere. Was this really how Loki's children lived? He'd mentioned their world was a prison, but this was beyond depressing. At least Tartarus was warm – or so she'd been told. Then again, looking back at Hela, cold seemed to be a preference, not a hindrance. Perhaps the rest was as well. Loki did say there were many gods in the Universe, from many different pantheons, each possessing talents and ideals at odds with the Olympians. At the time, she'd found that hard to believe. But if they all lived in places as dull as this, it was no wonder she'd never heard of them. *And where were all the dead, anyway?* she wondered, staring into the pool. She thought she could hear something coming from it. Many somethings, in fact.

'Hello Psyche,' said a chorus of whispers.

'*Psyche, we've been waiting for you.*'

'*We welcome you.*'

'*You're one of us.*'

'*Join us,*' they echoed inside her mind.

Psyche peeled her eyes from the pool and shook her head to clear away the voices. She was now standing right at the edge of it and had no recollection of walking there.

"Be careful with creation, Daughter," Loki was saying.

"I am. I learned from your mistakes."

"I'm glad someone has," Loki replied glibly. "Where is… Psyche!"

He pulled her back from the edge of the pool before she fell in.

"Are you all right?" he asked, sounding genuinely concerned.

Psyche only nodded, her mouth too dry to confirm the lie. Whatever was in that pool was dark and thick like blood – definitely not water. Several roots dipped into it; one was pulsating.

"Don't stand too close to the well. We don't want you to accidentally fall into it." Loki acted nonchalant as he gently pulled her further away. But he also kept his distance from it, she noticed.

"Are these the roots of Yggdrasil?" she asked.

Loki cast about. "Some. This is where they mingle with the roots of our World Tree."

"What's the name of this world's tree?"

Loki's mouth twitched. "It doesn't have one. Only Yggdrasil, the largest and mightiest World Tree in the Universe, has a name."

"Doesn't seem fair."

He smiled, amused. "Why? Do you want to name it?"

"It's not my place," she said, then asked what she really wanted to know. "How can worlds be connected by trees?"

Loki's expression turned blank, and he blinked a few times. He often did that when he was searching for words to explain some abstract or bizarre aspect of the gods' reality to her. However, this looked more like he was trying to figure out the answer himself. As if he'd never even considered the question.

"Well, they… hmmm. I guess they – er, no.… I don't know." He finally admitted. "With the Tree's will, I *assume*." He winked.

Psyche bit her cheek so she wouldn't smirk. *Even gods don't know everything, apparently.* It was a troubling rather than a comforting thought, but at least she didn't feel so hopeless trying to get her head around the notion of worlds being connected or held together by tree roots. She reckoned that a mortal trying to imagine how gods, their realms, or world trees worked was akin to a blind person trying to imagine a rainbow. The idea made her sad.

"Don't worry about it," he said in a cheerful tone, misreading the reasons behind her sadness. He'd promised not to Reach her mind, and for the most part, he'd kept that promise. Of course, spoken words only widened the chasm between them, larger even than the one between the living and the dead. That thought made her even sadder.

"Where's your brother?" Loki asked Hela, taking his attention off her, thank the stars.

"Outside," Hela said.

"The *other* brother," he enunciated tautly.

Hela sighed and stopped touching the statue. She bit her lip and looked suddenly smaller and much younger when she faced him again.

"Oh, for fuck's sake, Hela."

"I've asked you not to call me that! My name is Hel."

Loki groaned with frustration. "Must you always be fighting, *Hel*?"

"It was the last time. I expelled him," she said.

"You what?"

"I expelled him from Niflheim," she repeated, louder this time.

"Please tell me you did not send him back to Midgard! After everything I did to bring him here, you –"

"He's here. And he's fine! He wanted independence, his own realm. So... I melted a lot of ice and made him an ocean. It's not nearly as big as Midgard's, but he fits well enough. Last I checked, he was trying to build land." She shook her head. "He has no talent for it, though. So far, he's only managed to make rock and sand, but at least he's occupied, out of my sight and, most importantly, out of sight of my souls as well."

Loki went very still. Psyche did not understand the meaning of half of what the goddess said, but she understood him and knew his stillness meant he was livid.

She stood at his side, touched his hand and felt some of the tension drain away.

"Are *you* all right?" she asked with a complicit smile. His eyes were incandescent blue with rage, but he almost smiled back when he squeezed her fingers.

"I'm trying to run a proper Underworld, Father," Hela continued. "Half the souls on my doorstep turn around and flee to Fólkvangr the moment they see him. I don't want to give Freya more souls to feed her vanity, and I certainly don't want Niflheim to be associated with torment, monsters, or punishments. We're not Olympians."

"He was just having fun!" Loki snapped.

"I don't care!" Hela snapped back. "I asked him to be discreet – which he's perfectly capable of being when he wants to, you know that. He needs to learn to respect my will."

Loki pressed his temples. "I really wish you wouldn't fight. The whole Universe is willing to pick a fight with you three. There's no need to fight amongst yourselves!"

"And I really wish Mother was here. Instead, I have to meet with… *humans*," she sneered at Psyche.

"We're not a couple," Psyche clarified, letting go of his hand.

Hela looked her up and down, then askance at Loki before rolling her eyes. "In that case, mortal, you really should not be here."

Psyche didn't need to be told to leave twice and stomped out of the cavern, cursing her and the cold in equal measure.

Who would have thought gods had family issues?

Sure, the Olympians were one big family issue, but still, she'd never imagined a god like Loki even had a family never mind that it might comprise a giant wolf for a son and a half-dead girl with an attitude for a daughter. There was a lot Psyche did not know about gods, this one in particular. And she certainly couldn't allow herself to care for him, his children or their damned issues.

He's a means to an end, she reminded herself.

The ground shook again.

∞

Loki found Psyche right outside Helheim's gates petting Fenrir, who was, to his astonishment, reduced to a normal-size wolf lying belly up, his paws flapping in the air, tail wagging like a puppy, a wolfish grin on his muzzle.

"I see you two are getting along," Loki said.

"Can I keep him?" Psyche asked playfully.

He laughed. "Eros would be delighted."

Fenrir rolled over, licked her cheek and leaped away with what looked like a resentful – or perhaps regretful – glance at his father.

Psyche got to her feet and began brushing the falling snow off her cloak as if she'd never encountered the stuff before – maybe she hadn't.

"The meeting with Hel didn't go as well as I expected. I apologise," he said. Whether the apology was to or for her, Psyche couldn't tell.

She shrugged. "It's all right. I wanted a distraction, and I got one. It's quite impressive – the world, I mean, and er… your children, too." She paused, tilting her head up at him inquisitively. "Funny, I never pictured you as a family man. And when you mentioned children, I imagined them young and… well, different. I don't know what I expected, really, but I certainly did not picture this. You're full of surprises, god of mischief."

He snorted. "When it comes to gods, it's better not to picture anything. Just expect everything, and you'll never be surprised."

"I'll keep that in mind."

"There's no time to go meet Jörmungandr, unfortunately. We have to go back. Unless you'd rather stay here permanently."

"Is that an option?"

He pretended to consider this. "Not while you're alive, and it would probably start another war between the pantheons."

She smiled. "It's not a bad idea, then."

Loki frowned. "I thought you were past self-pity and suicide."

"I am. But I will die one day. Can my soul come here when I do?"

He doubted it. Souls tend to travel to the Underworlds linked to their pantheon's realms. The idea of Psyche dying aggravated his temper, but she was mortal, and a short-lived one at that. Of course she would die. Already her youth had started to wane; soon her health would too. And yet, looking into her dark eyes gleaming with wonder, her slightly parted lips puffing misty breath, her cheeks flushed with cold, the pink tip of her nose, he replied yes for some reason.

Psyche beamed with hope.

Loki swallowed the lump that had lodged itself in his throat. "Ready?"

She nodded. "Take me back to my prison, Trickster. I guess I'll have to meet Jörmungandr next time."

He also doubted that. Hel was right. This venture had been too reckless, even for him. He could not afford risks, not when Psyche was so close to achieving his vengeance. *Vengeance…* The idea suddenly seemed so petty. Breaking Eros' heart would not save his children, nor Psyche or himself. What was he doing? He had to put an end to this ploy. It had already gone too far.

"Thank you," Psyche said. The words felt like slaps.

"For what?"

"The distraction."

He just stared at her, bewildered and ashamed. She was thanking him for bringing her to an Underworld, of all places, while he was planning on abandoning her to her fate once they returned. It was like having a dog licking your hand after you've beaten him. He clenched his fists. She was so infuriatingly *human!* Even now, even after everything she'd seen and been through, after everything he'd taught her, she still thanked a god for a reprieve to her misery.

What have I done? he thought, disgusted with himself. Not just to her, but to all humans. All Prometheus had wanted was to create a race to rival the gods. But they had it all wrong. Only gods can rival gods. Even gifted with creative fire, the only way humans would ever stand toe to toe with gods is by losing their humanity. And that meant losing the one thing capable of making them better than gods in the first place.

She kept smiling at him. It was such a lovely smile – a lovable smile. His fist unclenched, and before he knew it, he was caressing her cheek, cold and wet from the snow melting on it, as if she'd been crying. She seemed surprised, and a bit amused with this sudden and uncharacteristic burst of affection, but she didn't pull away, just raised an eyebrow questionably.

"You're welcome," he finally said.

Chapter 5

Too Much Drama

"No… That's not true. I don't believe it!" Psyche's complexion turns paler than mine. She braces herself against Xylo as if he's a piece of furniture. Her emotional distress is too uncharacteristic and overdramatic to be believed by anyone who knows her as well as I do. The physical distress, however, is not. As the swirls inside the butterfly pendant glow brighter, she grows weaker.

"Truth doesn't require belief, nor agreement," Zeus says. He's loving her distress and the attention he's getting for causing it.

"How did humankind leave Midgard in the first place?" she asks, as if the question just occurred to her.

"Some were taken by gods to their worlds and forced to wage war for them or to adopt simpler lives under their protection – like the Narrum, for example. Others ventured alone out into the vastness of space with no protection or guidance other than the intricate vessels they crafted for the purpose of finding other worlds to destroy. Humans have always been driven by curiosity and greed. A few were somewhat successful in their pursuits; most are now dead or changed beyond recognition, stranded in worlds governed by primordial forces. It suits them well."

Psyche furrows her brow. "I can relate to the desire to see what's beyond the stars, but it would never occur to me to build a vessel to get there. If humankind had indeed evolved to the point of being able to create such a thing, they also must have known what a futile endeavour it was to do it. It would have taken them generations to reach another star. Not to mention there are very few worlds worth visiting in that part of the galaxy. I can't believe humans evolved to be so ingenious and so stupid at the same time. Unless..." She trails off.

Unless they learned how to warp distances like we do... Loki finishes her sentence in thought.

"You don't know the half of it," Zeus says, eager to enlighten her.

"Apparently not, because what you say makes no sense. Something on that scale would take aeons to accomplish, not mere millennia."

"Chronos is not as patient as he claims," Zeus continues vainly. His desire to patronise blinds him to her deception. "In his haste to Merge these worlds and gather as many souls in the same Underworld as possible, Chronos broke his own rules." He speaks as if the God in question is not there. He's even more arrogant than Odin!

'I know, right?' Loki chirps into my mind. I want him out of my head so badly... yet, without his insight, I probably wouldn't have a clue about what's going on. If only I understood the why...

"Time is not constant; it has always been subject to His will," Zeus is saying. "Details like relativity and vast distances mean little to us gods, but to mortals – humans in particular – learning how to overcome them was all the motivation they needed. No matter the cost."

"But they don't possess the ability to deal with, nor the intellect to fully understand, such forces," Hecate says, joining us. "Even my most talented students could only grasp the concepts of time and realm. A flea might glimpse the sky, but it can never leap that high."

"And yet one did," Psyche sneers – she just can't help herself – always looking for ways to be disliked.

The witch pointedly ignores her remark. I can sense how much she hates Zeus. However, she respects him as well. I wonder why… She has no respect for Psyche, though, only contempt and a resigned resentment for her existence. She's changed into a black travelling cloak and tall leather boots as if prepared to embark on a journey to the Shadow Mountains. Beneath it, the fabric covering her skin is so thin she might have been wearing cobwebs. What a strange combination.

'If I were a betting man, I'd say she's meeting a lover,' Loki replies to my unarticulated question.

Now?! Who has a mind for such things?

'She does, apparently.'

"Hecate has a point," Gaea says, joining the conversation. "Time should have had the opposite effect. The vast distances between worlds and their brief lives should have limited their expansion. As to intelligence… a spark of genius is wasted on decaying flesh. I told Zeus as much when he sentenced Prometheus. And yet the Nephilim were resourceful enough to overcome that particular limitation." She narrows her eyes at me. Loki flinches.

Zeus sucks his teeth as if he's tasted something foul. "Every god thought I was a monster. I assure you, my judgement on Prometheus was just and the hardest I ever made." He sounds sincere, almost regretful. Then his expression and tone change to vindication. "But don't just take my word for it."

I follow his gaze.

A tall man, taller than I am, heavily built but showing signs of sickness and emaciation, enters the clearing. His skin is brown, covered in dirt and dried blood. The hair long and tangled, like his beard. He wears a blood-stained loincloth, and his abdomen looks as if it's been repeatedly ripped to shreds by talons. I don't recognise him; I don't need to. Everyone's reaction is as good as an introduction.

Medusa gasps and falls to her knees. Gaea places a hand to her half-open mouth. Ideth's eyes open wide. Hel narrows hers while Psyche's lower deferentially. One of Hecate's faces lights up in a smile; the others do not.

"There you are," Zeus says, standing tall. "Why don't you explain yourself to the old mother?"

The man ignores everyone and walks straight to me, wrapping his thick arms around my torso in a tight embrace. Loki disallows me from preventing it.

A knot of emotions rushes through me, and I find myself returning the embrace in the way I would had I the chance to hug my father again.

"Prometheus, my friend," I hear myself say as we pat each other's backs.

The man's beard tickles my neck, and he smells of blood, sweat and… urgh, bile!

Loki, that is enough. I demand you release me from this unpleasant display of affection. He doesn't.

"Took you long enough," Prometheus' guttural voice rumbles behind my ear.

"I was detained. But a promise is a promise," Loki says.

"I know." And they pat each other's backs again, hugging tighter.

No Dharkan deserves this.

A few more pats and the men – finally! – put some distance between them.

"Many of those in Tartarus are aware of what transpires in the Universe. But can do nothing about it. It's part of the punishment," Prometheus says.

"So you know *everything* that's happened in your absence?" Loki asks sheepishly.

"Not everything. Only the events set in motion by my actions," Prometheus replies, his steady gaze on Zeus and Xylo, not just Loki. "Although this could be more because of my talent rather than malice by those who sentenced me."

The Trickster forces a smile. "It's good to have you back, old friend." And they embrace again, for flame's sake.

"Coward! Have you no honour?" Ideth storms towards the Titan, mouthing some sort of incantation under her breath. Her hands glow green again. "You traded an innocent for your freedom. How can you stand here fraternising while he's being tortured in your place?"

"Chiron is not being tortured, unbridled one," Prometheus says patiently. He reminds me of the centaur in tone and manner, but his words are heavier, laden with the confidence, wisdom and suffering of ages. "We've exchanged places, but my curse is still my own. He wants you to know he accepts his fate."

"Well, *I* don't accept it." Her hands glow hotter.

Prometheus' sigh defines weariness. "Hurting me won't bring him back," he says.

"I can do a lot more than hurt you, Titan," she retorts.

Ideth aims a large ball of magic fire at us and then vanishes along with it as if neither had existed in the first place.

Hel ambles in our direction. "I warned her."

"Goddess, did you actually…?" Loki advises me not to finish the sentence.

Hel scrutinises Prometheus with dispassionate rigour. "So this is the mighty Olympian Trickster: god of fire, champion and creator of humanity." Her mouth twists in distaste. "Do you realise how much trouble you've caused us?"

"Yes," he replies, unfazed by her wrath, much as he was with Ideth's. He seems above emotion. I admire that.

"Can you undo it?" Hel asks.

"No."

She points at Xylo. "Can you do anything about him?"

"No." But a less emphatic one.

"What about them?" She points at the Stump.

He shakes his head, glancing at me sidelong.

"Then what is the point of you?"

"Hel…" Loki starts.

"Father, he's your friend, not mine. You've fulfilled your promise, had your reunion and so forth. Now the Titan must go to wherever Titans go when they are not hiding in my world or being tortured in Tartarus."

Prometheus chuckles, the sound as unexpected as it is humourless. "Thanks to Zeus, those are pretty much our only options these days."

Hel spares a disgusted glare at the Olympian king. "Indeed. Nevertheless, I have a world to fix. If you're not helping, you're hindering."

"I've helped more than you'll ever know, goddess of the dead," he says with an almost imperceptible hint of pride. "The rest is up to you."

"What do you mean?" She turns to me. "Father, what does he mean by that?"

Fuck if I know…

I repeat what he didn't say.

Hel stares Prometheus down. "I don't like you, Titan. I don't like your tone, your presence, your attitude, your… everything. I already have enough to deal with and have as much use for legendary deities in my realm as I do for talentless Olympians or artificial constructs."

"I understand your frustration, Hela."

"Do you? Do you *really*?"

"Yes. I can't undo humanity. Nor the Merge. But I'm not without talents. I can help prevent the fate of this world. If you allow me."

"And what do you think you know about my world and its fate?"

"He has the gift of foresight," I hear myself say.

"So he claims," Hel says. "How does a god with such a gift end up in Tartarus?"

"By choice." He winks at me. "And with the certainty of release."

Hel crosses her arms in front of her chest and scoffs. "Huh, I should have let the nymph have her way with you. You claim to have foresight, to be aware of what's happened in your absence. And yet you still call me Hela. How can you help prevent the fate of a world of which you obviously know so little about?"

"I know how it ends."

Her face twitches. "Do share."

"In ruin."

She laughs mirthlessly. "You really think you can intimidate me with false prophecy?"

He shrugs. "You're right. It's not the prophecy that should concern you. It's the prophet."

The whole clearing freezes. "Ruin will be *your* fate if you don't leave immediately."

'*Say something. She listens to you,*' Loki urges, sensing how close Hel is to losing it.

What do you want me to say? Your estranged friend arrives here from the Underworld, is greeted like a long-lost hero, rattles everyone, refuses to leave and then foretells the thing she cares about the most is doomed to ruin. She's taking it pretty well, I reckon.

Flaming sun, what am *I* still doing here? Ileana is waiting for me. I'm so tired of gods and their age-old disputes. They are bad enough when there's hope for a resolution. Without it, better to just return to the Shadow and enjoy the shade.

"Before you go, mighty Prometheus," Psyche says meekly. She looks impassive, almost lovely, but I feel her anger and tension like an aura of strain, her knuckles white around the butterfly pendant. "Zeus asked you a question when you arrived."

Prometheus sighs. "He did."

She's trying to keep us distracted, arguing. I wonder why… I see Gaea wondering it too. Loki forces me to gesture her to stop talking. We could not have given her a better incentive to continue.

"We are all eager for an answer," she says.

Prometheus doesn't reply right away, as if debating if he should at all. When he does, he purposely addresses everyone, not just Psyche.

"Zeus' punishment was… harsh, but not unwarranted. To most mortals, time is a limitation, yes. But to a mortal possessing a god's will and imagination, a mortal capable of invention and culture, limited longevity is something to overcome no matter the cost. A work of generations, of entire civilisations. I gave them more than intellect; I gave them the will to accomplish whatever they set their minds to. I gave them souls. Memory and luck took care of the rest." He shoots a pointed look at Chronos. "We all need a bit of fortune, don't we?"

Xylo's remaining eye flashes green deep within the stone.

"You're telling me Tyche and Mnemosyne are the ones responsible for the Nephilim?" Hel asks suspiciously. She obviously never gave much thought to humans or their evolution until they landed on her world.

"No… not them. Even with souls, intellect and all the luck in the Universe, humans could never have challenged us, no more than a planet can challenge its star. Regardless of how much they learnt and evolved, of what they did to Midgard, humans were never a threat or enemy. They worshipped us until the very end, in fact. Even now, their descendants still name settlements and significant geographical features after us." He pauses, glancing at the Stump. "The Nephilim, on the other hand, are not humans; they are their creation. Their ancestors left Midgard long before it became uninhabitable, guided towards an ideal world for a wicked purpose from the very start."

'Prometheus, please don't do this,' Loki says.

The Titan glances apologetically at me. "I'm sorry, old friend, they need to know."

'No, they don't.'

"Know what?" Hel asks, her tone icier than ever. The way she looks at me now. Flaming sun! I know it's not really me she's looking at, but I can't help but shrink under her gaze. Medusa may turn others to stone with one glance; Hel turns them to nothing.

My entrails coil. The sinking feeling in my abdomen nearly makes me double over in pain. My heart pounds against my chest. I want to run, to scream, to burn! Loki is a trapped animal. I'm his cage.

"After my trial, and with my permission, Loki took several of the best and the brightest members of humanity to a safe place. Enough to start a colony in another world. Away from gods. When we realised humankind's true potential, we figured Zeus would stall their development if not eliminate them completely," Prometheus says.

"I did. And I would. I just had to play with them first. They are so lustful and easy to breed with."

"You make me sick," Medusa says.

He replies with a rude gesture.

Ice spreads between the two Olympians: a clear warning for them not to say another word to each other.

"I figured as much," Hel says. "Odin took his share as well, only he selected the best warriors, not the best minds. As Zeus said, many gods populated their worlds with humans back then, most for no better reason than to amuse themselves. What made the Nephilim's creators special?"

"Their purpose: to enslave gods and take over their worlds."

"Father, is this true?" Hel asks incredulously. "Did you inspire the Nephilim to destroy us?"

"No!" Loki says defensively. "I... I merely did what Prometheus asked. I facilitated their evolution by keeping them secure in a world with abundant resources, no predators and no deities." He made me face Zeus. "And if they were to destroy anyone, it would be the Olympians."

"Loki..." Gaea says, shaking her head reproachfully. "Everything you touch..."

Something ignites within me. "I touched nothing!" Loki shouts. "That's the problem. I had a plan. I wanted to create an advanced civilisation free of worship and superstition, where reason prevailed and tricksters were appreciated instead of blamed for every misfortune caused by ignorance. I was *guiding* them until fucking Odin put me in chains. Then they were left alone. Orphans with too many toys, no adult supervision and all the time in the Universe to play. I'm less to blame for their evolution and actions than Prometheus is for their creation, or Zeus for Prometheus' incarceration, Odin for mine, Chronos for the reckless use of his talent, and Hel –"

"Hey! What am I to blame for?"

The burning spreads. "You, dearest daughter, are guilty of letting Apollo into Asgard to kill Baldur. I didn't have to pay for a crime I didn't commit. You could have stopped it. You could have let her" – he points at Psyche – "stop it. But you enjoyed having Baldur in Helheim for no better reason than to rub it in Freya's face. Have you learned nothing from Odin and me? The truth is that every god here is to blame for the Nephilim. Even you, Gaea. If not for souls and Ambrosia, Chronos would never have bothered with us gods, let alone mortals. So well done, everyone! Fuuuuck!"

Loki has me so tense I fear my very bones may shatter. I've never felt such rage, despair and torment. As a Dharkan, I've experienced plenty of injustice and indignities in my life, but this… this is eons of frustration and justified resentment. Sparks spread over my skin. *Loki! Control yourself!* I can hardly keep Zeus' talent under control, and Loki's energy is too chaotic to contain. If he unleashed it now, we'll all be burned to oblivion.

An ice bolt fires from my hand, blowing the nearest tree to splinters. The next one smashes the cabin, leaving only a crater. Everyone takes a step back, except Xylo, who can't.

"Loki, my friend. Hear my voice," Prometheus says to me.

This only makes him angrier. *'You're not my friend.'* His thoughts overrun mine. There are so many emotions, so many memories – too many to keep track of.

Millions of years' worth of them; billions of lives, deaths and worlds pass before my eyes all at once. Is this what it means to be a god? How could they be sane with so much inside their heads? My body aches; my own mind breaks. There's too much! Too many images, too much noise. More energy shoots from me, through me. I have lightning in my veins! Someone screams – It's me. I'm the one screaming! I'm burning from the inside out. My body's being torn apart by Loki's rage. He's trying not to hurt anyone, so he's turning it on himself. Flaming sun! That's where his power comes from. He feeds off himself!

"Loki…" Psyche whispers. Her touch on the back of my hand is like tasting Prana for the first time – a breath of life. A heartbeat of peace. It only lasts a moment. But it's how long it needs to last. I see her staring up at me – at him. At both of us. And in that moment, it's as if everything is right with the Universe again. Like the pain was just a bad dream. And then I'm free. My body is healed, and Loki is sitting on the ground, his head buried in his hands, shoulders heaving.

No one makes a sound; even the very ice around us refuses to crack.

But something surely did.

There are many, so many creatures hidden in the surrounding forest, drawn to witness the gods quarrelling. They are terrified. As well they should be. Yet they remain here, silent, watching, hoping the gods pull themselves together because their existence depends on these entities with so much power and so little inclination to use it responsibly.

"Father…" Hel murmurs hesitantly. "You have to move past that."

"Why should I?" He shakes his head, still bowed. "How can I…"

"Because…" Hel takes a deep breath. "I need you to."

Loki looks up at Hel. His eyes are red but dry. "I know… I'm sorry. I shouldn't have brought up Baldur again. You did what you thought was right. And it probably was. But then, when the Nephilim arrived, you chose to remain hiding in Hades' Underworld instead of dealing with the Suzerain when you had the chance. Whatever happens, this you brought on yourself, Hel. I don't know how or even if I can help you anymore."

Hel takes a second deep breath. "Yes, I am guilty of underestimating the Nephilim. I figured they would leave once there were no more mortals to cull. They were doing me a favour." She glances apologetically at Gaea, who doesn't look like she's taking apologies anymore.

"And now, what's stopping you from taking matters into your own hands?" Loki asks.

Hel clenches her jaw. "You know what's stopping me." Her anger is a feeble thing compared to his. "Fenrir is still inside."

Loki nods to himself as if he's reached a resolution. "It's too late to change anything now, and blaming me won't solve our problems. It never has." He looks around. "Where the fuck is Hades?"

Hel winces. "By the sea."

Loki briefly buries his head in his hands again. "For fuck's sake. He must really love you," he snorts. Hel smiles the saddest smile I've ever seen on her.

Psyche still holds my hand. "Thank you," I say to her. And I mean it. Loki's chaos would have destroyed me.

She tilts her head to glance at me, her mind clearly someplace else, then looks away. Strange, for once I feel nothing from her. And it perturbs me.

Hel closes her eyes as if to face her fears. Medusa reaches for her goggles, ready to petrify us all. Gaea is a mother disappointed with her children, and Prometheus remains indifferent to rage or pain, fear or the cold. Not sad; certainly not pleased. But nothing else either. It's as if he's not even there.

Now that the gods have vented their grievances and their secrets, they look older, tired, less than themselves. Just ordinary beings with celestial burdens and an innate animosity for each other. I pity them.

Zeus stares at me hungrily. "Give me my talent back, Dharkan."

"No."

"I refuse to remain here amongst *them*."

"Then don't."

"And how will I leave with meagre power and no talents?"

"Find another talent. Is lightning all you are? All you can do?" I ask.

"No. But it's the lightning that sparks life. You have no use for it. You're dead!"

"Seriously. You Olympians need to update your definitions of life and death."

"Make him give me my talent back, Psyche. You owe me that much."

She seems to return to herself. "Fuck you. I owe you nothing."

"Neither do I," I say.

Zeus takes one step towards us, loses his balance

on the thin ice and falls on his arse. There's cursing. He stands up again as if he'd never fallen in the first place, head high, shoulders squared. I have to give it to the god, even butt naked and talentless, he still commands more authority than most, and he's not done quarrelling yet. I can tell. "I can't go back to Olympus like this!" Zeus insists, turning flush with rage.

Gaea and Hel exchange glances.

"Good. Because Olympus is no longer where you left it," Hel says. It sounds like she's been waiting a while for the perfect moment to say it.

Zeus' tenaciousness falters. "What? Where did it go?"

"We don't know. We – as in Hades and I – never bothered to look, truth be told. After the Merge and the desolation of Midgard, Olympus simply became... unimportant, untethered from the world."

Zeus blanches. "You mean any god could have taken it?"

Hel shrugs. "I suppose."

He jumps at me. Literally jumps, gripping my shoulders like a gryphon snatching its prey. "Give me my talent back! I can't stay here! Can't live like a glorified mortal with no talents. I have a world. I rule a pantheon. I am Zeus!"

"Aah, good. You know how it feels now," Psyche says.

"To have and to lose," Loki says to her.

"The best vengeance." She nods at him. They smile at each other.

"Odin would love to see this," Hel says almost wistfully.

"You icy bitch. Go and describe it to him, then!" Zeus suggests spitefully.

"Perhaps you'd like to describe it to him yourself instead."

The former Olympian king is a portrait of indignation, chest heaving in outrage, frustration and fear. It would not surprise me if he started crying. "Do something!" he demands of Gaea.

"I've done enough."

"This is very disappointing," Hecate says, joining the conversation again. She's been quiet this whole time, only shaking her heads now and again. "I had plans to make him suffer. But what can we do to him now? It really takes the fun out of it."

"I disagree," Medusa says, staring intently at Zeus. "I've been waiting a long time for this."

"Quit staring at me, creature! I had nothing to do with your fate."

"No. But in the absence of Poseidon and Athena, you're the best I've got to exert my revenge on. Tell me, do you like what your daughter did to me?"

Zeus leers back at her, arrogant and defiant even now. "I've seen worse."

Medusa's snakes hiss at him.

"You think you can intimidate me? You pathetic creature. I've faced Typhon in battle and won! You wouldn't be so bold were I not as powerless as a Wyrd."

"Odin was powerless as a Wyrd and still caused a lot of trouble," Psyche says.

"Then you should have destroyed him."

"Noted."

"Shame on you. Shame on all of you!" Zeus says.

"Take a good look at yourselves. What a bunch of hypocrites you all are. You all judged me for the very same actions you're now taking. Don't you understand? We're all the product of strife between Life and Time while Nyx laughs at both. At all of us! You really can't see what's been eating away our existences? I used to think power was what corrupted us until Chronos told me how we came into being. Now I know power is the only thing keeping us whole while souls are what corrupts us, and their goddess will be our doom! Release Chronos, return my talent, and you'll still have a chance to survive this. Otherwise, we're all doomed!"

"I've never heard that one before," Loki says sarcastically.

Hecate tuts. "I, too, am done with being doomed and already spent enough time on Time and vengeance. I'm bored now. Goodbye."

She takes a pouch from her bag, sprinkles something foul in the air, spreads her arms out and vanishes.

I wish I could vanish like that.

Hel, who took most of the powder carried by the wind, sneezes. "Freezing witch. She could have just translocated like a normal deity."

"Where did she go?" I ask.

Hel's eyelids flicker. "Not far. She's still in the forest," she says, suspicious.

"Are you sure it's safe to let her go?" I ask. After all, she escaped Tartarus and hid Chronos from us.

"There's no moon in Niflheim. She's all but powerless without her ingredients. Let her go to her lover."

"She has a lover?" Medusa asks indignantly.

"No woman dresses up like that without one."

"And she's going to meet with him now?" The idea clearly revolts her. Even the snakes act disgusted. "Does she realise how dire the situation is?"

"I daresay that's the reason she's in a hurry."

"Selfish whore."

"Give it a rest, Medusa. It's better this way. I don't trust her, and I'd rather not have her around on top of everything else. Her work here is done."

"And who's going to make sure Chronos remains restrained, huh?"

"You will. For now… Until Ideth gets back. Father?"

"I'm working on it…" Loki says tonelessly. "Although, I might have a better use for our unbridled one," he adds with a hint of mischief.

Hel puffs her cheeks. "Do what you must."

An awful noise assaults our senses: laughter. It comes from the block of petrified wood in the middle of the clearing. Loud, genuine, mocking laughter.

And that's when everyone notices Prometheus, too, is gone.

Interlude 3

Prometheus

Prometheus stood at Xylo's side, assessing everyone with patient resignation.

"Whatever you need to do, do it fast. I can't hold this illusion for long," Hecate said, glancing at him, then at her illusion of him standing passively amongst the quarrelling group.

"Fates, is that really what I look like now?" he asked, frowning at himself.

"Yes. Don't change aspect or you'll ruin the spell," she warned.

"I wouldn't know how... I've been like this for so long, I can't see myself as anything else," he stated not as complaint but as an irrefutable fact.

"I forgot how attached Titans are to their aspects." Hecate's faces shared similar expressions of annoyance. "Had I known you just wanted to look at yourself, I'd have conjured a mirror. Come on, say your piece so we can go."

They stood outside everyone's Reach. Even Gaea didn't seem to notice the small disruption in their reality. Like the others, she'd listened intently to Prometheus as he revealed Loki's role in the Nephilim's creation and had too much on her mind to even suspect anything was amiss. Gods need to know what to look for in order to find it, and Prometheus made sure that by the time he'd finished speaking, everyone's attention was on Loki, not him. It was unfair. After all, Loki had only done what he'd asked him to do.

"I'm sorry, old friend. Some gods are born to be antagonised. And that requires focus." Prometheus knew Loki couldn't hear him, but his conscience demanded he said it, nonetheless.

"What a bunch of idiots," Hecate said appraisingly.

"They're not idiots; they're ignorant. There's a difference."

"If you really believed that, I wouldn't need to deceive them. Honestly, I don't know how you endure it." She meant how he could stand there, watching the gods wasting their breath with petty arguments, knowing what would come – what *could* come, he reminded himself. There was still a chance things would change if his plan worked.

"I'm a Titan. I've endured much worse than a little strife." He gave her a sympathetic glance. "I could ask you the same. I don't know how you endured your time here, pretending to do his bidding."

Hecate pressed her lips; her faces overlapping to stare at him expressionlessly. "I'm a woman."

He almost laughed. "Ah, of course. There's that. And what's the point of suffering if not to teach you to do whatever is in your power to end it, right?"

"It had better end this time, Prometheus. Hermes paid a high price to deliver that message," she warned him.

"I've made many mistakes in my existence, but never the same one twice."

"Once is enough for some mistakes."

"Having second thoughts?"

"No. Just… concerns."

"Concern yourself with the spell and leave the rest to me. Are you sure no one knows what we're doing?"

Hecate suppressed whatever else she was about to say next and narrowed her eyes at the goddess of the soul. "Sure? No. But as far as I can tell, the only ones with the ability to perceive these illusions are Loki and Ideth. Loki's talents were blocked inside the Dharkan when I cast the spell. He won't be able to see us unless he knows exactly what to look for. And Hel did us a favour regarding Ideth."

Prometheus raised an eyebrow at her. "Do you think it was a favour?" It'd been such an overreaction, even for a goddess.

"I think Hel's the sort of deity who prefers to give others enough rope to hang themselves with rather than doing it herself. Like I said, be quick about it. I have places to be."

Hecate was good at her craft. The best; or she used to be. It was sad how reluctant she was to use her powers now. Zeus' punishment had left a mark. More than that, it had left her jaded and selfish, like so many others punished for no other reason than being themselves. But while his resolution to avenge the injustice had been reinforced by his punishment, hers seemed to have weakened.

"Can you give us some privacy?" he asked.

"Seriously?"

"Yes, please."

She complied, uttering a few words never before spoken outside Tartarus.

The gods kept shouting at each other like mortals, not even bothering with Reach for fear of what they might reveal. The louder the shout and the more indignant the statement, the greater the truth it hid.

"Look at them," Prometheus said to Xylo. "They spend so much time in reality, their senses are bound to it. I never understood why gods crave ownership over matter. Worlds make us weak. We were never meant to bow to gravity or property. Do they even realise how much their behaviour has changed in the last age? Likely not… It's the thing about change: if it happens gradually enough, you don't even notice. Isn't that right, Chronos?"

Chronos did not reply.

Prometheus sighed, then leaned on Xylo, poked a finger in his eye and pretended to inspect the contents. "The lengths we go to get what we want." He snorted inwardly, his face and thoughts betraying nothing. "I know you can hear me, so hear me well. I know I can't free the Universe from you. You're part of it now. To expel you would unravel everything. Personally, I don't care anymore, but this is not about me. This concerns everyone. We didn't ask to exist, but we will persist. In life *and* death."

Xylo's mossy eyes glittered slightly in his direction.

"It was a mistake to merge these worlds. Of course, you know that already. I daresay you knew beforehand, yet you did it anyway. When I saw it coming, I thought it was a hallucination caused by agony. What happened,

Chronos? You used to be patient. Did you tire of waiting? Nah, that's what you want us to believe, isn't it? You are the God of Time. For you, waiting is simply existing. You'll never tire of existing. Not an entity like you. So, what was it? You saw something, didn't you? An opportunity, perhaps? One of those rare moments where the fates lose a thread and anyone can pick it up to weave what they want? Must have had quite the impact, for you not only broke your own rules, you did it after humans spread across the stars, after they'd created the Nephilim – after many gods had perished. You waited until the Underworlds were bursting with souls, desperate for another taste of life. And for what? So you could torture them? Make life hard and the afterlife even harder? You thought you could eliminate us by shattering our souls into smaller and smaller pieces until nothing and no one could ever put them together again."

Chronos remained silent.

Prometheus took a deep breath. "You were right. In fact, you succeeded. You could have left it at that, but it wasn't enough, was it? Too late you realised causing pain to others did little to relieve yours. So you literally tore yourself and the entire Universe apart trying to excise Nyx's soul out of you." Prometheus looked at Psyche. "She wasn't a fluke but the inevitable reaction of the Universe to its pain. The pain you inflicted with your arrival and kept inflicting just by being here. I wonder when you saw her first? Right after you shattered the Universe's soul or after I created humans?"

Again, no reply, only a slight shift of his hateful gaze towards Psyche.

Prometheus appraised the goddess of the soul again. "She didn't quite turn out as you'd expected, did she? You thought you had everything figured out, but you forgot to account for two things: chaos and free will. What a combination! Stars, and I thought Pandora caused trouble."

"Psyche is greedier than Pandora," Chronos said. Prometheus found it strange that he chose this moment to speak, but he was too absorbed in his narrative to hold the thought. "She turned out exactly as she should. She's taking Nyx's soul for herself. I will soon be free and stronger than ever."

"Is that what you think will happen?"

"Yes. I *know* it will. I can feel it already. Nyx's soul was like your eagle: tearing me apart, making me vulnerable." The tone defined contempt.

"Vulnerable? Can you even grasp the meaning of the word? I didn't. Not until I had my liver ripped out of me again and again… and again. The pain wasn't the worst. It was bad, excruciatingly so, but the worst was the moment just before the pain. When I knew it was coming and I couldn't fight, couldn't run, couldn't avoid it in any way." He paused to collect himself. "Funny how knowing that it will stop doesn't have the same effect. You never get excited with the prospect of not feeling pain. You have no energy for it."

"Sounds like you understand me better than anyone," Chronos said. "So why do you judge me? I'm not a villain, Prometheus. I just fit the role better than most."

"Because this was never about the souls in the Underworld. It was about the soul in *you*. You needed someone to take it from you. A new type of god, born from a new type of mortal. Add a bit of spark, and boom. The rest, as they say, was just a matter of time. I judge you because you used me to create your weapon, and I could do nothing about it except trick you into believing you would succeed."

"Is that what you think you did?" Chronos laughed.

"Yes. We are bound to our talents, after all. Of course, I wouldn't have done it without Loki's help – may he forgive me. Between you and me, he's a much better Trickster than I am. Had he foresight as well, we wouldn't be having this conversation."

"Foresight." Chronos mocked the word. "You think yourself enlightened and mighty because you stand atop a hill, able to see the herds moving across the plains below. I can see the entire world."

"Ah, but not while you're part of the herd, like you are now. You'll soon find that things might not turn out *exactly* as you saw."

Chronos laughed. "I can see all the worlds in all the galaxies. Just as I've seen your deception, Titan. You think these… *tricks* will hold me for long?"

"No. Just long enough. Once Psyche is done with you, you will only be yourself. No longer able to cut strings. Not a master but a fixture of the Universe, with no power over death."

"I never wanted to be anything else. What need have I to cut strings when I can just stretch them, knot them and pull them at will? You have it all wrong, Titan. Once I'm free of this vessel and the curses suffered upon it, I will be unstoppable. I will be myself again, and she will perish, for no mere god can ever contain Nyx's soul without being consumed by it. You cannot fathom my strength, nor my patience. Just being here, listening to them, to you, is the very definition of patience. That's how much I'm willing to endure for my freedom. For I will be free and master of this Universe once again."

"Yes, you're the very personification of freedom," Prometheus gibed.

"One thing surprised me, though," Chronos said. "I expected Medusa to betray me, but not Hecate. It's remarkable how she managed to conceal her true intentions from me. Perhaps, instead of souls, I should have looked more closely into this ability of hers. Tell me, how did you convince the sorceress to help you?"

"Why would I?"

"Why not? If you are so sure of your success, what harm is there in granting such a small boon to a doomed entity?"

"It wasn't hard. She's in love, you see. Those under Eros' curse are easy to manipulate. You may be able to hear anything, anywhere – except in the Underworld. Oh, and in dreams, of course. But who gives a shit about those? It's not like they ever come true."

"Then you haven't been paying attention." Chronos laughed again. An impossible sound to conceal beneath the spell. "Aahh, love, you say… of course. Thank you."

The gods no longer argued. Hecate signalled for him to hurry up. It was all right. Prometheus had gotten the answers he wanted and given the one he needed.

"You have to leave now. Take this." She handed him a piece of snake's skin. "It will shield you from their Reach."

He took the skin and her hand in both of his. "May we never meet again, goddess of magic."

They looked at each other for a moment in a silent goodbye, eyes gleaming with unspoken words, then she nodded abruptly and pushed him away. "I surely hope not. Now go, go! Damn you."
He left.

INTERLUDE 4

Hades

Hades kicked the pebbles under his feet as he paced the long beach separating the Gharb from Aegea.

Many believed Niflheim to be a frozen world. Perhaps it had been once. Ice still covered most of its surface, true, but a significant portion of it had long been melted to create an ocean. This did not surprise Hades when he first found himself translocated there, along with his entire realm. After all, Niflheim had been inspired by the polar regions of Midgard, and gods are far less creative than they think themselves to be. Of course, now he knew better. The expanse of water stretching before him was not the result of imitation or lack of imagination, but of necessity.

Since the Merge and subsequent trouble in the fiery bowels of his Underworld, this oceanic realm had grown substantially. And it just kept growing, much like its lord, while Niflheim melted away into it.

Hades disliked oceans: their constant turmoil, the briny smell, and he wasn't particularly fond of the creatures living in them, either. In his opinion, nothing good ever came from the sea. Fish were smelly creatures, sirens were just plain evil, and sharks! What twisted god came up with those? One thing Hades knew for sure: monsters loved water. Oceans had more monsters in them than any other place outside Tartarus. Creatures like the Leviathan, Tiamat and Scylla had made the cold deep waters of Niflheim their home after the Merge. Unfortunately for him, Hades wasn't there for them but to meet with the original inhabitant of Niflheim's ocean: the largest and most monstrous of sea monsters, the world serpent, Jörmungandr – Hel's brother.

Hades shook his head. As if Fenrir wasn't bad enough. He often thought the reason Olympians were so messed up was because of their inbreeding. Something he was not innocent of. After all, he'd married his niece. But Loki's children, free of consanguinity as they were, made a mockery of the notion of family planning. Loki and Angrboda had not even been remotely related, yet their offspring had the potential to destroy worlds. Loki himself was unlike the gods of any pantheon. What else could be expected when a creature like him bred with a Jötunn? Absently, Hades wondered how they had even met. The attempt at shifting his thoughts away from his task failed, for he really couldn't care less about Loki's or anyone else's personal affairs, except as Hel's consort, he now had to.

Cerberus breath, what have I got myself into?

"Find my brother. Convince him to help us," Hel had said, as if it were a trivial task.

"Convince him… yeah, right," Hades grumbled to himself. How was he supposed to do that, exactly? So far, he couldn't even find him! He'd tried every call and trick in his power to seek a monster. Something as large as Jörmungandr would not go unnoticed, surely. Either he wasn't in the ocean, or more likely, he did not want to be found. Hades pulled at his hair. The shortness of it made him want to pull it more often, not less. He was seriously considering just shaving it all off. But then, going like this, he would just claw at his skull. *What is a god to do...* he thought over and over. He could not return to Hel without at least finding the beast. Lying about it, seducing or kidnapping weren't options either. Not with him.

"Damn it, Hel!" he said out loud, worried sick. He understood why she'd ventured inside the barrier without him, but she still hadn't reappeared in his Reach. Whatever hex Hecate put in the forest, it was still active and everyone in it was as good as gone from the Universe. How Hades hated witchcraft. Hecate all but founded her own pantheon of sorcerers with little more than herbs, bones, and the promise of elevating the wills of scorned women. No wonder Zeus punished her – for all the good it had done. Women, mortal or otherwise, were definitely more power hungry than men. Perhaps because they had less of it to begin with. Or perhaps because they were never content with what they had. Their hunger for power was so strong, many risked being burned alive for a chance to wield it. Didn't they know that just by being a woman, they had all the power they'd ever need over their male counterparts? He was a prime example of that fact. No, he decided. Women already had their own special power; they did not need another one.

He sensed a presence swimming under the grey waters. *Finally!*

"I know you're there! We need to talk." A ten-foot wave crashed on the beach in reply. Not Jörmungandr, just the Kraken playing with him. "Don't you have anything better to do?" a soaked Hades shouted to the turbulent waters. Another wave came crashing down. This time Hades was prepared and fended it off back into the ocean, to the Kraken's greatest amusement.

"Piss off! I'm not in the mood to play waves." Disappointment, boredom and something like loneliness Reached him from the water. "I'm sorry, friend... We'll play when this is over, I promise."

A giant tentacle waved downheartedly before submerging again. He looked so sad. What had the Universe come to when even monsters needed a cheer?

Hades kept searching, feeling more anxious than ever.

As he paced the stony shore of the Gharb, he couldn't help but notice what a miserable place it was. More than that, the peninsula didn't make sense. Hel would never have created such a landscape. This was definitely Jörmungandr's domain, designed purposely to be inhospitable to the Dharkan – Hel's creations – which spoke volumes about their relationship.

Hel had described their quarrel as a trivial thing, not a world-splitting grudge, and yet, looking at their world, that was exactly what it was. There's nothing trivial about quarrels between gods, especially between those related to each other. He'd enough of his own quarrels with his brothers to know that, and the stars knew he was as used to dealing with them as he was to dealing with monsters, but this… Cerberus' breath, the world serpent was just a bit too monstrous for his nerves.

A lone figure appeared strolling along the beach in his direction. Hades squinted to get a better look since nothing of note appeared in his Reach. He unconsciously went to pull on his cloak, but of course it wasn't on him. Hel had taken it with her inside the hex. Cursing to himself and simultaneously hoping for the umpteenth time that she was all right, Hades used his talent instead. The cloak was just an affectation, after all. He could become invisible whenever he wanted. For most of his existence he'd been invisible without even willing it, but there was something dignified about swirling fabric around you before vanishing.

The figure was male, his bone structure a bit too slender for a Narrum, his height too short for a dryad. He wore a simple tunic and sandals, stopping now and again to pick up a shell or a stone and throw it in the water. A Narrum scout slacking at his duties, or more likely a runaway, Hades reckoned. As he got closer, though, Hades thought he looked too young to be a scout. Not a child, but still a boy. *An idiot, then.* Many Narrum youngsters fancied themselves explorers. They usually preferred the Mountains for their explorations and would climb their icy peaks just to get a glimpse of the ice beyond them right before they died of exposure. But a few chose to prove their bravery by making their way into the Gharb and trying to snatch themselves an Aossi maiden. Some even managed to escape with their lives and their manhood intact. Such basic creatures,

Narrum, almost exclusively driven by their impulses. Hades missed the beauty and complexity of the original humans. He never learned where these poorly evolved specimens came from, but he would bet Thor dumped them here just to annoy Hel. There was no room in Asgard for ugliness, lest it remind their rulers of their own inner aesthetics.

Hades' digressing thoughts came to a halt.

The boy's body cast no shadow; his spirit had no presence. Hades cursed. Could this be another one of Loki's tricks? He really had no frame of mind to deal with him right now. Maybe it was a Wyrd.

The boy waved at him.

Damnation, Hades cursed again, realising he'd been spotted. Not a Wyrd, then. Of course not. Wyrds cast shadows for one, and they would not be fated to a Narrum. So... probably a demigod, or some other attention-seeking deity like the one who played the martyr to the wrong crowd back in ancient Midgard. There were plenty of those in Aegea. Hades knew he should pay them more attention, instead of aggressively avoiding them. But they were just so dull! Those self-righteous types always preferred to stay near the ocean. Preaching to the monsters, no doubt. Hades would rather deal with a Narrum or a Wyrd, for he definitely had no patience to be preached at. Vanishing again wasn't an option, so he considered translocating back to the other end of the beach – good manners be damned – but before he could do it, the boy translocated to him.

"You seem lost," the boy said, now standing so close he was practically stepping on his feet.

And he's here. Great, Hades thought with annoyance.

"I'm looking for some – one," he replied, stopping himself short of saying some-*thing*.

"Who? I know everyone along these shores."

Hades' patience was thin, and he had no time to waste so he simply said, "I'm looking for Jörmungandr," hoping the name would make the creature leave Hades alone to continue his search in peace.

"On a beach?" the boy asked.

Hades winced at him. "Where else?"

"You're more stupid than I thought if you really expect to find the sea serpent lying on the sand," he said mockingly.

"Now listen, you –" Hades stopped short of giving the boy a piece of his mind when he noticed the Suzerain's insignia embroidered on his tunic. He also had one of those contraptions they called keys strapped to his forearm, concealed under his sleeve. *A Nephilim. Of course.* Now it made sense. Funny how the mind often refuses to consider the most obvious possibility when it's also the most unpleasant.

"I have no quarrel with your kind at the moment and no time to talk. Move along. We can both pretend we never saw each other. Deal?"

"What is your business with Jörmungandr?" he asked, obviously refusing the deal.

Hades' patience ran thin. "*My* business. And who the frost are you anyway to think you can talk to me like that? Do you know who I am?"

"I do, Lord of the Underworld. You're the one who's forgotten yourself to come here and talk to *me* like that." The boy grinned. There was something familiar about that grin – too many teeth. It reminded him of Mika.

Oh…

As soon as Hades thought this, the boy began to grow. First in height, then in length, then in every other conceivable dimension, until a scaled giant loomed over the land, staring him down with deep blue eyes shining brightly through vertical slits. Hades nearly fell backwards as it flicked its tongue at him. Around them, the tide surged. The creature was taking over the entire beach and the ocean as far as Hades' eyes could see, and despite that, there was still nothing in his Reach. The combined result of Loki's talent of illusion and Hel's affinity with the world, he realised. *Cerberus brea…*

Hades knew size was not the measure of a god's power or monstrousness, so he closed his mouth and told himself he'd faced worse monsters. Actually he hadn't. But he had dealt with monsters before and he would deal with this one as well.

He cleared his throat. "Ahh, there you are! A pleasure to finally meet you, Jorma."

The massive snake head left the world in shadow. It tilted slightly, letting a ray of light through to momentarily blind the Underworld lord, then the flickering tongue slid slowly across scaled lips, an action more offensive to Hades wretched state than any smirk.

"It's Jörmungandr for you."

"Right…"

"I see my sister has made you her servant." Jörmungandr's voice echoed through Hades' senses. It seemed to echo over the entire world as well, straight to his soul. It probably did…

"I'm a lot more than her servant," Hades said, trying to sound both proud and calm. Quite the undertaking.

The snake hissed in dismissal. "You are her pet. She always liked to have others carrying her messages, fighting her battles. Is Fenrir not good enough for the task anymore?"

"Fenrir is in trouble."

The snake's head seemed to flatten slightly at the news. "Be more specific."

I just did, he almost said, but then he realised Jörmungandr had not heard him. He couldn't Reach. Every talent had a price. That was his for staying out of everyone else's Reach.

Hades fought the urge to pull at his hair again. This conversation would be even more unpleasant than he'd imagined if he had to use words. He stared up at the serpent again. He couldn't talk to *that*. Not only was it terrifying, it made him feel so tiny.

"Er… is there a chance you can return to your previous aspect so we can talk eye to eye?"

"No."

"Didn't think so…" Hades cleared his throat again and put on his best smile. "Very well. You know why I'm here, yes?"

"I can guess. My sister wants something. And she must want it pretty badly. I think she wants me to eat you so she can finally have her world back."

The smile froze on Hades' face. That possibility had not occurred to him. *Could Chiron have been right about Hel?* He shook his head. "No. She wants something from you, but not for her sake. She would come herself, except she's engaged with Chronos."

The scales on top of the snake's nostrils crinkled in a sort of frown.

Yes, there's always a bigger monster, Hades thought.

"So it's true. What's it to do with me?" Jörmungandr said.

"The God of Time? Well… nothing. I suppose. But the Nephilim –"

"I'm already onto them."

"You are?" That explained the outfit and ornament. Although Hades could not fathom the snake's angle regarding their use.

"This is my world too, Olympian. In case you have forgotten."

"I just learnt it," Hades mumbled. Jörmungandr ignored him.

"We are very different, my sister and I. When the Nephilim landed, she did nothing. Just hid away with you, like the girl she is, pretending they did not exist, much like the living, while she studied your side of the realm. I haven't been idle. Yet despite my efforts, she and her… *friends* somehow took the Stump before I could. Then she lost it again!" Jörmungandr flattened his neck. "I wasn't even informed of her plan, and now that it failed, she has the nerve to come to *me* for help?"

Hades was well versed in family feuds. This one would not be solved. It didn't even matter how or why it started. If Jörmungandr was half as stubborn as Hel, this entire discussion would have the same impact on their argument as kicking sand. He had to try another way.

"Things changed. I have a stake in this world as well, whether you like it or not," Hades said.

"Then I suggest you go tend to it, god of the *Un*derworld. The oceans are safe. And always will be. I personally guarantee it."

"Plenty of monsters in there," Hades said, glancing at the water.

"Precisely."

"Plenty in Tartarus too. Monsters love water. Things could get pretty crowded for you." Hades gave him his best grin, eyes aflame with defiance.

Jörmungandr lifted his top lip, serrated fangs glimmering in the light – his version of a menacing grin. Hades had seen many disturbing things, but seeing a snake's actual grin beat every single one of them.

"Feel free to send your monsters to me. I'd like to find out how they taste. Especially the old ones, the Titans. There's much life and soul in them." The way Jörmungandr said this gave Hades pause.

In a flash of revelation, Hades understood why Jörmungandr was so feared, as well as where Hel got both the inspiration and the ability to create the Dharkan. They called him the World Serpent, but Jörmungandr didn't feed on worlds. He fed on the life force of gods. He ate their souls!

Cerberus breath… maybe the snake was right. Maybe Chiron had been too. Hel had sent him there, hoping he would be devoured. Then brother and sister would rule the world together without him. But in that case, why was he still alive? He pushed the thought away and pulled himself together.

"I'm not here to argue, nor threaten."

"You just did."

"Yes, well – old habits. I'm here to do what gods do best: negotiate. We do need your help."

"More than you know," the snake said. How Hades hated being interrupted by conceited deities. *Breathe.*

"There has to be something you want in return."

"This ocean is too small," Jörmungandr said.

Good, we're getting somewhere. "I can appreciate that. Once we win, we'll gladly find you another ocean. I've once heard Poseidon talk about worlds with no land at all, only water. I'll personally make sure you get one of those."

"I want to go back to Midgard."

Hades cringed. "Why?"

"The reasons are my own."

Hades scratched his head. As the situation stood, getting to Midgard was as hard as any other world. Of course, Zeus would not be happy with this. Then again, he was no longer around. Neither was Odin. Their arrangement was null. Midgard was unclaimed and still had plenty of water. *Sure, why not?*

"All right," Hades said, starting to feel good about the situation.

"The Aossi come with me."

Oh, dear… Moving mortals to other worlds would be far more complicated. Hades had to force his hand away from his skull. "Of course," he said cheerfully.

"One more thing."

"Sure." *There's always one more thing,* Hades thought bitterly.

Ulla suddenly dropped out of thin air, coughing her lungs up. She was covered in stone dust, her clothes shredded and torn. She looked like she'd crawled out from under a pile of rubble. He was aware of the riots in Relicum but didn't think they'd got this bad.

"Tell my sister not to send mortals to do a god's work. They make poor spies and, fortunately for them, even poorer meals." Jörmungandr flicked its tongue in disgust.

"Where's Ulcan?" Hades wondered aloud.

"He didn't make it," Ulla said, more to herself than him. Even before she spoke, though, Hades had a vision of an intoxicated Ulcan on the bank of the river Styx arguing with Kharon about the exorbitance of the fare. *Oh well, I did offer him a priority ride.*

"Don't expect any help from Seshat. She has other plans," Jörmungandr said.

"Can you be more specific?" Hades asked.

"No."

Ulla looked up to see who he was talking to, gasped and immediately prostrated herself. "Mighty sea serpent. Forgive me for not recognising you sooner. I'm Ulla of the Aossi. Your humble servant." She closed her eyes, shaking with fear. "Please don't eat me. I'm pregnant." Her voice was barely a whisper.

"I know who you are, as well as your condition and devotion, Ulla of the Aossi. It's the only reason you're still alive. I want you to return to the Gharb and prepare the people to leave this world upon my command. Do as I say and you'll live to see your child grow up."

Ulla hesitated. Her mind filled with protests, questions, and inarticulable horrors. "Thank you, Lord," she said sensibly.

Jörmungandr turned to Hades. "Tell Hel I'll hold the world together for as long as I can. For my sake, not hers. Only she can help herself in the end, if she's willing to sacrifice."

"Sacrifice what?"

The snake dove out of sight without giving him an answer.

Hades pulled out a handful of hair, then channelled his frustration at the dryad. "*That's* your lord? I'm kin to your creator, guardian of your spirit. And *he's* the one you worship?"

Ulla frowned at him. "Wouldn't you?"

"You butch nymph, I'll have you know that –"

"I can't go back to the Gharb alone and order people to pack up everything for no better reason than the sea serpent told me to. That's even worse than trying to convince the population of Relicum to move to the Gharb!" Ulla said, talking over him.

There is something to be said about being a monster, Hades thought. Mortals no longer had any respect for reasonable, compassionate gods like him. Any other day, Hades would have sent the insolent dryad's spirit to the deepest pit of the Underworld as a lesson. Today, he was simply too tired, too distraught to bother. He took a deep breath.

"I'd be more concerned with the fact that most of the Aossi are at the Grove, not the Gharb..." he said, trying to figure out a way out of his own tasks.

"Is Arianh with them?" Ulla asked.

"No, and I wouldn't count on the queen's help, either."

"Why? Where is she?"

"The question is not where, but when. And the answer is, I haven't a clue."

Ulla blinked. "Was she...?"

"Stupid enough to travel? Yes."

"I was going to say ambitious…"

"They tend to go hand in hand."

"Frost!"

"Yeah…" Hades spared another glance at the ocean. He was starting to understand why monsters liked it so much. You couldn't talk underwater, and there were many places to hide.

The world trembled. Not the sort of tremble caused by Hel's temper, or the menacing rumble of volcanoes and tectonic plates, not even the soul-piercing rumble of Tartarus in uproar. This was deeper, older, a graver sort of tremble.

No no no no! Not this!

Hel appeared in his Reach. And for once, he was not happy to see her.

ANAMNESIS 4

Beneath the Stars

"Eros took you to Olympus to meet the gods? Ah! He really is in love."

Loki was dumbfounded. Not because Eros was in love or that he'd taken Psyche to meet his family, but because he felt somewhat glad he'd taken her to meet his own family first.

Psyche grunted in annoyance. "He's in love with the idea of love."

He agreed. Still, the difference was inconsequential to the outcome of his plan.

They were lying side by side on the balcony floor, heads touching, staring at the stars – the closest to relaxed he'd felt in a while – but Loki wasn't there to enjoy himself stargazing. He'd told Psyche stars were just enormous balls of fire, the primordial gods' first attempts at creation. They had no agency or sentience. Each one would just burn itself out and then trap light instead of giving it. He'd hoped this would dwindle her fascination with them. Sadly, the outcome had been the opposite to his intention. And so here he was, staring at the dull sky with her, wondering why gods kept repeating the same mistakes again and again.

"Tell me, what did you think of the Olympians?" There was the hint of a test to the question. He did not bother to disguise it.

Psyche sighed dramatically. "They are all arrogant, vain, petty, self-absorbed. You should have seen the way they looked at me… as if I were a stain or an insect fouling their otherwise immaculate surroundings."

"Most mortals are."

"Thanks."

"To be fair, it's not our fault. How often do you notice the ants at your feet or the spiders lurking in the corners?"

"I would if they talked to me," she quipped.

"Ahh, but imagine them all talking at once. Would you be more inclined to reply or to squash them?"

She turned her head to face him. "Is that really all we are to you? Noisy bugs?"

He stayed silent a moment, choosing his words. "Until we pay closer attention, yes. Then we might see some pretty specimen and take it as a pet."

"You're devastatingly honest today, god of mischief."

"Contrary to common belief, I rarely lie. And when I do, it is mostly to spare weak-minded creatures from the truth and myself from their complaints when they learn it. You're not weak-minded, so don't start complaining now."

"It was a fucking observation, not a complaint," she replied defensively.

Ever since their clandestine trip to Niflheim, Loki

had vowed not to let himself dwell on emotional dilemmas or stray from his plan. That meant he had to be stern. She was a mortal, a means to an end. He was a god. Gods go after what they want. And he wanted revenge. There would be no more kindnesses, distractions or reprieves from his goal.

"I promised to teach you how gods think. Our sensibilities may seem blunt for your standards, but remember, a god will dote on a pet as much, if not more, than any mortal master."

She grunted in acknowledgement before snuggling her head back into the crook of his shoulder. "You've been on edge lately. More than usual, that is. Is it something to do with your new project? The one you avoid talking about."

Loki didn't think she'd noticed. He had underestimated his lessons.

"Tell me about the Olympians," he demanded, refusing to indulge her curiosity. "How did they react?"

She bit her cheek, resigned to his mood, and did not pursue the subject. She'd learnt to pick her battles. Like him, she had a goal, and it was clear she would not compromise it for the sake of idle curiosity.

"The twins were fairly amused. Artemis made many spiteful remarks regarding the pitfalls of lust as she pretended to be Eros, shooting arrows with appalling accuracy. Apollo composed a mocking ballad to our love. Hermes couldn't stop laughing. Poseidon looked bored and eager to return to the depths of the ocean. Hades was the only one who didn't look down on me or insult me. He actually talked to me as if I was a person." She shrugged. "I know it was not for my sake. He was trying to annoy Persephone and Zeus. Still, he was quite pleasant. Unlike Hephaestus, who made no effort to disguise how much he despised me. I couldn't tell if it was for my sake or Aphrodite's. It doesn't matter, really. I didn't like him either. Athena wasn't there. She would not demean herself to meet, let alone engage in conversation, with a mortal. Neither was Demeter, since she refuses to be in the same realm as Hades."

"What about Zeus? What is your opinion of him?"

"He's a prick – a clever and powerful prick."

"A fair assessment."

"He wanted to take me from Eros."

"Did he say that?"

"He didn't have to. His wife, Hera, saw it too. She hates me for it." Psyche puffed her cheeks. "All I said to either of them was hello."

"With those two, it's all it takes. He's a hound, and she's a jealous hag."

Psyche snorted. "Speaking of jealousy. Eros took me to see my estranged family, too."

"Really? That must have been fun."

"Oh, exceedingly. My parents were so mortified they couldn't even pretend to be happy or even relieved to see me alive. My sisters were livid. You should have seen their faces, their envy. The hunger in their eyes, gazing at Eros' beauty. They think I've done so much better than them. Which I suppose I have, judging by their standards. Their poor husbands will have to deal with their disgruntlement for the rest of their lives."

"Must have felt good after how they treated you. To be vindicated."

There was a moment's silence. "I felt nothing, Loki.

No pain, no anger, no satisfaction. Definitely not vindication. I just wanted it to be over. I never wanted to go back, and I don't want to stay here. I just want to… go."

"Where?"

"Anywhere. Everywhere!" She sighed longingly at the sky.

"You will."

"So you say…"

She was sceptical. He'd taught her too well.

"It's a great love story," he said, hoping to steer the subject into a different perspective. "How the god of love fell for a human. I bet it will be told thousands of times through the ages. A beacon of hope and inspiration for mortal girls everywhere."

"I never wanted to be part of a story. I want to be part of history."

"And I want to be king of Asgard," he said dryly.

"Why?" Psyche asked, genuinely puzzled.

"Because…" *Because I've wanted it for so long, I can't remember ever wanting anything else. Because if I'm the king, Odin isn't. Because I enjoy giving orders.* "Because I was born to rule. It's my purpose," he said instead.

"I thought your purpose was chaos and your talent, mischief."

"Precisely. It's what kings do."

"The bad ones," she scoffed.

He wasn't taking the insult lightly. "Your father is a king; is he a bad one?"

She hesitated. "No. He's not great, mind. But he provides for his people. We've never known famine or war."

"And how much chaos does he foment in

neighbouring nations so his can stay at peace? He went as far as sacrificing one of his daughters to appease both the gods and the masses."

Psyche pressed her lips. "Point."

"Here's another piece of advice for you: personal peace often comes at the cost of someone else's turmoil."

"Noted." Her tone was colder than Hel's in a bad mood.

He turned his face to whisper in her ear. "I know how much you crave freedom, so let me tell you: freedom gets tiresome. When you're a god, even the universe eventually runs out of novelty, believe me. After seeing a few hundred stars, a few thousand worlds, you end up returning to familiar places, to the people you can bear. Or just like Poseidon, hiding deep in the ocean, bored with it all."

"It would be nice to have options," she said crossly, her mood growing sour by the word. "It was the most disappointing thing about the gods, you know. To see how miserable they were, how miserable they made each other. I kept wondering *why*. Why choose misery when you can do anything, go anywhere?"

"Being a god is complicated. We have… responsibilities to each other."

"Tsk. You are fools."

"And what would you do if you were a goddess?"

"I'd travel the Universe – alone. I know my human soul would never get bored." The reply was almost immediate. She'd given it some thought, as he supposed many mortals did. Poor things, they had no idea how difficult it was to be alone when you're a god.

"Would you miss me during your travels?" he asked without thinking.

"Do you wish to be missed?"

Did he? He was just making conversation. No one ever misses him. Then again, it could be interesting. He frowned, reminding himself of his goal.

"No. No, I do not," he lied.

CHAPTER 6

Game Changer

Transferring Xylo onto the glider is no easy feat. The gods' powers are useless against the curses holding Chronos inside his host, so they are forced to use their muscles – a far less effective way to get things done.

Everyone agreed Prometheus' disappearance was intentional. Whether it was triggered by Hecate's magic or Chronos' obscure power is still a point of discussion. The problem is, neither Hel nor Psyche can locate him, apparently. Fortunately, the gods have tired of arguing and begun acting for a change. Even Zeus is pretending to help with the ungodly task of fitting and securing Xylo to the glider.

"How fascinating. Is it powered by light, like a dryad?" The former king of Olympus peeks under the levitating metal as if he'll find the answer there. He seems to have calmed down substantially since his breakdown only moments ago. Or more precisely, since Prometheus left. Which means he either knows something we don't or he thinks he can find another solution for his problem.

"Must be." Gaea indulges him with the obvious reply.

"Ingenious. The Nephilim are truly ingenious," he says, a flitting amusement in his eyes as he glances at Loki.

"You're awfully keen on your old captors," I say.

"I merely recognise *talent.*" The strain he puts on the word confirms my suspicions. He's as livid and desperate as he was before. But now he has something else on his mind.

"And yet you let yourself be overpowered by them," Loki says. I wish he hadn't. The flames of their argument might have been put out, but it will only take a bit of kindling to reignite the fire.

"A miscalculation," Zeus replies with dignity. "No god is perfect. We all make mistakes – once in a while."

A very short while, I think but hold my tongue. This fire doesn't need more fuel.

"And still, you punished Prometheus for his mistake," Loki insists. He just can't help himself, burn him.

"Always so quick to defend your friend, Trickster. Even after what he did to you just now." He tuts. "Prometheus took credit for his creations, alone. I believed him. Too late, I discovered he wasn't the one who provided the spark. But by then, punishing you would be pointless. Not to mention, it would have made Odin exceedingly happy. I couldn't have that." Zeus grins maliciously. "You have much to thank him for, you know. Your enmity allowed you to get away with so much mischief in my realm. Had I been the one deciding the terms of your punishment, you would not be free now."

Loki frowned.

"You don't need to explain yourself to me," Zeus continues, feigning humility. "I, better than most, know how humans can be irresistible to gods, with their innocence, their flaws and their damned souls. It's funny, I created dryads to be beautiful, self-sustainable and obedient. The perfect pet, completely nonthreatening to us. And they became utterly boring because of it. Humans are not so easily manipulated or subdued. They are a challenge, are they not? I don't know about you, but I, for one, felt very challenged."

I don't like the tone of his voice: not threatening but teasing, almost mocking.

"You knew?" Loki sounds offended rather than surprised.

Psyche stops inspecting the glider's controls, her face blank, her eyes open wide and fixed on Zeus.

The Olympian smiles smugly. "About your little affair? Oh, please, I knew everything that happened in my domain."

"And you did nothing?" Loki says.

Zeus acts shocked. "I would never interfere in another god's fall for a beautiful mortal. I always liked you, Loki. It's true! I was a big fan of your… deeds. Anything that made Odin pluck the hairs off his beard pleased me no end. Besides, Eros is a cunt. The boy deserved the pair of antlers you put on his head. Oh, Trickster, don't look so surprised. It doesn't suit you. Did you actually think you could just fly into Olympus unnoticed? And they accuse *me* of having a large ego." He laughs.

Gaea leans back on the splintered tree, massaging

her forehead as if soothing a headache. Hel's glance to her father says 'I told you so' as clearly as if she'd spoken it. I just feel a certain pride at having been right myself.

"You mean the trials. The wedding… It was all…" Psyche shakes her head.

"Very entertaining, yes. Also part of the plan to make you a goddess."

"You wanted me to become a goddess?"

"Yes," he admitted frankly. "I was curious to see if Ambrosia worked in your condition. Do you know how many mortal women died giving birth to my children or just from carrying them? How many lovers I lost… and how much I loved them…"

"Sure you did," she scoffs.

Zeus went very serious. "Each and every one of them. Eros' love may not be real, but it sure feels like it. Lust, love, and loss. Over and over again… The boy is a sadist. He didn't care for my pain, or theirs. He just loved to see Hera's rage and what she did to the poor women. You all mocked my affairs. They were no laughing matter to me."

I reluctantly sympathise with the Olympian. *How many Ileanas has he lost?* I wonder.

"Lust is the root of all evil," Medusa says, nodding to herself. No one cares to comment.

"Since we are on the subject, I think you should know Loki wasn't the one who helped you gather the water from river Styx. I did," Zeus says smugly.

Psyche looks at Loki. He buries his head deeper into his hands.

"Why would you help me?" she asks.

"I was curious. Well, mostly I wanted to teach

Aphrodite a lesson. And truth be told, since Eros became *occupied* with you, life in the pantheon became much more bearable. Besides, I liked the idea of having another pretty goddess around. A god can never have too many pets."

"You tried to kill me!"

He lifts his hands in a placating gesture. "I did, yes – but only after I made you."

"Zeus… don't," Gaea says, glancing at Xylo. "Not here. Not now…"

"He knows! And if he doesn't, he has the right to." Zeus turns to Psyche again. "Ambrosia is not enough. Even for my offspring. It also needs my energy. My talent is the catalyst for apotheosis." He turns to me. "That's why it's so important I have it back. You owe what you are now to me, Psyche."

"I owe you shit."

"I didn't try to kill you because you became a goddess. I tried to kill you because you became the goddess of the soul," Zeus says.

The silence that follows is interrupted by the ice at our feet as it cracks when Psyche shifts her weight from one foot to the other. "I know," she admits almost to herself. "I know!" she shouts, in case anyone missed it.

Loki lifts his head, confused.

"I always knew. That's why I didn't kill you." There are unshed tears in her eyes. One moment there, the next gone, replaced by a scorn like no other. "Death was too good for you. But now we are even. No more secrets. No more debts. You got what you deserved."

His nostrils flare. "I got what you gave me! Neither fate nor merit had anything to do with it."

"Are you sure?" Loki asks. "There was a prophecy, as I recall. An Olympian prophecy involving my children."

Zeus grimaces. "She's not your child!"

Loki gets up and pulls the dagger out of Xylo's eye, set on using it on Zeus.

Hel stops him. "Do you really want Zeus to join Odin in Helheim?"

"Maybe that's what they deserve for what they did to us."

"Being as it may, the decision belongs to Hades as well. So pull yourself together."

Loki grunts in frustration and walks away to calm down.

Xylo's mossy eyes – or should I say eye – the only thing not truly petrified by Medusa's stare, shine behind the ice, sucking the strength if not the will of those who dare to glance at it. Except I can swear it's the shine of amusement, not anger.

"Gaea, dear. Aren't you proud of your creations?" the stone rumbles.

"Chronos, don't you start too."

"Well, well. He laughs and now he speaks!" Hel's not pleased with this. Neither am I for fear it will trigger yet another argument.

"This voice box doesn't require air to work," Chronos says.

"And yet you remained silent until now," Hel says. She's talking almost for the sake of it. It's unlike her. She's afraid. Which is also unlike her. Whatever concerns her is not the God of Time – not exactly – or the missing Titan, or even the Nephilim. It's something more personal. Could it be Hades? Probably her father. We're all concerned about Loki. He's working on something, I'd bet my left hand on it.

"Talking is for minor deities," Chronos says. "Do you even realise how pathetic you sound when you bicker at each other like mortal children? I am a God who listens and learns."

I can relate.

"So why talk now?" Hel asks.

"To ask the thing I haven't yet learned before it is too late for you to answer. What have you done with Ideth?"

"Wouldn't you like to know?" Hel snorts, fastening him firmly to the glider with a length of Gaea's conjured ivy.

"It's why I'm asking," he says, thunder in his voice.

Hel stops to properly address the God. "I'll tell you where she is if you tell me why you went to such lengths to infiltrate my world."

"I don't negotiate for information. You'll tell me because I have asked."

As a Dharkan, I was never intimidated by time. Not like the living or even the gods. Time for my kind is kinda like air. We are aware of its existence, what it does; sometimes we even breathe it into ourselves. We take it into consideration in our travels, our plans and actions, but we never rely on it. The only reliable thing about time is how inconsistent it is. On the other hand, this treelike construct, or more precisely, the conscience animating it, intimidates me a great deal. No creature in his position should act so arrogantly, not even a God. The way he talks to them and how they react to his words, to his very presence, is the scariest thing about him.

"He wants the souls," Psyche says before Hel can say something ill advised.

"My souls?" Ice spreads along the vines. The goddess of the dead isn't known to suffer bullies lightly. In this case, however, a little circumspection wouldn't go amiss.

"Careful! They'll shatter." Gaea pulls Hel away from her task. "You're doing exactly what he wants."

"He wants to insult me."

"So let him."

Hel scowls. "That's even more insulting!"

Just moments before, Hel stopped Loki from reacting the way she's reacting now. My father once told me, gods need other gods to keep them in check and maintain balance in the Universe. *'There's nothing more dangerous than a god who is alone,'* his words echo in my mind. He was trying to convince me that the Dharkan were more than hosts, we were company, a conscience of sorts. I did not believe him until now. Loki would have self-destructed earlier if he hadn't been trapped in me. Who knows what Hel might have done were she not bound to her souls and Hades? Then it hits me: Chronos has been alone for a very long time. And so has Psyche.

"Deal with it, Hel. It's what we all do. I, for one, would like to listen to what he has to say," Psyche says. The butterfly pendant is no longer glowing. At first glance, it looks like an ordinary piece of sculpted amber discarded on the grass, but upon closer observation, it's almost as if it holds a collapsed star inside. I have to avert my gaze for fear it might suck me into it.

"You think yourself victorious, goddess of the soul?" Chronos asks.

Psyche snorts ruefully. "I really don't."

"Do you think I'm the sum of what's inside this vessel? You better than anyone can grasp the extent of my being. What do you expect to gain from your effort?"

"Time."

"That you will," he threatens.

"What is he talking about?" Hel asks suspiciously.

It's Psyche's turn to give everyone the silent treatment. She isn't looking so good, and I don't think that, unlike her distress for her home world, is a pretence.

"Don't let him inside your head either, Psyche. He'll never leave." Gaea speaks as if from experience. Like Psyche, she looks drained, ill even. *Can gods get sick?* I wonder.

Another bitter snort from Psyche. "If he felt as confident as he claims, he wouldn't be talking." She curses at the ivy. "I can't work with this shit. We need a proper rope."

"Here." Rope, thick and precisely woven, appears in Loki's hand. Psyche takes it suspiciously and gives it a pull. "It's real," he says. He seems calmer now.

"Thank you." She ties it around Xylo with Hel pretending to help, her attention divided between them and Zeus, who is, once again, looking far too pleased with himself as he studies Loki and Psyche's interaction. When he sees me looking at him, he transfers his focus back to the glider.

"Do you forget you were once mortal, girl?" Chronos says. "Some ties are not easily broken, not by willpower, not by force, certainly not by Ambrosia. You may have spent an age as a goddess, but to me, your apotheosis happened only yesterday, and your end may well happen at any moment. Such is the fate of those who play with forces greater than their own."

"Ah! Then you definitely won't have a goddess of the soul to do your bidding."

The rock rumbles. "You stated your disapproval, had a little tantrum. Proved your stubbornness and so on. Now be a good girl and get on with it. We both know you'll do it, because you have to."

"Do what?" I ask in unison with Hel. Is this something to do with her passage through time? A debt waiting to be collected, perhaps? If the butterfly necklace wasn't meant to protect her, maybe the God of Time has reason to be so confident.

Psyche shakes her head. "You think yourself above all other gods. The Mighty Chronos, unfathomable, unbeatable, ineffable. And yet your wishes are the same as any other man or deity who bullied me. You want me to serve you, to obey you. To move souls around for you. Except my will is not bound to yours. Isn't that why I upset you so?"

"It's one of many things."

She scoffs, adding another loop to an intricate knot. "You know, I liked Xylo. Could even have liked you, Chronos. I probably understand you better than most. I respected you. Stars, I worshipped you! Time was all I had for so long… and all I feared to lose. Time was important; more than that, it was sacred. When I became a goddess, I mourned the fact that I no longer had time to worry about, only consequence." She scoffs again. "Gods think they are free of you because they are eternal, and yet every game they play is on your board, by your rules. It's their actions and their consequences that create what mortals perceive as the passage of time. You would be meaningless without them; they would be pointless without you. But mortals would still be mortal, no matter what. I can't change that. I can't change the game." She leans closer. "But I can change the board."

I catch Loki smiling at her, entranced.

"Straight to the point. I do like that about humans. They have no time to waste," Chronos says.

"I'm no longer human. It's not time I don't have to waste, it's patience." She fastens the rope tight.

"Then give me what I want."

"Aah. There lies the problem. Want comes from the soul. I only just learned that recently." She smiles at me. "So I'm giving you what you need instead."

Chronos laughs, a cosmically disturbing sound if there ever was one. "You're healing my wound because you think it's what I need? No god or mortal is that kind. Not to me. Save your righteous speech for these fools. The truth is, you're far greedier than them. You want Nyx's soul fragment for yourself. You think it will make you more powerful than the other gods. It won't. She'll consume you. Annihilate you. It's what you deserve."

"You're right. I'm not doing it for you." She picks up the butterfly pendant and hands it to Gaea. "Here. Take it. It's yours."

"NO!" Chronos' protest sounds like an explosion, its echo bouncing off the mountains, silencing everything in its path.

Gaea stares at the pendant, dumbfounded. "Psyche, I can't take this, I –"

Psyche presses the pendant into her hand, cutting her off. "Death should be Life's responsibility. You don't get to just waste away in peace after what you've done. You owe us, all of us: gods, mortals, animals, plants, everything that lives. No more blaming Chronos for their death or your losses. He's the consequence, yes. But you're the cause. Make it worth it."

Gaea holds the pendant as if it's scalding, eyes wide. Her mouth opens and closes a few times before she speaks. "But Kali is anathema to me. Psyche, I really can't –"

"The soul itself has no power, no will of its own. It reacts to the mind it's connected to. Kali is Nyx's soul's reaction to Chronos' mind. The only way she could survive, even control him to some degree. Her essence is already in you. It's in all of us. I'm just giving you more of it, for you are and always were the greatest and the best part of her."

Gaea keeps shaking her head. "I'm the Goddess of Life. I can't kill. It will destroy me."

"I didn't say it was going to be easy. Or pleasant. As humans liked to say in ancient Midgard: what doesn't kill you makes you stronger. So be strong, damn it!"

Gaea sets her jaw, chest heaving, eyes darting between Psyche and Chronos. Now the personification of old age, she shows anything but strength.

Nevertheless, she takes the pendant and leaves.

"Psyche, did you just give Life the power over Death?" Hel asks incredulously.

"Don't worry. Gaea can't stop death. The same way she can't undo life."

"It's her only goal! It's why she created Ambrosia. Why she challenged Chronos in the first place." Hel's eyes flash blue with rage.

"And now she has the means to fight him on equal ground," Psyche says calmly, resuming her task.

"She has the means to make every Underworld in the Universe obsolete. That's what she has! You should have given it to me, Psyche." I've never heard the goddess of the dead sound so desperate.

"Then you wouldn't be you anymore, Hel. Is that what you want?"

"I want to save my world and the souls in it. It's all I've ever wanted. How could you do this? Father, tell her. Father?!"

Loki, to no one's surprise, is no longer in the clearing. Hel screams in rage.

"What's in the pendant is not enough, though. Gaea's going to need souls – trillions of them," Psyche says in the same placid tone.

A glimpse of Hel's true form breaks through her illusion, such is her strain to remain coherent. "For what?"

"Nyx's rebirth – the new board," Psyche explains. "The Universe still needs three deities. Two opposing forces, and a neutral one to keep them in balance."

"I will not command my souls to –"

"You won't have to. They have free will. You just need to give them the choice. Most souls are too fragmented, too weak, merely inclination more than will. They know they belong together. They just don't know how to come together. I will guide them."

"You can't have my Underworld, Psyche. I'd rather let it burn."

Psyche sighs. "I don't want your Underworld, or any world for that matter. And I said *most*. There'll be many souls left that are whole and content with the minds they're bound to. They'll always need a place to go to when Life ends. You have more than your share in Helheim. It's time to let some go."

Hel shuts her eyes and lets out a deep growl of frustration. I almost expect her to cry. When she speaks, it's in a haunted, heartbroken voice. "They still ask about you. My souls. Since you came to Helheim, back when you were still a mortal. You talked to them through the Well. I don't know how. But you did. They've never forgotten you. For centuries, all I heard was *'Where is Psyche? When will she come back?'* Never met a mortal who had such affinity with death. At first I didn't understand what drew Loki to you. I mean, you're not that pretty, not that bright either. You're a freak. And he turned you into a monster." Hel covers her mouth as another realisation hits her. "The prophecy wasn't about us. Not all of it. It was you! You'll destroy not only the worlds and the Underworlds but the Universe itself!"

Psyche takes a long, deep breath. "Honestly… I can't be arsed. I'm sure you'll all find a way to do that eventually without my help. Believe it or not, Hel, I'm doing what I can to save it. I'm taking him" – she nods to Xylo – "out of your hands and freeing Fenrir as I promised."

"You're coming?" she asks me.

I nearly jump in surprise. "Er… Yes, sure." I thought we'd never leave.

"Hey, move over. I told you next time I'd drive. Watch the cargo," she says.

"And what exactly am I supposed to do if he gets loose?" I ask.

"He won't."

With Xylo tightly settled on the rear of the glider, Psyche sits herself in the driver's seat, looking more tired than ever. "Talk to Hades, Hel; this concerns his souls too. Then come and find me. I can prove to you I don't want your souls for myself." She raises an eyebrow at me, still addressing her. "I'm sure we can work something out."

Hel seems appeased by this and whatever else Psyche suggests telepathically.

"What do you think you're doing?" I ask Zeus as he prepares to climb aboard.

"I'm going too," Zeus says.

"The flame you are."

"You may have taken control of my talent, but you don't control me."

"But I do," Hel says, regaining some of her coolness. "Medusa, keep your gaze on your deposed king until Hades returns."

"I'm sorry, Hel. That was not part of our agreement."

"After all you just learned, you still think there's an agreement?"

Medusa's snakes dangle limply over her shoulders, seemingly lifeless as she shakes her head. Not just in denial or sorrow, but something more. "No, I guess not." She turns to us. "You can't have my soul, Psyche. But you have my support. Go, before I change my mind. You too, Hel. Hades needs you. I'll guard this one. And then..." She shrugs wearily. "I'd forgotten how violent life can be. I'd rather return to the Underworld."

"Let's hope there's one to return to," Hel says to her, then narrows her eyes at me. *'Keep your promise, Aedan.'*

I will, goddess, I pray to her. *Whatever happens, I will.*

INTERLUDE 5

Oric

"My hair!" howled Ileana, her voice breaking through a stream of sobs and snot as she clutched her partially bald scalp.

"You just had to wait until the very last moment, didn't you?" Oric hissed over her cries. There was not much left of his own luxurious hair, even his eyebrows had been scorched away, but never mind that. The raw skin on most of his face and chest was far more grievous, not to mention excruciating. His leather boots had shrunk tightly around his practically cooked feet, and with just one blistered hand and a barely functioning half of an arm, he could not get them off. He thought about cutting them free instead, but he'd lost his knife in the fire, along with its holster, and what was left of his trousers now hung precariously around his waist, leaving most of his legs and one bum cheek exposed. His left foot throbbed in agony. He had no feeling in his right one. He reckoned that was a bad sign.

"He burned my hair," Ileana sobbed again, staring in disbelief at the remnants of a lock of her once lush dark green hair.

"He burned a lot more than that," he replied, struggling with his own disbelief. Her dress was little more than a scarf around her neck. Her hands, legs and most of her back were badly burned. The loose pieces of skin peeling from her calves made even Oric's stomach turn at the sight, and yet her only complaint was about the loss of her hair.

"Burned it all away…" she mewed.

"For frost's sake…"

Could someone really be that vain? Maybe she was too burned to feel it, or in shock, perhaps. Most likely, the Suzerain had altered the pain receptors in her body. Lucky for her; not so much for Oric. The last pain he needed was a headache triggered by her noise.

Oric rubbed his nose in a failed attempt to get the stench of scorched flesh out of his nostrils while he assessed the situation.

They were right outside the Stump, next to the teleportation ring. Wisps of smoke billowed from several vents. The studding of the hull of the docked ship flashed glaringly. A blaring sound followed.

"Frost! Think, Oric. Think!" They couldn't stay there, and there was nothing closer than a half day's walk in any direction. Tattered trousers aside, his attire had more or less survived the fire. His burns were extensive but fairly superficial. They would heal… eventually. The med kit on his arm still worked, and he was confident he could still walk if not run – for a while, anyway. And walk he must if he wanted to live, which he very much did.

He stopped struggling with his boots, having

decided it was better to leave them on, and got to his feet, teeth gritted against the pain.

"Give me that thing!" He snatched the deathwand from Ileana's lap before she accidentally fired it again.

Ileana let go of her hair to scrabble in the air after it. "Give it back! It's mine. Or are you going to shoot me now?" she asked spitefully.

He wanted to kick her. "You weed. I should shoot you! You deserve to die, to burn alive the way Iosh and Oreth did because of you. *I* nearly died because of you," he shouted. By the gods, it was impossible to remain reasonable in her presence.

"You should have died. And they deserved to die!" she said vengefully.

Oric remembered Iosh crawling through the flames at their feet, begging for help. And how she had stepped on the burning man. He shuddered.

"You really are an unfeeling bitch."

"I feel plenty!" she shrieked back at him.

He'd disliked Iosh intensely – as he did most people, to be fair – but no creature deserved to be burned alive, not even the Dharkan. As a half Dharkan himself, he took burnings very seriously and had always tried to make sure the Wraiths were dead before he chained them to the wall. The last burning still did not sit well with Oric, especially after he realised they'd burned the wrong man. It was his fault. He should have sent Aedan to the Shadow when he had the chance. He'd failed. Since then, everything in his life had turned to slush. He'd tried to make things right. From the moment he'd noticed the lack of a scar on the Wraith's face, he'd tried to get to him before the sun to finish the job but had been distracted by Ileana and her Wyrd. He'd told himself then that not even he could have fought through the madness of a mob. The truth was, he'd let his aggravation for the woman get the better of him. Later, that same aggravation had led him into that cave where he'd lost his arm, and now, here he was again, aggravated and about to lose a lot more.

Oric shook his head to clear it of such thoughts. Regret had no place in a sensible mind. What was done was done, and he would not dwell on it.

"You're welcome," he said, rising above his misgivings and his antipathy for the girl.

"For what?!"

"Saving your life." His greatest regret, of course. He should have cut her arm off to get the bracelet and spared himself the ordeal of dragging her through the fire. Sure, the Suzerain would not be pleased with that. But burn the man for raising such a despicable creature.

"Ah! As if. I saved *you*!" Ileana threw the bracelet at him to prove her point. "Without me, you'd still be in there, burning to a crisp." Realisation dawned on her singed face. "I… *saved you*. Oh, frost!" She acted as if she was going to be sick. "Frost… no! This is not fair!"

"Tell me about it." He picked up the discarded gem key and took a tentative step forward, trying and failing not to wince with the strain.

"Give me the key back," she commanded, glaring at him from the ground. "It's an order."

"To the Shadow with you! Giving me orders. Who does she think she is?" he grumbled to himself, still testing his unsteady stride.

"I am the daughter of your sovereign. You can't leave me. You owe me, metz," she spat behind his back.

He would laugh if it didn't hurt so much to do it. "I owe you slush."

"My father, then. You owe him."

"And I paid my debt," he shouted over his shoulder. "You're alive and free to do whatever you want. Go back in, if you wish. And good riddance."

He would heal, but healing took time, energy, and rest. All the things he lacked standing there talking to her. He pushed on further.

"You can't leave me here!" she protested.

"I just did." He waved his good hand without looking back. "Bye." He was so done with her. Keeping some distance between them was all the motivation he needed to pick up speed.

He hadn't gone far before he heard the shuffling and grunting behind him. She was crawling after him. Her legs were too injured to support her weight, but she kept trying, dragging herself along the dirt when she failed. A pitiful sight if there ever was one. Enhanced as she was, she would definitely survive until the Nephilim got themselves organised enough to search the perimeter, and when they resurrected the Suzerain, her report on his conduct would be less than stellar. *What a bloody mess…* Oric stopped and looked at the sky. The day had barely started. He took a long, rattling breath before turning around.

"Come on," he said with an outstretched hand. "We can't stay here. They will come for us. I know you don't want that." Actually, he was surprised they got out in the first place. The Stump was on lockdown even before the fire automatically triggered it. The Suzerain's bracelet overrode many security protocols, true, but Namrive's command overrode everything. That meant she'd been focused on something else during their escape, or that she'd slacked on her own protocol. Namrive never slacked.

Ileana slapped his hand away. "I don't want your freezing help! I want my key back. I can't go anywhere like this. I need a new body! With hair!"

"You need a new brain!" he spat back. "Your precious hair will grow and your skin will heal. Faster than mine, I bet. Your father wouldn't build you to break easily." He inspected the bracelet in his hand. One gem had cracked in the heat. It was no longer working. He tossed it back at her. "The key is broken. You can call them on the ring and ask them to pick you up if you wish." He could tell she didn't. "Or you can take my hand. I'll help you get to Portum and then –"

"I'm not going to Portum."

Oric inhaled through his teeth. "Then where? The Grove?" He exhaled through his nose. "Sure, at least it's closer."

He'd drop her at the Grove with her kind and then continue to Portum to seek shelter in Jonas' sanctuary.

She scowled. "No. Not the Grove either. You're right." Ileana glanced fearfully at the Stump. "I can't go back right now. I'll heal. Yes, I just need a bit of Ambrosia, and I will be good as new. Take me to the caves."

He didn't want to believe what he heard. "What for?"

"Aedan is alive. I need to find him."

"The Wraith?!" What had possessed this creature to be so obsessed with a Dharkan? The things weren't even alive! It had to be a curse. There was no way a woman – Oric frowned at her – or girl, as the case might be, could be that stupid. Yes, love was a curse. And Oric was immune to curses thanks to the Nephilim. If only he could be immune to her presence as well.

It was tempting to take her to the Wraith so he could kill him in front of her. After all, Oric had vowed to kill the creature. He hated leaving tasks unfinished, and he very much wanted to cut him open even more than Anubis did him. But the caves… He shrugged his left shoulder unconsciously. The very mention of the place made him sick. The memory of Aedan feeding off him came unbidden – as it always did, for who wants to remember such things? – making both his step and his resolve falter – as it also always did. Alek once told him the reason he'd removed his body's ability to feel sickness was not so he could murder in peace, but so he could think about it without nausea. One day, Oric would like to understand how memory and imagination can cause so much physical distress.

"I'm not going back to those caves," he said. "You can come to Portum with me or go anywhere else you want, alone."

"What about the Grove?" she asked.

"That offer expired." He set off again, painfully aware that his feet wouldn't take any detours.

"If something happens to me, my father will not forgive you."

"And I wouldn't care because I would be dead already." The Wraith would finish his meal, for sure.

"If that happens, my father will bring you back just to punish you. You know he will."

Oric looked up again. The smoke was thicker. Red lights flashed alarmingly all over the ship. The labs had probably been destroyed by the fire. What were the chances of Alek coming back this time? *Slim…* What about the consequences if he did? *Dire…*

He cursed, then sighed.

"Girl, I can't protect you. Look at me. I can hardly walk myself," he said truthfully.

Ileana grunted and whimpered her way to a standing position. She held herself there a moment before taking one stilted step, then another, her face contorted with the effort. "I don't need your help or protection. Just your escort."

He snorted. "You think you can cross Aegea in that state? Even the women will stop you."

"Not, if I'm, with you," she said through gritted teeth.

She was right. She wouldn't be the first battered female 'escorted' by a man. Husband, brother, father, the relationship wasn't important. Neither was her state, as long as there was a man nearby to take responsibility for it.

Oric wished he still had his blade. Wished he still had his arm, wished his feet weren't cooked inside his boots, wished he'd never returned to the Stump, wished he'd killed the Wraith. More than anything, Oric wished he'd never met the Suzerain's daughter.

If only wishes were weapons, as Hephaestus liked to say.

He shrugged exaggeratedly and kept walking. His body might be ruined; he would not compromise his sanity as well.

She fell over. "You'll pay for this! Father will return,

and when I tell him what you did, his punishment will make you wish Anubis had dissected you."

Oric stopped and scratched at his throat while trying to gather as much restraint as he could muster. It wasn't much. He turned around and pulled her up by what was left of her precious hair. She screamed as more of it came off. "What about I end you right now, huh? Beat your brain to pulp so no memory can be recovered from it."

Her breath caught. That possibility had not occurred to her. Bodies can be rebuilt, but we are nothing without our memories.

She stood on her knees, tears in her eyes, hands on her hips. A broken portrait of stubborn indignation. "You can do that. Or you can take me to the caves like I asked."

She was her father's daughter, all right.

"You're worse than nettles, creature!"

Gods always go on and on about curses. Oric never really understood them until now. She was his curse. He could break her. Even with one arm and injured feet, he could destroy her and he would certainly enjoy it. Of course, this close to the Stump, he would not get away with it. Even if she didn't remember, his guilt would be a simple matter of deduction.

Not here, then.

"Very well. I'll escort you as far as where the road splits to Portum. Then you are on your own. And you better catch up. I won't carry or wait for you." Lights were now flashing all around the Stump as well as the ship. Birds flew from their nests as a tremor rocked the dirt at their feet. That put an end to their argument. "Move!"

She stood, only to fall again as soon as she tried to walk. Oric pulled her to her feet and put her arm around his shoulders. He would help her walk but would not carry her, dammit.

They limped on.

∞

Ileana tripped over her feet, and Oric caught her by the arm just before she fell over again.

"Get your filthy hands off me," she said, as if he hadn't been holding her all day.

"You ungrateful cunt."

She snorted. "You're the second person to call me that."

"Because it's true."

"The first was Psyche, when she was usurping my body to hide from her lover and kill my father. Gods' notion of gratitude is hilarious. Yours is just petty."

He gritted his teeth. *I'll kill her and say the Dharkan did it, or a snake did it. Oh, I know, a gryphon! They often prey on young dryads.* He smiled at the notion.

"You find that amusing?"

"Oh, more than you know. We should keep going. It will be dark soon." Actually, according to his calculations, it should have been dark already. But with all that had happened, he figured his calculations were wrong.

"You were thinking about killing me again, weren't you?" Ileana asked.

"A man can dream."

"You're not a man."

He stopped, ready to let her fall. "Say that again."

"A man defends his woman, he doesn't daydream about all the ways he can get rid of her."

"You're not my woman! I can daydream about whatever I want. And that's rich, coming from you and your taste in men."

"Aedan would never hurt me. He loves me."

Oric gaped at her. "You really believe that?"

"Of course he loves me. How could he not?"

Oric bit his lip. It was too easy to fall down the insult hole again. "Maybe he does, or maybe he was just hungry. Dharkan can sense emotions better than gods, but they have very few of their own, believe me. He's no better than a corpse with needs."

"You're half corpse yourself."

More than half at this point, he thought bitterly. His body was a mess, and this excursion was only making it worse. Still, the revolting accusation demanded retaliation. "I'm nothing like them! Or you! You're neither dead nor alive. You're a *thing.* I have a Dharkan's strength and resilience, but I'm very much alive. I can walk in daylight without being host to a god. I age and I feel and I have to feed like any normal creature. Wraiths feed on the life of their women. Often killing them in the process. My mother was one of them. I bet she thought my father really loved her too when he abandoned his brothers and ran with her to the forest where they lived happily until the day he came home just a little bit too peckish."

She was silent for a long moment. "Is that why you hate them so much?"

"Would it make it easier for you to accept my hate if it was?"

"Yes," she replied, to his surprise. "It would make me hate you less. I would just pity you instead."

He stared at her, stunned. "Congratulations. I now officially despise you more than the Wraiths."

She lifted her chin. "Then you now have an idea of how I feel about you."

That's it. He dropped her to the ground. "I know you're sick. Traumatised by your life. And I cannot imagine what you've been through in your time. Alek told me things, horrible things that defy belief. If any of those were true, you have my sympathies. But girl, you're the worst creature I have ever met! You're hazardous to my health. We're done."

"We're here," she said, ignoring everything he'd said.

"Huh?"

Her eyes and index finger fixed on a point beyond his head. "Portum."

You can't see Portum from here. He turned around and blinked, all his pains momentarily forgotten by what he saw. A massive white marble dome shone through the trees. It was larger than the temple in Relicum. Larger than anything he'd ever seen besides the Stump. "What in the Shadow…" That couldn't be right. He checked his surroundings. The dome's location did roughly match where Portum should be, but that was definitely not its temple.

"Help me up," she demanded. "I always wanted to see the grand temple in its prime."

The grand what? The hairs on his nape stood on end. He didn't like this one bit.

"Er… you wanted to go to the caves. I think perhaps

we should." Oric did not trust whatever the frost was ahead of them.

"After. I need to hydrate first." She pushed herself up again, invigorated with a new purpose and extraordinary healing ability. "There will be gods there. One of them will fix me."

Oric had no doubt there would be gods. No mortal could build something on that scale, never mind in such a short time frame. The question was… which gods?

"I really don't think that's a good idea," he said.

She huffed. "Why do you always have to dispute everything I say? You're the one who wanted to go to Portum."

That's not Portum! he wanted to say, but she had a point. As challenging as she was to reason with when she was wrong, it would be impossible to do so when she was right. And he really didn't want to go to the caves.

"All right! All right, stop shouting. We'll go quietly – through the woods, not the road – and we'll check the area before entering the settlement. Understood?"

"Whatever."

Oric groaned inwardly. His hand unconsciously clutched at his absent holster again, looking for his knife. Life was easier when you were armed and able to defend yourself. His only defence at the moment was her, and he would gladly leave her behind as a decoy if things went wrong. Yes, he would.

ANAMNESIS 5

Free Will

Psyche marched back and forth across the room, wringing her hands and chewing on her cheeks, her thoughts an incoherent mess of dread, anger and worry. Loki alighted on her shoulder in his guise of a fly to better make sense of the situation before manifesting his arrival – as was his habit these days – and barely dodged the hand aimed at splatting him.

"Careful!" he bawled out as he shifted to his usual form. Insects were dangerous things to impersonate, he reminded himself, especially around ill-tempered humans.

"Loki! I've been praying to you for days! Where the fuck have you been?"

"I was with Hel, deep in Helheim, out of Reach," he lied. "You seem to be all right." Another lie. "What's the urgency?"

"Eros wants to marry me!" Psyche announced, clearly displeased with the prospect.

"I thought you were married already."

She blew out a lungful of air. "He only calls me

wife to annoy his mother. But now he wants to make our" – she hesitated as if trying not to choke on the word – "*union* official in the pantheon."

Loki chuckled. "Aphrodite must be furious."

"She is. And so am I!" she practically screamed in his face.

"I can see that," he said, leaning away from her fury.

"It's been over a year, Loki. You're no closer to your revenge than I am to my freedom. And now this? We have to do something other than lazing about talking."

"I thought you liked to talk."

"That's not the point!"

Loki sat on the bed. "So marry him," he said, feeling uncharacteristically tired. Tending to the birth of an entire civilisation took its toll, even on a god like him.

Psyche remained standing, gaping at him in confusion. "I'll do no such thing!"

"Why not?"

Her jaw dropped further, eyes wide in disbelief. "I don't love him."

The understatement of the age, Loki reckoned, but a moot one. Every god knew marriage had nothing to do with love.

"If Eros wants to make your relationship official, then Zeus will have to turn you into a goddess. There's no place for mortals in the pantheons. Surely that's a good thing? Once apotheosized, you can do whatever you want."

"Zeus wants to give me Ambrosia, yes. Except you told me Ambrosia only works with demigods."

"I did," Loki admitted.

"I'm human! Most humans die at the mere taste of the stuff. It will not work. I'll either die or… or nothing. It was all for nothing!"

"It's still worth trying, no?"

"No! How can you even suggest that? I don't want to die anymore. Not yet. And if I don't die –" She pressed her hands against her temples and inhaled deeply, letting the air flow in and out of her lungs slowly before she continued. "Don't you see what they're doing? It's the ultimate humiliation, the proof I'm not even worthy of being Eros' pet."

Eros and Psyche's relationship, mostly ignored at first, had become increasingly frowned upon and was now a prominent source of gossip and concern amongst the pantheons. Rumours of Eros' infatuation for a mortal had reached as far as Asgard. Opinions were divided between those who were amused at the irony that the god of love had succumbed to his own talent and those who'd rather he got a grip on himself and his damn talent, for everyone's sake. They all agreed on one thing, though: the Universe didn't need more gods, especially Olympian ones.

Psyche winced as she chewed on her cheeks. They had to be bleeding by now. "The gods wanted to get rid of me for years, and this is the perfect excuse. An execution disguised as a wedding. Just like before, when my parents offered me to the monster. I'd become too much of a nuisance, so the oracle's suggestion suited them perfectly. They could finally get rid of me and still be seen as the injured parties in the deal. That's humanity for you. Divinity, it seems, it's even worse."

Her voice was taut. She had tears in her eyes, caused

by rage more than sadness. And fear, of course. Her usual cynicism often acquired a dramatic edge when she was afraid.

Loki sighed. She had good reason to be afraid. Zeus was a cunning bastard. Up until then, Loki hadn't given much thought to Ambrosia besides the fact that its tree was planted in Niflheim, or even bothered to learn more about the schemes between the King of Olympus and the Mother of Life. As long as Odin remained ignorant of the arrangement (which meant it was likely he would suffer from it, not benefit) it was fine with Loki. But Zeus had to know Ambrosia would not work on Psyche. Unless he had some other way to transform her, it would never work. Why bother with the pretence, though? Zeus could just take her for himself, kill her with no reason, explanation, or even apology. It's what gods do. Why go to the trouble of indulging Eros? Maybe he was afraid of the consequences if he denied the god of love this. After all, few gods had been shot with his arrows as often as he had. Hera would not tolerate more infidelities, that was for sure. Then again, perhaps this was Hera's idea of revenge on Eros for all the trouble he'd caused in her own marriage. She was the type of woman who always punished other women for the offences suffered upon her by men. He really couldn't fathom what motivated those two to remain together, not even what brought them together in the first place except power. Is power really worth so much personal misery? Loki had to admit one thing, though. He was glad Zeus reigned in Olympus and not Asgard. He'd rather not have him as an adversary. Odin was clever and ruthless, but he was also honourable in his own way and fairly predictable because of it, while Zeus had a twisted way of thinking that often challenged even his own twisted thoughts.

"What am I to do?" Psyche asked, staring up at him with pleading eyes. How could she ask him that? How could she even trust his answer? *Haven't I taught you anything?* he wanted to scream at her, but she looked so vulnerable and so… lovable. *Fuck.*

"You need to get pregnant," he told her.

She blinked a few times, her upper lip curling in incomprehension, then her brow began to furrow as if the idea was a mathematical equation, impossible to contemplate, let alone solve. "That's the last thing I need!" she screeched, then stomped out onto the balcony as if she needed fresh air, despite the fact the doors were wide open.

He followed.

"If you will not take this seriously, get the fuck out!" She kept her back to him as she spoke, shaking, her thoughts a self-destructive howl of apprehension, anger and frustration. He'd never seen anyone this upset. He touched her shoulder. She immediately jerked it away.

"How much do you know about how Ambrosia works?" he asked gently.

"Probably the same as you do about Yggdrasil's roots," she replied acerbically.

He regretted the question. Of course she wouldn't know anything about the properties of the resin. He himself had only just begun to make enough sense of the substance to formulate his theory.

"Ambrosia was meant for soulless mortals. It acts on the flesh, makes it repair itself faster, more efficiently, and indefinitely. Its purpose is to heal and prolong life. It doesn't work on gods because we do that naturally and our lives are practically eternal. You can say Ambrosia runs through us from the moment of creation. Turning demigods into gods was an unexpected effect. Gaea herself was surprised since, despite appearances, we have very little in common. My theory – and it's only a theory – is that it has something to do with fragments of a god's soul passed on to their otherwise soulless offspring."

Psyche huffed. "I don't give a fuck about Gaea's surprise or how and why Ambrosia works. It won't work on me. I already have a fucking soul. And having a child will not get rid of it. I have enough problems already!

He turned her around and pulled her wrists away from her face, forcing her to focus back on him. "Hear me out. The souls of humans are similar to those of gods, but much less powerful. Just powerful enough to repel a god's soul in case he wants to take over the human's mind. They are what gives you free will."

"Ah! Free will to a creature who is bound in every other way to the laws of gods. What cruel entity would do such a thing?"

Loki had to force himself to breathe. "That's not important right now. I'm trying to explain something to you. It's difficult enough to explain using words, so stop interrupting me and listen." He held her steady in his grip to force her to pay attention. "In theory, Ambrosia should work on humans, and yet it doesn't. My guess is that whatever prevents gods from taking humans as hosts also prevents Ambrosia from affecting them. Now, demigods are mortals with vestiges of a god's soul, but their talents are atrophied – for lack of a better word. Yet Ambrosia has the ability to boost their bodies enough to accommodate and somehow enhance their soul to its full potential, allowing them to develop their talents."

"Your point?"

"If you had the blood of a god or even just a wisp of a god's soul in you… it could work."

"That's crazy! And even if it did, you know what Olympians are like. Do you actually believe Zeus, Eros, or even Aphrodite will go soft on a pregnant woman, especially if she's carrying the offspring of a god? Stars! They'll probably give me to Hera!" Psyche covered her mouth at the thought. "Oh, fuck… I'm so fucked…" she mumbled into her hand. "What about my own soul? Wouldn't it fight off the god's? Or worse. I could go insane."

"It is a possibility, yes."

She considered this for a heartbeat. "No. It's not worth the risk. I'm perfectly capable of going insane by myself. Besides, it's not like I control the matter."

"More than you think," he said.

She clicked her tongue. "If I could get pregnant, I'd have been by now."

Loki tried to sound jovial. "Well, you know. When a mare can't conceive, changing the stallion often does the trick."

"I'm not a mare! And there will be no fucking children," she snapped adamantly, releasing herself from his grip with far less conviction than she put in her words. "Stars, Loki. Even the thought makes my skin crawl. Changing stallions, indeed." She puffed out another breath, then eyed him askance. "You're volunteering?"

"My fertility has been proven." He grinned.

"I've met your offspring. You're not impregnating me." She pushed him away.

"Ouch, my pride bleeds."

The overture of a smile died on her lips. "Enough play. This is serious, Loki. What do I do? They're going to kill me. I'm not a demigod, so I can't turn into a goddess. I don't want to be a wife and certainly not a mother."

"Well, then you'll remain a slave and a mortal."

"Are those my only choices?"

"I'm afraid so."

Psyche took his hands in hers, pulling him close. "If mortality is to be my fate, let it be one of my choosing. Take me away. Take me to Niflheim. Permanently," she whispered. "They will never find me there."

"You don't understand what you ask."

"I'm asking for help. For freedom. Freedom from this place, freedom to spend eternity as I choose – with those I choose." She gripped his hands tighter, getting up on her toes to whisper her plea close to his ear. "I'm asking you to take my soul to where it might be accepted. Where I might belong. I'm asking for peace."

Peace, not happiness, he noted.

He breathed in. The combined fragrance of the lily in her hair and green apple on her breath delighted his senses. He wanted to kiss her, hold her and, yes, take her with him. Vengeance and consequences be damned. He wanted her. He always wanted the things he couldn't have: respect, Mjölnir, Asgard, a world to rule as he willed. But to want something he could actually have and knew he shouldn't? That was a whole new torment. He pulled away from her as if he'd been scalded. The disappointment on her face was almost too much to bear.

"You're praying to the wrong god, mortal. I deal in chaos, not peace."

And with that, before either said or did something they would eventually regret, he vanished from her sight.

INTERLUDE 6

Loki

Loki found Prometheus knelt by the Chronodéndron, hands clasped together in front of him as if in prayer. "I knew you'd follow me here," he said without even lifting his gaze.

"Must be great to always know what's going to happen," Loki replied. There was no accusation or resentment in his tone, just a fact stated with resigned wistfulness.

Prometheus grunted ruefully. "Depends on what you see."

"At least you knew you'd be freed. I had doubts. Sometimes I still do..." A realisation more than an admission. "I still feel those obsidian walls closing in on me. The heat, the hisses, the stink of the putrefaction caused by the snake's venom. The flesh might have healed, but my mind makes the experience real again every time I think about it. Which is pretty fucking often," Loki added tiredly.

Prometheus nodded. "A mind like yours is torture enough."

"Ain't that the truth... Did you know I would be imprisoned?" Loki asked after a moment's pause.

Prometheus half shrugged, eyes still fixed on the swirls in the Chronodéndron bark. "I suppose. Not thanks to my talent or because of what we did, just common sense. You being you, Loki, sooner or later you would end up in chains. Imagination amongst the unimaginative is a cruel gift. Much like foresight amongst the sightless."

"That's why we became friends."

Prometheus finally turned his gaze to face him and smiled nostalgically. "Amongst other reasons. Ah, the mischief we pulled together. Remember Utgard? That was fun."

Loki remembered. And yet he felt no nostalgia, only regret. "What happened back there, Prometheus?" he asked, more angrily than he'd intended.

"Apologies, friend. I needed everyone's attention away from me so I could have a private word with Chronos. I wish there had been another way, but if there's one thing I've learned from you, it's that in order to control people's attention, you need to give them what they want to see. And they all wanted to blame you so badly." Prometheus sounded almost contrite as he spoke.

"How convenient," Loki sneered. "You knew. You saw all this happen. You *made* it happen. And now you blame me."

"No," Prometheus roared. He stood up to his full height, eyes ablaze, pinning Loki down with his gaze, lest he forget the Titan was also a god of fire and, even broken as he was, not one to be trifled with. "Foresight is not the same as prophecy, and it's certainly not destiny. We all chose our fate. Don't act all righteous, Loki, it doesn't suit you. Their blame might be misplaced in this case, but we both know you are to blame for much pain and suffering in this Universe. How dare you make a fuss because, in this particular case, you didn't actually mean to cause the harm you did?"

Loki held his stance. "What about Psyche? How is she to blame as well? What choice did she have in all this?"

"She's the product of your choices. Not mine."

"You brought her here!"

"And you're welcome!" The Titan winced and unconsciously covered his gaping wound. Sickly sweat ran down his temples. "Psyche would never come for you. Not willingly. But in doing so, she freed you. That was the fault in Odin's plan, Chronos' plan, the Suzerain's plan – in everyone's plan, including mine! I didn't do it for you, Loki. I wasn't even aware of your connection. How could I have been? I just needed her ability." He sighed. "I thought she was a fluke. Of course, now, in hindsight, it all makes sense."

"You must have known something," Loki insisted. "How did you lure her here?"

"With a dryad's prayer," Prometheus said simply. "She wouldn't answer to humans or anyone she feared might remember her, so Alek Dveer groomed his daughter to be the perfect vessel for her."

"Except she wasn't. She was her father's pet. Psyche should have seen it."

Prometheus' mouth turned slightly into a crescent. "She did, but I convinced her otherwise. As to Ileana,

Hecate has a way of turning women against men. Brother, lover, father. It makes no difference."

Loki snorted. "I can't believe you've been working with the Olympian witch."

"Tartarus is a lonely place. We shared a common enemy. Sometimes that's all it takes to build an alliance."

Loki wanted to hit him. He'd been in Tartarus too, and they'd shared many enemies. Hecate knew he'd been held there. She could have contacted him, helped him escape. She didn't because he hadn't featured in their plans. He was just an unintended consequence. More than that, they didn't need him. Didn't need his chaos. They feared he would inadvertently ruin their plans because he was Loki. That's what he did, even without trying. "Yes, Hecate is indeed very skilled with illusions," he said tartly, then looked at the Chronodéndron. "Tell me, is the future as incredibly bleak as they say, or just… incredible?"

There was that mouth twist again. "Depends on the future."

Loki frowned.

"What if I told you that in most futures, Alek Dveer never marries, never meets the Nephilim, never even travels? He's butchered, like so many others of his kind, without having done anything more remarkable than improving the desalination method used by the Aossi. Then in one future, he meets the woman of his dreams and has a child, who then becomes his whole world and gives him the strength to survive capture by the Narrum. And when that child gets sick, he defies time itself to save her. Not for the child's sake, but for his.

Because he cannot bear to lose another loved one, another battle, another day living a life he hates."

"What are you saying?" Loki asked, taken aback.

"I'm saying we have it all under control. Your part in this ended the moment you left Psyche to her fate. Now you're just complicating things."

"Then tell me how to simplify them!" he snapped. "Control? What control? Niflheim is breaking apart! I don't want to complicate things, I want to solve them. So far, all I've seen you do is aggravate the problem. It's my children who are in danger, Prometheus. You don't get to tell me only half the story. I need to know all of it."

Prometheus turned back to the tree. "I know many things. It does me no good." He winced again, and dark blood oozed from the wound in his stomach. Zeus' curse was still active outside of Tartarus. For as long as Prometheus would live, even without the eagle, the mere thought of what he'd done was enough to trigger the punishment. Loki had to respect the meticulous viciousness of the Olympian king. And he could learn a few things from it as well.

He swallowed his next accusations. There was no point in debating who had suffered more or what could have been done differently, so he skipped all the personal grudges to address the next grievance on his list. "Have you seen what Chronos would do to this world?"

The Titan exhaled. "No... not exactly. I saw humanity's downfall and the Nephilim's rising. I told you, I'm not an oracle. I can only see my future and the outcomes of the things that either affect me or have been set in motion by my actions."

"Then why did you ask me to take humans to another world?" Loki almost pleaded. "Why didn't you at least warn me about giving them too much intellect? You wanted to. I saw it in your eyes, at your trial. You looked at me as if I was the one to be pitied. I didn't understand it back then. I expected you to blame me. Fuck, I almost wished you'd revealed my presence to the Olympians. But no… you just took it all upon yourself. Why? So you could dump it all on me now? I would have shared the burden, taken the responsibility. I'd put measures in place. I would have believed you! As I always had…"

Prometheus' long-suffering sigh defined resignation.

"Because change requires sacrifice, Loki. Gods don't just evolve on their own."

"They don't need to evolve."

"Yes, they do!" the Titan thundered.

"Ah…" Loki said, glimpsing the truth. "So you did want me to inspire humans to create the Nephilim so they, in turn, would destroy the gods."

The Titan shrugged. "Just the Olympians. And I confess I was curious to see how far they would go. How far *you* would go, yes."

"I went to a cell in the Underworld! That's where I went. Meanwhile, the pantheons fucked up humankind to the point they self-destructed in their pursuit to become gods themselves. They even destroyed Midgard, Prometheus. They are probably destroying Asgard as we speak. For what?"

"Loses were to be expected. Stars frequently consume worlds. No one blames them for it."

Loki's temper threatened to get the best of him. "I, for one, liked that world! For fuck's sake, the Nephilim are not stars! They destroy every world they set foot on so they can control it on their terms. Niflheim is about to be next! They think they are gods. They imitate us, but they'll never understand us. They don't know how to rule, how to lead, only to conquer and dominate. It needs to end. I need you to end it, or the stars help me, I will!"

The Titan gave him a long-suffering look. "That is what I'm doing, old friend. Believe it or not. I see what's connected to my future, but I don't get details for this knowledge. The visions are always murky, deceiving. I knew humans would be crucial for the gods' downfall and the Titan's survival. I knew you were involved. I assumed the involvement was limited to the Nephilim. I was wrong... Psyche was the key."

Loki shook his head. "If she ever hears you calling her a key…"

"She is your greatest creation."

"I very much doubt she sees it that way."

"I'd rather not leave such important matters in the hands of a woman. We all remember what happened with Pandora. But this Universe has always favoured the feminine."

"No wonder. Nyx was female. She was here long before Chronos," Loki said.

"And we wouldn't be here if he hadn't come."

"Speak for yourself." Loki puffed out a breath. "Do you really think it's a good idea to bring her back?"

The Titan shrugged again. "Honestly, I don't know. But the 'key' unlocked the secret, and the process is already in motion."

Loki shook his head. "She didn't know what she was doing. You could have given her a heads-up. You should have asked her!"

"So she could decline or do the opposite?"

Fuck, she probably would, Loki thought. "You could have given *me* a heads-up. How about that?"

"We did all we could to keep you out of it. Forgot to account for the Dharkan, though." Prometheus' forehead creased slightly. "What's up with him, anyway? Why does he keep following her around?"

"He's in love."

"With Psyche?"

Loki grimaces. "No. I don't think so. It's… complicated. But that's the problem when you only take one thread into account. Fate is not linear, Prometheus. Everything's connected. The full ramifications of Nyx's return are unforeseeable. Which means, so is this new future of yours."

"Well, it is done," Prometheus said gravely.

Loki shook his head. "For fuck's sake… Do you trust Gaea?"

"I trust her hate for Chronos, and I trust her desire to protect her creations."

"She means well, but she's like a lioness amongst kittens, trying to blend in and play. Except they don't really like to play with her. They just like having her around for protection, and they like to taunt her, to pretend they can beat her. She suffers their scratches and their bites because they don't really hurt her. How could they? Until one day she loses her temper and accidentally kills one of them with a flick of her paw. Then she realises how big and strong she is and how she would never, ever be a kitten or be accepted as their playmate again. What will you do then?"

Prometheus' eyebrows rose halfway up his forehead. "Gosh, Loki. You've been spending too much time with Seshat."

Loki exhaled and got to the point. "*I* could have taken Nyx's soul."

"Yes, I know you could. And you might still have to if all this goes pear-shaped. I can only see so far, after all."

"So why risk giving it to Gaea in the first place?"

"I didn't. It was Psyche's choice. I can't see souls. Maybe she saw something I missed. Maybe she cares for you too much. Or more likely, she doesn't trust you."

And who can blame her... Loki mused bitterly.

"Let me tell you a story," said Prometheus. "Zeus and I got really intoxicated once and, in friendly spirit, promised to answer each other one question truthfully. It was the sort of stupidity we mistook for fun back then. Back when there was trust between gods, before worlds became coveted as a symbol of status and worth was determined by how many mortals worshipped us." He sighed, as if gathering strength to tell the rest of the story. "Anyway, Zeus asked me what I feared the most, so I asked him the same question. I expected him to answer Hera or Chronos or eternity in Hades' realm. Instead, he replied Nyx. Nyx was the thing he feared. I hadn't even known who Nyx was until then. And it was like the very Universe was pulled from under my feet."

Loki remembered those ages well. As a deity who always craved a world and worshippers, he found them quite boring. Then realisation dawned on him. He felt himself pulled downward by overwhelming gravity. Back then, only two gods had known about Nyx, besides Chronos and Gaea, of course, and that was Odin and himself. A secret shared back when they used to be brothers, much like Zeus and Prometheus had been. The very secret that shattered their friendship. He'd never mentioned Nyx again. He supposed Gaea could have told Zeus. They were close, after all, but he very much doubted it. And that meant…

Odin and Zeus were friends long before they were enemies.

"Now you understand," Prometheus said morosely. "We were tricked long before we became Tricksters. The title itself was given to us by them, was it not? We took it for ourselves and wore it proudly, but to them we were nothing but a flame that had to be extinguished."

"What was your answer?" Loki asked in a whisper.

Prometheus took a long, deliberate breath. "Eagles…"

Loki closed his eyes.

"You were wrong too, about the Nephilim," Prometheus said.

"Pardon?"

"It wasn't intelligence combined with imagination that created the Nephilim. It was logic. Cold, calculating logic. They weren't alone. Their technology is not the result of cunning or trickery, but equations." Prometheus pressed his lips before he spoke. "They found another mentor in your absence. Or should I say, she found them."

"Who?!"

"Athena," Prometheus said, too tired to play

guessing games. "She used them to claim Olympus after it was conveniently no longer linked to Midgard or Hades. She won't stop until she has control of every world in every pantheon."

Loki's eyebrows rose. "Athena? Nonsense. She's the most predisposed to being neutral." Then he remembered Troy. "Oh, fuck..."

"Exactly. She's her father's daughter. Born fully grown and armoured from Zeus' own head. What a remarkable feat: to personify and weaponize your own mind. Was Gaea involved, you think? I never quite figured it out." He shrugged again, more forcefully this time. "I suppose it doesn't matter now. The sad conclusion is we can't beat the Olympians, Loki. They've already won. Either through deed, feat, legend or record, they are part of everyone's subconscious. Take Pan, for example. Even the most remote and primitive tribes of mortals, long abandoned by their gods, will recognise some of their names. But who will recognise ours?"

Loki felt the extent of the realisation hit his ego with a similar effect as a kick in the balls.

"Odin didn't know. He was tricked, too." Loki held on to that small consolation, as if his very sanity depended on it.

"Perhaps..."

They were silent for a long moment. Words were too loud, too violent and crude to express what passed between them.

Prometheus broke the silence first.

"May I ask, why Psyche?"

Loki spread out his hands. "It wasn't about her. She

was a means to an end. I infiltrated Eros' realm for the same reason I do pretty much everything: for fun, to keep boredom and anger at bay. To annoy others. I wanted to stir up a little trouble. I never meant for… any of it."

"What about your feelings?"

His breath caught. Loki hadn't even realised he had been breathing. "A miscalculation."

"Funny, I did not foresee that bit. You knew your offspring would bring about unparalleled destruction. Why risk another one?"

"I… I didn't think… I wasn't ready to let her go," he admitted.

"Are you now?"

"I have to be. She's free, even if she doesn't see it yet."

Prometheus bobbed his head. "And what is an end if not a new beginning?" He winked and turned to face the Chronodéndron again.

"Are you really going through with this?" Loki asked.

"Of course. I already have, in a way. Better to do it now, while Chronos is shielded. Yewlow has agency to do as she wishes."

Loki winced at the tree again. He wasn't fond of Chronodéndrons. He'd rather put himself through a wasp nest than one of them. The product of Chronos and Gaea working together could not be good.

The swirling movement in the bark was imperceptible to anyone but a god. She heard his thoughts and didn't approve.

Apologies.

"She accepts your apology," Prometheus said.

"At the risk of causing offence again, how can you trust a Chronodéndron?"

"Trees carry the marks of time like scars. They are alive; they give and sustain life but have no agency over their own lives. They are often used, abused, pruned, neglected, dismissed, ignored, treated worse than rocks, really. They can't move away from fires, can't stop axes. Most have no real intellect, so at least they are not aware of the injustice of their existence. Trees like Yewlow, though, they have more reason to hate Chronos than we do. So yes, I trust her. Her foresight is far better than mine. She sees every outcome clearly because she's already there."

"But she can only see what's immediately in her vicinity – again, no offence!"

"It's far enough." Prometheus tilted his head to the bark. "What's that? Oh. She wants to speak to you."

Loki narrowed his eyes sceptically. "I'm listening."

"You have to touch her."

Loki laughed. "As if!"

Prometheus gave him a long-suffering look. "All right. Touch me. I'll deliver the message."

Loki did as he asked, confident he wouldn't be sucked into the time portal this way. He was right. Although, after what he learned, he almost wished he had been. After all, one does not risk chrono-travel for the experience but for the redemption.

"No creature can hide their desires from a Chronodéndron, especially not one with a soul," Prometheus said knowingly.

"Thank you." Loki had tears in his eyes when he

spoke. *It's not too late,* he said to himself, then turned to his friend. "So… is this goodbye?"

"Yes."

"Where will you go?"

Prometheus looked fondly at the tree. "Wherever."

Loki didn't like the way he said that. "Are you trying to trick me?"

"It doesn't take much to trick a trickster. Always remember Utgard."

Prometheus winked and smiled. It was a cryptic sort of smile. Not pleased, not sad, not amused. Loki wouldn't understand the emotion it conveyed until much later, when, like most things lost in time, it no longer mattered.

Chapter 7

Breakdown

The glider makes an eerie noise. A red light glows behind the main control unit. Psyche curses. Before I can ask what's wrong, the Nephilim contraption slows and jerks, moving in bursts like a reluctant horse determined to throw its rider, until we shudder to a stop not far away from where we crashed into a tree not too long ago.

"Shit… I'd hoped to reach the Stump by nightfall," Psyche says.

I squint at the sky. The sun hasn't moved since we set out on this ill-advised quest. "You still might."

"Godhood made you optimistic," Pan says mockingly. We found him along the way, and Psyche invited him to ride with us. I was against it. He's less belligerent now but more determined to regain his freedom than ever.

"I'm not optimistic; I'm in a hurry," she says.

He chuckles. "So am I. Time might be by our side, but he's sure not *on* our side. Oh well, I needed to stretch my legs, anyway." He jumps off, agile as a goat and, balancing on one hoof, pulls the other leg up to his horns. It hurts just to watch.

"Maybe it's tired or scared, or maybe it stopped to pay its respects to its fallen brother," I suggest, averting my gaze from the satyr and pointing to the other glider.

Both goddess and Wyrd stare at me as if I spoke in my native tongue.

"Its battery died," she says matter-of-factly.

"What? You killed another one?" I say.

"No, you idiot, it's" – she takes a deep breath, then forces a reassuring smile – "it's hungry, that's all."

"So am I. But I'm not having a fit about it. Tell the thing to keep moving. Force it if you have to. Isn't that what gods do?"

"Stars give me patience…" she murmurs as if I can't hear her, sat right behind her. "It's *really* hungry, Aedan. It can't go on. It, er… it's fainted. We've put too much weight on it, made it run too hard, and it spent energy faster than it could feed from the sun." She frowns at the sky. "At least it won't get dark anytime soon. Let's dismount. It will recharge faster – I mean, rest better – if we're not sitting on it."

I'm confused by her answer. "Huh. The other day you told me these things weren't alive. Now you're telling me they need rest."

She curses me under her breath again. "I updated my definition of the word, as you suggested. Now I'm explaining the problem in a way you can understand." She twists around in her seat to scowl at me. "Do you remember everything I say?"

"Yes."

"Well, you shouldn't. The stars know I don't…"

She dismounts gracefully, one leg at a time as if coming down a dais. I jump off and massage my stiff legs.

These things are far more uncomfortable than horses. They cramp your limbs in unhealthy ways, much like chairs.

"Now what?" I ask.

She glances up again. "Well, it feeds on light, so we better move it from under the trees, find a sunny spot."

"Might as well move it up the hill, to the caves. We can shelter in my place while we wait."

"Yes, you two do that," Pan says.

"And what will you do?" she asks.

"Hunt," he says, already walking in the opposite direction.

There's nothing to hunt in these hills but snakes, so I'm not sure what he's up to. Whatever it is, I probably won't like it, and I'd rather he just stay away. I don't understand what Psyche sees in the creature. I wouldn't trust him as far as I could throw him. She doesn't either. Not since his confrontation with Loki. Still she acts as if it never happened. I wish the gods would give me some insight into the reasons behind their actions, no matter how unreasonable they might be. I'm so tired of guessing at their motivations, of being thrown blindfolded amongst their conflicts and schemes. I only want to find Ileana, make love to her and forget the world's problems.

"Did you just sigh?" Psyche asks incredulously, with a hint of derision.

"No. I blew out some steam. There's a difference."

"Hmmm," she says, biting her lip in an effort to remain serious.

As if conjured in empathy for the thought, boiling water suddenly spurts from a spring a few yards away in a magnificent display of the world's immense power and discontentment.

"Flaming sun, I haven't seen one of these since the Merge!" I say in wonderment. Another one shoots into the air, reaching higher than the treetops. Then another from further away. "And never this far from the lake."

Psyche is very still, squinting at the ground. "Ah, fuck…"

"What?"

"Nothing. I… I remembered something, that's all."

"About Ileana?"

She acts annoyed. "No. The spurt of water, it's called a geyser. That's what I remembered."

It's my turn to act annoyed. She's not lying, but she's not being honest either. She's learning to subvert my ability to detect her lies by concealing the truth with other truths. *Flaming goddess, what are you not telling me?*

"You're grumpier than usual," I point out. In fact, she's not. She's worried, her mind clearly busy trying to solve a problem she doesn't want to share.

"Dharkan, for all your affinity with emotions, you still can't tell the difference between grumpiness and tiredness."

"You're a goddess." I regret the observation the moment I hear it spoken.

"So?" she snaps. "I'm not allowed to be tired, is that it?"

Not too tired to argue, apparently. "What are you spending your energy on anyway?"

She bites her cheek. "Right now, on putting up with you and climbing this hill."

"Do you wish me to carry you?" I ask playfully.

"Insufferable man," she murmurs. "I should take you up on that offer. If not for the fact that I know you'd just toss me over your shoulder like a sack of grain, and then I'd have to kill you for the insult."

I laugh. She smiles for a moment before turning melancholic again. "You would be tired too if you had to wrestle with the souls of primordial entities," she admits.

"Humph… You're not still draining Nyx's soul, are you? You gave it to Gaea."

"I did…"

"So what's wrong?"

"I'm not sure I did the right thing. Or if I did it right, I mean."

"How so?"

"I don't know…"

"Psyche…"

She turns sharply to look up at me, and her neck cracks again. It hasn't been the same since she broke it the last time. "I don't want to lie to you, nor myself. So please don't ask me any more questions to which I can only give you lies as answers."

I nod slowly. "For all it's worth, I hope you did the right thing. And I hope you know what you're doing now, little goddess. Because not even I can host Chronos' soul."

Xylo's mossy eyes glint at me in instigation. He's playing with us. I'd bet my right hand that he's exactly where he wants to be. I only wish I understood why Psyche and the rest of the gods are playing along with him.

"The truth is, I don't know what's wrong with me,

Aedan." She sounds sincere. "I couldn't transfer the soul directly into the pendant, so I had to channel it through me, and now... something's not right. I'm not quite myself." She speaks as much to me as to Xylo, hoping he takes the bait and explains what she cannot. He's not like the other gods, though. His pride doesn't demand he give long speeches or explanations for his actions. If anything, I think he relishes silence as much as the ignorance of others.

But I think I know what's wrong with her.

"You're low on Prana," I say.

"How is that possible? I'm a goddess."

"You were mortal once. Maybe you could become one again if you're not careful."

She halts. "Don't even joke about it." The horrified expression on her face hardly does justice to the terror she feels.

"Don't you think it's too much of a coincidence that the glider stopped here, so close to the other one?" I ask, changing the subject, for I see how much it distresses her.

She relaxes a bit, considering this, then casts about us first with her eyes open, then closed. "Perhaps. There is definitely something different about this area. It's warmer, and I can sense a strange energy field around it. No wonder snakes love it so much. Mushrooms too, it seems. Could be intentional or simply geological; most likely it's both. I cannot fathom for what purpose, though. Still, I'm fairly sure we're safe here." She glances at Xylo again. "Or as safe as we can be under the circumstances."

The glider moves easily over the vegetation with

little effort on our part. I can't help wondering if it is indeed hungry or just lazy.

We stop by Cornus' grave to pay our respects. The loss of my friend still hurts and always will, but I have to admit, he looks mightier than a Titan with his beauty immortalised in stone like this. I wish Loki hadn't wasted his horn on the God of Time. It had no effect that I could see. If not for the combined talents of Hel, Psyche, the witch and Medusa, we would not be here dragging him around, and personally, I'm not convinced by Psyche's plan. The only reason I'm going along with it is because Hel asked me to. And Ileana, of course. If it was up to me, I'd dump our cargo in the Boiling Lake. Nothing ever comes out of it. Then again, what do I know? I'm just a Dharkan.

INTERLUDE 7

Ann

"Hello, Ann," Agnar said when the woman who had once been Arianh appeared next to the Chronodéndron, Huginn and Muninn perched on each shoulder.

Ann's smile turned to joyous laughter when she fell into his arms.

"You remembered me! I knew you would remember." In truth, for a long time she didn't believe he would, but everything changes with hindsight.

"I wasn't sure I did," he admitted. "Not until you went through. Your voice sounded familiar, but I couldn't trust my memories... Most are like half-remembered dreams. There's too much of Odin's own memories in them." Agnar pulled back from the embrace to touch her cheek. "But this face." She tried to hide it. Even after all those years, it didn't feel like hers. "I remember it well." His eyes came alight with joy. "It's real. It's you. It's always been you!"

"You waited for me," she sobbed with relief.

"Well, it's only been a couple of days," he said modestly.

"It doesn't matter." She spoke to the crook of his neck.

"You waited." Her heart beat so fast, almost bursting from her chest. But happiness, Ann realised, is like feeding. The hungrier you are, the better it feels when you feed. But once you're full…

She pushed him to arm's length, no longer smiling. "Did Odin know about us? Before, I mean."

"Er… no. I don't think so." Agnar staggered, taken aback by the sudden change in her mood. "My personal life never much interested him, and for my part I did what I could to keep it uninteresting. All he knew was that I had an affair with the Suzerain's wife. Odin believed that was the real reason he threw him – er… me – off the Stump." He moved his head from side to side, pondering the issue, then shrugged. "Maybe it was."

They sat down under Yewlow's shade, still holding hands as if afraid if they let go, one of them would vanish again.

"He came to see me," Ann said.

"Who? Odin?"

"Yes."

Agnar considered this. "I suppose it's only a matter of time until Odin finds his way back from the Underworld."

"I'm not so sure he did…" she said.

"I don't understand."

"Neither do I. But… he asked me – no, he ordered me – to give something to my father." She became very serious. "There's two problems with that."

Agnar stared at her in suspense.

"Do you know who my father was?" she finally asked.

He raked his hair. "Er…"

"Agnar?" she pressed.

"I can guess," he admitted meekly.

Ann forced an exhale through her nose. "I always figured my mother was ambitious enough to seduce a god; I just never imagined it would be him."

"To be fair, Zeus would hump anything that moved." Agnar cringed at his words. "I'm not saying that's what happened! According to all accounts, your mother was gorgeous and resourceful." He cringed again. "I don't mean she didn't have feelings or standards. She was the kind of woman who got what she wanted." He raked his hair again. "Which doesn't mean they weren't in love or that you weren't wanted. I…"

"Relax. I'm fairly certain love was beyond my mother's abilities. Regardless, that's not the problem. I never gave my father's identity much thought. Never even felt the absence of a father. My mother always took all the emotional space," she said with a hint of resentment. "But if that's true, if Zeus is my father, then why didn't I turn into a goddess when I ate the Ambrosia? Feel free to chime in with an opinion," she added to Yewlow.

'I'll let you figure out this one yourself,' Yewlow said through their bond.

Did you interfere? Ann asked. The idea hadn't occurred to her until now.

'No. I'd much rather be linked to a goddess than a queen.'
I bet you would.

Agnar's eyes shifted from Arianh's tightly pressed lips to the object of her annoyance.

"You are linked," he said.

"It's one way to put it," she said tartly.

"Must be amazing," he said dreamily.

"To suffer the thoughts of the most opinionated tree in the forest? Yes, it's been great."

He recoiled at her sarcasm. "She seems nice."

Ann blinked a few times.

Have you been talking to Agnar while he waited?

'It would have been rude not to. I was bored; he was bored. We entertained each other.'

You didn't talk to me for years. I nearly went insane with boredom!

'You were less entertaining, always moaning. It's not my fault we exhausted all interesting conversation rather quickly.'

Ann's nostrils flared. *I will fell you branch by branch!*

'I'm shedding leaves in fear.'

"Ann?" Agnar whispered tentatively. "Is everything all right?"

"Yes," she said rather stiffly, making a tremendous effort to compose herself. "It's just…" She glared at the tree again. "Everything's great! Back to Zeus: Why am I not a goddess?" The question sounded unbearably petulant to her ears, but she still wanted an answer.

"Maybe there's more to it. Maybe eating the resin isn't enough."

"Or maybe he's not my father," she retorted. His face told her she was wrong in that assumption.

"Frost, Agnar. Is that why Odin took an interest in me? Because I'm his rival's daughter?"

Agnar held her hands tighter and looked her in the eyes. "He *was* fond of you. In his own way…"

"He wasn't when we last met." She absently clutched the pouch dangling from the cord tied around her waist.

Agnar made light of her comment. "He was a hard man to understand, even harder to like. But rest assured, he respected you more than he did most mortals."

"High praise indeed," she grumbled, realising that she didn't actually care that much about her uncle's opinion of her anymore and focused back on the topic at hand. "Odin asked me to give something to Zeus. But Zeus is dead, right? Aedan killed him. Or Psyche did. Or both! It really doesn't matter who did it. The thing is, Odin acted as if he wasn't. What do you make of that?"

Agnar pondered this. He looked particularly dreamy when deep in thought. She indulged herself in the sight.

"I felt him leave. He went to the Underworld, believing himself dead. Something must have changed, then. Maybe Hel brought him back? Or he didn't die in your future?"

"Is that possible? A different future, I mean." The gods seemed to think so, and the stars had changed after Ileana went through. Of course, she had no idea what that meant. She'd never paid much attention to the sky before, and it was daylight now.

"Odin used to say we make our own future. But he was just repeating the mantra from his wife. He never really believed it." Agnar turned introspective again. "I never quite understood why he regarded her with such bitterness. She sounded like a wise woman."

"She's the harpy who gave me this face," Ann said, struggling against the negative emotions the memory still triggered.

"Ah..." Agnar said cautiously. "Then... I don't know."

"We must find out!" Ann sprang to her feet, pulling him with her.

He quickly caught up with her enthusiasm. "Where do you want to start? The caves?"

"Goddess no! If I never step foot in that place again, it would be too soon."

"But the books –"

"They are not there yet. Besides, we've already read them. Let's go to Portum first. It's closer and I need to pay a debt to someone. I'll tell you everything on the way."

Interlude 8

Jonas

Jonas wiped the sweat from his brow, taking a moment to appreciate everyone's work with an ebullient grin. It was such an unusual sensation for him: grinning. His long-neglected facial muscles were sore from being constantly contracted, his lips almost cracked with all the stretching, but he just couldn't help himself. He was so happy! His heart beat inside his chest as furiously as it had when that Manticore dragged him to his lair, except now it wasn't beating in terror but overwhelming exultation. He was intoxicated with bliss.

"I need a drink," he said to no one in particular, then glanced at the half-full bottle of spirits in his hand and decided that wouldn't do. In a moment of prideful liberation, he tossed it aside and strode towards the fountain where Iva and a half a dozen of her Dharkan hydrated under the wary gazes of the Narrum and Anann waiting for their turn. Still, their wariness had more to do with their surroundings than Dharkan's presence.

Jonas had always believed a little alcohol went a long way in bringing people together; a lot of work went even further. He'd ended many disagreements over the years, not with words or fights, but with spirits. He used to think only drink was able to make folk forget their grievances, their differences and pretty much everything down to their own identities. But then, of course, they would sober up and the conflict would restart with the added aggravation of a hangover. It was a full-time job keeping them drunk. If only it had occurred to Jonas earlier to keep them busy instead.

He looked beyond the temple. Everyone had their hands full. Dharkan carried rock, Narrum carved it, women polished it, children ran errands. They all had a purpose, including him – a purposeful purpose. He always knew he was made for more than pouring ale and listening to peoples' complaints or preaching non-sense and performing assisted masturbation for a cause he despised. The world didn't need more children, just as it didn't need more conflicts.

He'd never picked a side. Not only because he couldn't but because he didn't think he should. After all, it was taking sides that caused conflicts. He was and always would be a peaceful man. Ulcan once called him a dreamer. Well, when you despise every moment awake, what else can you be?

But not anymore, he reminded himself, and the grin returned to his face like the sun beaming from behind a cloud. This day didn't seem to end. And he was fine with that.

"Excuse me," he murmured as he pushed his way through the crowd of Dharkan gathered around the spring. He dipped his hands in it and bent down so as not to waste the precious liquid they held and drank deep.

"Are you sick?" Iva asked, eyeing him suspiciously. She looked better than she had when she first showed up at his temple, prepared to take everyone there as provisions before an assault on Relicum. Better dressed, for one thing, slightly less deranged and a lot more resigned to her situation. Whatever disagreement she had with the entity she hosted, it seemed to have subsided.

"No. I'm just thirsty." Jonas bent to drink more. He didn't remember water tasting this good.

"Thirsty… for water? Let me ask again: Are you ill?"

He understood her suspicion. He was, after all, known for his aversion to basic hydration. It was one of the reasons he'd built his sanctuary – the one that'd burned down – in the first place, to turn his habit into a business. To give it a purpose beyond the need to numb the pain and frustration of having to live in a nonsensical world, dealing with those who made it so. This strange craving – or the lack of it – surprised him too at first. It was the sort of thing a deity might trigger in a host. But in his case, its cause was sheer happiness. He no longer felt the need to numb his senses, to intoxicate his body in order to spare his mind from the ugliness and misery around him. It was a happiness derived from a sense of accomplishment and security. The happiness of a dream come true. This new sanctuary would be his means of making a stand in the world. It would give him the power to choose who was allowed in and for what purpose. And if all else failed, he could just close himself off, turn his back on everyone and finally find some peace.

He finished gulping down the refreshing water with

a satisfied "aaahh," the grin back on his face. "Never better."

Iva's fleeting expression – if the slight twitch of her eyelid could be called an expression – appeared to be one of concern.

"I'm fine," he said soberly. "I am myself. No one's possessing me. I just needed to hydrate. I am part dryad, you know."

"I do. You are the one who's always acted as if you didn't."

He gave her his best annoyed glare to reassure her of both his identity and sanity, then changed the subject.

"Isn't it marvellous?" he asked, surveying the tall marble walls. "I still can't believe we've built so much, so fast."

"We hardly built anything at all," Asher pointed out. He was the one always by Iva's side. Jonas supposed there were not many ways to stand out amongst the Dharkan.

"It helps to have a god doing most of the hard work," Iva said reproachfully.

"Yes, it does." It was clear this had been the subject of the Dharkans' discussion prior to his arrival at the fountain. The construction of his new temple had happened fast indeed. Impossibly so, one might say. But nothing is really impossible when a god puts his mind to it.

Suddenly, Jonas felt like a cat surrounded by hungry dogs. And the only way to survive in these situations, he'd learned from observing a stray tabby, was to remain still and show no fear.

"When do we get to meet this benefactor of yours who not only provided us with both the material and the tools for this endeavour but also built most of the foundation and walls overnight?"

"Could be more than one," Jonas said gaily.

"That's really not the point," Iva replied acerbically.

He shrugged. "I suppose we'll meet them whenever they're ready to reveal themselves to us."

"Jonas, gods are many things. What they are not is altruistic or charitable. I've yet to meet a god who does anything without expecting something in return." Iva's guest spoke hauntingly. He'd learnt to differentiate the tone of voice, but the identity of the goddess who, by all intents and purposes, ruled the Dharkan in Iva's name remained a mystery. Normally, Dharkan could not be bound to their guests, but something had happened to those two, leaving them stuck with each other.

"Do you know every god in the Universe?" he asked her.

Her host frowned. "A god who builds something of this magnitude overnight, without waking anyone up, is definitely not talentless or humble. So yes, we would have met."

"Maybe that is why they chose to remain incognito."

She stepped closer, looming over him. "You claim you've made no deal. I don't believe you."

"Why would I lie? I'd proudly admit to any deal to have this built. All I did was draw it out on the wall. You saw me do it. Maybe there are still benevolent deities in the Universe, and the reason you don't know about this one is because you're not one of them."

A bead of ice appeared on Iva's forehead. She took

a few deep breaths. Jonas tried not to wince. He found the action disturbing from a Dharkan, to whom breath was meaningless.

"You may not remember the deal, might not even be aware there was a deal, but I bet that there was one." She glanced at his artificial leg, proudly on display, for he no longer felt self-conscious about it. "Now, I know it's not Hephaestus, and that's the only reason we're still here. I agreed we would help you build this, not that we would stand idle while it's being built."

"Then don't. There's plenty of work to do. Try it. Contribute. You might even feel better about yourself afterwards."

"Listen to me, mortal. This has nothing to do with my feelings. There's little difference between a temple and a tomb, for gods can as easily erect walls as they can knock them down. And until I know exactly what sort of bargain prompted something on this scale, I refuse to be a part of it. Our deal is broken. The Dharkan are leaving tonight."

"Great!"

"Along with what they are due."

Jonas pressed his lips.

"Their lives are not mine to give," he reminded her.

"Then you shouldn't have bargained with them. Tonight, metz. Either your god appears, or we take what's ours."

He tried to grin and failed, so he sneered instead. "Try to make yourself useful until then." He pointed in the direction he was heading. "That hole needs digging. I've designed it for the Dharkan, so they would have a place in the shade. You're welcome!"

In truth, the underground room was supposed to be a pantry for the Narrum, but Jonas figured it could well function as both.

Aedan, you better return soon.

CHAPTER 8

The Narrative

Aegea is truly a place of punishment, I muse as I walk up to the caves. Ever since I arrived here, all I've done is go back and forth running around in circles, and every time, I end up here, in these hills. No matter what I do, I can never get too far from this place, it seems. I'm like a celestial body trapped by a singularity's gravity. *But not for long,* I tell myself, hoping that it's true.

We find Loki lazing on the grass, sunbathing right outside Aedan's caves, seemingly without a care in the universe.

"Ahh, there you are. I figured you'd stop here," he says when he sees us. Unlike mine, his mood appears to have improved substantially since we last saw each other. He talks as if nothing out of the ordinary happened earlier, as if the world isn't breaking apart or time magically frozen inside an artificial tree. It's why I can never trust him. He takes nothing seriously.

"Yes, here we are again," I mutter.

"I love this place," he says, looking around.

"Why?" I ask as I steady the glider between two boulders.

"Because I made it," he replies proudly.

I pinch the bridge of my nose. "Of course you did."

"You don't like it? I made it for you." He winces. "With your kind in mind, I mean. After your visit, back when Niflheim was... well, Niflheim. I thought about what you said and made this place purposely so the world wasn't so harsh on the living."

Aedan shoots me a pointed look.

"The dead liked it too, apparently," I shoot back.

The two men frown at each other.

"No hard feelings?" Loki says, beaming insincerely at the Dharkan.

"Just stay away from me," Aedan replies sternly.

"Why are you here, Loki?" I ask. After what happened earlier and the surreptitious way he vanished after Prometheus, I did not expect to see him again so soon.

"I owe you an apology," he said.

"Only one?"

"Don't push it, Psyche."

I walk up to him. "Oh, I'll push and pull and tear it apart if I have to! That was a nice trick back there. What did Prometheus have to say for himself?"

The look of surprise on his face is short-lived. "Quite a lot, actually. So did Yewlow."

"Anything that concerns me?"

"Yes." He grins.

I glare, for I can guess what the tree said, and it has no place in this moment.

He reaches for my face, still grinning like an infatuated boy. "Psyche, I –"

I turn my cheek away. "Not now, Loki. After. When

all is done. When the Nephilim are gone, Fenrir is safe, and the world set to rights. If we're still here. Then we'll talk."

The grin fades. "If and when, huh?"

"Hel needs you more than ever."

"While you don't."

"Correct."

"Is that why you push me away? Because you don't need me or because you don't want me?"

"Neither. It's because we do a lot more harm than good together. Especially to each other. Besides, I didn't push you away, you left of your own accord."

He snorts. "I came back. After we argued. I came back."

It's my turn to snort.

"You don't believe me…"

"I do. I just don't want to listen to it right now."

"Why not? You listened to everyone else. What is it about gods like Odin and Zeus that makes everyone listen to them? Why doesn't anyone listen to me?" he asks glibly.

"They believe their lies," Aedan replies flatly.

Loki narrows his eyes at him. "Don't presume you know me just because we shared a body."

"We shared a lot more than that."

Loki's eyes flash blue in anger.

"Enough, you two. Loki, unless you're carrying a spare battery for this glider, there's not much you can do to help right now. I can take care of myself as well as our *bribe* for the Nephilim."

He clenches his jaw before he speaks. "Why is Pan spying on us from behind those trees? Actually, why is he still here at all?"

"I don't know. I haven't figured out what to do about him yet."

"You don't owe him anything."

"No. But I owe it to myself to be right before I act."

"What did he tell you, Psyche? During the trials."

I chew on my cheek as painful memories creep up my soul. "He stopped me from killing myself," I admit. "Then told me to pray to Eros. That he would keep me safe."

"Excellent advice," Loki says sarcastically. "Now why would Zeus punish Pan when he himself admitted to helping you?"

"Who can guess a god's whims?" I reply pointedly. *Why didn't you tell me about the Nephilim?* is what I really want to ask him. But of course I already know why. I was mortal. I would never have understood his intentions back then. And now… What is the point of understanding something when you can do nothing about it?

Loki takes a deep breath and turns to Aedan. Lightning crashes between them.

"I think you should go," the Dharkan says.

Loki laughs insincerely. "Very well. I better go check on Gaea, then." He turns to leave, then stops. "By the way, you're wrong, Psyche. Hel doesn't need me anymore. She hasn't for quite a while. She needs Hades, and the stars help us if he doesn't live up to her needs. You know, for once, I almost wish Eros was here."

A chill runs through my spine. "Don't."

"Yeah, I suppose if there is one silver lining in all of this, it's that he's not involved."

Except he is, Trickster… very much so, I want to tell

him, but remain silent. This battle, like so many others, I need to fight alone.

He's about to speak again but stops himself, his thoughts as guarded as mine. "As you will," he says and walks away.

"Loki…" I call back. He glances over his shoulder. "Be careful. Don't get distracted and don't accept anything from anyone," I say, hoping he'll understand.

He half smiles and nods before vanishing.

"So…" Aedan says. "How much of the end of that conversation did I miss?"

"Not much. We don't use telepathy with each other." I shrug in reply to his unarticulated query. "Old habits…"

He smirks. "*Old* habits, you say. Interesting."

"Oh, fuck off."

A shadow crosses overhead, putting an end to the Dharkan's teasing. "Flaming goddess!" Aedan's expression changes from smugness to horror when he catches sight of the creature that caused it. "What is *that*?"

"A sphinx," I reply calmly.

She perches atop the hill, right on the tip of the Nymph's Bosom.

"We must hide!" Aedan says.

"Tsk. Stay here," I say, walking up to her rider. "Hello, Seshat. Have you been flying in circles, waiting for Loki to leave, or does my talent deceive me?"

She forces a chuckle. "Hello, Psyche. Perceptive as usual. I don't enjoy writing epilogues."

"Me neither…" I sigh. "I'm afraid you missed the main plot – again. The story unravelled back in the forest and left quite the impact on the world. If you fly over, you might still see the crater, right next to a resurrected Zeus."

Seshat taps her lips. "You know how to tempt a chronicler, goddess of the soul. However, I've written enough about Zeus and the Underworlds. I wish to speak to Chronos."

I glance at Xylo. "Speak. He'll listen."

Aedan gives me a 'what the fuck are you doing?' look.

"Is it really him, in *that*?" Seshat asks, trying to adjust her concept of the God to the reality on top of the glider.

"Yes. He's all yours and your responsibility until the glider recharges. If I sense his soul move, I'll crush yours," I say, and I mean it.

She hisses at me.

"Manners, Seshat. You'll need them to deal with him."

She narrows her eyes at me and makes her way down the hill on foot, while the sphinx remains majestically perched atop it, guarding both her mistress and our cargo.

"Are you sure this is wise?" Aedan asks.

"Someone needs to keep an eye on Xylo while the glider charges, unless you want to stay in the sun and guard him yourself or drag him with us inside the cave. No? Perhaps you'd rather I leave him alone with Pan, then?"

His sneer deepens at each suggestion. "No. But I don't like the idea of leaving him there either. I don't trust her," Aedan whispers in my ear. "She's made of starlight, for flame's sake!"

"Precisely. She'll burn anything and anyone who gets near."

"Including me or even Xylo. Have you thought about that?"

"Yes. Don't worry, she won't do it unless she feels threatened."

"That's not reassuring. The entire world feels threatened right now!"

"I trust her, Aedan. She only cares about the narrative. And she has the right to learn his account."

"I appreciate your confidence," Seshat says dryly when she joins us. She spares one brief glare at Aedan, then studies me with the intense appraisal of an art critic. "I really can't tell if you're the villain or the hero of this story, goddess of the soul."

I smile. "I am myself. Those definitions always depend on who's telling the story and how it is told. What I won't be again is the victim."

"I hope you're right. I really do." She leans closer. *'Eros is coming for you.'*

I know…

Interlude 9

Namrive

Every alarm went off at once.

The flood of warnings and error messages bombarding Namrive's mind was overwhelming. She barely had time to unplug herself from the system before it fried her matrix.

"Bugs!"

The lights went out. The backups came up shortly after. She hated them. Red did nothing to soothe the senses.

She consulted the system for a report. There was none. She hit the console. Still no report.

Fire. She'd seen that much on the screen before the system crashed. A ruptured fuel tank in the incinerator room had ignited the entire level. She'd immediately closed the fuel pipes and vented the oxygen from the room. That should have stopped the flames, and yet they'd kept spreading. How? There was hardly anything to burn on that level, no more fuel or oxygen. Except…

"Apollo."

How she hated sun gods. Glitching pyromaniacs, the lot of them!

She plugged herself back in, directly into the surveillance network. As she feared, most cameras inside the soul source were not only offline, they were destroyed. Fire alone wouldn't do that. Those things were designed to withstand the conditions inside active volcanos. She accessed the last recorded feed from inside the room, and sure enough, there he was, turning a spark into an inferno.

The Olympian blacksmith had built the soul source so that any god inside it would be powerless – exactly as they'd asked him. *Powerless*, not *talentless*. Too late, the Nephilim realised those were not the same thing.

She accessed the other cameras on that level and glimpsed an incandescent hand as it closed over the last one still working. Namrive cursed and proceeded to activate the link to the bug she'd implanted in Judoc so she could monitor him and Anubis on their journey to Relicum. It wasn't supposed to be activated yet. Those bugs needed time to adjust themselves to their host's brain, and a premature activation could damage it, rendering any information collected by their senses useless. But she was out of options. No device dependent on biological sensory information was ever one hundred percent reliable, anyway. At least her bugs had the advantage of recording observations without either the observer or the subject knowing about it. After all, you can never accurately analyse an intelligent creature who's aware of the analysis. That she'd learned from the gods. The best way to study the minds of her subjects is to be inside their heads, see what they saw, hear what they heard and – unfortunately for her in this case – feel what they felt.

Namrive screamed as every fibre of her body burned. The heat, the pain, the fear and despair nearly unmade her. And above it all, the betrayal.

"Illy!" she croaked. The words, like the pain, were not her own, but by the Maker, they sure felt like they were! That's why one couldn't trust biological bodies. They had too many pain receptors, and pain always impairs perception. She had to decide whether to stop Ileana and Oric from going through the ring or seal the soul source before the twins escaped. A simple choice – just not when you felt yourself on fire. She'd hesitated for only a moment, and as a result, both parties had escaped.

"Bugs, bugs, bugs!"

She cut the connection to readjust the parameters of the link. Being aware of *everything* the subject felt and thought was not the best way to learn, she decided. Anubis had once accused her of not being alive because she'd never experienced the pain of living. He was wrong. What she'd experienced was not living. Quite the contrary. And she could have done well without the experience.

She hit the console again, forcing herself to think past the lingering haze of agony and aggravation. Communications came back on. Warning messages kept flashing in quick succession – too many even for her to keep track. She linked to the ship instead and accessed the system through there. It was bad. Every camera in the Stump was either offline or destroyed now. She had no idea where Oric and Ileana teleported to. They could be outside the structure or right outside the door, while Apollo and Artemis could be anywhere. Oreth was dead. She'd seen the footage of him dying. Iosh was still alive, according to the status of the tracking bug, but she'd be fried if she was going to link with him again. The pain had ruined his senses, if not his mind. She kept monitoring his life signs, hoping to devise an educated guess as to the gods' location and the state of the fire.

Namrive typed every command she could think of as fast as her enhanced abilities allowed. Fire alone could not explain this chaos. There had been a breach. The Stump had been on lockdown before the fire started, and yet an override command activated the ring, allowing the dryad to escape along with the metz. *Did someone else get in? How? Who? Why?* She had no way to answer those questions. Nothing worked. She'd never witnessed so many systems collapsing at once. Whoever caused this chaos knew what they were doing.

You cunning bug, you think you can lock me out of my system? I'll show you.

She reactivated every ring so she could at least see which ones were still working and when they were used. Then, with remarkable adroitness, she put most of the fire out and restored the motion sensors not damaged by the flames. Sure enough, the Olympians were no longer on that level. She found them on their way to the top, heading towards the ship. She smiled. Her faithful would handle them. This left her with a few moments to replay the footage from the incinerator room to find out how the gas leak happened. She did not like what she saw.

"Ileana had a deathwand?"

Namrive felt her circuits coil. Those were severely restricted and linked to their user to avoid situations such as this. The girl must have found it in the Suzerain's room. And of course, her genetic material was more than enough of a match to her father's to use it. Namrive had been against the blending of their DNA, but the Mentor thought otherwise. She'd doted on the Suzerain's daughter, for some reason. And sure, the girl would have perished without the treatment, but she was defective. Her ailment was one of the mind, not the body. And Alek's mind, as brilliant as it was, had not improved things. If it was up to Namrive, any creature with Ileana's mindset should not be given the opportunity to hold knives, let alone deathwands. She tried to contact Anubis. There was no signal. He, too, had managed to leave. Luck or good planning? She didn't believe in luck. The Nephilim had captured Tyche long ago and after many years of study concluded that her influence in large-scale events was negligible and that, given enough tries, probability always overrode luck. The conclusion being that luck, like many gods' talents, was obsolete. Gods knew it too. They made their own luck. Still, as much as Namrive wanted to believe Anubis was the primary suspect in this failure, she knew better. The god was illiterate in her technology. Whoever hacked into the system was not.

Think, Namrive, think, she commanded herself.

She didn't have to think too hard. The protocol in these situations was clear. She began uploading her memory, along with all the data from the Stump's computer, into the ship, and from there, relayed it to her home world.

Because of the bizarre time dilation surrounding the planet, transmission would take much longer than normal, but it would get there eventually, even if her body never did. She disliked that idea. Transferring her consciousness to new bodies was always such a nuisance. Another option was to go to the ship and wait for the next optimal window for take-off. She much preferred that option even if it meant risking an encounter with the Olympian twins. She turned to leave and found the exit blocked.

"Hello, love."

Namrive blinked several times, her mind in glitches, trying to make sense of what she saw. "How did you?" She retracted the question. "Your body is still –" Her eyes darted from him to the black screens behind her.

"I have many bodies," Alek Dveer said. "But you know that already. I can hide what's up here" – he pointed to his head – "but not what's in there." He pointed to the computers. "So… why bother, right?"

The question in her mind was not why he hadn't bothered to cover his tracks better, knowing she would find out his illegal experiments, but why he was standing there talking about them to her now. More importantly, where had he been hiding in the first place? His body was not ready. She was sure. Chances were, it had, in fact, been destroyed by the fire. And the first thing she'd done when she landed was to sweep every room for life forms as protocol dictated. Where the blip had he come from?

"I took the liberty of making a few modifications to the Stump's configuration," Alek said. "I'm surprised you didn't notice. Then again, I suppose even your brain can't account for every little inch of every world tree."

A secret lab? her mind suggested.

"No, just a room," he said, guessing or – the Maker forbid – reading her thoughts. "We all need privacy away from prying eyes. I've always found hiding to be a viable survival strategy. I am a dryad, after all." He smiled in that overly cunning way of his. "Hiding is often considered a coward's choice. I disagree. It's an excellent strategy. Good for hunting and survival. Hence, both predator and prey use it. It takes courage, forethought, planning and a great deal of patience to remain hidden for long." He spoke almost to himself, throwing words in the air, each one a weapon aimed to set the listener's mind off balance.

"You can't kill me," she said. It was technically true since, like Anubis said, she wasn't really alive, and thankfully, her link with the ship still worked.

He tutted, waving a dismissive hand at her. "Killing is overrated, love. I'll let Apollo try. I bet he's dying to melt your core."

She had to put that image away. "Why reveal yourself to me now?"

He acted annoyed, almost impatient, something she knew Alek Dveer was anything but. "Things have escalated faster than I planned. You know how it is: a plan is only as good as those employed to execute it. If I could do everything myself, believe me, I would. But not even Chronos is that talented."

"So you *were* working with this God of Time." She didn't even resent Anubis for being right. That's how disconcerted she was. Nephilim didn't fear gods. Neither did Alek Dveer, apparently.

He half shrugged. "We share common goals. Of all gods, he's the only one who can be called as such. He earned my respect. As for working together… Let's just say we helped each other out. Now he's on his own. And so am I," he added bleakly.

That's good to know, she thought. But if that was the case, he knew better than to accost her like this.

"Here's the thing. I need your ship. I don't have the access codes, so you will give them to me. That's why I'm here." His attitude, like his words, was offensive to her senses.

"I won't give them to you." The nerve of the creature to even suggest she would.

"Oh, but you will." He showed her the remote control pad in his hand. "I always said minds are more useful than souls. It's better to possess a god's power than his soul. But since a god's true power lives in their soul… what a conundrum. Then I met your kind, and you taught me how to harvest a god's soul and control it with my mind – quite the revelation. Then you taught me how to duplicate a mind, change memories, merge personalities." He sighed in reverie. "Such wonders you people come up with. I figured if all that was possible, then controlling a mind without a soul should be as well. You see, biological minds are complicated. The Nephilim, however, not so much." Alek looked at the device with a mix of irritation and appreciation. "Even so, it took me years to figure out your… technology. And your mind…" He whistled. "No one has a mind like yours, Namrive. I'd never have cracked it if not for Zeus. I wanted to thank him for his help, but sadly I see he's no longer accepting favour. Oh well, he fulfilled his purpose, I suppose."

Alek pushed a button on the remote, and something began stirring inside her matrix.

Bugs.

"Precisely. A little bug inspired by your own cunning spying methods. Hidden in the Stump's computer and released the moment you accessed my files. Secrets should be shared. Don't you agree, love?"

She tried to move and failed. He had assumed control of her motor functions. Her mind would be next.

"It amazes me how anything can be turned into a puppet if you know where its strings are," he mused malevolently.

"Except you," she replied, afraid for the first time in her existence. She'd rather be disconnected than aware of her lack of control.

"On the contrary," he said with fake humility. "I was a puppet for many years and freed myself at great cost."

She remembered when they'd first met. His memories and the awful marks of predation on his original body made even some of her kind avert their eyes in distaste.

"You, too, can be free again – if you're willing to pay the cost."

"Which is?" Namrive asked. But, of course, she already knew the answer.

"Give me the codes. Or I'll find them myself." He showed her the control pad again. She resisted. He tutted. "Circuits are a bit like flesh: so fragile. One wrong command, one wrong push of a button can cause so much damage – irreparable damage." He began pressing buttons at random. "Imagine the things I might accidentally delete while searching for something when I don't know where it is. You can guide me. Or…" – his tone hardened – "I will delete everything in my path until I find the information I want."

She screamed. He'd definitely pressed something. Her mind sizzled. The fear of losing information, of losing herself, was too much. She could not allow it to happen. Not like this.

"Stop! I'll tell you. I'll tell you anything you want."

"I thought so."

INTERLUDE 10

Ideth

Ideth gasped from the sudden cold. One moment she was about to burn Prometheus from existence; the next she was pitched into darkness, flapping in freezing slush.

Had Hel really sent her to Helheim? She couldn't have. Ideth was still alive! …Wasn't she? She felt cold and wet and furious. All pretty good indications of being alive. Then again, how could she tell? She'd never been dead for a comparison. No, she had to be alive. Helheim was not as inclusive as the Olympian Underworld. Hel only took in those with souls. Right?

She decided – for the sake of her sanity – that if she felt this cold, she couldn't be dead. So that meant she was in the Shadow. For a dryad, that was as good as dead. Except she was no ordinary dryad. Not anymore.

Ideth cast a spell to dry herself, another to descry the area beyond the icy puddle her fireball had created and, uttering every curse that came to mind, trudged up to a better vantage point. She didn't like what it revealed.

"Frost…" In every direction, as far as magic allowed her to see.

Her body was numb with the cold, her lungs burned with the effort of breathing in the frigid air, her nose dripped, her teeth rattled.

This is a big *problem.*

If she wasn't dead, she would be soon. She created a shield around her and recited a warming incantation with unsatisfactory results. Hecate loved to control the weather inside her little realms, but Ideth never paid much attention to those minor tricks; she never thought she'd need them, which she now realised had been short-sighted of her. Most of the world was, after all, frozen.

She had no idea where she was exactly or where to go, but she couldn't stay there. She had to move, even if it was just for the sake of moving. Ideth picked a direction at random and began walking. The shield soon became a hindrance. She had to move it along with her constantly, so she gave it up and conjured a blanket instead. It was a crude thing – since learning how to conjure fabric had also been something she thought she'd never need – but it would have to do. She wrapped herself as best she could and resumed walking.

She walked for what seemed like days, powered by outrage and the need to avenge what the Suzerain and the gods had done to her, to Chiron, to Orion and even to Oreth – ungrateful little thorny weed that he was – when she saw what looked like the glow of a campfire. The perception spell was a poor substitute for eyesight, but there was definitely light and warmth in the distance. She ran towards it.

She could almost see Aegea in her mind's eye when she heard someone crying.

"Who's there?" she asked, casting in every direction for a clue.

The crying continued. It seemed to come from the glow, which was now all around her, except Ideth still couldn't actually see anything but snow. She followed the sound until she stumbled on what she first thought to be a root, but her fingertips told her it was a foot instead. One about five times the foot size of a male Dharkan. It had golden skin, and Ideth had to take several steps before she finally found the rest of the creature it belonged to: female, sort of dryad looking, apart from the smooth gilded skin and enormous size. A giantess, perhaps? She'd heard of such creatures but figured they only lived in Jötunheim. Was that where Hel had sent her, then? Ideth felt sick.

"Excuse me. I don't mean to interrupt… but… er… where are we?" she asked the crying giant. Under closer observation, Ideth noticed she was cradling something in her massive arms. It looked like the mummified corpse of a large cicada. Ideth stepped back.

"Niflheim," the giantess answered in a surprisingly small voice, without even looking up at her.

Ideth sighed with relief. Now that she thought about it, the enormous creature didn't fit her idea of a Jötunn. She might be giant, but she was as lovely as a nymph. More importantly, she was warm.

"Who are you?" Ideth asked.

"I am – I was… the dawn," she sobbed.

"Ahh," Ideth said politely, without knowing what to do with the answer. There was no shortage of strange deities in Hel's world. They all had two things in common: they were broken and likely had a story to tell. "But not anymore? What happened? Is that why it's dark?" Ideth talked gently, as if addressing a child. She had no interest in the sob stories of others, but she was tired. She could use the rest as well as the company while she figured a way out of her current situation. Besides, the giant's warmth was doing wonders for her own misery, so she curled herself against her shoulder, ready to listen to any clue as to her exact whereabouts and how to return to Aegea.

"I lost the sun," the woman said morosely.

Ideth perked up. "The blue sun?"

"That one too…"

Realisation dawned on her. "Eos?"

A large eye blinked at her. "Yes, I remember that name. Where have you heard it? I think it used to be mine. Have I lost it as well? Where did you find it?"

Her mind was clearly gone. Ideth didn't care. She was about to pounce on the Titaness with questions, a truth spell at the ready if needs be, when the thing in her arms moved, reaching out to Ideth with a withered limb.

"Freezing goddess! What have you done to… to… What is *that*?!"

"He's my love." Eos caressed his shrivelled body tenderly with a finger. "Do not fear Tithonus. He means you no harm. I've made the wrong wish and now he ages, so I brought him here, away from Olympus, to the world of the dead. But death won't take him. And life doesn't want him anymore. Zeus made it so. No matter how much youth I feed to him, he keeps ageing – forever. A punishment for my mistake," she said with unbearable sadness. "Beware of wishes, mortal. They are treacherous…"

Just when Ideth thought her revulsion for the gods couldn't get any worse, something like this made her reassess the very definition of hate. How exactly was Eos the one being punished when Tithonus was the one truly suffering?

"I can help," Ideth said before she could stop herself.

Eos looked at her again, her eyes two nebulae filled with hope and unborn stars. "How?"

"Tell me where the blue sun is, and I'll help him." If Ideth had learned one thing, it was that the best way to communicate with a deity was to bargain.

Eos frowned. "You have power, unbridled one, but you are not a goddess."

Ideth was annoyed but not surprised that Eos knew who she was. It made no difference. "No. I am a sorcerer. I can undo a god's design," she said, adding a bit of magic to her words.

The Titaness tilted her head in blunt assessment until the hairs on Ideth's nape stood on end with both expectation and apprehension. She had to be more convincing. "I know Loki took the sun."

Eos lost interest in her and focused back on the thing in her arms. "Your power is vast; your knowledge is not." The words were hot with reproach.

"So enlighten me," Ideth strained through clenched teeth. "Do you want me to help your love or not?"

Eos took her time deliberating. Olympians relished dazzling mortals with their brilliance, but Titans – except for Chiron – felt no such need. Their egos required no admiration. They were forces of nature. The very notion of an explanation was beyond many of them. Fortunately, not this one.

"Loki took the sun. Took it from me as payment for saving my love. But it was an illusion. It wore off." Her eyes glowed hot. "He tricked me. Then he gave the sun to the wolf. The wolf ate it. It is gone. And the deal can't be undone," she moaned pitifully. "My mistake… again."

Ideth stood there shivering for a long moment, thinking that perhaps there was something wrong with her hearing. "I'm sorry… the wolf did *what* to the sun?"

Eos cradled her precious bundle closer. "He was so beautiful. Can you make him beautiful again?"

"Yes, yes. He'll be gorgeous," Ideth said hastily. "Please explain what you mean by the wolf ate it."

"It is his talent."

"Whose?!"

"Loki's child. The wolf. He eats stars."

Had Ideth something in her stomach, she would have retched. She felt hot, even surrounded by ice as she was. She'd spent days in Fenrir's company at the Stump. She knew what he was, how monstrous he was. But how could he – *how* could anything! – eat a sun?

"A bargain we struck. Payment is due." Eos lifted Tithonus to Ideth. "Make him young."

Ideth stared at those pleading eyes, the only thing still remotely recognisable as once having been a person. The truth was, she had no idea how to make him young again. She'd just said whatever nonsense came to mind – as she often did in stressful situations. And even if she could give him youth, it didn't mean she should. And then what? She had to negotiate a better deal than this.

"Can you take me to the wolf?"

Eos moved her head in that disturbing way again. "Why?"

"I'm small. My legs are too short. It's too cold here. I'll freeze before I get back to Aegea, and I need to find him."

"Why?" Eos repeated in the same impassive tone.

"Because the sun is mine. I want it back." Ideth spoke the way she'd often heard Arianh speak.

"You are wrong, unbridled one. The sun never belonged to you. It belongs to the huntress, and she to him."

Ideth felt her lip tremble. "That's not for you to decide! You lost it. So it certainly doesn't belong to you. If you want your lover restored, take me to the wolf. I'm freezing."

"I don't know where he is."

"The Stump, then. Take me there."

Eos stood – by the gods, she was tall – and began to glow. The heat, welcome at first, turned to a furnace of pure light. Ideth cursed.

"All right! I'll do what you ask first."

And how am I going to do that, exactly? She tried to remember her lessons. Rejuvenation was not something she learned. Her focus had been on healing and countering a god's designs. Healing was a sort of rejuvenation, she supposed. Except she had no ingredients with her, nothing to work with, so whatever she did, she could use only her magic, which meant it would probably not work. Or last, if it did…

One problem at a time.

She placed her hands on the living carcass and murmured the incantation she'd often used on Chiron.

At first nothing happened, then the creature seemed to unfold from itself. *Was she actually doing this?* Gnarled limbs grew new muscle. Leathery skin became smooth. Hair began to grow, and the agony in his human eyes became unbearable. *Kill me*, they said, as plain as if he'd spoken the words.

Ideth winced at the creature, feeling dirty. She was acting like a goddess, selfishly hurting an innocent for her own benefit.

Eos' smile was one of a vicious child with a new pet. "Tithonus!" she said again and again while crushing him against her chest.

Ideth closed her eyes so she wouldn't have to look into his when she said, "I'm so sorry. We all have problems." And before she could say anything else, reality imploded.

CHAPTER 9

The Goddess and the Jackal

Psyche holds me back as we're about to enter my cave. "Wait. There's someone in there," she says.

"I can't sense anyone."

"Hush. Trust me." She motions me to stay put. "I'll handle this."

I know she's a goddess, and it's all well and good that she's finally grown into her divinity, but I'll be damned if I'm going to be treated like a helpless nymph. She takes two steps forward, I take one, and we end up pressed side by side in the narrow opening. She spares me an exasperated glare before addressing the walls as if they were a crowd.

"You can hide your light, but you can't hide your soul!"

I'm beginning to question her senses when a god steps out from the gap between worlds, manifesting himself just a few strides away. He's short for a deity, with a crest of black hair standing on end atop his head as if to make up for his lack of stature. He has long vulpine ears and a muzzle for a face, different-coloured eyes, dark bronze skin similar to Seshat's, and he wears a golden cloth wrapped around his slim waist like a skirt.

I have never seen the like.

Psyche's eyebrows rise a fraction. "Anubis," she says with the confidence of a goddess. "I see the statues to your honour did not do you justice."

I frown. *Is she flirting with this scrawny dog?*

The god's ears flicker at her. Our scrutiny, and I suspect the fact Psyche was not only able to recognise him but was not caught off guard by his presence or appearance, unnerves the god, but he does his best not to let it show. "You recognised me from a statue?"

"Yes. My father accepted one as levy once; the poor merchant had nothing else of worth. He kept it in his waiting room to discombobulate petitioners and scare the children. Had you chosen a different aspect, I probably wouldn't have recognised you. You have quite the unusual soul for a god of the Underworld."

"Do I?" His snout twitches – a canine version of a cryptic and insincere smile. "Well, if you know who I am, goddess of the soul, and what I am, then you know I'm also a connoisseur of souls."

"So I gather," Psyche replies cautiously.

Anubis crosses his hands behind his back and straightens himself, as if proud and at ease, but his emotions betray him. He reminds me of a cat negotiating a puddle. "I'm able to measure the soul of every god and mortal, except mine. I always wondered what it looked like, though. Do you mind describing it to me?"

"A blinding light mixed with gloom, like most of

your kind. A brutal mix in your case, full of angles, not swirls. It lacks harmony," is Psyche's prompt reply. Unlike him, she makes no effort to hide her annoyance.

"Makes sense," he says to himself, then turns his ears forward suddenly, like a dog who's just heard his master's call. "I am delighted to finally make your acquaintance, Psyche. I confess, you are not what I expected."

"Sorry to disappoint," she says sarcastically.

"You absolutely have not. Your soul, too, is unusual. At first it barely registers, like a mortal's, but your will is certainly that of a deity. Just not an Olympian deity." He grins, an unsettling sight in a god with a snout and fangs.

"I have no pantheon," Psyche states defensively.

He takes one step closer, hands spread out in front of her, palms facing up. The grin stretches to a snarl. "I have weighed your soul against a feather." He sounds like an oracle now.

"And?" she prompts, a hint of apprehension in her tone.

The snarl widens, and he nods to himself as if at a joke only he understands. "You have powerful wings, Butterfly. Fiery and chaotic."

Psyche is a string about to snap with tension. I bet there's a lot more being shared between them than words. Gods just can't help themselves. I suppose I wouldn't bother to speak either had I the ability to Reach others' minds, but I don't, and I resent missing out on their private conversation.

"Words. Care to use them?" I say unceremoniously.

The canid glares at me before he speaks again. "No wonder you keep such *charming* company, Psyche."

"You're judging *my* company? How exactly did you arrive in this world?"

He chuckles. "Touché."

"So we understand each other," she says.

"In this matter, at least. And only until it is resolved. Then, ah, it's so easy to get confused, don't you think?"

"Let's hope not."

"Humph," I say. That's great. Now they're talking, but talking in riddles. I think I prefer the silence. I leave them to their wordplay to go sit by the pool. I figure if they wanted to fight each other, they'd have done it by now.

I feel Anubis' gaze on my nape. "Moody, isn't he? Perhaps a little scorching is in order to teach this cat some manners."

Ice forms at my feet. "What does he mean by that?" I ask Psyche.

The god glows in reply, much like Seshat does when upset. No wonder he's so cocky in my presence. This dog is a scion of Ra!

I stand up, alarmed by this revelation. "Flaming sun! A god of light *and* the Underworld?" I say, a bit too loudly. "Fantastic. We all needed more of *those*." I think I'm getting the hang of this sarcasm thing. It's very useful in situations where violence is not an option. No wonder the gods love it so much.

His smile is too genuine for comfort. "Technically, I'm just a humble god of the dead. I abdicated the responsibilities of an Underworld in favour of pursuing

my true passion," he says, pursuing me to the edge of
the pool.

"Which is?" I ask, knowing I won't like the answer.

"Corpses." He licks his snout hungrily. "How I would
love to dissect you."

I think I finally understand how a dryad might feel
in our presence. "Psyche?" My voice nearly breaks.

She does an excellent imitation of a bored sigh.
"Anubis, stop coveting my property and tell me what
in the name of Ra you are doing here?"

"In the name of Ra, indeed," he muses, annoyed and
still very much interested in my flesh. He gives me one
more craving sniff before moving away. I have to stop
myself from exhaling. Burn me, that was unpleasant.

"Since this meeting has already taken a turn for the
unexpected, I will skip the customary threats and boasts
and get to the point."

"Please do."

"As you've so cunningly deduced, I've made
questionable alliances for survival. I won't explain my
choices beyond that, nor will I apologise for them to
you. Regardless of what you might think of me, I have
not completely turned my back on my kind. And as
it happens – however it might have happened – you
qualify as one of my kind."

"I'm flattered," she says flatly.

He's vexed by her attitude but continues nonetheless. "I've only recently learned of your presence in this
world. Unfortunately, so have the Nephilim."

Psyche frowns. "I thought they already knew."

"No. The Suzerain was extremely circumspect and
protective of his interests. But now, you're not safe."

"Ah! I've never been safe. Thank you for your concern."

"You misunderstand me. My concern is not for you; it is for all of us. In their hands, you'd be our end."

"As if I'd ever let myself get caught by the Nephilim."

He gives her a sour look. "You've spent days in the Stump as a prisoner already. If Alek Dveer had had his way, we would be finished. And you want to go back? The Nephilim know about you now. They will be ready. They have weapons, instruments, things that defy comprehension, but they work. I know how efficient they are. They'll catch you, and they'll link you to one of their own, and there's nothing you can do about it because they have no souls. Believe me, I tried." His features change. Muzzle replaced with a comely face expressing genuine concern.

"I appreciate the warning, Anubis. And I understand the threat; however, I must do this."

"Because of the wolf," he says.

Psyche's arrogant stance falters. "You've seen him? Is he –"

"Trapped. Willingly, I might add. He asked for you." Those mismatched eyes seem to dissect her for clues as to her intentions. "He's your bait. But I'm not sure who's setting the trap. Aahh, I see you're not either. And yet you're going there anyway. Why?"

"I've made a promise."

He shakes his head, and the jackal aspect returns. "This conversation is pointless. Seshat was right about you."

"Was she?"

"You're too young. Too naïve. You're too human to be a goddess."

"Well, Seshat can write a poem about it once she's done interviewing Chronos."

His ears twitch in irritation. "My motives differ from hers. I'm not neutral in this. I came to meet you because I was curious, and now that I've met you, I'm concerned. You're not as strong nor as clever as you think, goddess of the soul."

"You're right to be concerned, just not with me. I'm as strong as I need to be. But are you? Your presence here is causing quite the disturbance. Hel is not pleased. Neither is Hades."

"I'm not their enemy."

"But you're not their ally either. And you're trespassing in their world."

"That was not my intention," he snarls.

"I doubt they'll believe you once they find out Apollo is free." She tilts her head coquettishly. "Or was that not your intention, either?"

His chest heaves, nostrils flaring. "Don't be so quick to judge. You better than most know we do what we must to survive. My work here is not done yet. I will leave when it is." He sounds sincere and almost as tired as Psyche. He walks to the cave mouth, then hesitates and turns to face her once again. His tone is more casual, almost humble. "Is that petrified tree really the God of Time?"

"A part of him, yes."

"And you're gifting it to the Nephilim."

"I'm bribing them with him."

Anubis clasps his hands behind his back and nods resignedly. "Their eyes and sensors are likely non-operational after the fire, but the entire structure is designed to detect souls and life forms. They'll know you're there the moment you arrive. I suggest a disguise," he said, arching an eyebrow at me. "Don't talk to anyone but Namrive. Oh and, if she asks, we never met, Psyche, goddess of the soul."

"Not under these circumstances, you mean," she says pointedly.

He growls deep in his throat and leaves, head shaking, ears flat against it.

ANAMNESIS 6

Promise

Psyche waited. For what, she couldn't say exactly.

It was late. Eros wouldn't come tonight, she was sure. Ever since the marriage decision – for it couldn't be called a proposal – he'd given her ample time alone so she would miss him. Stars, how could the god of love be so blind to the lack of it? She despised him more than ever.

She'd thought through Loki's suggestion at length until, grudgingly and reluctantly, she'd come to agree with him. If he was right, if Ambrosia indeed worked as he said, then if she got pregnant, she might have a chance of apotheosis. Or at the very least, an elevation in status from pet to mother of a deity. The idea revolted her. Psyche had never wanted to be the mother of anything, and she felt nothing but contempt for women who use pregnancy to bind men to them, but she supposed that – under the circumstances and as far as maternity went – it couldn't get much more purposeful than this. And it was not like she had much of a choice, anyway. It was either pregnancy or death and eternity spent in the Olympian Underworld, where she would never know peace, for Eros would just keep tormenting her there. And besides, she'd come too far, endured too much to die now.

The more she thought about it, the more she hated the idea, but that didn't make it any less reasonable, or her any less resolute.

"Loki," she prayed.

"You called?" His voice came from a short distance away.

He had to have been there already. Like Eros, he rarely came to visit her these days, always busy elsewhere with his 'project,' and when he did, he mostly pretended to not be there, watching her every move, her turmoil, maybe even her sleep. Waiting for her to break. She pretended not to notice, but over their time together, she'd developed a sort of affinity for his presence. She could always tell when he was around even when she couldn't see him, and unlike gods, she did pay attention to the ants and the spiders lurking in the corners, mostly because there were none in Eros' palace except him.

She turned around and smiled. Not the way he'd taught her to, but the way she wanted to. "I did. It's good to see you." The words, much like the smile, spoken before she could stop herself. She meant them. Stars, it always felt good to see him, to know he was there. Her legs urged her to run to him, her arms to hug him, her mouth to – *No*. She allowed herself to relish the happy feeling for a heartbeat longer before she buried it deep under less dangerous feelings.

Love had no place in her decision, especially when lust would do just fine.

"Did you miss me?" he asked, his grin a reflection of the joy she'd repressed.

"I thought you didn't want to be missed."

The grin faded. Lips forced together into stern lines. "Good. You were paying attention. What is the purpose of your prayer, mortal?" he asked formally.

"I have come to a decision."

"About?"

"The future – *my* future."

"And?"

"I'm ready to do whatever it takes to get what I want."

"Is that so?" he said, trying not to sound too pleased with himself. "And what do you need me for, exactly?"

"We had a deal, if you remember. You want your revenge. I want my freedom."

He gazed at her intently. "How could I forget."

Silence.

The bastard is going to make me say it. Psyche took a deep breath. This was not the time to be prideful, nor bashful.

"You've taught me well, god of mischief. I'm ready to fulfil my end of the bargain."

"Just like that?"

"Just like that." She coyly shrugged out of her nightgown. Now that she'd made up her mind, she just wanted to get it over with. She sauntered to him and ran her hands up his chest, absently wondering what the fuck was he wearing and what it was made of. The fabric felt like hardened cobwebs covered in fur and not a seam, pin or lace in sight. It just clung to him, like a second skin. She covered a bit more ground with her fingers, relishing the lean lines of his body, still searching for an opening. It had to come off, surely. But for the life of her, she couldn't figure out how.

She gave up on his garments and caressed his ears instead. They were so fascinatingly pointy and one of his most sensitive spots; she knew.

"Psyche, what are you doing?"

She was getting ahead of herself, that's what she was doing, and he was far from convinced by her sudden change in behaviour.

She took a deep breath and tried to sound earnest when she spoke. "I may die at the ceremony. Or be taken away to a new prison where you can't visit. Whatever happens, you promised me the best night of my life, did you not?"

"I did."

"Do you always keep your promises?"

"I am a god."

"That's not what I asked."

He traced the line of her jaw with his index finger, then brushed a thumb over her lips before he tilted her face towards his. "What do you ask?"

"Kiss me."

He kissed her shoulder, then her collarbone, her neck, her ear. Each kiss a rippling wave of pleasure from her skin down to her core. Her fingers laced through his hair, curling as he kissed her breasts. His tongue swirled around a nipple until she gasped. One hand slid to her waist, followed the curve of her hip down to her thigh until it stopped between her legs. His touch was skilful and so audacious, her legs began to shake.

Sex held no mystery to Psyche, but she was a stranger to tenderness, and the care he devoted to her made her feel vulnerable and insecure. But stars, it felt good. She had to fight the urge to avert her eyes from his like a blushing maiden. She told herself her nervousness was due to impatience, not excitement. Her body, though, said something else entirely.

The kiss that followed put most other kisses to shame. Gentle and meticulous at first, it quickly turned breathtakingly chaotic. Skill gave way to eagerness, powered by overwhelming desire. Stars, she wanted this man, this god, this unfathomable creature. There was no denying it or fighting it now. Her pride crumbled under his passion, her moans muffled by his lips, her misery forgotten in his bliss – much like herself and all her plans. She let him carry her in his arms to the bed, her defences discarded along with her gown on the polished floor. His hands kept caressing her face, her hair, her breasts, her legs. There seemed to be dozens of them now, touching everywhere she wanted to be touched.

There probably were.

Her own hands were still trying to figure out his outfit.

"Take it off!" she finally demanded. Suddenly there was no longer fabric between them. Nothing was. No pretence, no lies, no games. Nothing but the chasm of mortality, the impossible summit of divinity and their own insurmountable wills, of course.

"Ask me," he rasped in her ear.

She wrapped her legs around him, caressing, grinding, pulling him closer, aching to be fulfilled.

"Ask!" he groaned, hard in her hand.

Never, she thought as she guided him inside her in reply.

CHAPTER 10

Heart to Heart

Anubis leaves the same way he arrived: surreptitiously. And as soon as he's gone, I slide down against the wall, claimed by exhaustion. Stars, I'm so tired… I can't even spare any energy to pretend otherwise. It took everything I had left to stand up to him and his canny talent. So he weighs souls against feathers, does he? I'm surprised my soul didn't break the scale! Only the most insipid would pass such a test. It's clear the scions of Ra don't want any wilful creatures in their Underworld.

Aedan stands brooding by the pool, arms crossed over his chest. I expect his foot to start tapping any moment now.

"What?" I ask. His stance could be the result of many things; better not assume anything in particular in case it's wrong. I really don't have the energy for empty arguments caused by misunderstandings.

"Your property?" he says indignantly.

"Would you rather I'd let him dissect you? He would, you know. He would cut and burn every inch of you until he figured out exactly how your body works, how you're able to host gods and absorb

their talents and why light affects you the way it does."
Actually, I too would like to learn those things.

"Humph." Aedan tries to hide his apprehension with annoyance. "What did he mean about you not being Olympian?"

I bit my cheek. "I never said I was."

"So what are you?"

"The last true human, apparently." The notion is still appalling and, to be fair, not entirely accurate either. I always had so little in common with my species, and if the Narrum are any indication, I have even less in common with their descendants. I don't know why this bothers me so much. It shouldn't. I'm a goddess now, as different from any spin-off of the human race as I can be, and yet I can't help feeling purposeless and somewhat... alone.

"You can talk to me," he says.

I raise an eyebrow at that. Talk? The most laconic man I've ever met wants to talk? To *me*? *Oh, Loki, what have you done to the poor Dharkan's mind?*

"Talk about what?" I ask defensively.

"The things that eat at you the way you eat at your cheeks could be a start."

"You have your frost fits and lightning displays; I have my cheeks. Or would you rather I start picking at souls instead?"

I swear the idea is more appealing each time I have to put up with a pretentious deity. I'm running out of patience for their shit, tired of their prejudice, of being accused of being something I don't want to be. And I wonder: What's the point? What if I am as bad as they say? Regardless of why or how it happened. This is what I am now. Maybe it's time to act accordingly. Everyone else does… Unravelling their souls would be so gratifyingly easy, it almost excites me to consider it.

"What happened to you?" Aedan asks. It's like he can Reach my mind sometimes.

What the fuck do you care? I think. "Why would I tell you?" I say.

"I'm the closest thing you have to a friend."

I chortle. "Stars, wouldn't that be sad for both of us."

The temperature lowers considerably.

"Give me a break, Aedan. What does Loki want to know?"

He grunts something acrimonious to himself. "You want to talk about Loki? Very well."

"That's not what I said!"

"I encouraged you to talk, and the first topic you picked was him."

I'm too enraged to argue. Too drained to engage. I just bring my knees to my chest and wrap my arms around them in silence.

Aedan takes a book from his shelf and sits himself on his bloodstained cot.

"*To Trick a Trickster* written by *Wouldn't you like to know?* How clever," he says sardonically. "Unlike the other books in my collection, I did not buy or steal this one. I found it right here, in this cave, and so I kept it. It's also why I chose this cave, but that's beside the point. You've read it, right?" I don't reply. He knows I did. "I didn't particularly enjoy it, myself," he admits with a partial shrug. "It's meandering, self-indulgent, the characters have no names... How are we supposed to enjoy or even follow a story like that?"

I still don't answer.

"But it's not a story, is it? It's a diary. The autobiographical ramblings of a megalomaniac's mind. I'd always assumed these events happened in Asgard – and I think some did, but not all."

"You know what they say about assumptions," I warn him.

"I do. It's right here. And so is one of the main characters – the pet princess."

I shake my head. "You think I tricked Loki?"

"Is that why he gave you his heart?"

I laugh despite myself. "Loki has no heart to give."

"Because he gave it to you."

"Tsk. He has less use for his heart than you do, Dharkan."

He puts the book down, unoffended. "I hosted him before, you know. Before I even knew he was Hel's father."

"My condolences," I say insincerely. "You should have been more selective with your guests. Once he gets inside your head, there's no fixing it." *I should know…*

"It's hard to be picky when you need to walk in daylight. When a god offers to empower us in exchange for protection and anonymity, we accept. It's what we were made for. To a Dharkan, hosting is more than a duty or a necessity to survive in the realm of the living. It is an honour."

It seems Aedan is the one who needs to talk about Loki. "He already got inside your head, didn't he?"

"Yes. But I also peeked into his. I know how he thinks. I've seen his soul."

This makes me lift my head to face him, and I have to ask, "Then why are we having this conversation?"

Aedan leans back against the rock, pensive. "Because after what you said to Anubis, I wonder if you see souls the same way I do."

"What do you mean?" I say, unfolding myself away from the wall.

"I see intentions and emotions. Not shapes."

"The shapes inform me of the god's personality and motivations. A sort of body language of the soul," I explain.

"Language is open to interpretation. Emotions are not."

"But what causes them is. The same emotion can be triggered by a dozen different reasons. What are you getting at, Aedan?" Stars, I'm really not in the mood to speculate about souls, Loki or anything else right now.

A tiny spark appears above his palm, and he freezes it. I can't tell if he's showing off or trying to intimidate me with how he's learning to combine his talents. He places the frozen spark on the warm rock. We both watch it as it melts away.

"Loki's obsessed with you, as I am with Ileana. Except, while I welcome my feelings, he does not."

I snort. "Why would he? I'm such a lovely creature, after all."

He smirks. "Yes, there's that. But it's also because you terrify him. More precisely, how he feels about you terrifies the darkness out of him."

"There you go. Fear and denial are not exactly the basis of a healthy relationship," I say glibly, hoping he will drop the subject.

"Goes both ways, it seems."

I shake my head again. "I *can* see his soul, Aedan. I see it clearly through all his illusions, down to his true self. He doesn't fear me because of how he feels about me – however convoluted that might be. He fears me because he knows what sort of monster he created. Because he knows what I can do to him. But more importantly, because he knows I *know* him, and what's worse, I know myself as well."

"Mmm," Aedan says.

"Mmm?!" I echo.

"Then you should know better."

"Do you think this is funny?"

He smiles. The spark is completely melted now. "No. I think it's sad. Most gods believe they have free will, but they don't. They are slaves to their wants. We talked about this back at the Stump. Gods like to think of themselves as asocial individualists, but they are gregarious. They constantly seek each other's company, even if it's just to have someone to argue with. I mean, look at Hades and Hel. Some are more hostile and open about their altercations than others, of course: Zeus and Odin, for example. But deep down, they all seek company."

"No, Aedan. They seek an adversary."

"Ahh, but only because they don't allow themselves to call them anything else. Gods crave recognition and respect, especially from their peers. I don't think it's out of rivalry – at least not all of it – but affinity. You're all connected. But you'd rather argue than admit you need each other. That's why it's necessary for you to make deals amongst yourselves to keep appearances and pride intact. You're all jaded and frustrated because you have all that power and cannot use it as you wish, so you lash out, you blame each other. That's what happened back in the forest. That's why it's so hard for you to say no to mortals, for only they can make you feel like gods.

"Loki, however…" Aedan continues before I can find fault in his arguments. "He was born to say no. He's anathema to rules and conformity. Whenever someone tells him to do one thing, he has to do the opposite. His talent is to contradict, more than trick. He's chaos and deceit. His soul is raw, uncompromising, different than the rest. I've only sensed three others like it: Hel's, Fenrir's and" – the silence only lasts a moment, but it feels like forever – "yours."

"So we're soulmates. Is that it?"

He blinks in confusion. "Soulmates?! What a preposterous notion. Souls don't have mates. No. My point is, that explains the attraction between you two."

I drop my head. "No, it doesn't…"

"If a dryad can love a Dharkan, why can't two stubborn, selfish gods love each other?"

I sigh with relief. He'd almost got me concerned for a moment. But as it turns out, he's still just a lovesick puppy filled with romantic notions. "Ileana doesn't love you, Aedan. She lusts for you, longs for you, obsesses over you. That's not love."

He clenches his jaw a few times. "All right. What is love, then?"

ANAMNESIS 7

Trials

When Psyche finally surrendered to Loki, she made no effort to please anyone but herself, and in doing so, she pleased him like no other. All that she gave was freely given and greedily accepted as much in ecstasy as in wonderment. He'd never experienced anything like it. Never allowed himself to be carried away like this. And for the first time in an age, he felt at ease.

"I thought you'd never ask," he said truthfully.

She lifted her head from his chest, cheeks still flushed, smiling mischievously. "I never did."

Clever and cunning, much like a goddess. She'd never said the words, true. But she'd asked all right, with every gesture, every breath, every movement of her body against his.

"Ah, but you would have, were you not so lost in passion."

"Perhaps, had you let me catch my breath long enough to speak the words. I do need to breathe, in case you have forgotten."

Sadness pierced his bliss. How could he forget? But

for now, he would ignore it. "You must forgive my oversight. I've never been with a human."

He let her have her way. The technicality wasn't worth the argument. For once, he didn't feel the need to be the smartest one in the room, to win an argument or have the last word. Fuck, what had she done to him?

"Psyche, I –" *I what?* What was he going to say, exactly? *I love you?* An absurd notion, and to her, deeply insulting. Even in his head, it sounded wrong. *I want you?* A waste of breath. She knew that well enough. *I need you* sounded too desperate.

"What?" she asked, smoothing his brow. He'd started to frown.

"I like you." His eyes widened. *Did I just say that?!* He was tempted to translocate away in shame.

She was silent for a very, very long moment to his perception, then raised an eyebrow and patted him playfully on the chest. "Good. I like you too, god of mischief."

He grimaced.

"Well, this was quite entertaining," she said, her tone aloof. "Your pillow talk leaves some room for improvement, though."

"I don't tend to cuddle or talk afterwards." *That came out wrong.*

"You're sweeping me off my feet!"

"I thought I already did."

What the fuck was he doing?! Trying to make her regret this? Of course he wanted to talk and cuddle, but he didn't dare say another word or move a muscle for fear of another blunder. He just lay there in silence, staring into her eyes, breathing in her breath, feeling her warmth, her heartbeat. He felt so content. And that not only terrified him, it made him stupid. There was only one sensible thing to do.

"I should go."

"Yes, good idea," she said, her voice taut.

And just like that, reality asserted itself. He was a god; she was not.

But the thought of leaving her behind – again – was suddenly too much to accept.

"Come with me," he heard himself say.

Her eyes widened at the prospect, shining with hope and delight, then suddenly teared up with disappointment, a hint of resignation at the edges. She broke eye contact for an instant; when she looked up again, she was smiling the lovely smile he'd taught her.

"Don't presume you own me now, Trickster. My place is here."

"Since when?!"

She pressed her lips, then bit her cheek, smiling no longer. It seemed that she, too, was tired of the game. "I can't go with you, Loki. Not anymore. The trials begin tomorrow." She sounded serious.

"Trials?"

Her head tilted. "Haven't you heard? Stars, you really have been busy elsewhere, haven't you? I wonder what wondrous and wicked things you're working on. Wonder if I'd ever recognise them if I saw them… Likely not." She spoke to herself, looking away.

He forced her to face him again. "What trials?"

He could tell she was about to lie, but she thought better of it and took a deep breath instead.

"Aphrodite wants me to do four tasks before I can marry her precious son." Psyche rested her head back on his chest as she spoke, her tone dark and glib. "First, I need to sort a huge pile of poppy, corn and barley seeds into separate piles. I have to do it at night – in one night – in the dark, so that should be easy. The second task is to get the fleece of one of those golden rams the Olympians like so much. I've been told they tend to be extremely aggressive and protective of their fleeces, so that should be fun. The third task is to fill a flask with the water from the spring that feeds the river Styx. It's located atop an unclimbable cliff and guarded by dragons – apparently! And the final task – my personal favourite – is to descend into the Underworld itself and bring Aphrodite a box of Persephone's beauty ointment." She tutted. "Gods are so insecure and vain. What use has the goddess of beauty of more beauty? I must have really pissed her off. She'll never allow another mortal to overshadow her worship again."

"Trials… interesting," he mused, his mind racing at the implications.

Psyche stared at him with a pinched expression. "Are they? To whom? They are fucking bonkers! Aphrodite could have at least pretended to give me a chance."

"On the contrary, she has – Ouch! I'm serious! It sounds like Aphrodite believes there's a chance you might actually become a goddess."

"So she wants to toughen me up. Is that it? To teach me something?"

"No. She wants you dead, all right. But it is a pretty convoluted way to go about it. Sounds more like she's covering all bases." He chuckled. "She has no idea what you're capable of, and I bet that gives her wrinkles."

"No shit… Well, there's no way I can complete any of those tasks, so that's that."

"Isn't Eros going to help you?"

"No. Zeus forbids it – Yes, he's in on it too, of course."

"Huh." That complicated things. Still… "Don't worry. I'll help you," he said.

"How? I can't cheat, Loki."

He gave her a condescending look. "I am a god, remember? *The* god of mischief. Cheating is my speciality."

"It's their playground."

"So is this palace." He winked.

"All right. How are you going to help me?"

He sat up on the bed; she rolled over, arms bent behind her head, staring intently at him. Stars, she was stunning. He wanted to take her again and had to focus to peel his gaze away from her perky breasts before he spoke.

Focus. "Don't worry about the first task. I'll sort the seeds out for you."

"They'll see you."

"Not if I'm an ant," he said cheekily.

"One ant sorting through thousands of seeds in one night?"

"A god ant."

The raised eyebrow said she was still sceptical.

"Leave it to me. It can be done," he assured her.

"If you say so. What about the fleece?"

"That's the easiest one. Aphrodite only asked you

to bring the fleece, not that you had to shear the ram, right?"

"Yes. I was given specific instructions not to harm the beasts, in fact."

"So all you need is to wait until sundown. Those rams are famous for spending the days fighting each other amongst the reeds. You just need to wait until they're done and collect the clumps of wool from the brambles they've brushed against. It's a test of cunning, not power."

Psyche hummed, lips parted slightly in understanding. "I see."

"I taught you to think like a god."

"You did. But gods rarely need to think. They have the power to just act."

"Not against other gods. And not without consequences. Sometimes the best way to get the upper hand in a conflict is to keep the enemy engaged in some other futile endeavour, like collecting stuff or talking."

"Humph."

"The third task is the trickiest… I can't help you there. I mean, I can take you up there and fight the dragon, but everyone would know I did it."

"Can you keep the dragon distracted for a while?"

"Sure," he said, not entirely sure. Dragons were single-minded beasts and very attached to their possessions. "You'll still need to get up there, though."

"Could you cut a series of hand and footholds up the cliff wall without being noticed?"

He pondered. "I suppose so..."

"Then I'll climb."

It was his turn to look sceptical.

"What do you think I did all day in this place before we met?" she asked.

"I… never really thought about it," he admitted.

"I climbed. I've climbed every wall, every pillar, roof and rail of this prison, looking for an exit. I've fallen many times too, but the wind always brought me back. I've gotten pretty good at it over the years."

Loki found himself grinning at her. "Aren't you full of surprises? All right, then." The grin slipped. "The last task…" He trailed off. There was no way he could help her in the Underworld.

She nodded, understanding his limitation. "Getting in is not an issue. Hades will make an exception for me. I'm far from the first mortal to travel to his realm. Like Niflheim, Hades made it bearable for mortals, so I don't have to die to gain entry. Getting out, though…"

"You'll make it," he said more confidently than he felt. "Take a treat for Cerberus. I heard he likes honey cakes. Don't get distracted. Accept nothing from anyone, especially not food, and you'll be fine."

She gave him the saddest of smiles.

Realisation dawned on him. "Is that why you called me here? Because you think you'll die soon?"

She bit her lip. "Yes."

The word cut through his soul. For once, he'd rather she'd lied. He would gladly believe the lie.

"Wasn't that always the deal? One good night before an eternity in the Underworld?" she said.

Of course. Now it made sense. She would never have bent if she wasn't already broken. What a fool he'd been to think she might actually have grown to *like* him. No one could like him. Not without a spell or curse. Especially not her.

"You used me," he said, surprised at how much that stung.

"Yes. I used you as you have used me for your revenge. I used every trick you taught me. Aren't you proud?"

No. He was not proud at all. He was sorry.

Humanity… he mused. So close to divinity in so many ways… Maybe Prometheus hadn't been wrong after all. Humans were indeed ruthless creatures. Vile. Survivors as selfish as their creators. All they needed were stronger bodies and longer lifespans. He would give them that. He would teach them to break the gods as she'd broken him. After all, if there was one thing he'd learnt from all this, it was how good a teacher he was.

He leaned in to kiss her. "Very proud," he lied.

He got off the bed and summoned back his clothes.

She followed him with her gaze and sighed. "My mother always said men are all the same. It's not true for gods." She spoke almost mournfully.

He cringed at the idea of being compared with the Olympian god of love. "Is there a compliment somewhere in that statement?"

"Nah. Just an observation."

He wasn't in the mood for observations.

"I must go. There's a lot to do: carve rock, gather ants, and so on. Whatever happens, we'll meet again. In this world or another."

"Is that a promise?"

"No."

She chuckled bitterly to herself, as if laughing at a joke only she understood. He Reached for her thoughts, but whatever it was, it had already been put out of her mind.

"Goodbye, Trickster." She turned over, away from him.

He clenched his jaw and left without another word.

CHAPTER 11

Mind to Mind

Psyche's expression hardens. Her dark brown eyes fill with grief and pain and sadness. I've struck a nerve. Not the one I was poking at, but definitely a raw one.

"Do you want to know about love, Aedan?" she asks defiantly.

"Please, enlighten me," I sneer.

"I was married to it," she says.

I can't disguise my astonishment.

"Remember when I told you love is a god's talent, like dreaming, lightning, or life itself? Eros' talent is love. Not the sort of love bards and damsels like to sing about, sweet, altruistic and blissful, but an all-consuming obsession that takes over the minds and bodies of gods and mortals alike. It brings down kingdoms, pantheons, worlds. It breaks hearts, alliances, ideals. No spirit or will stands a chance against the might of Eros' arrows. And neither did I when I was mortal. At first, anyway."

She shakes her head ruefully. "I felt so lucky, so proud – unworthy, even! When the wind took me to his palace amidst the clouds, I thought I'd be happy ever after. I was lover to a god, not some vain man who called himself king just because he had more land and gold than his neighbours. And not just any god, but one of the most beautiful, powerful and sought-after gods in the pantheon. I know how much you respect Hel, but Dharkan are used to gods. To you, they are just another race of creatures. You talk to them, argue with them. You take them within yourselves, for fuck's sake. Can you even comprehend how much gods meant to humans back then? How much we worshipped them?"

"No," I say truthfully. The Dharkan are taught to respect and honour the gods, not worship them. Still, I get a glimpse of the magnitude of their devotion in the heartfelt way she speaks. It is Psyche the human telling me this, not Psyche the goddess.

"Good or bad, they were the Universe made flesh, a paragon of unattainable power, beauty and perfection. To be loved by a god was the greatest gift a mortal could receive. Many would lay down their lives just for a touch of divinity." Her wistful manner is replaced by bitter hatred in a blink. "But then... that first night, I learned love is nothing but the whim of a cruel being, a monster. It's overwhelming, maddening, agonising, even. And while we're in its throes, the monster plays with us as he wills." She bites her cheek again, choosing her next words. "He would suffocate me," she whispers. "Strangle me until I lost consciousness. Then he would bring me back, maybe even from death. *Breathe...* he always said before he smothered me again and again."

Burning light, no wonder she's so protective of her neck.

I clear my throat. "I'm sorry. I... didn't know."

"Still not the worst thing he did to me," she says, talking over my apology.

Flaming sun, I asked her to talk, and now she's talking all right. I don't want to hear any more of it, but I have to. I owe her that much.

"He would torture me: razors, fire, acid, fists, spikes, whips… He used them all just for the fun of tearing me apart like a rag doll and putting me back together again. But that wasn't enough. I had to laugh at his jokes, moan for his pleasure, pleasure myself for his pleasure. Listen to him with a smile on my lips while he talked all night about his despicable deeds. I had to constantly nod and praise his every action and opinion, never allowed to express my own. And the worst of it, each morning, I had to thank him for his love and attention. I had to tell him how grateful I was to have been chosen to be his. And I'd better sound convincing… or else. I had no control, no agency over my life or fate. Every word of his was a command I could not refuse. And the things he would make me do…" She shudders. "When he was finally gone, bored of playing with me, there was nothing left in me but the dread of his return. Every god in the pantheon knew about it. None protested or lifted a finger to help me. They either despised me or were waiting for him to get tired so they could have their turn." Her face is almost distorted by loathing. "Fucking gods."

"But you are a goddess now," I say, unable to come up with anything better to say after all that.

"Ain't that ironic…"

I think I finally understand the reason behind her constant turmoil, her anger and selfishness. Why she has this constant need to run away. She has the power to do to them what they did to her and more. Would I show such restraint? Goddess, no. I would have burned them all.

"I wished for the power to defend myself," she says morosely. "And promised myself that if I were a goddess, I would do better, be better than them. Look where it's got me."

"That's why you replied to Ileana," I realise.

She nods. "I wanted to use my power to help mortals fight the gods' injustices. More than that, I… I guess I fancied myself a champion of mortalkind. Ileana held such hatred for the Narrum. She believed them soulless. Tsk, as if souls were the magic ingredient for a conscience. She was so wrong, so misguided I had to do something. Of course, I suspected a trap. Deep down, I knew that idea could only have been planted in her head by a god. What do dryads care about souls? How did she even know of my existence? But then I realised I couldn't stay hidden forever. I've been through so much to earn my power, I owed it to myself and all the others who have suffered at the mercy of men or a cruel deity to use it to stop the abuse. I would set the gods straight."

"How did you end up a Wyrd, then?" I have to ask.

She shrugs. "Prometheus asked me to. He was the last god I ever expected to find there, and probably the only one the mortal in me still worshipped. He showed me what had become of the world, what the Nephilim had done, and he convinced me Ileana was the safest way to get close to the Suzerain unnoticed. The Suzerain would try to free Ileana and release me instead – exactly as he did. I would then release Zeus – as I sort of did. Then Zeus would release Prometheus."

"But Prometheus had to be free already to find you in the first place," I point out.

"He'd been free because Tartarus ceased to exist. Most Olympians were gone; the Titans ruled again, which incidentally was exactly what he'd wanted. Except Gaea had exhausted herself trying to save her creations and faded into oblivion as she almost did now. Chronos had his victory over her, cutting the link between life and death. As a result, worlds, stars, life, everything was being extinguished all over the Universe – permanently. There was little left to rule, and soon Titans would perish too. It was more than Prometheus could bear. He had to find another way. A way to trick time itself."

"How did you stay alive during all that?"

She smiled ruefully. "I was asleep."

"Why take away your memory, then? You'd have done a better job had you known what you were doing, no?"

"It was as much for my benefit as Ileana's. A precaution in case I got caught – which I did – or Ileana's mind was probed – as it was. Besides, no one should know their own future, especially not gods. He told me to trust my instincts. I guess I did. The memory loss wasn't meant to be permanent. It was a spell, a good one, but intended to fade. It relied on my willingness to forget more than anything else, really."

"But," I say, still confused, "you brought Chronos' soul inside the butterfly pendant. Why? And who put it there?"

"Hecate. She, too, was freed when Tartarus collapsed, and she did it at Chronos' request. You see, like most tyrants, he changed his mind. With life gone from the Universe, he became redundant. Alone but for the soul in his mind, the only one he could not send to the Underworld – the only soul he truly wanted to be rid of. Hecate used a dagger infused with my talent by Hephaestus. It's how she got hold of Mnemosyne's talent as well. The Blacksmith had a way of collecting talents," she adds sourly.

"Still doesn't explain how they got hold of that specific pendant. It was crafted specially for you. And didn't Loki kill Hephaestus before he could craft it?"

"This time around, perhaps. Who knows what the Blacksmith crafted or when? Regardless, once an object or piece of information is sent back in time, it becomes trapped within an infinite cause-effect loop in which the item no longer has a discernible point of origin. If a future event causes a past event, which then leads to the future event, that event loses its origin. It just exists apart from its own causation because its future is the past."

I'm getting a headache… "All right…" I say, rubbing my temples. "How do I fit into all this?"

"Good question." She spreads her hands. "You don't. Time may be a loop, but Fate is a web, a mesh of interlaced strings so convoluted that it's nearly impossible to unravel. That's why everything seems random. But it's not. Prometheus spent eons studying fate, and he saw this moment in time as a crucial point to change the outcome of Chronos' plan. The problem is, they were not the only gods with a plan. Zeus had a plan to conquer Odin's nine worlds by using the Nephilim. Odin had a plan to triumph over Zeus, as well as the Nephilim. Gaea had a plan to make time as irrelevant to mortals as it was to gods by turning them immortal. The Suzerain had a plan to destroy all gods. And Eros planned to find me and punish me for ripping his soul to shreds."

I blink.

Psyche sighs deeply, as if the admission has left her empty. I say nothing.

"After my apotheosis and after I was sent away from… never mind. After I was left alone. I was very angry, and I didn't hide right away. I travelled the Universe first, visited a few stars, a few worlds… Eros found me. He was determined to make me his property again, to punish me for something that wasn't even true. I tried to undo him. I took away his soul, but I had nowhere to put it, and no Underworld lord would have it. I could have kept it with me, but I didn't want that! I realised I would never be rid of him, so I did the worst thing I could do. I made him suffer first, though. Once I had him in my power, I inflicted on him all the pain he'd caused me tenfold. When I was done, there was nothing left of him but the godly equivalent of a vegetable." She smiles mournfully. "I guess I am as bad as the rest of them after all."

"That still doesn't answer my question," I say with a newfound respect for the goddess, as if I'm seeing her for the first time. Seeing what she'd always wanted yet dreaded others might see.

Psyche massages her neck absently, her face contorted in anguish. "He's here. In Niflheim. Stars, I really thought I'd destroyed him. But gods are resilient creatures. I felt his presence even while I was a Wyrd. At first I thought it was my imagination or fear. Then when

I met Iosh, I recognised his *gift*. He's not completely himself; otherwise we would not be having this conversation. But he is here. He's involved in all this. He made you and Ileana fall in love, I'm sure of it. I still don't know why. Maybe he thought you would kill me to 'save' her." She snorts. "As you nearly bloody did! He won't stop there, though. And he doesn't give a fuck about anyone else's schemes. That's the sort of god he is. Ask any deity who they'd rather have as an enemy: Eros or Chronos. They'll pick Chronos. No one wants Eros as an enemy."

"Or you," I point out.

"They don't want me as one of theirs, period. I never fit in with mortals. Now I don't fit in with gods either."

"Might have more to do with your personality than your talent," I point out.

Psyche narrows her eyelids to slits.

"Just something to consider. If you were –"

"If I were what? Meeker? Nicer? Lovelier? Fuck that! My personality is the result of a lifetime of mistreatment, not the other way around. I'm too old to change. Even if I wanted to – and I don't! – my temper has always served me well. It kept me alive."

"It also brought you here."

"And it will get me out! I can change who I am as much as you can change your freezing moods."

I feel the energy running through my body, its manifestation on my hands. It gets stronger as I get angrier. One power feeds on the other. I could raze these hills with lightning and freeze every hot spring. She's right. I can control it, but I can't change it.

Silence follows.

"Why do you fear Eros? You beat him once. You can beat him again." I was always aware of her fear, but not what caused it.

She shakes her head. "He would not risk another confrontation. You saw Chiron. He was mortal. Whatever can turn a Titan mortal can turn me. I think that's what he wants. It's the perfect punishment."

"I think you are right," I admit, unsure of how to feel or what to do about it.

She guffaws. "That would be the day all stars in the universe burn out."

"Perhaps they have, and we don't know it yet. The light we see is thousands, even millions of years old," I say offhandedly, trying to lift the mood.

She raises both eyebrows at me, her temper subsided. "I didn't know you cared about stars, Dharkan."

"I bet I can see them better than you," I tease. "Stars are all we have in the Shadow. We've probably been looking at the same ones, aeons apart."

Her eyes glaze over for a moment in contemplation, then narrow sidelong at me, sharp as ever. "One friendly observation would have sufficed to lift the mood. After all, I did pour my heart out to you. So much rapport is troubling, though. Either you're trying to seduce me, which I doubt, or... What are you getting at, Aedan?"

"Can't I just be nice? I understand you better now. And I'm tired of arguing with you."

"You're being nice because you're afraid I'll go away, and I'm still your best bet to getting your precious Ileana back."

"Am I wrong?"

"No."

"Then I'll keep being nice."

"Tsk."

"Does that mean you'll help me find her? We are in this mess because of –" I stop myself when I see the warning on her face. "Gods," I say.

She chews on her cheek, eyes glaring. "If the opportunity arises – and there's no extra cost to my well-being and freedom – yes, I will help you. And may you forgive me for it one day…"

"Why would I need to forgive you?"

"Are you familiar with the adage 'Be careful what you wish for'?"

"Yes. It's another of those Narrum contradictions. It makes no sense."

"Doesn't make it less true."

"I'll take my chances."

She leans back against the wall, eyes closed, looking bedraggled and sleep deprived like a mortal. Her Prana is so low, I can hardly sense it. She's in no condition to fight a dog, let alone a god.

"Do not mention a word of this to anyone… please," she whispers.

"I won't." And I mean it. *Goddess, to whom would I mention it? Which part?*

I take a moment to absorb all this, at a loss for what to say next. I have questions, many questions, but I won't get any more answers right now, for it looks like Psyche has fallen asleep.

INTERLUDE 11

Anubis

Anubis left Aedan's cave feeling denuded, dissected, and discarded like an old bone. He'd heard Psyche had a temper, and he'd been prepared for it. But her talent and, more specifically, her soul had caught him off guard.

Did Seshat know? If not, he sure wouldn't tell her. Some things should remain off the record for everyone's sake.

He found her outside with the anguished expression of one to whom no words come to mind.

"Are you done?" he asked, eager to get back to the Stump. This world made him utterly uncomfortable. Not just because it was breaking apart but because it belonged to gods who made it too tempting for him to join in with its breaking. If anything, this detour had reminded him of why he'd joined the Nephilim. He hated abstracts and subjective realms with no measurable or even reliable attributes. As a pragmatic god, he'd lived by the scale, and if there's one thing the Nephilim understood well despite all their flaws and misguided perceptions, it was scales.

"Yes… I guess I am." She glanced down at the stack of blank sheets in her hands.

"He gave you nothing, hmm?" Anubis sniffed at Xylo, wondering what had possessed the God of Time to submit to such humiliation. The Suzerain could at least have built him a more practical construct, surely.

"No… he gave me plenty. I can't write any of it down, though."

"Why not?"

"Who would believe it? Cats, what would it do to those who did?"

Anubis had no answer to give her. He was still pondering the pros and cons of presenting Chronos to Namrive. On one side of the scale, it was in his best interests to do so. Not only would the God of Time improve his status amongst the Nephilim and satisfy all of Namrive's ambitions, it would keep her and the most influential of her kind busy – or at least distracted – for a while, giving him a precious opportunity to achieve a few ambitions of his own. On the other side of the scale, it might mean the abrupt end of everyone's ambitions. If only choices were as easy to measure as souls were to weigh.

"How did it go with Psyche?" Seshat asked.

"Enlightening," he said sardonically. "She's a liability to us all. She doesn't know how strong she is, nor does she fully understand her weaknesses. And she's too stubborn to take any advice from us, whom she so rightly distrusts. If Namrive, the Suzerain or any of the Nephilim get hold of her…" He trailed off.

"Then we must make sure they don't."

"Easier to bathe a cat," he grumbled wearily. There

was something else on Seshat's mind he couldn't quite Reach, but he was too weary to care. "Can we go now?"

"Soon. First, I need to stash a few things."

"Here?!"

"Yes. This network of caves was not designed by Hel. It will remain as long as the world remains, regardless of what happens to it. I may not have recorded everything, but what I did, someone needs to read. Someone *will* read it," she said pointedly to Chronos. His eye seemed to lighten slightly in amusement or rage. Anubis couldn't tell.

"Very well, do what you need to do. Let's keep it brief."

∞

They returned to find Aedan flirting with Quetish. He was feeding her apples while she made a show of savouring them.

"Just what do you think you're doing to my sphinx!" Seshat shouted in outrage. She'd left her there to guard Chronos, not to flirt or be fed like a pet.

"Cornus loved apples. I figured your mount would like them, too. Everyone loves apples."

"Get away from her, you dead cat, before she eats you. I should burn you for your insolence."

"That would be a shame," Quetish purred.

"Ah! I didn't realise you could speak," Aedan said, only slightly surprised by the revelation.

"I can do many things," the sphinx suggested lewdly, running a sharp claw up his leg.

Surprise turned to unease. "Right. Humph, well... maybe some other time. I really need to talk to Seshat."

Quetish stretched her wings leisurely. "Pity," she said and – thankfully – flew away.

Aedan shook himself, then took Seshat's manuscript from his bag and threw it at her feet. "You gave this to Psyche. Why? Why her and not Hel?"

Seshat's eyes flared in recognition. "Hel wasn't around. I tried to warn Psyche. She had the right to know what she was getting herself into."

"Had I or Odin access to this information sooner, it would have saved us a great deal of pain."

"I didn't know you could read. Had I known, I wouldn't have written it." Seshat picked up the book and walked to the Dharkan, an aura of flame glowing around her. "Your pain is not my concern or responsibility. I would have shared my knowledge with Hel had she been around – had she cared. But I would never, ever have trusted Odin. Whatever machinations you two had going on, they did not include me, so mine certainly did not concern you. And I warned you not to confront me again. If you think you can judge or intimidate me, you're mistaken."

A sheet of energy coursed over the Dharkan. "There are many things you don't know about me or my kind."

"I know all I need to." Seshat glowed.

I wish I knew more, Anubis mused, curious to find out.

Seshat waved the book in Aedan's face. "You better forget what you read in here, or I will burn it from your memory along with your brain. Oh!"

Ice wrapped around her to the hissing sound of drenched coals. "Don't come any closer, dog!" Lightning crashed at Anubis' feet before he even had a chance to intervene.

Seshat melted the ice away and glared at the Dharkan, furious and wet like a cat in the rain.

"I may not be able to take away your light, scion of Ra, but I can surely take away your heat and the delicious Prana that comes with it. Let's not dwell on past offences. I've had enough of gods babbling about them lately. I want a solution." He considered this. "No, I *need* a resolution. More than that, I need to be done with your lot, find my woman and do what none of you idiots seem able to: live. Yes, I'm sure you see the irony. Now, can we put threats aside and talk like civilised beings?"

"Loki, is that you in there?" Seshat asked, bewildered.

"Not anymore, but he left me some entertaining memories."

Seshat's angry flush turned to a blush. "Where is Psyche?"

"Asleep."

"Curious. She doesn't know you're here, then." Anubis chuckled.

Aedan narrowed his cold gaze at him. "No. You see, contrary to what she believes, I'm not her property; she's mine. And unfortunately for all of us, so is he." He glanced sidelong at Chronos. "An arrangement I'm not happy about, but I'll be burned if I'm going through all this slush just to have him delivered to our enemies — and I mean *our,* as in Hel's and mine, not yours and Psyche's. So, dry yourself, sit down, have an apple. Let's see if you can talk as persuasively as you write."

"I admire your audacity, corpse," Anubis said. "Alas, we only talk when we negotiate, and you have nothing of interest to us, except yourself. Besides, we're in a hurry."

"It's all right. Time is frozen, after all," Seshat said almost in a coo.

'Seshat, what are you doing?' Anubis Reached to her.

'I just revised my opinion of this character. I believe he might still play an important role in our story.'

'It's not our story! Cats, Seshat. Namrive must have the fire and the twins under control by now. The ship might leave at any moment. What happened to not interfering?'

'I'm merely steering events in a different direction, perhaps even towards a swifter solution.'

'And you're doing it with words uttered in front of the God who's been meddling in the plot since the very prologue?'

'Sure. Why not?' She smiled at Chronos. *'After all, the God of Time is always listening, is he not?'*

Anubis rolled his eyes and sighed.

∞

"What an amazing specimen," Anubis said appreciatively once Aedan had returned to the cave. "I really need to get my hands on one of those before we leave." He rubbed his palms at the prospect.

"I hope you do," Seshat said.

"Do you think he'll do it?"

"He'd better. A lot depends on it."

"Oh well, let's go, then. Ready?" Anubis asked.

"Not yet. There's one more thing I need to do before we return to the Stump."

"What?" He almost barked the question.

"I need to find Hermes."

INTERLUDE 12

Oric

Oric squinted at what had to be an illusion: a nightmarish scenario that defied comprehension.

Portum had been overrun by Wraiths. But that wasn't the scary part. Nor was the impossible structure being erected atop the hill. What terrified Oric was how lively they looked, working at its construction alongside the Narrum and Anann. Oric watched, mouth agape, as one Wraith put down the massive dressed stone block he was carrying to help a frail Narrum lift a basket brimming with tools. In return, she gave him a crown of flowers, which he placed atop his head with a beaming smile. Another Wraith carried a dryad toddler on his shoulder and stopped so both could pet a shaggy dog. It was hard to tell who was more excited by this: the Wraith, the boy, or the dog.

"What the…?" Oric breathed, unable to close his mouth long enough to articulate the rest of the sentence. He knew the people of Aegea were nothing if not adapted for survival. They would follow and praise any lord – mortal, divine or dead alike – as long as they had something to gain, even if it was just another moment alive. But what in the shadow was the meaning of this?!

Was he dreaming? Had he died in the fire? Or had the teleportation ring malfunctioned and somehow transported him to another realm, perhaps? He'd heard Alek mention alternative realities and worlds set so far apart in space, magic was the only way to travel between them. But this... this was inconceivable in any reality.

"There's Jonas," he heard himself say, relieved to see someone familiar, something that made sense – at least it did until he saw the metz pat a Wraith on the back and both bend over with laughter for no apparent reason. It wouldn't have been the first time Jonas socialised with Dharkan, but laughing? He never laughed. Certainly not like that!

"Aedan!" Ileana squeaked.

"Ileana! Come back here," Oric urged in vain. She was already limping towards the madness.

She made straight for the tallest Dharkan. "Aedan! Oh..."

The man looked down at her and offered her a flower. "You're hurt. Let me help –"

She shook her head, not in denial but disappointment. She turned to the next Dharkan. "Aedan?" More disappointment. "Where's Aedan? Has anyone seen Aedan?" she shouted.

The whole town stopped to look at her.

"For frost's sake..." Oric covered his face. Some creatures were just naturally born prey.

"What do you want with Aedan?" a woman called from the temple under construction.

"Slush…"

It was Iva, the mad Wraith queen herself. She looked more deranged than ever, wearing little more than boots and a cape. It looked like Oric hadn't been the only one put through fire recently.

"I want to see him. Is he here? Aedan, is that you?"

Iva exchanged a glance with the Dharkan at her side. He seemed to be wearing the rest of her clothes and he, too, had a scar across his face. A very different scar, though. Fresh, and the skin looked scratched, not burned.

"No. This is Asher. Who in the flame are you?" Iva said.

Don't answer and don't look at me! Oric thought as she did just that. All other eyes followed her gaze.

"I'm Ileana. Ileana Dveer."

Iva's expression could have intimidated the sun. "Are you, now?"

Frost frost frost!

Before he could hide, or do anything really, a severe Dharkan was standing at his side. "Come with me." It was not a request.

Please, please don't say my name, Oric pleaded when he saw Jonas staring over at him.

"Oric?" Jonas said. "It's all right. I know this man. He's my friend," he announced loudly and proudly to the others.

"He's not our friend," the Wraith beside him said. They all knew who he was and what he'd done to their brothers. What he'd still do, given the chance. His hand drifted unconsciously to his waist, then closed into a fist. He felt utterly exposed without his blade.

"Oric, by the gods, what's happened to you?" Jonas asked, aghast.

"He looks like he fell asleep under the shade of a treacherous tree," a Dharkan said.

"Those are not sunburns," another replied in chastising tones.

Oric was about to list for Jonas the series of unfortunate events that had befallen him since they'd last seen each other, but there were just too many of them, so he abbreviated his account. "She did."

"You're Ileana?" Iva, now standing between them, sounded sceptical.

"And who the frost are you?" Ileana demanded petulantly.

Both of Iva's eyelids twitched; the surrounding air turned frigid.

"Nonsense!" Jonas said. "I've met Ileana. That's not her." He further scrutinised the girl. "She could be her daughter or younger sister, perhaps…"

"She is the Suzerain's daughter, all right," Oric said. She would never deny it, so he hoped maybe the truth would provide him with some leverage. After all, the Suzerain was the one they really despised.

No one dared say anything for a long moment until suddenly Iva burst out laughing. Oric had never heard a laugh like that. There was no joy in it, only madness and despair. It went on for an unnerving length of time. Even Ileana seemed taken aback rather than offended.

"Take her inside," Iva said sharply and mirthlessly. Several nondescript faithless moved to carry out her order. Ileana kicked and screamed to no avail, losing a few more strands of hair in the process.

"Oric! Do something!"

He wasn't particularly inclined to.

"Remember, this is still a sanctuary," Jonas warned.

Iva narrowed her grey eyes at him. "Don't make me regret our agreement. The girl needs healing and shelter, does she not?" She turned her gaze on Oric, intrigued by the layers of cartilage and bone of what would eventually become a hand. "What about you? What do you need?" A trick question, if there ever was one.

Had he been asked that a day earlier, he'd have said he wanted nothing more than to rest, get his arm fixed, have a bath and a woman. Not necessarily in that order, mind. Now he just wanted to stay alive with all his remaining body parts intact, if possible.

Before he could answer, though, another voice spoke from Iva's mouth. "*How* are you alive, creature?" Iva, or more precisely, the soul inside her, placed a hand flat on his chest.

"Hey, get your hand off me. Don't you dare feed o –!"

Her eyes flashed blue. "The heart beats too slowly. The flesh is confused. You should not be alive. You're an aberration," she said in that different, more feminine – and a lot more sinister – voice.

Oric forced a chuckle. "You're hurting my feelings."

"I'll hurt a lot more than your feelings, killer." It was definitely Iva who spoke this time. "How many of my kind have you put to the flame? Tell me, what should we do the Suzerain's right hand?"

"I'm not. I've quit." He showed them his stump again, almost pridefully. It was the left hand he was missing, but he didn't think the detail mattered overly much.

The Dharkan closed in. If there was one thing Oric recognised well, it was predatory behaviour motivated by murderous hate.

"Where's your magic blade, killer?" one asked.

"Gone. I'm a peaceful man now, honest," he lied.

They knew he was lying.

"Easy to claim to be peaceful when you know you won't win a fight," the one called Asher said.

More Dharkan surrounded him, all with scowls on their faces and flowers on their heads. They had to have been gifts from the women and children. Narrum always liked to give each other flowers, convinced it would make them more attractive and less smelly. Oric reckoned they'd probably tried to make the Dharkan less scary. It failed horribly.

"Sanctuary!" Jonas' reminder fell on deaf ears. There would be no sanctuary for Oric after all he'd done to their kind. He closed his eyes and did something he'd never done before in his life: he prayed.

INTERLUDE 13

Eros

Eros trudged up the Nymph's Bosom, thinking about what he would do to Pan if he'd sent him on a fool's errand. Amoral creatures were the hardest to punish. There was hardly anything the god of the wild wouldn't hump, so a proper punishment required a fair amount of creativity.

Eros hated walking. More than that, he was fed up with it, and this little detour would add many more steps to his journey back to Portum, where he hoped Freya hadn't done anything stupid in his absence. Still, if he could retrieve the box from Seshat and catch up with Psyche in the same place, it would be worth it.

It would be reckless to engage Psyche prematurely, but if Pan was right, she would be weak from her efforts with Chronos, and he doubted her pet Dharkan would attack his own brother. Even without brotherly love, their notions of honour would prevent him from any sort of bloodshed.

He ran through the list of things he would teach Psyche – for he had much to teach her. He would make her mortal first, to teach her a lesson in hubris, then he would take his time with the other lessons. She'd pay for what she'd done to him and his child. And he would enjoy that payment. This would be a good day; he could feel it. The entire world trembled in expectation of his reckoning.

He found one of the Nephilim gliders basking in the clearing, just like Pan had said. And that meant the stunted petrified tree strapped to its backseat had to be the host of the God of Time. It was hard to believe the mighty Chronos would subject himself to such treatment, but then again, Eros was wearing a corpse. Every god had to compromise something in someone else's world; might as well be their appearance.

"Well, hello." Eros sat himself on the glider, appraising Xylo. "Fancy meeting you here, Chronos. If only it had been in less embarrassing circumstances, huh? Fear not, I won't mention it to anyone. Say, would you be so kind as to tell me in which one of these holes Psyche is hiding? I'm without Reach and sort of anxious to meet her. Hello? Can you hear me?" He knocked on Xylo's head. What a nuisance it would be if the host couldn't speak. Then he figured he should at least pretend they were both free gods and offer something in exchange for the information. "I can untie your host if you wish. I taught Psyche these knots," he added, pleased that she still remembered them. "Or I can drive you to any location – after I'm done with her, of course. I don't suppose you're in a hurry." He laughed at the idea. Unlike most gods, Eros was not intimidated by Chronos. Quite the contrary. He knew well how the God was susceptible to his talents, much like any other deity. Even if the ways he would manifest his affections were far from orthodox.

"How considerate of you to offer, god of love," Chronos replied tonelessly. "I confess I am intrigued by your presence here and your constant interference in my affairs. Why have you taken it upon yourself to rescue me now?"

"Rescue?" Eros guffawed. "I'd never presume you of all gods need rescuing. As to my interference, it's quite coincidental, I assure you. My motivations are personal. I have no interest in the intricacies of the fabric of the Universe, its politics and power struggles, nor even souls really. Just the one soul, which belongs to me." Eros uttered the last statement gravely, in stark contrast with his previous blithe tone. "Any action that hinders Psyche's plans is good enough for me. And I'm definitely interested in this glider. Can you imagine how tedious and degrading walking is to a god who can fly? I've done little else but walk since I arrived in this world. Hey? Are you still in there?"

The laughing started as a rumble, then a chuckle, until it became a full-hearted bellow. Eros felt himself grow cold, the only physical reaction available to him in Emil's body. If there was one thing he hated more than being ignored, it was being laughed at. He would not tolerate it, not even from his mother, and certainly not from one of the Three.

"Aphrodite once told me love is the most powerful force in the Universe because it's the only one ruled by whim," Chronos said.

"That is true," Eros replied grudgingly, intrigued by why Chronos found it so amusing.

"I delivered her to the Nephilim for her insolence – an

offering in the Suzerain's name to guarantee his place in their pantheon."

"What… did you say?"

"You heard me. My pride would not accept such a statement. How could a whim be more powerful than a goal? Or a meticulously planned objective be subverted by a fancy? My logic would never allow such perversion of the laws of cause and consequence. She was right, of course. I see it now. Love has been the bane of my existence from Nyx to Ideth and now Hades and Hel, Psyche and –" He paused, green eye flashing with mischief in Eros' direction. "I'll answer your question. Your *love* is in the third cave from the top, on the left."

"Why, thank you very much," Eros said peevishly. "We'll continue this conversation once I acquire the right tools to do it justice, I promise you. Don't go anywhere," he added balefully.

Logic, Eros mused as he stomped up the rest of the hill, deliberately crushing every flower and plant in his path. Only the God of Time could still believe anything happened for a reason. Gods make their own reasons, and their actions shape the Universe, not the other way around. The fates always favoured the whimsical – his mother taught him that. The idea of her being held by the Nephilim disgusted him, but there was nothing he could do about it just yet. Still, this was exactly the sort of information he needed to put him in a vicious mood. He would need it to deal with Psyche.

She would finally get what she deserved. Chronos could wait his turn.

ANAMNESIS 8

Turmoil

"You're back!" Loki squeezed Psyche in an embrace. "You've made it. You passed the trials!" He'd thought he'd lost her, and he made no effort to disguise his relief.

"Hello, Loki." She spoke so abjectly, he almost flinched.

"What's wrong?" He could tell something was by her stance but refrained from searching her mind for the reason. "When did you return? Psyche, where have you been?"

"Right here. Where else would I be?" A statement rather than a question.

"You weren't before." He'd searched for her everywhere he could think of in the days after the trials. He hoped maybe she'd lost track of time in the Underworld. The stars knew he did often enough. But something much worse had happened, it seemed. "Why didn't you pray to me?"

She shrugged. "I wasn't sure you'd come."

He supposed he couldn't blame her, considering how often he'd pretended to miss her prayers lately. He regretted that, as well as the way they'd parted, and had nearly made himself mad with despair, thinking she'd failed the tasks because of him and ended up trapped in the Underworld for eternity. Of course his pride would not allow him to admit such a thing, so instead he said, "I'll always answer your prayers."

Psyche smiled dutifully, then turned her attention back to the sky. Her apathy cut deep. He figured she'd be upset after how their last meeting ended. So was he. That was why he'd left in the first place.

"Thank you for helping me with the tasks," she said. He couldn't tell if she was being sincere or not.

"You're welcome." In truth, Loki had only helped her with two of the tasks, and he'd been pretty discreet. Maybe she was upset because she thought he'd abandoned her. That he didn't care. He wanted to explain, but this was Psyche. If that was what had upset her, she'd have told him the moment he arrived. No, this was different. She felt different. Whatever happened during the trials had changed her, and his absence certainly hadn't helped. Maybe an apology would.

"I'm sorry. I could only help you with the ants and the climbing wall. I couldn't get near the damn rams, nor the fucking dragons. They were impervious to my charms." An understatement. Oh, how he hated dragons.

"It's all right. Pan helped me with the fleeces," she said.

"Pan, really?" Well, if anyone could handle those wild beasts, Loki supposed it would be the god of the wild himself. He sucked his teeth. "He's full of surprises."

"He knows about us."

Loki bit out a curse. He was being facetious before. The truth was, he hated surprises, especially those from a god who had given his name to an entirely new – and unpleasant – emotional state: panic. Why hadn't Loki thought of that? He, too, should have an eponymous emotion. What would it be? Lokic? Lotrick? Tlokick?

"Did you hear what I just said?" Psyche asked sharply.

Loki anchored his mind back to the subject. "Yes. Yes, of course I did. I was just thinking. That's bad – that he knows, I mean. One should never trust a satyr."

"Is that another piece of advice?"

"More like a personal mantra."

"Huh. He really doesn't like you, you know. Is there any god in the Universe you haven't pissed off yet?"

He pretended to consider this. "Sure. Even I can't have met every god in this Univérse."

Psyche rolled her eyes. "In any case. He's not fond of Zeus, either, so we can count on his discretion."

"Thank the stars for small favours." Loki doubted it had been a favour. The price for his help and discretion would present itself eventually. "What about the Underworld?"

"I don't want to talk about it," she replied assertively before he even finished the question.

"Did you bring the box?" Loki asked instead.

"Yes." She dragged the word reluctantly.

"Did you… open it?" He knew how curious she could be.

"No."

"You're stronger than Pandora, then." He chuckled.

"The first woman?"

"You heard of her?" He was impressed. Even the Aesir preferred to overlook that unfortunate chapter in Olympian history. Too awful to make fun of.

Psyche lifted an eyebrow, showing the first wisp of interest in the conversation since he'd arrived. "Every girl has. It's the first thing our male elders teach us: That women are wicked, especially if they are beautiful. That they are the cause of all the suffering in the world and therefore cannot be trusted to make decisions for themselves. My father often called me Pandora. Any time a crop failed, a house burned, cattle died, or a sickness swept across the land, he would say it was my fault, that my very existence made people ill."

"That's not fair."

"You think?" she snapped sarcastically. "One woman, ages ago, opens a box she wasn't supposed to, and now every woman has to pay for her mistake. Tsk. I understand why men make it so, just not why goddesses allow them to."

"Oh, she was supposed to open it," Loki said sheepishly. "It had nothing to do with gender. Zeus made it irresistible for any human to not open the box. He was trying to prove a point to Prometheus."

"What point?"

"That humans were a bad idea."

"Fucking gods." She shook her head. "What happened to Pandora?"

Loki scratched his head. "Last I heard, she married Epimetheus, Prometheus' brother. I haven't heard from either of them since. Rumour has it he'd rather share his brother's fate in Tartarus."

Psyche puffed out her cheeks.

"Didn't you want to peek inside?" Loki wasn't sure he could have helped himself.

"Of course I did. Persephone even offered to open it for me so I could make sure everything was as it should be. And that's precisely why I didn't. She reminded me of my sisters. I just wanted to get out of there. I didn't even look at the thing when Aphrodite opened it, thank fuck."

"Why? What happened?"

"It was ageing cream. Aphrodite looks like a crone now." Psyche couldn't keep the smirk off her face. "Suits her well." The smirk vanished. "But now the wedding is postponed until she's fixed. Hence I'm still stuck here."

"How is she going to fix old age?"

"Apparently she knows a goddess who can work beauty back into flesh."

Freya. It made sense those two were acquainted. And the consequences of such acquaintance gave him the creeps. He shook himself.

"I'm so sorry. I know how much you were looking forward to the wedding," he said sarcastically. Then he thought better of it. She probably was, if it meant leaving the palace.

"Yeah…" Her hand drifted to her stomach.

Through Reach, he saw what his eyes couldn't. She saw him staring at her hand and moved it. It was too late, though. His jaw had already dropped.

Psyche clicked her tongue. "Turns out the new stallion did the trick. You didn't know? I thought gods could sense these things even before we did," she said. What she didn't say was, *I thought that was why you left me.*

"I don't use Reach with you." A lie and she knew it. "Not… consciously. But that's not the point!" He moved closer to her side. "Why didn't you tell me?"

"I prayed once. You didn't answer. I figured you weren't interested." She looked down at her stomach again. "The wedding is tomorrow, so I guess we'll find out soon if your theory was right."

He stepped back. "You… planned this. Was that why you –"

"You're listening in on my thoughts again."

Actually, the realisation came as much from intuition as from Reach. Which was also not the point. "You knew there was a good chance you'd get pregnant if we…" *Oh no.*

"Don't pretend you're shocked, Loki. And don't play the victim. It doesn't suit you. You knew it too. You let it happen. You suggested it, for fuck's sake!"

"That was before I –" *What have I done?*

"Before what?"

I can't tell you. "Thought better of it!" he retorted.

"Ahh. I bet this change of heart had something to do with your new project. Or the prophecy, perhaps?"

Damn the woman and her ability to read me.

She tilted her head. "What is this project, anyway? More children?"

How the fuck does she…? "Something like that," he said almost desperately. "But… I… I might have been wrong," he admitted.

"About what?"

He had to tell her, and there was no easy way to do it. "Ambrosia will kill you," he said bluntly. She just stared at him, unblinking. He persevered. "I discovered that the chasm between humans and gods goes further than their souls. Souls are actually the bridge, the easy part to convert."

"What are you talking about?" she asked, stoicism replaced by concern.

Fucking words! If only he could just communicate what he'd discovered directly into her brain. He took a deep breath. "It's the way we created you. Your bodies can't transcend this reality. Not on their own. It takes a huge amount of energy and will to transform or transport living matter through realms while it's still… how to put it… performing functions like, you know… breathing," he said gravely.

Psyche took it better than he expected. She just pressed her lips into a line, nodded once and released a resigned exhalation. "I guess it was all for nothing, then."

"Is that what you think it was? Nothing?" He wanted to grab her shoulders and shake her. How could she be so calm and so cold towards him?

She lifted her eyes to his. "You tell me."

Except he couldn't. Not now. Not like this. She would die and it was his fault. He should have taken her away when she asked. He'd had so many chances to do it. He'd chosen vengeance and games and keeping her his prisoner as much as Eros. The truth was, he couldn't face her limitations, her growing old, her mortality, her… humanity. He couldn't face himself either. How he felt for her. How he'd let her down at the trials, how he'd turned her passion into stoicism. Anger boiled up. And so he did what he did best. He left.

∞

When he returned, much calmer and determined to take her to Niflheim, even if it meant fighting both the Aesir and the Olympians to keep her, she was no longer there. Nor was the palace. Both were gone as if they had never existed. Gaea once told him he ruined everything he touched. She'd been right.

"I'm so sorry…" he said to the wind. Then he gathered his guilt and turned it to anger like he always did.

He couldn't dwell on his mistakes or his loss. He had to go to Asgard, support Hel while she presented her creation to the Aesir.

And then he would show them his.

ANAMNESIS 9

Peace

Psyche stared at the place where Loki had stood long after he'd left her – again – without so much as a goodbye. She knew he'd gone to spare her his anger. The problem was, he was always angry. Leaving didn't spare her; it punished her. Because she couldn't follow.

She cradled her stomach again. "Well, it seems one way or the other, you'll be the death of me."

She was actually relieved. Motherhood was such a burden. The very idea made her sick – as if the customary nausea wasn't enough. How could she ever create life when she hadn't even lived her own? She was done with self-sacrifice and punishment. The best thing she could do for a child was spare them her resentment.

She felt a presence behind her.

"Who were you talking to?" Eros asked. He had a lovely voice. Smooth, warm, caring. She turned around and saw the most beautiful man beaming at her – proof that mortal senses were deceiving.

"The baby," she said as she smiled at him. Thanks to Loki, it took no effort to make him believe it was sincere – proof that gods were not as discerning as they thought themselves to be.

He hadn't hurt her once since he'd found out about her condition. If anything, he'd been what any young girl imagined the god of love to be. The perfect lover and partner. A proper god. He looked at her with such love and devotion, the sort of look the god of mischief would never manage, even with his talents. *Is this really all it takes to please a god?* she wondered. *To give them what they want?*

Psyche could have cried.

"It's time," Eros said. "Everyone's waiting for you."

"I'm ready," she said truthfully. And without doubt or regret, she took his hand.

CHAPTER 12

Love

There is no escape, love.

Alek Dveer's voice echoes inside my mind. The words remembered so vividly, it's as if I'm actually hearing them. I never did. They weren't meant for me, but Ileana. The reason they perturb me, more than any of Ileana's other memories, is the similarity with another voice, another phrase uttered in similar honeyed tones, foreboding and final as a sentence.

There is no escape from love.

I start to run. I'm in the woods. It's dark and I can't see where I'm going. I run and run and yet get nowhere. The voice becomes louder, closer, as if I'm running towards it instead of away.

No.

I look down and see footsteps. They're mine. I'm running in circles.

Escape

The voice echoes from every direction. It's inside my head!

From

A face suddenly appears in the darkness: beautiful and cruel.

ME.

I wake up with a start, wide-eyed and nearly blind with horror, to see Aedan frowning quizzically at me from across the room.

"Damnation! Why did you let me sleep?" I sit up, pushing the memory away. *It was just a dream,* I lie to myself.

"I was curious. Never seen a god sleep," he says casually, then he pauses as if pondering something important. "I have seen you unconscious. I suppose if gods can lose consciousness, they can sleep." He tilts his head like a bemused puppy. "Why do you sleep?"

"For the same reason you do." I sound more abrasive than I intend and take a deep breath to calm down. "All gods sleep. Or have to from time to time. Either through tiredness or boredom, Hypnos influences us all."

"The god of dreams?"

I shake my head. "Morpheus is the god of dreams; Hypnos is the god of sleep."

"Huh. A god for everything," Aedan murmurs to himself. I consider telling him Morpheus is Hypnos' son and his talent merely an extension of his father's power, but I'm still too bleary and exhausted to bother with words, let alone lessons.

"Dreams are good. They guide you in your choices," Aedan says to ease the silence that follows.

"Did it seem like a good dream to you?" I sneer.

He chuckles. "No. But you learn more from bad dreams than good ones."

"Yes, you learn not to fall asleep."

I stand up with difficulty. My head throbs. My heart's still beating out of control. My mouth tastes of blood. I'm so tired and weak, I feel almost human again. Pulling Kali from Chronos was like playing tug of war with a star. I succeeded, but I'm not sure I actually won. Then it hits me: Seshat is no longer close by. "Shit! Chronos!"

Aedan motions me to relax. "He's still outside."

I confirm with great relief that he's right. Which reveals a whole new set of problems, for I'm fairly confident the God of Time could have escaped his vessel while I was unconscious. Hecate's magic and Medusa's stare only work on the body, not the soul animating it. So why is Chronos still here? He's already got what he wanted. He's free of Nyx's soul. What else could he, a God with an astronomical sense of self-importance, possibly want to warrant such a humiliation?

"The mount is fed, but it's not going anywhere," Aedan says unconcernedly.

"Where the fuck is Seshat?" I can't sense her anywhere, which means she's either at the Stump, the Blacksmith's smithy, under some other hex, or has left Niflheim entirely.

"The scions of Ra left a while ago. The chronicler asked me to give you a message when you woke up. It goes like this." Aedan lifts his head and does a pretty good imitation of Seshat's voice and demeanour. "Remember our first meeting? The only way to survive in this world is to play a different character." He shrugs. "She said you'd understand, and I hope you do, because I don't. Like I said, the mount is fed, but I took its brain." He reveals a small key. "The jackal explained that without this piece, it won't move or allow itself to be moved."

"Stars, Aedan. You're lucky he didn't take *your* brain. I shouldn't have left you alone with them." I guess I'll have to thank Seshat for keeping both men civilised. She's so much better than I am at solving conflicts. Then again, she has a lot of experience recording them. I bet she's able to predict their outcome the moment they begin. I wish I could do the same...

He half smiles, pondering his next words. "It was... awkward, to say the least. But you know, for creatures of light, they are not so bad."

I don't know what stuns me more: his nonchalant attitude or his newfound assessment of the scions of Ra. "Are you hosting, Aedan?"

The smile turns to laughter. "No. Never again, Psyche. We just had some time to talk."

"How long was I asleep?!"

He spreads his hands out in mock helplessness. "Hard to tell. Time is frozen."

"Very funny," I say. *And a good thing it is,* I think. Otherwise, the world would've broken apart completely by now. Hel's talent has some pretty deep inner depths to hold it together this long, but time cannot remain still forever. Life requires movement and energy and warmth. It rebels against inertia as much as entropy.

I walk to the pool and splash scalding water on my face. It works even better than cold – if you can heal, of course – then I brace both hands on the edge, lean forward and stare at my blurry reflection for a long moment, my mind   flooding with questions. *Am I doing the right thing? Will I be able to go through with it if it is? What else can I do? What would she have done?*

Aedan sits by my side. "What are you thinking?"

"Nothing," I lie. He knows it's a lie. And a bad one at that. No one thinks of nothing. "My grandmother…" I say.

I can tell he still expects more of an answer.

"She was an extraordinary woman, what Hecate would call a daughter of the moon."

"You mean a witch?"

I narrow my eyes at him askance. "I mean, a woman of exceptional intellect, willpower and talent – for fuck's sake. Do you want me to tell you about her or not?"

He presses his lips together with his finger. "Carry on."

"If my grandfather hadn't been an educated man with an open mind, she'd have been left in the forest by her family to be devoured by beasts, same as I was left on a cliff by mine. Not for the same reasons, mind… I was the prize everyone wanted to claim, and so they gave me to a monster and called it an offering. No one wanted to claim her. They thought she was crazy, a bad omen. She died under mysterious circumstances when my mother was still young. They say she accidentally poisoned herself. I never believed it. She worked with herbs and made medicines, elixirs and ointments for healing, not killing. I'm sure she knew how to concoct poisons as well, but she was too skilled, too sensible and clever to allow herself to be poisoned. So… make of that what you will. The point is, I never met her, except in my dreams. I figured she was part of my imagination. I had no one to talk to as a child. Or as an adult, for that matter. My mother and sisters talked at me, and of me, but never with me. Over the years, I convinced myself I'd conjured her in my sleep for company. She would tell me things… Sometimes those things would come true. She taught me a lot, and I took her teachings to heart. I would not have survived without her or my dreams…" Despite the tiredness, I feel my countenance getting lighter at the memories. Then it becomes heavy again. "But as soon as I woke up, she would be gone. I only realised dreams aren't just dreams after apotheosis, when I was able to peek through the layers of realms. I met her before that, though – in Hades' Underworld. She helped me complete a series of tasks designed to trap me there. I only escaped because of her advice. I am what I am because of it. But… lately, I… let's just say, I don't think I'd have made her proud of my choices."

It feels like I've been talking for a very long time. I'm flushed and slightly dizzy.

"What was her advice?" Aedan asks, transfixed, moving closer to my side. There's something about the way he looks at me that makes me suddenly very much aware that I'm a woman and he's a man – and a particularly attractive one at that.

I lick my lips, almost tasting his. "She told me to… to…" *Learn to say no.*

I hear a whistle. It's a familiar tune – a dreaded tune. I go cold, then numb, then desperate. Vertigo overtakes me. I'd have fallen had Aedan not steadied me.

"What's wrong?" he asks, his eyes searching for threats, his hands seizing me for more than stability.

He's coming. "Aedan, you must leave. Now!"

"Leave where?" he asks, holding me closer.

He's right. There's nowhere to go. No other exits from the cave. *Fuck.*

"Then you need to hide! In the pool. Go!"

The whistle is getting louder.

"Why?" Aedan asks, holding me tighter. "I'd rather kiss you."

I touch his face and have to cover his mouth so I won't kiss him. "Please! I know you don't trust me. You have no reason to. But for once, just this once, do as I say."

He hesitates a moment, ruled by desire. And goddess, so am I. Then finally reason prevails and he jumps into the pool. I will the water to remain still. Mask his presence as best I can with the little power I have left. At least it's easy to conceal a being who has no soul, and thank the stars he doesn't need to breathe.

A young Dharkan enters the cave. I recognise him: Emil, Aedan's younger brother. He pointed him out to me back at the Boiling Lake. The only Dharkan who did not cheer Iva's speech. I should have known, for I felt then what I feel now. Even trapped inside a host, Eros' power is too great to ignore. Wherever he is, lust follows.

"Well, well. What do we have here? My loving wife," he says coldly.

I will myself not to glance at the water. I fear if Aedan sees his brother, he will not remain hidden. Of course, of all the Dharkan, Eros had to choose this one. His youth probably made him easier to control, and he needed a host others would be sympathetic to and less likely to harm, especially Aedan.

"Fancy meeting you here." He grins maliciously, glancing around. "Is Seshat with you, by any chance?"

"No."

"Do you happen to know where she is?"

Far away from you, would be my guess. No wonder she cut the interview with Chronos short. "No." That's all I say to him.

"How disappointing. I suppose some of us can't have everything." He clicks his tongue several times in mocking reproach, then moves closer, forcing me to back into a corner. Try as I might, I cannot Reach his soul inside the Dharkan. I should be able to. After all, I was able to liberate Aedan from Loki's soul, even with Ambrosia in his system. But Eros is more than a guest in Emil's body. He's the owner. Emil is long gone. Aedan will be crushed, but right now, I cannot feel any sympathy for his loss, for I'm so consumed with dread and hate and disgust I can hardly think.

"Are you alone?" he asks, still searching.

"Yes."

He's not convinced by my answer, but he's not concerned either. And that concerns me.

He shows me his teeth in a caricature of a smile. "I hadn't planned to deal with you yet. However, one doesn't look a gift horse in the mouth." He feints an attack to throw me off guard, then while I'm still reeling from it, pushes me against the wall, covering my mouth, his face inches from mine so I can clearly see the sadistic hate of the soul behind the white irises of his dead host.

"Shh, shh, shh. I was saving our reunion for when we were both in the Underworld, but oh well, this could be fun too."

If he thinks he can physically overpower me like this, he's gravely mistaken. Even as weak as I am now, I'm still a goddess. In one swift motion I kick him in the groin with my knee, then his stomach as he bends over, and next his face for good measure. I'm about to hit his lower back with my elbow when I realise his moans and convulsions are not from pain but laughter. His host is gone, so of course, he feels none of his pain.

He pulls both my feet out from under me simultaneously, the motion too fast and unexpected for me to react or brace properly. Gravity is unforgiving even for a god, and my face hits the stone pretty hard. My nose takes most of the blow. Pain fills my senses; blood fills my mouth. He drops onto my back with all his weight, pinning me to the ground, grabs a handful of hair, roughly jerks my head back and whispers in my ear.

"Did you miss me that much?"

"Fuck you."

"I will. But not without some foreplay. After all, I am the god of love." He pulls my head back further and smashes my face into the stone again, breaking my skull. "Are you wet yet?"

I don't reply. I don't think I could even if I wanted to.

"You really thought you could torture *me*? That my soul would be so easily unravelled? Or did you actually think I'd let you get away with it? Silly girl, you just made me want you more. You and I will have so much fun together. Forever."

I laugh. All I can think to do with my horror is to laugh. It's a pitiful attempt, more of a gurgle, and painful to boot. "You can't harm me anymore, Eros."

"But I can make you hurt," he drawls hatefully, his hand reaching between my legs. And he does. "Before, I had to be careful. The human body is so fragile. But now…" He sucks his teeth. "Imagine the possibilities. I will have justice for what you did to me."

A rebel tear slides down my cheek from both pain and shame. How could I have allowed myself to become so weak? To be at his mercy again?

"Never leave your enemies alive," Zeus had said. How I wish I'd been crueller back when I had Eros' soul in my grasp. So much could have been avoided had I done what I wanted, what I could do, instead of what I thought I should.

A spark of angry defiance still burns in me. "My body will heal. Yours will not. And when your soul leaks out of it, I'll be waiting. You've already done everything you could do to me. But I still have a few things to show you, *husband.*"

"Show me, then," he dares, hitting my face against the rock again. "Show me how much you love me."

A god's power is their will. I'm weak because I let it falter. I allowed myself to wallow in self-doubt, to question my choices, to fear their outcome, to feel guilty, undeserving, and even ashamed of what I've become. Gods are not weighted by such concerns. So why should I be?

As I realise this, power surges through me again. Not just mine, but whatever is left in me from Nyx as well. My weakness came from fighting this power, from smothering it while telling lies to myself, for being afraid to be what I am. The moment I accept this, it's like a dam bursts inside myself, much like during my apotheosis. More than a liberation, it's a revelation. I no longer feel pain, guilt, or fear. Not even hate. My flesh mends instantaneously and my mind is finally clear.

"Thank you," I say to him, still facing the rock.

"For what?"

"For showing me who I am. For destroying everything I was. Everything I could have been as a mortal. For teaching me what it means to be a goddess. There was hardly anything human left in me after the years I spent with you, and there's no humanity left now. You killed me. And I hate you."

He releases his hold enough for me to roll away and face him. "You loved me."

"No. I never did."

His surprise at my quick recovery is short-lived. "Liar. Such a liar, even to yourself. Only love – real love – would have granted me a child. The child you sacrificed to become what you are now."

I'm taken aback by this. "You knew?"

"Of course I knew!" He scowls. "You bought your godhood with the soul of my child!"

Now it makes sense. Eros loves pain, yes, but it wasn't just pain he wanted to inflict; it was revenge for the damage I did not just to his ego and soul but to what he'd considered his greatest possession.

"It wasn't your child," I say frankly.

"What did you say?" he demands, grabbing me by the throat.

"It was not your child," I spit the words in his face.

"More lies," he hisses.

I hold his gaze. "How many years had you held me prisoner? How many lovers did you, god of love, have in your existence? Have any of them ever carried your child? You can't conceive with either god or mortal."

"I did with you."

"No, you didn't. You can't create life, only destroy it. And all you give others is the drive to create life by destroying their own. As for love… Was that a prophecy?" His expression confirms my guess. I laugh again. "Love? Who would ever love you of their own free will?"

The lines of Emil's face, so similar to those of his older brother, become unnaturally distorted by his host's state of mind, as if unable to express it fully. "No god could have entered my realm."

"Not an Olympian. There are many other gods out there."

"Who?" A guttural growl more than a word.

"I'll never tell you," I purr.

"How?" He shakes me by the neck as if that would force the answer to drop out of my mouth.

"You'll have to ask him."

"I don't believe it. You lie! All you did, all you ever do, is lie."

I keep smiling. "At first, he pretended to be you. But I knew he wasn't. You know how? In the dark, with nothing but the flawed five senses of a mortal? Because I enjoyed it." He punches me with all his strength. I still laugh, unscathed. "I sacrificed the soul of my unborn child to get away from you, and I don't – I will never! – regret it. I owe you nothing, Eros. The curse you put on me broke long ago, since the first time you killed me, and no matter what you do to me now, know it will not change the fact that I love another."

He believes me now.

"So, you found real love, have you?" His voice is smooth, cutting through words rather than speaking them.

"I found self-esteem."

He's silent for a long moment, upper lip curling, first in a scowl, then a snarl, until finally there is only insolence on Emil's innocent face.

"Well, in that case, I'll just devour your Prana instead." He grabs my neck with both hands and begins to feed.

I fight him with all the strength my power allows but immediately realise my mistake. Dharkan are immune to a god's power while feeding. Hel knew what she was doing. The more I lash out, the more he takes. I thrash, kick, scratch, curse to no effect.

"You're mine. And mine alone. Body and soul. All mine. Forever."

Panic overtakes me along with the cold. *No, not like this. Not when I'm so close!* And yet, somehow, it feels so fitting. All my life I've been playing a rigged game. I lose every time I get close to winning. It's like the fates themselves are against me. And why wouldn't they be? I broke the laws of the Universe. *"You are an accident, a mistake, an anomaly born of chaos and disobedience,"* Chronos had said. Of course, something like me would never be allowed to exist, let alone succeed.

My vision blurs, then fades out completely. I think I can hear the souls in Helheim calling me again.

'You belong with us.'

No! Not yet!

Then I think better of it. Whatever happens, I can't let Eros take my talent. So I give him my life instead.

"Emil?!" Acdan's shout carries over the voices in

a mixture of confusion and outrage. "Emil, stop! She's on our side. Iva deceived you. Listen to me, brother."

"Guess again, *brother.*"

"Let go of her," Aedan growls.

"By the fates, the arrow really missed the mark with that one," Eros whispers to me before turning to Aedan again. "Wait your turn."

We are all blind to the changes in those we love, I think absently.

Something knocks me back. I can breathe again. But it's not breath I need, is Prana. And Eros has taken most of it. I'm cold and numb, stuck in the place between realms. In the distance, I hear lightning crackle, the heavy thuds of fists hitting flesh and men grunting like beasts, snarling at each other.

I try to act, but there's hardly any life or energy left in this body. Most of my soul is already on its way to the Underworld, and no amount of willpower will bring it back without a living body to go back to.

A boot steps on my outstretched hand. The pain barely registers.

"Psyche?" Aedan's voice sounds like it comes from another realm.

It's too late. I'm already gone.

CHAPTER 13

Loss

"We're even now," I say to Psyche.

She looks up at me, one hand pressed to her chest, as if trying to touch the Prana I've given her. I can't tell if she's grateful or disgusted. Much as I can't tell if I'm proud of or disappointed in myself for having done so.

"How…" She rubs her throat. "How much of our *conversation* did you hear?"

"All of it."

"Right…"

"Is it true, then? Actually, don't tell me. I don't want to know. What I witnessed was brutal enough, regardless. I wasn't going to interfere. You asked me not to, and I didn't want Emil to know I'd seen him like that… doing that. I figured you could handle him. But when you didn't, I began to worry. I kept waiting for my brother to take charge, while listening out of curiosity and, I suppose, the lack of agency that comes with shock and denial. Until I'd heard enough."

I sit next to her, leaning back against the wall, dejected.

"When I realised you'd rather relinquish your life than let him have your talent, I knew my brother was gone. *He's not Emil,* I reminded myself as I beat him. A Dharkan can protect the soul of his guest against any attack, but soon I realised that wasn't the case. Even if it was, my brother might protect that piece of ash against you. But against me? Never. The rest wasn't hard... Even charged with your Prana as he was, Eros presented no challenge to me. He's no fighter. I doubt he ever hit anything that could actually hit him back. His feeble attempts at retaliation were no threat, merely an annoyance."

She snorts in acknowledgement.

"I kept thinking, *Come on, leave my brother's body. Face me like a god so I can suck you dry.* But he was too clever, or too cowardly, for that. So I just kept beating him." *And losing myself a little with each blow,* I think grievously. "I'd still be at it had I not felt you slip away."

There's no clue on her face to her thoughts, nor any emotions I can discern. The silence stretches on. It suddenly occurs to me that maybe she hadn't wanted to be saved. After all, she told Hel she needed to gather souls from the Underworld. Maybe this was her way of doing that while simultaneously freeing herself from her obligations to Chronos, Gaea and myself.

"You better say something," I growl.

"Thank you."

"Humph," I reply with a mix of aggravation and relief. Two emotions I'm beginning to associate with being in her presence.

"It mustn't have been easy for you," she says.

"It wasn't," I admit. It would be so easy to let her go – and burn Hel's wishes – but much as the idea of having Psyche subdued in Helheim appeals to me, I'd rather not be the one in charge of Xylo outside. And then there's Ileana, of course. Psyche better keep to her promise now.

"I'm sorry about Emil."

"Me too…" I can't allow myself to think deeper about it now, so I lash out. Besides, she's too damn calm for someone who's just been to Helheim and back. "By the Shadow, Psyche. How did you allow yourself to be defeated like this?" Deep down, I'm furious. I want to say, *Psyche! You stubborn bitch, how could you be so stupid?* Flaming sun, I want to hit her myself.

She averts her eyes, as if guessing my thoughts.

I sigh. "I understand why you fear him. And fear clouds judgement. But –"

Her expression hardens. "Judgement clouds judgement. I was overconfident and underestimated him. It won't happen again," she says vehemently.

"It better not."

She casts around, animated with purpose. "Where did he go?"

"Nowhere." I point behind the wall. "I knocked him unconscious and tied him up. Like I said, he presented no challenge to me," I reply, to her astonishment.

She jumps to her feet to stand by the restrained shape of Emil and touches his forehead cautiously.

"Is Eros's soul still in him?" I ask.

"Must be. I can't feel him anywhere else."

"Bring it out, then."

"I can't." The look she gives me confirms my worst

fears. Emil is truly gone. "We need to force Eros out of his host."

"Burn it, Psyche. Don't ask me to mutilate my brother."

"I'm not. I – I'm asking permission to do it." She picks up a stone.

Icy tears sting my eyes as I look upon my brother's youthful face. He was good. He's never killed, never taken Prana from the living. Never even argued with me or judged me for leaving. He was too young to host. All he'd ever wanted was to see the world beyond the Shadow. I suppose now he has… I hope he has.

"What happens to Dharkan when they die?" Psyche asks.

"Nothing. We have no spirit, no soul, so all that is left of us are the memories in our brothers."

"Turn around, then," she says, emotionless. "You don't want this memory, trust me. He's waking up."

I watch her kneel with what's now a stone hammer in one hand, the other pressed to his chest, steadying him. His eyes open just in time to see the crushing blow coming. Mine close the instant before it lands.

Lightning fills the cave along with Eros' scream of eminent defeat. He tries to force his way into me. I'm assaulted with overwhelming lust for his soul. Goddess, if not for the rage, I might have let him in. Then suddenly – thankfully – he is gone.

Psyche stands with her eyes closed, seemingly unaffected by the spent energy or emotion. She'd placed a black sheet over Emil's body. I leave it there.

I'll remember you, brother.

She says nothing for a long moment. I don't believe

she's grieving. And even she's considerate enough not to celebrate under the circumstances. Still, this lack of reaction troubles me.

"Psyche?"

"We have to go to Portum." Psyche speaks slowly, almost in a trance.

I rub my eyes, trying to come to terms with this new development on top of everything else. "But that's taking us further away from the Stump."

She looks up at me, dark brown eyes coming into focus. "Yes."

"Why?!"

"Hel's asking us to."

INTERLUDE 14

Ann

"I'm tired of walking," Ann said. As pleased as she was to see green again, she'd become quite out of shape during her ordeal in the future. "Oh, why did you let Chiron take the glider?" The memory of driving it through the trees with the wind in her hair was still glorious to her.

"It wasn't mine to keep. Even if it was, how would I have stopped the gods from taking it?" he asked patiently, trailing after her and looking twice as exhausted.

An invisible force swept through the forest, beating them back like a gust of wind, and spared her from giving him an answer.

"You felt that?" she asked.

"How could I not," Agnar replied, still steadying himself. "What was it?"

"I'm not sure. But I've felt it before. After Ileana went through the Chronodéndron. I think it's the sorcerer. The one I told you about, with the torch and the heads. She's done something."

"Are you certain about the heads?" Agnar had had a hard time believing her account of the gods' final meeting. And no wonder; she herself was still trying to make sense of it all, but that particular feeling and the image of that goddess would be forever branded in her memory.

"I know what I saw! I might have lost my youth, but I still have good eyesight." Her eyes widen. "Hide!"

They flattened themselves against a tree, then crouched behind a conifer to get a better look at the group that suddenly appeared ahead of them.

Hel, Aedan, Psyche, Gaea and Ideth – even though they weren't quite as she remembered – shouted at each other in a patch of snow around what looked like a statue of Xylo. Joining in on the argument was a naked Narrum with white hair and a long beard and a strange woman with glass over her eyes and snakes for hair. Chiron was there too, lying on his side, hind legs strapped to the glider, his head resting on Ideth's lap. He looked dead. They had not been there a moment ago, nor had the cabin beyond them.

"Where did they come from?" Agnar asked.

"Shhh."

Ann tapped him urgently on the shoulder. "There! Behind the cabin. See? That's her! Now tell me she doesn't have three heads."

"They're more like faces…" he said cautiously.

She glared at him.

"Oh…" he said.

"What?"

"That's Zeus."

Ann squinted. She vaguely remembered seeing Zeus suspended in mid-air inside the vault. "Frost! It is. I didn't recognise him without clothes. So he *is* alive!"

"Odin must be furious," Agnar said.

She couldn't care less about Odin's fury after the way he spoke to her last. She cared, however, about what this meant. "Well, we came all this way. Let's find out what the fuss is about, as my sister likes to say." Occa wasn't part of the group, which was just as well. Ann had no desire to deal with her.

Agnar held her back. "Let's wait here for a bit."

"I want to hear what they're saying," Ann protested.

"Send the ravens."

"Excellent idea, Agnar. And then what? Do you speak raven?"

He frowned at her. "Yes. Don't you?"

She twisted her mouth. "No."

"Oh… Odin used to talk to them constantly, so I picked it up over the years. Don't worry, I'll translate for you," he said cheerfully.

"Worried is not how I feel right now," she replied crisply.

They focused back on the group.

Hel was making a speech. She rarely spoke, but when she did, she did not hold back, apparently. There was no need to send Huginn or Muninn. The entire forest could hear her well enough.

Ann shook her head. "The goddess of the dead could use better communication skills, as my mother used to say. She always goes for vinegar instead of honey."

"I think it's because she knows we are here," Agnar said.

"Slush, Agnar. I shouldn't have sent the ravens. Of course they would be seen."

"Maybe *we* were seen. Regardless, I think the speech

is for us. She wants us to know what happened, who's with her. I don't think she wants us to reveal our presence or intervene, and she's telling us this the only way she knows how."

Ann was sceptical at first, but she soon agreed with his assessment, especially once they realised the petrified Xylo was in fact a vessel for Chronos.

"I never trusted that creature," she said. "Always staring at me as if he knew something about me I didn't. Frost, I guess he did… How can so much have happened in a couple of days? Look at Ideth. She looks older than I am! And she has powers now?"

"You have a new face, a new name, and a new understanding of the world, don't you?" Agnar pointed out.

"I ate worms for that Ambrosia and got nothing but a bit of longevity and fast healing while she's conjuring flames with her bare hands! It's not fair."

"Power, much like time, is relative."

"No, it's not. Power is power. And I deserve some. I did not cross time, lose my youth, my face, my identity and nearly my sanity to stay hidden behind a bush while the fate of the world – the very Universe, it seems! – is being decided on that clearing. Enough of this slush." She stood up, determined to make herself heard.

Agnar pulled her back down. "Wait."

"I'm tired of waiting!" she snapped.

"Someone's coming."

She crouched low again.

"It's him!" Ann squeaked. "The Titan."

"Prometheus…" Agnar breathed reverently.

"You didn't believe I talked to him either, did you?"

"I… did. I just… Did he actually kneel at your feet?" She glowered at him again.

"Perhaps we should go, away, I mean," Agnar said.

"But I need to talk to Zeus!"

"Yes, of course, but it doesn't have to be here or now. Do you really want to add more wood to that fire? If we were meant to interfere, Prometheus would have told you to. He definitely knows we're here. He looked straight at us!"

"But –"

"What would your mother do?" he asked her in his tutor's tone.

Ann didn't have to think too hard. "She would have listened and learned all she could before she acted."

"And?" he insisted.

Ann took a deep breath. "She would have put the interests of her people above hers, but her self-preservation above everything else."

"So, what will we do?"

She understood what he was doing, trying not only to protect her but also hoping to gain some insight about the situation. She still wanted to hit him, though. "We'll wait," she said in a tone that bade no further argument.

He grinned. "Yes, my queen."

∞

"That was a lot of arguing…" Ann said after the gods had left. *And a lot to take in,* she thought.

"That's what gods do." Agnar yawned. "They argue. Half of Odin's memories are of arguments with Thor, Freya, Loki, Baldur, Tyr, Zeus, Huginn and Muninn. The other half are of bloody battles, eating meat and getting drunk. Actually, he was often drunk and fighting while he argued as well."

"Lovely."

He shrugged and said, "Gods," as if that explained it all.

"Can we approach now?" she asked the ravens.

They cawed in unison and flew away. That was all she ever heard them say – caw. Agnar translated their account in great detail, claiming that in order to understand them, she had to listen with her mind. Well, her mind was linked to a tree and had enough voices already.

"Yes, we can go talk to Zeus. Avoid looking too hard at Medusa. She's not homicidal like most gorgons, but still." He made a gesture that implied her mind was as coiled as her snakes. "Let me go first and introduce ourselves, just in case. You are, after all, a queen," Agnar added in a well-intended and totally misguided attempt to make her feel less frustrated. "I'll beckon you when it's safe."

Ann walked up to the white-haired Narrum, hand clutching the pouch at her waist, the one given to her by Odin sometime in the future with the instruction of giving it to Zeus, before she'd even known he was her father. After everything she'd lived through and everything she witnessed now, she resented the task more with each step.

"Are you Zeus?" she demanded, not sure why. She had no doubts about his identity. It was mere petulance or perhaps even defiance. She just wanted to hear him say it, for more than her father, he was the creator of her kind, and a part of her still didn't know how to accept that he'd chosen to look like the metz offspring of the Aossi's greatest predators.

Medusa laughed as if reading her thoughts. "When a nymph needs to ask that question, you know you've fallen from grace, Z."

Zeus stiffened in outrage. "I am Zeus, King of Olympus. The fall – more like a stumble really – is temporary, I assure you."

"Are you my father?"

He looked her up and down, tilting his head from side to side, insultingly. "It's possible. If your mother was as beautiful as you are."

Ann had heard Zeus was a lecher, but she hadn't really understood the meaning of the word until now.

She took a calming breath. "My mother was queen of the Aossi."

His face brightened. "Ahh, yes. I remember her. An excellent specimen. Shame she had to die."

Ann blinked. "What?"

"Don't blame me. The Suzerain gave the order when she refused to send tribute to the Nephilim. The blue-haired metz carried it out after their child was born. I had little say in the matter." He spoke airily, dismissively, as if discussing someone else's fancy. "She should have accepted his offer. It was a good one." He sniffed at her. "I guess you are the reason she didn't."

"Me?"

"Who else? The Nephilim execute all demigods. They only offer immortality on their terms." He laughed, as if remembering something funny. "Clever bastards. Oh! You didn't know? Didn't Odin or Agnar tell you?"

He laughed again. "Looks like he's still Odin's pet, not yours."

Ann glanced at Agnar and saw the horror on his face. "My queen. Ann, I didn't tell you because –"

She motioned him to be silent. She would have to discuss this with him later – at length. First, she had to come to terms with what she'd just learnt.

"Apologies," Zeus said sardonically. "I figured that's why you were here acting all mighty and stupid, asking questions to which you so obviously know the answers. Why bother me then? For your information, I'm having a terrible day. If there's something you want from me, pretty thing, you're out of luck. I have nothing to give but my body, as you can see. But I don't sleep with my daughters – as a rule," he added, as if considering making an exception.

"Men are devious, evil creatures, girl. Gods are worse," Medusa said. "I'm not allowed to petrify him – yet," she added, in case he'd forgotten, "but I can make a pretty statue out of your manservant if you wish."

"That won't be necessary, thank you." Goddess, but those eyes were disturbing, never mind the snakes. She gripped the pouch harder, determined to see this through.

"I came to –"

"To do more than assert your lineage, surely," Zeus talked over her. "Odin's pet told us you, too, are a queen and on good terms with the rulers of the world. And yet you hid and waited for them to depart before coming to me. This suggests that whatever you want, you know they don't want you to have it." He leered at her again. "Ahh, you want to be a goddess, don't you? All beautiful women want to be goddesses. I'd turn you in a heartbeat, but alas, one of those undead Aesir things has stolen my talent. Perhaps we can make a deal. Help me get my talent back – by whatever means you deem necessary – and I promise to turn you into a goddess. In the meantime, you keep me safe and comfortable, preferably away from the judgemental stare of this reptile. What do you say?"

"You have some nerve," Medusa said with disgust.

He glared at her. "Your task is to stare at me, not tell me how or with whom to conduct my affairs."

Ann knew she had no chance of convincing Aedan to give up anything, nor the right. More than that, she didn't want to give Zeus anything, not even for a chance of achieving her greatest wish. What was she doing? She hadn't missed having a father; she'd never needed one. No, that wasn't true. She'd had an uncle, Odin. He had been her father. And this despicable man had been his greatest enemy. Why would he want her to give Zeus his eye? The eye he'd sacrificed for knowledge. Did he want to empower Zeus or destroy him? More to the point, what the frost was she doing running errands for him? Hadn't she learned anything during her decades of suffering? She travelled so she would learn to rule, not obey. She'd been Alek's wife. And if there's one thing the Suzerain had been right about, it was refusing to be a pawn. That's what she was now: a pawn in a petty rivalry between two old men.

She released the pouch.

"You're not the god I thought you to be. My mistake. We have no deal."

She turned around, ignoring Zeus' protests and

attempts to bargain, feeling more empowered and determined than she ever did in her entire life.

"Ann?" Agnar ran after her. "I was going to tell you about your mother and Oric, I swear. It just, it hadn't come up yet! I didn't want to add to your troubles. It's not like we can bring your mother back. And Oric –"

"It's all right, Agnar," she said with a sad smile. In a way, she now respected her mother more. She'd been a formidable woman and ruler. Now she knew she'd been a formidable mother as well. She'd saved her.

He looked relieved, but utterly confused. "Why have you changed your mind?"

"On the contrary. I've made up my mind for the very first time in my life." She winked at him.

'Took you long enough,' Yewlow said proudly.

Yes, let's hope it's not too late.

Ann waited.

Yewlow! This is the part where you tell me it's not too late.

'I wish I could, but you know I don't lie. It is late. So much so, we are practically on the verge of never. I suggest you hurry.'

"Frost!"

"What is it?" Agnar asked.

"Run!"

CHAPTER 14

The Road to Damnation

"Since when do you so willingly do what Hel wants?" Aedan asks as he drives the glider. I encouraged him to, hoping it would keep his mind off the awful events back at his cave and leave mine free to communicate with the many gods Reaching at it. He took the task with stoic resilience, determined not to let the mount disobey him again.

"When the world depends on it," I say. It's an understatement. The ground keeps shaking. For longer and with more violence each time. Soon it will start to properly break apart. Xylo's eye seems to twinkle at the prospect.

"Humph. Will this day ever end?" Aedan grumbles.

"You said it yourself. Time is frozen." I'm still not sure if Chronos can hear my thoughts or why he chooses to remain in his host, but I suspect it has more to do with curiosity than any actual grand plan. After all, he already has what he wants. Why help delay the end?

"Couldn't it have frozen at night?" Aedan asks, squinting at the sky.

It's good to see the Dharkan still has enough spark in him to attempt a gibe. He hasn't grieved for his brother yet. Not properly. He's doing his best to get through this. And so will I.

"It's a good thing it didn't. Can you imagine what that would do to the dryads? Stars, what would the Narrum do to them and themselves during a never-ending night? Not to mention we'd have no means of transportation."

It can always get worse. Ileana's words come to mind unbidden. I hope that, for once, that isn't the case. There's a point where worse becomes irrelevant, for what is the point of ighting for something you can't win or improve?

I give Xylo a sidelong glance and see Aedan's scowling at him. "Keep your eyes on the road, Dharkan – Fuck!"

A geyser erupts a few yards away. Aedan turns in time to avoid it, only to almost fly into another one. We zigzag out of control as the ground breaks all around us, spurting vaporized water and gas into the air accompanied by the grinding roar of earth splitting and the snap of roots tearing.

"Stop!" I shout while trying to bring the glider to a halt with my will before we plummet into the fuming depths of the chasm that's appeared just ahead of us. "Shit."

"What in the shadow is that?" Aedan asks, making no attempt to disguise his astonishment.

"The world's sundering." There's no point keeping it hidden.

"What? How? Who's responsible for this?"

"Well… technically, you."

He scowls at me.

"When you let Loki stab Chronos with the horn," I explain.

"I'm not responsible for his actions!" he protests. "And we were trying to protect you. No, wait." Realisation dawns on his face. "That flaming…! He knew."

"Huh?"

"Loki. He knew what he was doing. He knew this would happen. I saw the world breaking apart in his mind. He said it was to save you, but… he also said you didn't need saving, that you could handle yourself."

"I could. Hold on, are you telling me he wanted the world to break?" That's a bit much, even for Loki. He wouldn't do that to Hel. Unless…

"I don't know. His mind is tricky. But I remember one thing clearly. When he stabbed Chronos, he wasn't thinking of you. I mean, you're pretty much all he thinks about, but in that moment, he was thinking of Hel and Fenrir." Aedan hesitates. "And this enormous snake that pops into his thoughts now and again for some reason. I call it his conscience."

"Jörmungandr. It's his other son," I reply to Aedan's questioning look. "Yeah. He's a giant snake. I swear I could not make this shit up."

"For flame's sake." Aedan massages his forehead. Eyes darting from the chasm ahead to the sun above, the Boiling Lake up in the forest beyond the chasm and the Stump far away behind us. "What do we do now?"

"We keep going, of course."

"And how do we get from here to there, exactly?" he sneers.

"Well, obviously we have to move across," I say matter-of-factly.

"Can the mount go over it?"

"I doubt it. They're gliders, not fliers. But I might be able to move it across, like I did with the boulders. Get out, the less weight, the better." I frown at the petrified lump, unsure of the strength of my willpower when matched against gravity. "Mmm, we should take him out as well, just in case."

Aedan gapes at the chasm. It's only about as wide as he is tall, but I bet it goes all the way down to the Underworld. "I can't jump that far!" he nearly cries.

"Don't worry. I'll throw you." He's the only one I'm confident I can get across safely.

"You'll do no such thing!" he asserts with indignation.

"Come on, Aedan. You're lighter than a boulder. I'll make you land gently, I promise."

"No. Absolutely not! I won't be treated like a rock."

"Would you rather end up at the bottom of that pit? Looks like a straight path to Helheim."

"I'll find a way around it. There will be no throwing, and that's final."

I simply have no patience to argue right now.

Aedan flies above the abyss in a flurry of insults, arms and legs flailing ungainly.

He lands more roughly than I'd intended, chest heaving, eyes glaring at me, desperate to find a dignified way to deal with his humiliation. "You'll pay for that, little goddess," he says hoarsely.

"Sure." I proceed to unfasten Xylo from the glider, cursing myself for having been so diligent with the knots in the first place, when I'm caught by another jet of steaming water launching me, the glider, and its cargo high up in the air. It all happens too fast. I land on the other side of the abyss, in far worse shape than Aedan. The glider is not so fortunate. I stretch out my hand, as if I could ever grab it and pull it back up. I'm too disoriented to focus properly, and I deal with souls, not matter, for fuck's sake. And so all I can do is lie precariously on the edge, watching it and Xylo fall away into the darkness. Through the smoke and shimmering heat, I swear I can see him wink.

INTERLUDE 15

Apollo & Artemis

Apollo kicked Mika's corpse, wishing that Fenrir – wherever he was – would feel it. In truth, Hel was the one he really wanted to kick. More than that, he wanted to burn away her skin inch by inch, make it regrow and then burn it again until he tired of it. He should have known better than to mess with the Trickster's daughter. And she should have known better than to mess with him. The fates had decreed Loki would get what he deserved. But what Hel deserved, he would deliver himself.

"That was Orion's son," Artemis said, scowling at the other charred corpse at her feet.

"How unfortunate," Apollo replied dispassionately.

"That one's still alive." She pointed at Iosh. Only a god with the talent to detect life would be able to tell just by looking at him.

"Even more unfortunate."

"The mortal is gifted – by Eros," she added meaningfully. "He won't be happy about this."

Apollo was about to end Iosh's suffering but thought better of it. *Let him suffer.* After all, why shouldn't he suffer? He was suffering too. Fenrir had made sure of it. He kicked Mika again.

"Can you heal me, sister?" he asked, holding his mangled jaw.

Artemis scowled at the walls. "Not in here."

"Grumph." Apollo hated pain. More than that, he hated not looking his best.

"Why did you let the dryad escape?" Artemis asked, resentfully. "She was mine to catch."

"She's part of a prophecy."

"Which one? You have so many, brother." It sounded like defiance in her tone.

Apollo gave her a sour look. Only her eyes were visible against the grey walls. They confirmed her mental state. "Do I ever question your hunting needs or your colour-changing skin, sister? I mean, can you even control it?"

"To some degree." She went from anthracite to a lighter shade of grey. "Have you ever tried to control your prophecies instead of fulfilling them?"

"That's not what I do."

"Are you sure?"

Apollo wasn't in the mood for this. Even outside the cursed room, being inside the Stump drained him. "We need to get out of this place before we can have this conversation."

Artemis relented. "Sure." They rarely disagreed on anything, but when they did, it could take days to return to harmony. Fortunately, she was sensible enough to understand they did not have that luxury at the moment. And hopefully, by the time they did, she would have forgotten about it.

"Can you burn through it?" she asked.

"Do you want me to?" Unlike him, Artemis was not resilient to fire.

She considered this, her lip curling. "Not really. But we can't translocate, nor can we teleport out of here."

"Then we walk."

∞

"Stop holding me back, sister," Apollo said, not for the first time. Artemis' hunting habits made her too cautious. And caution slowed progress. "If we keep stopping at every corner, door and red light, we'll never get out of here. I swear Theseus had it easy."

"That's because the Minotaur was trapped in a labyrinth. We are in a maze."

"The difference being?"

"Labyrinths have only one path; mazes have multiple paths, and most lead nowhere. One is designed to stall and confuse, the other to trap."

"Huh." He sure felt trapped, and that made him impatient.

"I want to leave this place as much as you do, brother. But there are predators ahead," she said.

"So you keep telling me. And yet have we found any, sister?"

"Be glad none have found us." She sounded unusually concerned.

"What if they had? We're gods, not prey. And you're the goddess of the hunt! Act like it."

"I am acting like it," she snarled back at him.

Apollo was running out of patience to indulge her.

They advanced to the next corridor – empty like all the others behind them. "Artemis, this is ridiculous. The place is deserted."

"Deserted of life, yes. But not empty."

He showed her the flame still burning in his hand. "I'll burn anything that gets in our way."

"You've burned enough. Your recklessness and over-confidence nearly got us killed, or worse, domesticated by the Nephilim."

"*My* recklessness? You're the one who let yourself be frozen by a Dharkan."

"Not an ordinary Dharkan," she said, her skin rippling at the memory. They advanced a few more steps before she stopped him again. "Have you ever wondered how they function?"

"Who? The Dharkan or the Nephilim?"

"Both."

"No." *Not until recently*, he might have added. "All that matters to me is that they burn."

Artemis shot him the sort of look only an exasperated sibling could pull off. "Don't you think there's a similarity between the two?"

"Not really," he said, unsure of what his sister was getting at. "Technically, neither is alive. Beyond that… Why would there be?"

"I think this uncanny ability to animate things runs in the family: Loki's family."

Apollo was about to dismiss the idea as nonsense, but then he thought it through. Artemis' mind worked in strange ways. She was deranged, but she was also far cleverer than people gave her credit for, and able to see beyond the obvious. At first glance, there was nothing similar between the Nephilim and the Dharkan, and yet they were both lifeless and both able to host gods' souls and wield their talents. It was probably a coincidence. Except Loki and Hel being related was not a coincidence. Apollo knew this better than most because he had been part of its design. "What an unpleasant notion…" he murmured to himself.

"So you understand my concern," she said.

He did. "All right. Let's move cautiously, then."

When they finally reached the top, he sighed with what, in a mortal, would be described as relief. "See, what did I tell you sister? No predators."

Artemis was looking up, skin rippling through all the colours in the spectrum in distress. "They're all in their hive."

"Perfect," he said.

Apollo sent a burst of power up at the ship, strong enough to vaporise a small moon. The Nephilim's vessel erupted in an explosion that filled the heavens. Chunks of molten wreckage streaked away as far as the Shadow Mountains, leaving the Stump open to the sky once again. He smiled as he healed, relishing the weak sunlight on his face. "That should teach them not to mess with a sun god." Dead or alive, no creature was a match for him. Apollo disliked using his power like this, but they had forced his hand. Or Hel had. And she, her world, her creations and Loki would soon burn for it.

"Hmm, brother. The metal is moving."

Apollo interrupted his healing to pay attention to what Artemis was showing him. Far in the distance, where the debris had fallen, there was indeed movement. But not life.

He frowned and focused his Reach. Dozens – no, hundreds – of metallic humanoid figures moved away from the wreckage, leaving a burnt trail in their wake. It hadn't rained in days and so, within moments, great conflagrations had broken out wherever they fell.

"What are those things?" Artemis asked, bewildered.

"Those would be our faithful," Alek Dveer replied from the ramp.

Apollo immediately turned and sent a blast of energy at him, pulverising his clothes. The rest of him, however, remained unburnt.

"Silly boy, if you wanted to see me naked, all you had to do was ask, love," the Suzerain said as he inspected the strange object in his hand, charred and melted at the edges despite being shielded from most of the conflagration by his body.

"How?" Apollo mumbled, confused.

The Suzerain spared him a glance, as if the question hardly justified an answer. "It wasn't easy. But I figured if we could shield a room against the gods' talents, why not a body?" Then he shook his head at the object in his hand and added to himself, "Why not this as well, you idiot."

"My ship," Namrive whispered, coming up behind the Suzerain in a dreadful state, her body clearly lacking his immunity to Apollo's talents. Her eyes flickered at the sky in disbelief, then she saw what Artemis was seeing and glitched. "My faithful…"

"I'm glad you've upgraded them," Alek said appreciatively. "The original models were a tad too fragile for the job. These… well, they seem a bit too efficient, no?"

"The first ones were designed to blend in…" she explained tonelessly.

"And these?" Artemis asked tautly.

Namrive looked at her, and in that moment they were not enemies, not Olympian and Nephilim. They were two sentient creatures understanding the ramifications of a mindless enemy. "To annihilate anything that moves."

"Make them stop," the huntress said vehemently.

"I can't. It was their last given command. Without the ship or access to the Stump's computer, I can't."

"You can control them with your mind," the Suzerain said.

"You control my mind!" she hissed.

He laughed, shaking his head.

"We need to go back to the control room," she said, already turning towards the ramp.

"No one's going anywhere." Everyone shifted their gaze to the speaker, and the next thing the twins saw was a burning ball of green fire.

INTERLUDE 16

Ideth

"Frost!" Ideth said when she was able to talk again. She'd experienced some awful sensations in her life, but nothing, not even chrono-travel, compared to the whirlwind of translocation. She had to touch her face, then her arms, her chest, her legs, to assure herself everything was in its rightful place, for it sure felt like it wasn't. Hecate once told her in sorrowful tones that translocation was the only thing she couldn't teach her. That she'd have to learn how to make portals instead, and those required ingredients they didn't have in Aegea or, ideally, a moon. Ideth took it as ill will from the sorcerer, an excuse to keep her trapped inside her realm. Now she knew better.

There were gaps between realms, imperceptible to a mortal's senses. Most gods were able to step in and out of those gaps to cover any distance in what was commonly accepted as reality. But those were harsh realms, as unsuitable to mortals as the space between stars. She remembered how Chronos described chrono-travel and the role of the Chronodéndrons in keeping the traveller intact. Could the gap between distances and the one between realms be crossed the same way? Was reality just an infinite combination of realms separated by veils of cause and consequence? She steadied herself. Speculation was for the idle, and she had much to do, especially now that she realised she'd been cheated.

"Oh, you giant bitch." Eos had indeed brought Ideth to Aegea, but she'd dumped her on its edge, just beyond the Shadow Mountains. The Stump was still miles away and… "What the frost?" There was something on top of it, fuming like the Boiling Lake on a bad day! That was definitely a problem.

She dropped the blanket and ran.

∞

Ideth arrived at the teleportation ring exhausted, feet bleeding, mind reeling to find a way inside. The teleportation rings were portals – the Nephilim's solution to translocation. They were not as flexible as those created by the gods, but just as efficient. Sadly, much like understanding how birds fly, but having no wings, what good was it to understand how gods translocate or how teleportation works if she didn't have the means to do one or use the other? What the frost was the point of anything she'd learned?

She found a bracelet discarded on the ground not far from the ring. It had strands of green hair and blood on it. This should have been enough to activate the ring. Except it didn't because one of the gems was broken.

"Argh!" She threw it on the ground in a pique. How could she be so powerful and powerless at the same time? So close and so far from reaching any goal?

Calm, Ideth. This is just another problem, and problems can be solved, she kept telling herself.

Ideth had become pretty good at solving problems over the years. They say practice makes perfect. Well, she'd had a lot of practice, so where the frost was the perfection? The problem with problems was that they bred faster than the Narrum. The moment you solve one, two take their place. Her life had been one problem after the other. She kept finding new ways to solve them: cunning, seduction, chrono-travel, magic. And the only thing she'd gained from solving problems were more problems – bigger problems – but few or no solutions for herself or those she loved. The more she learned, the more powerful she became, the less agency she had. She'd failed to save Chiron. Oreth didn't want to be saved. And Orion was… frost. She didn't know what or where he was anymore. When – how! – had her life gone so wrong? It was like the Universe was mocking her.

Chronos said she'd been chosen. Frost that! She didn't choose to be chosen. When had she ever really chosen anything in her life? From the moment she was brought into this world, to finding herself stranded in the middle of an icy desert, what had she chosen exactly?

She picked up the bracelet again. Now it had two gems broken instead of one. Burn Hecate and her magic! She needed the power to fix, not destroy.

She felt something stirring inside her. She'd first felt it back in the forest when Chiron died, and it had been growing ever since, fuelling her frustration, turning it into something vast and ugly. Not hatred; it was worse than that, worse than any emotion she knew. Stronger, more focused. She didn't know what to do with it, only that she had to do something or it would soon consume her.

"I can fix it for you, unbridled one."

She spun around to face the speaker. "Trickster!" The word was uttered in a snarl. The look she gave Loki could have stripped bark from a tree, but it seemed to only amuse him. She conjured her fire. "What did you do to Orion?"

He tutted and conjured a burning flame of his own in warning. "Hel told me you were special. Now be smart. You know the answer to that question already."

"I need to hear you say it."

"For fuck's sake… I hate words," he mumbled. Then, as if reciting someone else's script, he said, "I tricked Eos into giving the sun to Fenrir. Satisfied?"

"So it's true." Her voice faltered. "Did he actually *eat* him?"

Loki half shrugged. "Yes… it's his talent. Something we try to keep in the family."

"Why?"

"Well, you can imagine how people react to that sort of thing," he said flippantly.

"Why give it to him?" she snapped, exasperated.

"I needed it gone."

"You said you hid it."

"It is hidden – very well hidden. I couldn't just cover the damn thing with a cloud, now could I? I create illusions, Ideth, I don't alter reality."

Yes, Ideth was familiar with his talents. They'd worked together alongside Hel, Hades, Chiron and

Aedan to defeat the Suzerain and take control of the Stump. He had given her the task of helping Mika – Fenrir's human aspect – enter the Stump, where he then mutilated and devoured most of the Suzerain's faithful. When she first saw what Mika did to those men, she wasn't afraid but rather in awe of his appetite for violence. As it turned out, she had more reason to be amazed than she thought, considering he had eaten Orion just prior to that carnage.

Gods were unnatural.

She shook her head in denial. "But I still sense him."

"That is part of the illusion."

Oh frost. She felt sick. However, the idea gave her hope.

"Can Fenrir… er… regurgitate him?" she whispered. It sounded crazy to even say it, and she sure could not imagine it, but she wouldn't put anything past them at this point.

"Sure, why not?" Loki said whimsically.

"So Orion is not dead?"

"Technically…"

"Trickster! Spare me the technicalities. Just tell me what I need to do to bring him back."

"All right. We're finally getting somewhere. Put that out."

She realised she was still holding the conflagration in her hands. What would he do if she used it on him? What would she gain? Chiron had always said violence was not the way. She wanted to believe him, so she let it go and took a deep breath. After all, it was doubtful he'd harm her. Loki wouldn't be there unless there was something he was unwilling or unable to do himself.

"What the frost do you want from me?"

"Do you really need to ask? I want you to use your powers for my benefit, of course."

She guffawed, momentarily at a loss for words. Few things were as disarming as honesty. "Be more specific," she said dryly. "In case you haven't noticed, my power is pretty limited. I can't even fix these stupid gemstones. Can't translocate. Can't do anything worthwhile in this world without a god's aid or say-so."

"Ideth, you are the closest thing a soulless mortal can get to a goddess," Loki said in earnest.

"Not close enough," she replied bitterly.

He moved closer and took her hands in his as if still seeing the fire held there moments ago. "You're making the same mistake Psyche did. Why do you keep trying to attain our level when you have the power to bring us to our knees?"

"Now you sound like Chronos."

He smiled. "Well, even a broken clock is right twice a day."

He had to want her help pretty badly if he thought he could seduce her with sweet gibberish. "Chiron warned me about you. He said of all the gods, you were the one he trusted the least."

"How wise," he said sarcastically. "Titans are primal creatures. Complicated in their simplicity. Like you." If the tease was meant as a compliment, it failed.

"While you simply pretend to be complicated," she said disdainfully.

His eyes narrowed, and for the first time, Ideth glimpsed the true nature of the god behind them.

"Unbridled one. You'll go places. But you need to

learn to bite your tongue before someone else does it for you."

Ideth had had enough of his slush. How dare he threaten her? She had dealt with both Chronos *and* the Suzerain. There was nothing this devious god could do to intimidate her. And since he refused to enlighten her about his motives with words, she would uncover them by other means. She took a step forward, grabbed his cheeks, pulled him down to her face, and plunged her tongue inside his mouth. She didn't ask permission, nor did she give him a chance to bite. She did, however, wish she could unsee what she saw of his soul.

She wished it until the end of her days.

Suddenly, what she'd seen in Psyche made sense. All that darkness. It had been him.

Loki smacked his lips. "Well, that was forward, even for a nymph. I hope it was worth it."

"Don't flatter yourself. And no. It really wasn't." She wiped her mouth in disgust.

"I'm not flattered, believe me. I'm deciding how to explain your death to my daughter. And here I was thinking you were just a witch. I see I've underestimated you greatly. A *soul taster*." He said the words as if they were curses. "Huh, haven't come across one of you since I left Nidavellir."

Curiosity overcame her horror. "Where is that? Is there more like me there?"

"Fucking hope not," he said. "I mean, yes, maybe. I do my best to avoid dwarven magic."

Ideth's eyes grew alarmingly disproportionate to her face. "I'm not a dwarf! I'm just short, for frost's sake!" She didn't know what made her react this way.

It was like the bigger the problem or the more dire the situation, the greater the need to lash out at the smallest of things.

He looked at her with newfound appreciation, a smirk on his lips. "Then again, unbridled one, I think you'll do just fine."

∞

The teleportation ring took her to the main hall. It was like stepping into a nightmare. There was no blood or viscera strewn about this time, but an ominous dark red light illuminated everything, making the walls seem like they were actually made of blood, not just covered in it. She tried to teleport to the vault, but the ring refused to work. She conjured her light. It was getting easier each time and also comforting, almost as if it was keeping her company. Ideth sure could use that comfort. The Stump looked deserted. It felt empty, too. No, not empty: dead. Like a tomb. There was an odd smell in the air. It reminded her of soot and cooked meat. It was disturbingly nauseating.

She was almost to the vault when something appeared in her way. She walked slowly toward it, then slower still. When she finally stopped, she stood there for a very long time, looking down. Her mind unwilling to comprehend what she saw. The sound that finally came out of her throat was more howl than scream – a mother's bawl of defeat, grief, and despair.

Oreth was dead. There was no doubt about it. Despite the state of his flesh, she would recognise her son even if little more than charred bones remained.

I can't solve it. I can't solve it, she thought over and

over again. Like Eos and so many like her, Ideth's mind had finally been broken by the gods and their cruel ways.

She fell to her knees, rocking back and forth.

I can't fix it. I can't... big problem. I can't solve it. No solution. Can't... No... no... no...

"Arianh? Arianh, is that you?" asked the other lipless, eyeless mass of burned flesh a few feet away from her. His voice brought her back to herself.

"Iosh?" She dragged herself from Oreth closer to him, unable to imagine his pain, as she was sure he could not imagine hers. There was no scale able to measure the weight of the agony of the body against the anguish of the mind, but in their case, she figured hers was less than his. If for no other reason than the fact she could still do something about her pain. Then again, hers would also last longer if she didn't...

"Iosh, what happened here?" she asked as she tried to heal him.

"Illy," he groaned.

She frowned at him. "Ileana? She did this?"

"She always liked to play with fire." He coughed. "What are you doing to me? Stop. It hurts!"

"I'm trying to heal you." And failing miserably, apparently. His flesh was too far gone. *But I healed Tithonus.* Then it hit her.

Loki, you monster!

"I'm sorry. I can't..." she admitted. She tried to pity him, but there was no room left in her heart for compassion, not even for herself. All she felt was hate, desolation and the nausea caused by the sight and smell of his ruined flesh.

"Where is Arianh?" he asked.

Probably lost forever in time or barricaded in the Gharb, she thought. "I don't know," she said.

"They both left me," he moaned.

"Where's Mika?" she asked before it was too late.

"Dead."

She became cold, the nausea receding along with the pain. "You're sure?"

His body spasmed. "What reason would I have to lie?"

None whatsoever, she thought bitterly. Her eyes were drawn to a small body beyond the vault's entrance, burned to an irreconcilable crisp. "Is there anyone left alive in this place?"

"Apollo and the huntress left not long ago."

Ideth felt the thing inside her ignite again. "Artemis is here? With Apollo?"

"Yes."

She had to find them. Which meant she had to leave him. "Hold on. I'll be right back with help."

Another spasm. This one looked like an attempt at derision. "Now who's lying?"

"I'm really sorry." She meant it, but she no longer felt it. Every emotion was being replaced by that ineffable thing she could not – and no longer wanted to – control.

"It's dark, Ideth. It hurts too much. She's not coming. Make it stop."

Her first reaction was to object, but it was an objection born out of habit rather than actual reluctance.

She'd never killed anything before. Not willingly or knowingly. She must have killed snails and other critters without realising. But to do it on purpose… *It's for a good purpose,* she told herself. And in that moment, she realised Ideth, the nymph, no longer existed, only the unbridled one remained. She stood up, the thing inside her burning hotter.

"If you see Chiron, tell him…" She hesitated. *Tell him what?* Then she knew exactly what to say. "Tell him Ideth is gone."

And then she drained the remaining life out of him. Immense, unmaintainable power surged through her. It was more than life; it was a gift. It was brilliance, beauty, love. All poured into her, and once there, they fed her flame, turning it into what could only be called magic.

She arrived at the top of the Stump burning with it. The first thing she saw was a tall woman with blue skin, a bald head, and a distressed look on her face. Then she saw the Suzerain, and it did not surprise her. Next she saw Artemis reaching for her bow, Apollo at her side starting to glow. She didn't think about what she was doing, didn't think of retribution or revenge, didn't see a problem to be solved, only an obstacle to be overcome. She didn't want to punish them, only to eliminate them from her life once and for all, for she knew, for as long as they existed, she would not. They would always have the upper hand, no matter what she did. They would keep reminding her of what she had lost. What they had taken from her. She couldn't take it back, but she could and she would make sure nothing else was taken.

Suddenly, the solution to all her past and future problems became obvious. Chronos knew this would happen. Of course he did. And that's why he'd chosen her. With that thought in mind, she unleashed the thing inside her that could no longer be contained, unfathomable and blinding. And when she could see again, the Olympian twins were gone.

INTERLUDE 17

Namrive

Namrive uncovered her eyes after the green light faded and saw Ideth on all fours, breathing heavily over a scorched lyre and a silver bow. The Suzerain stood a few feet away, by the main teleportation ring, tutting dispassionately.

"What. Was. That?" Namrive stuttered. Her senses had detected no power surges, and yet something pretty powerful had definitely happened.

"That would be magic," the Suzerain said. "Our unbridled one is a sorcerer now. How quaint."

"There is no such thing as magic," she assured him.

He gave her a pitiful look. "For beings of such intelligence and competence, Nephilim are quite narrow-minded. Just because you can't see or measure something, it doesn't mean it doesn't exist, love."

"What have I done?" Ideth murmured, staring at her hands.

"You've blasted two Olympians. Congratulations."

Ideth squinted at him. "How were *you* not blasted?"

"I'm not a god, love," he said condescendingly. "Magic doesn't work on me."

"Where did they go?" Namrive asked. She realised she was crouching and stood up awkwardly, still searching for a reasonable explanation for the event since *magic* was not something she could conceptualise, let alone use as an explanation for anything.

"Where we can't follow." The Suzerain smacked the device he used to control her on his palm several times, as if that would fix it.

She turned to him slowly, her joints badly affected by Apollo's conflagration. Her mind, however, was free.

"Oops, looks like I'm in trouble now," Alek said when he saw that realisation had hit her. "I'll advise you to stop right there, Namrive. If neither a sun god nor magic can touch me, you're smart enough to know you can't either."

"You'll never take my ship."

"No. I suppose I won't. Oh well..." He took a long, measured breath and threw the device away, then activated the teleportation portal with his ring. "Better luck next time."

Namrive moved to stop him. He flung her over the edge effortlessly, her fingers barely catching on the lip.

"I guess this is goodbye, Ideth. Thank you for bringing back my daughter. If you see her again, tell her... tell her I have not forgotten her."

"Yes, I brought her back. And as payment, you turn my son against me." The nymph's voice sounded unnaturally distorted.

"No, love. I tried to keep him a boy. But, alas, you took too long to return."

Namrive heard Ideth's guttural scream, Alek's grunt and the low-pitched sound of the portal closing. Then she heard nothing but the wind. Her hold began to slip. Her fingers had been designed to type, not to hold her weight. She'd fall before the new ship arrived. Her body would not survive the drop, there was a good chance neither would her mind. One would be an inconvenience, both… she'd rather not think about it.

"Hold on," a voice said, grabbing at her wrist. "Give me your hand. Now the other. Fuck, you're heavy! Hoist your leg over, that's it."

Nephilim weren't designed for strong emotions. Unless damaged, they had perfect mental balance, and yet when she saw her saviour, Namrive felt herself falter. Her mind began firing incoherencies too fast for her mouth to articulate them, so it just stammered sounds while she just stood there, paralysed, until one word finally came out.

"Maker."

He smiled at her. It was a beautiful smile, conveying both intelligence and amusement in an otherwise homely bearded face. They were alone atop the Stump. There were no signs of Ideth or the Suzerain.

"Namrive, a pleasure to finally meet you." There was something insincere in his words, but she couldn't tell if the lie referred to the pleasure or the meeting itself. She dismissed her concerns. It was probably a glitch in her perception or, more likely, in his expression. He had a large wound across his exposed torso. The sort of wound that should impair reason. Then again, this was far from a reasonable event.

"You need a new body," she said, words still failing her. There was no protocol on how to act when meeting the Maker, she realised. It was as if the Nephilim had never even predicted such a thing. Was she hallucinating? No, her mind would not allow such malfunction. Could magic have affected her senses, then? *Don't be stupid.* Then again, how could she tell?

He pushed her hand away from the wound before she could touch it. "This body has been serving me well for aeons. Fret not. This is nothing to a god."

"How are you here?" The Nephilim relation with gods was based on fact, not faith. They knew they existed and were ancient, near immortal creatures, able to bend the laws of the universe to their whim. Still, this was quite the whim!

"I live here. In the Underworld."

She blinked several times, unable to verify or dismiss this statement, unable to even carry on with the subject for fear of revealing the extent of her ignorance. Where was Anubis when she needed him? He should have returned by now, the bug. None of this would have happened if he hadn't left.

The Maker seemed to predict her next question. "I need your help with something."

"Anything," she said, relieved and grateful for the opportunity to redeem her recent failures.

"First, I want you to know how proud I am of your achievements. Never in my wildest speculations could I have imagined the Nephilim's outstanding development."

She bowed in humble acknowledgement of the compliment, feeling somewhat dazed – for lack of a better word – due to the amount of information being processed. *Can this really be happening?* she wondered. "We merely followed the Mentor's instructions," she said.

"Indeed." There was that feigned tone again. "Now I need you to follow mine."

"Of course. What do you instruct?" When in doubt, always gather more data.

"I need you to leave."

She glitched again.

"And never return."

"Maker?"

"This world and those in it are to be spared. More than that, they are to be forgotten, erased from your records permanently. I understand this is something you can do, yes?"

"Yes but... Why?"

"Because I am claiming this world for myself."

She quickly ran the implications through her mind. "Maker, if you wish to claim this world, it is yours. Why the need to erase it from our logs?"

His eyes blazed at her. An oppressive silence followed. The Maker was a Titan, and the thing Titans were famous for was their temper.

She bowed again in appeasement. "Apologies. You don't need to explain your reasons to me."

"I sure hope not," he thundered.

"I shall do as you ask."

"Good. One more thing. Can you tell me where the Suzerain has gone?"

Namrive promptly opened the control panel of the main ring to check its logs. The last entry read: 'unknown destination – locked'. She downloaded the records and ran a few diagnostics, searching for patterns.

"This tree connects to eight other worlds. The names of the worlds, as well as their exact coordinates, have been deleted. But I detect only five destinations have been used since our last visit, and of those, one has been used far more often than the others. Furthermore, its portal is locked, so it's a simple matter of dialling each world and finding which one we're denied access to. I can start now, if you wish."

"No. That won't be necessary, thank you," the Maker said introspectively while absently plucking notes from Apollo's lyre. "That will be all, Namrive. You should wait for your ship inside."

She moved to obey, for she had no intention of waiting for it on the landing pad, anyway. When she looked over her shoulder, he was no longer there.

Anubis had been right about one thing: there was something incredibly wrong with this world, and whatever it was, she wanted no part of it. Certainly not without reinforcements. The mother ship couldn't arrive soon enough.

INTERLUDE 18

Hades

Hades translocated back to the witch's cabin to find the area deserted apart from Medusa and… "No, no, no. You cannot be here!"

"Hello, Hades. Lovely to see you too," Zeus said.

Hades glowered at his brother. For it was him, of that there was no doubt, and yet it couldn't be. Zeus was dead. He'd seen his lifeless and soulless body at the Stump. Aedan had even taken his talent for himself. Did Hecate do this? Or had Hades somehow translocated through time without realising? He shook himself.

"By all the bastards you sired, what are you doing here? Wait. Never mind that. Where have you been? Were you just hidden away, drinking nectar and watching us struggle? Hoping that perhaps we'd annihilate each other? Did you fake your own death, you narcissistic prick? Are you disappointed that we didn't mourn? Answer me!" Hades shouted in Zeus' face.

"Hades," Medusa started patiently, but Hades wasn't ready to listen yet.

"Have you returned to witness our end and gloat over it?! Are you enjoying yourself, you piece of shit?

Medusa, take off your goggles. Petrify this asshole, and you'll be forgiven."

"I'd love to, Hades. Alas, Hel gave me specific instructions to –"

"You answer to me, not her!"

"In this case, I do answer to her because you are not in your right mind and you weren't here when the decisions were made."

"I was busy with…" He turned his attention to her. "What *decisions*?"

Medusa stood up from the rock she'd been primly sitting on and sighed. "Ask Hel. I'm tired of looking at his face. He's all yours. Now send me back to the Underworld, please. My work here is done, Hades. I'd rather die there."

"Die? No one's dying, not if I can help it. Except *you*!" he added to his brother, then pulled at his hair. "Cerberus' breath, a god can only take so much!"

Zeus remained calm, the very personification of royal suffering and patronising patience. "You think you have problems, Hades? I've been inside a Soulstone. Psyche kept me there as a souvenir. And I'd probably still be there had Chronos not demanded my release. He did not do it for my benefit, and there will be a price to pay, I'm sure. Before that, I was held prisoner: powerless, alone, forgotten. My talents usurped by an unnatural imitation of a dryad. Now, here I stand in a decaying body, still without talents, no kingdom, no realm, being stared down by this… horrible mistake."

Medusa's snakes hissed out at him.

"A woman claiming to be my daughter just scorned

me as if I was a worthless beggar, and yet I'm still here. That's how much a real god can take."

"My heart bleeds for you," Hades sneered. But for once he didn't feel the need to hurt or insult Zeus any further. He was past vengeance, past arguing. His world was falling apart. Their struggles now seemed so petty, so small in the grand scheme of things. He had no desire to engage in them, only to end them. Still, the fact remained, Zeus was there, and he would never be past engaging.

"It still doesn't explain why you're back here," Hades said.

"Hel left me for you. A gift. Or bribe. It's hard to tell with you two." He gestured to himself. "So, here I am, brother. Unwrap me."

Hades turned to Medusa. "Explain to me again why you won't petrify him."

"Do you want Zeus in your Underworld?"

"No."

"Do you want him in Hel's, along with Odin?"

"Stars, no!"

"That is why. I've agreed not to do anything until you chose."

Hades pulled at his hair again. "Is there a third option?"

"Leave him as he is. He may last a few more days or many more years – assuming any of us do. It will give you more time to decide, but eventually you'll have to," she said.

"Or you could help me retrieve my talent from that pet corpse of your mistress, and I'll do what no god seems to have the balls to do and set this world to rights," Zeus said.

"And how would you do that, exactly?" Hades asked.

"Oh please. Helheim might be linked to Niflheim, but your Underworld is much greater than hers. All the turmoil that's happened since the Merge was caused by its need to break out and assimilate hers. As well it should have. You could have taken it at any time. You know it. She knows it. I'm sure it's been a very exhilarating relationship, filled with denial and subterfuge, but it needs to end. The Merge is breaking apart. Soon, you won't be able to seize control of Niflheim. With Midgard lost, the Underworld will be lost as well. Are you really willing to give it all up for a dead woman?"

Hades turned darker; his eyes burst into flames. "Careful with what you suggest."

"I suggest you won't make the same mistake I did. I had to marry Hera to keep Olympus from the Titans and to give the mortals a motherly figure. And there was not a day I didn't think I should have left her to rot in our father's stomach. She never ceased to undermine my rule, to try to control my will, my decisions, my life, my cock. And now it appears she's finally taken Olympus for herself. Hades, you can become the most powerful god of the Underworld, or you can continue to be another one of Hel's pets." Zeus placed a friendly hand on Hades' shoulder. "I'll help you, brother. I know I haven't been kind to you, nor fair. I... apologise. The fact is, I was... intimidated by your power. Of all my siblings, you always were the strongest. That's why I gave you your own realm. I knew you could manage it. And you did! You and I, together. We can do anything: defeat the Nephilim, conquer the Aesir, even teach Chronos a lesson. Anything you want, brother!" He leaned closer, his eyes bright with purpose, his voice lowered to a compelling whisper. "Join me. Let's be gods together, and the Universe is ours."

Hades listened to the words he'd long wished to hear. And he believed them. The problem was, he could not imagine a worse fate for himself now than eternity at his brother's side. He made his choice.

"Medusa. Do it."

She removed her goggles.

"No! You can't!" Zeus protested. "You need me, Hades. This world needs me. You think I'd let myself be captured by the Suzerain without a backup plan? You don't know the state the Universe is in. What is still to come. Send me to the Underworld and Aegea will burn, I promise you that. Tartarus and Niflheim too! You already lost Hephaestus, Persephone and Chiron. How many more allies are you willing to sacrifice for *love*?"

"Open your eyes, brother." A command beyond Zeus' ability to disobey in his current human state.

Medusa grinned. The snakes hissed. Zeus turned into a startled-looking statue.

Hades huffed with disgruntlement. Even petrified, his brother still looked more godly than him. *Appearances aren't everything,* he always told himself.

"That felt good," Medusa said, putting her goggles back in place. "For all it's worth, I think it was the right decision."

"Thank you. Do you still want to return to the Underworld?"

"Yes…" She shook her head and looked up at him kindly from behind the glass. "Hades, I really don't like Hel. She's rude, abrasive, cold. No, wait, let me finish before I regret starting it." She pondered her next words carefully. "She's awful! There, I've said it. But I'm not the one who's going to have to live with her. And besides…" She sighed as if the next words were weights she had to drag out rather than spell out. "She really likes you."

He smirked. "You really think so?"

Medusa rolled her eyes. "Yes. The fates help us… You deserve each other."

"Well, thank you," he said, exceedingly chuffed.

"Just don't make a big deal about it. There are many souls in the Underworld who share my opinion of her and will resent any obligation to treat her as their lady."

"I understand."

"Good. Now, send me back, please. And go sort your shit out with her, for all our sakes."

Hades, still grinning like a kid, held her snakes back in one swift motion and kissed both her cheeks audibly.

"Hush! Get away from me!" Medusa protested half-heartedly, blushing furiously.

"I'll meet you back in the Underworld," he said. "I promise."

Whatever happened, he would fulfil that promise. Or die trying.

INTERLUDE XIX

Merge

Hades found Hel deep in her domain, where the roots of Yggdrasil entwined with those of Niflheim's World Tree. He should have known he would find her there. It was her favourite place. Where she always went when she was upset. Or afraid.

"Hel…"

"Hades!" she whooped, delighted to see him and, after a moment's debate with herself, hugged him tight. What was the harm of showing a bit of emotion? The situation certainly called for it. And she'd wanted to hug him, damn it.

Hades had arrived determined to give her a long speech about how he hated being used, hated being left out of her and her father's schemes, hated seeing his realm burn because of hers. He would not shut up until he told her everything he'd done for her and her family and how much he loved her. Until he made it perfectly clear that in love or not, he would not be used, abused or dismissed again, and under no circumstances would he allow her or anyone else to destroy what they had.

All that was dispelled from his mind by that hug.

"I'm glad you're all right," he said instead, breathing her in. "I was so worried. When I first returned to the forest and didn't find you there, I thought…"

"I'm fine. My world is not…"

"*Our* world," he said and even though she did not contest the correction, he felt her grow colder in his arms. He pretended not to be offended. "Yes, I know. I feel it happening as we speak. The Merge is being undone."

Hel nodded. Her bottom lip quivered rebelliously. She bit on it. She would not allow herself to appear weak in front of him. Not now. "At first I thought it was just another tear caused by the hex, but…" She let go of him and shook her head, eyes lowered, not daring to stare into his for fear he might see the turmoil behind hers. "It's breaking apart, Hades. The whole world, not just the Underworlds. The Dharkan are doing all they can. The World Tree, myself, even Jorma is doing all he can to keep it together, but…" She pulled herself together and gave him a melting look. "Thank you for talking to Jorma on my behalf. We promised never to speak to each other again, you see. It was stupid. We were young, and we were angry…"

Hades made a soothing gesture. "I totally understand why." He too would gladly not speak to the World Serpent again. "It was no trouble at all," he lied. "Charming monsters is my speciality, remember?" he added cheerfully. It sounded funnier in his head. Now he worried about the implication, that she might think he was calling her a monster. His anxiety was off the charts. He pulled at his hair and said, "I've put Atlas and

Hercules on the job as well. They have some experience holding worlds."

She almost smiled. "I suppose they do. Still, it won't be enough. The world will break, Hades. I never thought Chronos would actually let it happen," she admitted to both him and herself, then frowned in afterthought. "I'm not a monster... am I?"

"No! You're far too pretty for that." Hades realised he was making it worse now. "Er... What happened inside that barrier?" he asked, desperate to steer the subject away from treacherous compliments and back to their catastrophic predicament.

She closed her eyes as if to relive the events that had gotten them there. From her tone, she'd been practising the answer for a while.

"We tried to contain Chronos inside his host: Medusa, Hecate and I – yes, Hecate is on our side, as it turns out, so go easy on her. We almost succeeded, but then Father stormed in and stabbed Chronos with the Elysian horse's horn and everything turned to ash."

"Why would he do that?"

"To save Psyche."

"From what?!"

Hel huffed. "Herself mostly. She tried to take Chronos' soul."

"She didn't!" That was highly ambitious, even for the Butterfly. Then again, she'd taken Zeus' without anyone noticing. Hades would not dare to underestimate her again.

"Yes, she did. And she would have succeeded too, if not for Father getting in the way." Hel rolled her eyes. "I swear those two make us look well adjusted."

Hades had learned the gist of Loki and Psyche's tempestuous relationship. On one hand, it had explained a lot; on the other, he hadn't even begun to grasp the extent of its implications.

"Wait. How did Loki get through the barrier in the first place?" Hades might spare Hecate from another eternity in Tartarus, but he would not let her get away with excluding him from her little realm when Loki wasn't.

"He was wearing Aedan."

"Aaah." That option would never have occurred to him. Hades wished he wasn't so averse to the idea of wearing another man's body. Then again, no one's perfect.

Hel began pacing the cavern as she spoke. "And then Zeus aggravated everyone. Including me. Psyche lost her mind and took Kali's soul instead – who is technically not one of the Three, but a figment of Nyx, the original soul of the Universe, assimilated by Chronos during their battle. The rest lives in all of us, Gaea mostly."

"Huh?"

Hel waved her hand. "It's complicated. After that, everyone argued. I kept them arguing to give Psyche time to do whatever she was doing and to keep Arianh and Agnar out of it. Yes, she's back. I hardly recognised the Aossi queen. My guess is that Freya got to her. I honestly have no idea what's burning between those three and the Chronodéndron. I just know it has something to do with the Suzerain, and I probably won't like it. Anyway, that's not important right now."

Hades was about to disagree – anything related to the Suzerain had to be important – but kept listening.

"Then Prometheus, of all creatures, showed up. He's a twisted piece of work, by the way. Titans are all dogmatic pricks."

Hades found no fault there. He felt a sudden pang of sadness at the loss of Chiron. It wasn't like he couldn't visit him in Tartarus. He'd just rather not. Every creature there was after his hide, and he dreaded to think what might happen if the world broke apart and they all got out. Or worse… if he was made to join them. He forced that horrible notion away to focus back on Hel, who had not slowed down her pace or speech and was now gesticulating wildly as well.

"Then Ideth, who is now more powerful than Hecate, became *unstable* after Chiron's death and threatened to burn us all. I had to send her to the Shadow to cool down. There she stumbled upon Eos and learned what happened to the blue sun. As it turns out, she's in love with Orion and intent on burning everything in her path to get him back. Anyway, Father is confident he can use her power to our advantage."

Good luck with that, Hades thought. Poor Ideth… If she was unstable after Chiron's death, imagine how she'd be when she found out about Oreth's. Loki would do well not to cross her path when she does.

"But that's not the worst of it," Hel continued, her voice slowly rising in pitch with each word. "Prometheus told everyone Father was responsible for the Nephilim. Father nearly lost it. Then Prometheus disappeared. I can't find him. Can you?"

"Er..." He realised he couldn't. *That can't be good.*

"Hecate believes we're all going to die soon," Hel was saying "so she, too, left to do the fates know what, and I'm forced to trust Psyche to keep Chronos contained."

Hades opened his mouth to express his opinion of that decision, then promptly closed it again.

"Psyche then convinced me to take him to the Nephilim. Don't look at me like that, Hades. I know it was foolish. But at this point, I was like: sure, whatever. I can't deal with him while he's inside the construct. I'm not sure I could, even if he wasn't. But then she gives Kali to Gaea and wants me to abdicate half my souls to bring Nyx – or something like her – back into existence in order to restore balance in the Universe. And all through this, no one seems to give a shit about the fact the world is breaking apart! Oh, and Pan is in Portum, helping Morpheus build a temple, for flame's sake!" Hel was hoarse and breathless by the time she finished.

Hades scratched his skull. "All that happened while I was at the beach?"

"Pretty much, yes."

"Cerberus breath…"

Hel winced. "How is Cerberus, by the way? I'm sorry I had to freeze him…"

Hades waved away her concern. "Oh, don't worry, he'll be fine. He's been burned so many times, he probably found it refreshing."

They gazed at each other in silence, their minds filling in the gaps between sentences and working out the ramifications of recent events. Neither wanted to speak. And neither wanted the other to know their actual thoughts, either.

"Pan's building a temple. Are you sure?" Hades asked. That was highly out of character for the god of the wild.

Hel rolled her eyes. "He's a Wyrd, and he's stuck here since Psyche had the good sense not to free him. He probably believes he can gain favour with the god of dreams and outlast whatever is coming."

"I see," Hades said. Better stuck in a pleasant dream than in the Underworld, he supposed. Still, they had to do something about it. Pan could not be allowed into the realm of dreams. However, his talent might still be useful. A wicked idea began forming in his mind.

"What did you do with Zeus?" Hades had to ask, despite himself.

"I put him with Odin."

"You think that's safe?"

Hel puffed her cheeks. "They are as safe as we'll ever be. Thank you for sending your brother my way and adding another responsibility to my list," she added sarcastically. "Would it kill you to keep him on your side of the Underworld?"

"Yeah. It probably would. Hey, you don't get to judge my relationship with Zeus. At least we still talk to each other."

"Fine," she grumbled.

"Where's Psyche now?" Hades asked reluctantly.

"With Aedan and *Xylo* at the caves."

"And where's Loki?" Another question Hades would rather not ask but had to.

Hel seemed put upon by the question. "Here, there and everywhere. Trying to salvage relationships and organise a proper effort to… honestly, I don't know. There's so much he hides from me still – either to protect me or himself. I can't tell anymore." She moved closer, rested her forehead against his, and let herself sigh. "I missed you, Hades. I wish you had been there to help me figure it all out." It was the truth, and for once she wasn't afraid to say it.

"Then you didn't send me to your brother so he would eat me?"

She put him at arm's length. "No! Why would I do that?" *How did he know?*

"So you could have my share of the Underworld. Maybe even stop the Merge from… hmm, unmerging," he said, looking her in the eyes. He knew she was capable of that and much more. It was part of what he loved about her.

She held his gaze for a moment, her jaw clenching. She was surprised and oddly aroused by his deduction. Burn him for being so perceptive, so dark, so humble and so much more cunning than she was. For making her believe she had no choice in staying with him all those years and that she had the choice to leave him now without tearing herself and both their worlds apart. Above all, burn him for making her believe she would never fall for him.

"The idea crossed my mind," she admitted. "I told myself, had he done it, we would have deserved it."

"And now?"

"Now I mostly tell myself that I'm a fool."

"What about me?"

"You're an idiot," she teased.

He grinned. "So what's the problem?"

She pushed him further away. *No more games.* "You deserve to be lord of a unified Underworld. I can't give you that."

He closed the gap between them, eyes aflame. "Why not?"

She stared at him defiantly. "Because I'm the goddess of the dead. It's one thing to compromise, another to surrender. If I surrender my world, I'll just be a dead goddess." She blew out a breath. "It's probably what I'll end up being soon, anyway. But if I don't, at least I'll always have Helheim. I won't always have you."

"Why not?" he asked again. "Why does it have to be one or the other? Why can't you just be my lady? Hel, haven't I proved myself to you? I don't care about your world, your Underworld, your souls, and frankly I really don't care much about your family either. I care about you. I love what you are, your work, your place in the Universe. I don't want to rule. I'll happily let you run both Underworlds!"

Her expression darkened. Too late he realised his mistake. "There it is… the word I cannot abide: *let*."

He pulled at his hair again in exasperation. "Damn it, Hel. Words are too crude for this conversation. You know what I mean." He took her face in both hands. "I give it all to you freely. Our wills combined can hold this world together. We can outmatch Chronos' will."

She tried to shake herself free. He didn't let go.

"Hel, we *can* defeat the Nephilim. We can do anything we want. Us. Together. You just have to will it. Will you have me?"

She looked away, regretting the things she'd taken for granted. "It's not that I won't have you, Hades. It's you who won't have me."

"What's this nonsense?"

Hel did not reply immediately. She couldn't reply with words. Hades was right about one thing: words were too primitive to express the true meaning of her predicament.

How she wished to allow herself to be wrapped in his shadow, to be consumed by his flames. She believed he meant what he offered, except he didn't know what or to whom he was offering it. He'd never seen her. Not the real her. Never seen the face that was half goddess, half monster. The face even her mother would avoid looking at for too long. The face that had granted her independence, purpose and everlasting loneliness because no one could bear looking at it except the dead. It had made her enemies tremble and her lovers wince. The face that made Odin give away an entire world so as not to be forced to see it. The world she could not surrender because it was all she really had. It wasn't the aesthetics of the face that concerned her. Not really, or not until she'd met Persephone, that is. Hel had never tried to make herself look pretty, only... whole. Gods care little for the aspects of the flesh. They know beauty comes in many shapes and forms and are able to see past deformities. It was what the face represented, not the face itself, that truly concerned her. But she couldn't hide it any longer.

She let the illusion vanish in reply, showing her real self to him for the first time. No embellishments, no pretence.

He didn't even blink.

In Hel's face, Hades saw the reflection of his soul: half torment, half hope. He clasped her close and ran his fingertips from her forehead to her chin and down her neck, aware he was really touching her for the first time, and smiled. "I know you care for me as much as I care for you. You need me as much as I need you. You want me. And I want you. So I'm going to take you and your world. And you're going to take me in return. That's the deal."

Her vision blurred. "We'll fight for eternity," she said.

He smiled. "I look forward to it, my lady."

A tiny ice crystal formed in the corner of her eye. He kissed her eyelid gently, melting it away.

"Fine, then," she whispered. "Have it your way."

He laid her down on Yggdrasil's roots. Their eyes locked together, savouring every touch, every kiss, every gasp and moan of pleasure, the only language they shared until they connected. She shivered against him; he burned inside her. Hands clasped, legs wrapped, bodies entwined with the roots. Not worrying, nor hurrying. The world might be ending, but they were just beginning.

They fell into a rhythm, their souls aligned, their bodies lost in ecstasy. Their wills, their minds, their flesh, their passion, their very beings worked together towards a mutual, blissful goal. And as they shuddered, surrendering into each other, the world became whole.

INTERLUDE 20

Iva

Iva stared at Ileana, her lips pressed to bloodless slits, eyelids twitching, brow creased in what could only be described as scornful dismay. Try as she might, she could not come to terms with what she saw tied to the wall.

I refuse to accept that Aedan left his brothers, left me. *For* her.

'Men are –' Freya started.

No, Freya. Look at her, for flame's sake! No man would fall for that. She's barely more than a child!

Freya chuckled mirthlessly. "You obviously never met Zeus.'

Aedan is not Zeus.

Freya laughed.

What's so amusing?

'Oh, he's more like Zeus now than you can imagine. But no, I don't think his talent is the issue. In any case, that might not be the same Ileana.'

She was shouting for him as if she owns him. The ea-gerness with which Ileana searched for Aedan amongst the Dharkan was too raw, too real to come from an impostor. *I believe it is her. I just don't understand how... There's been talk of a witch in the forest. Can it be sorcery?*

'It's possible. Magic and lust often go together. Either that or Eros has done something pretty stupid,' Freya said.

Who?

'The Olympian god of love. He likes to manipulate lust in unnatural ways...'

The realisation hit Iva not from what Freya said but from what she thought. The longer they spent together, the thinner the veil between their minds became.

Emil?!

Freya gave a mental sigh. 'Yes. Not my brightest moment, I admit. Funny how not even gods of love are immune to its curse.'

Iva closed her eyes and took a long, deep breath. At least that explained her constant state of arousal around the boy. Had his intention been to keep her distracted or Freya humiliated? she wondered. Either way, it was personal. Her pride demanded she sorted this out.

"So you are Ileana, Ileana Dveer, the Suzerain's daughter." It was not a question, but an attempt to make the words fit the creature.

"That's what I've been saying. Are you deaf or dumb?"

Iva took a step forward, hand reaching for the girl's throat.

'Iva, breathe,' Freya cautioned.

No amount of breathing is going to make me spare this abomination.

'You can't feed off her.'

Nothing can, Iva thought in disgust. This Ileana was not only immature in every sense of the word, she had no Prana, and no spirit either. She was less than an animal. She was a thing.

I can freeze her and shatter her into tiny little pieces.

Iva snatched a hammer discarded by one of the builders in his haste to be working elsewhere and couldn't help thinking how ironic that walls were being erected all around her while her own inner world crumbled.

"You don't scare me," Ileana said pettishly, glaring up at her, head high.

Iva drew back the hammer.

'I strongly advise you to learn what you can before breaking her,' Freya interjected casually.

Iva cursed, then shouted, "What do you want with Aedan?"

"He's looking for me."

"Does he know you're here?"

Ileana hesitated. "Yes." An obvious lie.

'That doesn't mean he's not coming for her. We should keep her around as bait,' Freya said.

I don't want her around! Nor do I want to stay here much longer. All this – Iva cast about *– is too weird for my taste. What sort of god builds its own temple?*

'Many gods are as crafty with stone as I am with flesh.'

The silence that followed was like a vacuum in Iva's mind. *You know who he is!*

'I have my suspicions, since few gods work during the night, yes.'

What does that mean?

'It means there's no rush to leave. We're safe here. For now.'

What aren't you telling me, then?

The danger is not the temple, Iva. It's what's around it. Something has happened to the world. Something awful. All these tremors we've been feeling? The Stump is not the only thing burning. And I think Ileana's connected to whatever's causing it... somehow. So swallow your pride a little while longer until we figure out what's happening.'

Easy for you to say.

'No, it is not! You think it's easy to be a spectator in these events? To be stuck inside your body, reading your mind, feeling all your rancour and jealousy and indignation? You think it's easy to endure your ambition, knowing what it did to me? Or that I enjoy it when you hump Asher?'

Sure you do.

'I'd enjoy it more if you weren't thinking of Aedan the whole time! Every decision you make is clouded by your obsession with that man. If I didn't know any better, I'd say Eros shot you instead of Ileana.'

Iva bristled at that. *How dare you lecture me on obsession? You're the one obsessed with Hel and everything she has. Taking over her creations wasn't enough. You want her world, her souls. Why? Why do you hate her so much?*

'Because she's Loki's daughter.'

The vitriol that poured out with that admission was such that Iva nearly lost her balance. That was when she realised she was still holding the hammer high above her head and lowered it.

What in the shadow did Loki ever do to you?

A blurred image of a banquet came to Iva's mind.

Loki standing in the middle of a long table, pointing at Freya amidst a chorus of mocking laugher. *'He humiliated me. And he stole Brísingamen!'*

Before Iva could ask what that was, the clear image of a golden neck ring came to mind.

A necklace, Freya?

'It's a torc, and it was my favourite! He had no right to insult me or take what was mine!'

You convinced me to start a war with Hel and my brothers because of a bit of derision and a flaming necklace?!

'Oh, don't pretend you're any better than I am, because you're not. You needed no convincing, only an excuse.'

In that moment, it was as if the fates had placed a mirror in front of her conscience, and Iva truly comprehended the extent of her mistake. She stared at Ileana again – who in turn was staring back at a crazy Wraith brandishing a hammer in silence in the middle of the room – and felt nothing but pity. Pity for the brash and broken creature scowling at her. Pity for Aedan if he truly loved her. Pity for the vain goddess trapped inside herself. Pity for the faithless Dharkan she so cruelly misguided for her own misguided goals. And most of all, pity for herself, for realising it all now, when it was too late to take it back. She dropped the hammer. *Let the world burn*, she thought. *Let it all burn soon.*

"Mistress," Asher called.

"What?" she barked.

"There's a woman here to see you," he said meekly.

"Who?"

"An Aossi."

The Aossi had always caused trouble for the Dharkan. But now they were at the bottom of her concerns.

"Have Jonas deal with her. I'm busy."

He remained there, eyes darting side to side like trapped prey, struggling to articulate his next words. "The thing is, er… she doesn't really want to talk to you. She says she wants to talk to your goddess… mistress."

Iva glanced beyond the temple's entrance to see a head of green hair atop a body dressed in rags, conversing with Jonas. She had just handed him a flask, and he now stared at it dumbfounded, then produced an identical one from his coat, except hers was much worse for wear.

Do you know her? Iva asked Freya.

'No.' Freya sounded genuinely surprised, her anger subdued by confusion, followed by something too close to apprehension. *'But I recognise the man next to her, Agnar. He was Odin's host. The fool left him alive. With who knows what memories.'*

Great. It was fitting that Iva had to deal with Freya's personal affairs on top of everything else.

Her eyes swept dutifully across Portum, surveying the work and searching for potential threats before she decided how to act. They paused on Oric, tied and slumped against the remnants of the old temple.

"Why is that man still breathing?"

Asher made a face. "He… tastes funny. The men don't like his Prana. It's tainted."

"So kill him."

"We think he might be one of our own. Partially, I mean."

Iva rolled her eyes. Metz were an aberration almost as grotesque as the lifeless creature calling herself Ileana. Never the sort of thing a female Dharkan would allow to happen, but males had other standards. They liked to hump their prey.

"That's what happens when you can't tell the difference between your cock and your hand. Just cut off his head. I want him out of my sight. And send the dryad in."

He marched in place, torn between his duty and self-preservation.

"Oh, for flame's sake, Asher. What else are you not telling me?"

"Well, about Oric. We were about to do what you suggested when the dryad arrived and told us not to."

"And you obeyed her because?"

"Well, er… she was very assertive." He winced. "She claims he assassinated her mother, and she wants to deal with him herself. Of course, we would not take orders from anyone but you, mistress, but we can kill the metz at any moment so we… I mean, I thought it best to confer with you first. Jonas agreed." Asher completely deflated into a whisper under Iva's glare. "Mistress, she knows you're hosting. She says she and the goddess are old friends. She was so sure of herself, I…"

"Send her to me," Iva said coldly. She figured at the very least, she would get a decent meal out of the creature.

"Yes, mistress," he said obediently.

From the corner of her eye, Iva saw Ileana glaring at her. "You have something to say, girl?"

"Only that my father would very much like to deal with Oric himself. He might even forgive you for how you're treating me."

"I have no interest in dealing with your father."

Flaming sun, is that even a possibility?

'If the girl's here, I wouldn't be surprised if the Suzerain is too,' Freya said. 'We may not even recognise him.'

Iva had just begun running through the implications of that idea when the most beautiful woman she'd ever seen entered the sanctuary. Her gaze fell on Ileana first, and when it did, her assured step faltered. Ileana gasped in recognition.

"So you know each other," Iva said, unsurprised.

The woman opened her mouth as if to stammer a reply, then inhaled sharply, squaring her shoulders. When she spoke, she addressed both Iva and Ileana. "We all know each other. Or will, one day."

Iva frowned. "My concern is with the present, not the future."

"It should be."

"Who are you?"

"I used to be Arianh, queen of the Aossi. Now I am Ann, queen of all dryads in Aegea. I am the Suzerain's wife." She glanced at Ileana again. "Her mother."

"You're not my mother! You stopped being my mother when you left me to dry on a rock to fill the void in father's heart. So this is where you've been?" Ileana's gaze moved to the man at her mother's side. "Now I see why uncle favoured you all along." She practically spat resentment as she spoke.

Iva herself couldn't speak for a long moment. Whatever wrong she'd done, surely she did not deserve to be included in their drama.

She sauntered towards Ann. "If you came here to demand I release your daughter, you wasted a trip. First, she's not your daughter. Not the real one. I think you know that. Second, as poor a replacement as she is, she's mine to keep for as long as I see fit."

"No. I did not come for her."

"What?!" Ileana shrieked.

"I came to talk to Freya."

Iva frowned. *How does she know your name?*

'*I don't know.*'

The Aossi have been the Dharkan's enemies since even before the Suzerain's arrival. What scheme are you playing at, Freya? Don't lie to me!

'*I've never met this woman before, I swear!*'

Iva wasn't in the mood to take chances. She grabbed Ann's neck. Agnar moved to intervene, so she grabbed his as well. Two faithless appeared from the shadows, ready to protect their mistress and share the meal.

"Ambrosia," Iva drawled, savouring its taste.

'*Wait, Iva, I want to hear what she has to say!*'

"How do you know Freya?" Iva demanded.

"She gave me this face," the dryad replied in a manner too confident and dignified for someone in her position.

'*It's a fine job. It could have been me,*' Freya admitted.

"When? Why?" Iva insisted, straining patience.

"Sometime in the future. To help me undo your mistakes and save the world."

"What do you know of my mistakes, mortal?" Freya asked, taking over.

"Everything. Yours, Odin's, Zeus', Apollo's, Chronos', Psyche's, Hel's. I know of everyone's mistakes and how to fix them."

"And how will you fix *my* mistake, exactly?"

"I can convince Psyche to release you from your host."

Who is she talking about? Iva asked Freya.

'Psyche is the Olympian goddess of the soul. She's practically a myth, but I think if anyone can help us, it's her.'

Freya eased her grip on the dryad's neck. "What do you want in return for your generosity? I mean, if you're as knowledgeable as you claim. Why are you here? What do you need me for?"

Ann slowly lifted a pouch and dangled it in Iva's face. "I need you to carve this into my flesh."

A gasp of horror ran through Iva's mind. *'Let her go,'* Freya said. *'She's telling the truth.'*

"What is in that bag?"

'Our future.'

CHAPTER 15

The Butterfly Effect

"What in the shadow is *this*?" Aedan mutters incredulously.

I have no idea. Portum is definitely not how I remember.

From our vantage point next to the old temple, concealed by a pile of hewn stone – and some considerable effort on my part – it sure looks like the settlement we left, chased by an angry mob, not so long ago. It has the right number of shelters, arranged in the same order, and the burnt remnants of Jonas' sanctuary are still there, but everything else is different. Its populace most of all.

"How long were we inside the witch's realm?" he asks.

Another question to which I don't know the answer.

"I don't like this," he says.

There's very little to like, to be fair. The sight of Narrum, Dryads and Dharkan all working together should be a heart-warming one, and yet it's quite disturbing. Unnatural. And the temple… Even Seshat would be impressed by its splendour. But if the intention behind her pantheon's ostentatious architecture is anything to go by, this cannot be good.

"Are those Iva's faithless?" I ask, even though I'm pretty sure they are. The implication being that Iva has to be somewhere close by.

"Mmphm."

"Why are they wearing flowers?" Of all the things wrong with the scene before us, that particular detail stands out as the most bizarre to me.

"Persephone," is Aedan's curt answer.

"Oh… fuck. I see…"

"What in the shadow is *he* doing here?" Aedan points to a recess in the old temple's wall a short distance from where we hide. Oric, of all people, sits chained to it, fiddling with a device strapped to his left bicep. The arm below it resembles the gnarled member of a mummified child. He looks like he's been dragged over a campfire. How strange to see him without the haze of Ileana's hate, though... Stranger still to find him here, under these conditions. I'd sympathise, were I not more concerned with the general state of affairs. Jonas, looking far heartier than the last time we met, sits at his side. We move closer to them by silent agreement.

"What a pair we make," Jonas is saying, nodding at Oric's arm and tapping his leg. "Although, I think I still prefer mine."

"Jonas, I –"

"Shhh." Jonas hands him a bottle. "Drink this."

Oric takes a swig dutifully, then sticks his tongue out and gags a few times.

"It's wine," Jonas explains, unimpressed with Oric's theatrics.

"Blerk, it tastes like the rotten juice of overripened grapes."

"Like I said: wine," Jonas repeats with characteristic annoyance. "You are overly fussy for a condemned man. That's nutritious alcohol. It keeps you young. Or so I've been told."

Oric snorts. "Yes, I've always wanted to look young and well nourished when I die."

Jonas snatches back the bottle. "You ungrateful metz. Do you know there's a god whose single talent is to produce this? Pan says he'll introduce us."

"I thought you were drinking water now."

"I am. But a dryad can never have too much hydration." Jonas considers the bottle again. "Imagine if a god had the talent to turn water into wine. Wouldn't that be special?"

Oric sighs. "Jonas… You don't have to do this."

"Do what? Share a drink with a friend before his execution? What else is there to do?"

"Don't you have a temple to build?"

Jonas dismisses his question. "It's practically building itself. I can spare a few moments." He takes Oric's hand. His fleeting expression reveals what words never would.

Oric sighs again in that wearingly guilty acceptance of one who cannot reciprocate a gift. "I think the world is about to end, Jonas."

"Not here. Not for me, and nor for you, if I can help it."

"Do you really believe that?"

Jonas stares wistfully at the majestic temple before them. "After this, I can believe anything. Maybe the

Aossi queen will talk some sense into Iva. Maybe Aedan will come for the girl. Maybe the blue sun will return. There's still hope."

Aedan stiffens at the mention of his name but thankfully has enough self-control not to charge into the open. He gives me a look that is part eagerness, part exasperation, urging me to act. I want to hear more first.

"Jonas, if I hear the name Aedan one more time –"

"Frost, Oric. Why did you try to kill him?"

Oric releases his hand from Jonas' grip. "Because that's what I do! I kill Wraiths. And Narrum and queens, even gods. I'm a killer. Don't you know this by now?"

"But.. *Why?* You weren't always. I remember you cried when you accidentally killed that shrew." Jonas shook his head fondly. "What happened to you?"

"The forest happened. Hephaestus, the Merge, the Nephilim. In this world, it's either kill or be killed. Few have the luxury of neutrality. I made my choice, and if I die because of it, so be it. At this point, I just wish it to be over soon. I've been close to dying too many times of late. And you know what? It's tiresome."

Aedan growls a wistful curse.

I pull him closer before he does something stupid. "Don't even think about it."

"Well, ain't this a sight," Pan says from behind, grinning down at us.

"Pan?!" I hiss, gesturing for him to crouch before he reveals our presence. "Where the fuck have you been?"

"Here, mostly," he says sheepishly.

"Doing what?"

"Isn't it obvious?" He looks back at a young dryad half concealed by a tree, fastening a cloak around her neck. She blows him a kiss before heading back to town. He crouches behind the wall with us and speaks as if sharing a great secret. "Who knew that being scared senseless is as much a motivation to build walls as it is to destroy them? Amongst other things." He winks.

I narrow my eyes. "You were supposed to scare them *away* from the forest. Not gather them here!"

"Away where? There's nowhere to go, Butterfly."

"Where did all these people come from, then?"

"Everywhere. The Aossi arrived from the Grove, looking for their queen. Most of the Narrum and Anann came from Relicum. Not as many as one would expect… I heard things got pretty bad there. The temple is demolished – by a dragon, or so they say. The Stump is on fire. Snow is melting in the Mountains at an unprecedented rate. The nymphs talk of the Boiling Lake spilling over… It's bad, Psyche. If I'm to remain a Wyrd, I'd rather celebrate the end of the world with lots of sex and parties in monumental structures."

I shake my head. "How did you even build all this?"

"It wasn't me. I only manage the labour. Some other god did most of the groundwork during the night before I even arrived – not a Wyrd, obviously," he adds, clearly still cross with my refusal to free him.

"Who?"

He shrugs. "I don't know. Any god can move rock. Oh, how I miss doing simple things like that," Pan says dramatically.

Aedan shoots me a resentful glance.

Pan strokes his goatee, surveying the temple. "It should be completed soon. A good thing, since we're running out of time. Speaking of, have you lost track of it?"

"It's in a safe place," I lie.

He raises a bushy eyebrow at me. "We don't have those in Aegea, Butterfly."

"So what is this, then?"

"Shelter, for now. Soon, a tomb, probably. But I can't tell them that, can I? No work would ever get done. Now, are you going to tell me why you're here and not at the caves or the Stump as you said you would be?"

"We've encountered a few obstacles."

"Shit never goes according to plan, huh?"

"It seems not."

"Where's Hel?"

"Doing what she can. Freaking out. I don't know." It's the truth. I lost track of the goddess of the dead shortly after my encounter with Eros when she all but kicked my soul out of Helheim and asked me to come here instead.

"And Hades?"

"With Hel." It's my best guess.

Pan clicks his tongue. "You should have freed me, Psyche. I would have you on that Stump in a blink of an eye. I can still do it if you want."

It sounded more a dare than an invitation. "No, thank you. This is where I need to be."

"Psyche, why won't you free me?"

Because I don't trust you, and the last thing the world needs is panic, I think, but before I can even begin to come up with a better answer, a woman exits the temple.

I gape.

The bearing and walk are unmistakably those of Arianh; her face and spirit are not. Spirits are not as distinct as souls. They are more mutable – for lack of a better word – easier to change and evolve, to adapt. Hers sure has! So much so I failed to recognise her when we first met. And now... *Oh, dear*, I think as I relive the meeting with Ileana and Prometheus. *She'd been there too.*

Iva walks behind her. Unlike Arianh, she looks somehow less than she was before: frazzled, frail, but also more feminine somehow. I need to find out who she's hosting so I'm not caught off guard again like what happened with Eros. Agnar follows close behind the women, his mind deceivingly absent. And behind him, ragged, injured and nearly bald, is Ileana.

A half gasp, half sob escapes Aedan's throat. He looks at me, aghast and confused, then at her, then at me again, as if I'm to blame for both her state and his confusion. He rubs his eyes between his forefinger and thumb and curses in his native tongue, trying not to cry. Then he leaps from our hiding place.

"Aedan, don't!" I urge in vain. He already has his hands around Oric's neck.

"What have you done to her, you piece of ash!"

He lifts the startled Oric off the ground, pushing him high against the wall, deaf to both my and Jonas' protests.

"Aedan!" Ileana calls, limping in his direction.

He turns his head over his shoulder to look at her, his strength faltering. She throws herself at him, and he has no choice but to release Oric in order to catch her.

"I knew you were alive! I knew you'd come for me. I knew it! You would never leave me," she says, smothering him with kisses like an overbearing child with a puppy.

"How touching." Iva scoffs in disgust. A crowd is now gathered around us.

Aedan is a man who has just realised he's falling off a cliff, torn between the consternation that the ground is no longer under his feet and the realisation that he has nothing to look forward to but a swift end at the end of the fall. "What…?" he mumbles.

Ileana hugs him tighter and points at Oric. "He did this to me! And her" – she points at Iva – "she had me on a leash like an animal." Then her eyes fall on me, and the curl on her lips is one of pure contempt. "You!" she snarls. "She's the one who took my body. Kill them, Aedan, kill them all! For me. Father will reward you."

Aedan casts around indifferently, clearly having lost the lust for killing anything.

"You're not well, Ileana. You need healing. Psyche, she needs healing," he says.

Iva's eyes rest on me with layers of recognition and expectation.

Damnation.

"My talents only work on the living," I say as a means of apology. The truth is, they'd probably work on Ileana as well, but I'd rather decline than try and fail in this company.

Aedan, his agency restored by the power of passionate rage, pulls me roughly aside. "Psyche, do not fuck with me," he growls in my ear.

"I'm not!" I reply in similar tones through clenched teeth.

"Is that even Ileana?" he asks.

"Yes."

"How?! That's not the woman I knew. The woman I –" He's so tense, he's actually flushed. "That's not a woman!"

"New body. Give it a few years to fully mature," I suggest politely.

"Aedan?" Ileana asks, confused by this behaviour. His expression is beyond dismay.

Arianh shakes her head morosely. Agnar rakes his hair. Even Oric, absently rubbing his neck, seems to pity the Dharkan.

"I think we should all take a step back, find a quiet place and talk," Arianh says with masterful authority. To both my surprise and relief, everyone listens.

Interlude 21

Hermes

Hermes found Hecate in Hephaestus' smithy bent over a pile of assorted crafts, sorting through them without care or patience, pausing now and again to further inspect an object before tossing it over her shoulder with a disgruntled, "No."

"Witch," he said affectionately.

She turned. Her faces sharing the same expression of delight. "Hermes!"

He was winded from having run the length of Aegea to meet her but would happily run a little further. They embraced and kissed passionately for a long moment before he was forced to break the kiss to take a breath.

"We need to get you out of that body," she said.

"That would be nice…" Isko had been a suitable host, but his body was a curse in itself. If not for Hermes' strong will, it would not stand, let alone run.

"I'm so sorry, Hermes. I had it bad in Tartarus, but you… in *that*… I can't even imagine."

"You get used to it," he told her. It was true. So was the fact he'd rather have been in Tartarus, pleasures of the flesh non-withstanding. Still, he had not let his curse affect his good spirits thus far, and he would not now.

He glanced around the smithy: what a dismal place. The forge still burned and would continue to for as long as the world existed, but all it did was cast ominous shadows along the walls as if the thousands of forged weapons and armour were in danger of becoming animated by its power. The Blacksmith had been a compulsive craftsman. Nevertheless, this seemed beyond excessive, even for him. Definitely not the sort of thing a god does for leisure, but for a purpose.

"Found what you're looking for?" he asked.

"I have now," she said teasingly, then sighed. "No... I'd have a better chance of finding a needle in a haystack. There's a spell for that sort of thing. This is like trying to find a needle in a pile of needles. I have to touch each item to tell what incantation it holds, if any. At this rate, it will take me decades to sort through them all."

"We don't have that long..."

"I am aware," she said tautly and resumed her task.

"How much did you change this time?" he asked, pretending to help. As a Wyrd, he had no way to tell even which items were enchanted, let alone with what.

"Enough, I think... I hope. We weren't the only ones meddling with time."

"Who? Apart from the Suzerain, that is." Hermes gave up his futile task and sat down. The run had definitely been too much for his poor body.

"Eros and Freya," Hecate said.

"Oh..." That was bad news. Gods always expect interference from other gods, but some interferences are easier to handle than others. "Can Zeus keep a leash on them?" Since Odin obviously didn't.

"Zeus is trapped in a bag of flesh almost as bad as yours. I doubt he can even handle himself." She huffed. "Such a pitiful state. I couldn't even be bothered to curse him."

"Tartarus made you soft, witch."

Hecate gave him a sidelong glance that spoke volumes about what Tartarus had done to her. "I'm tired, Hermes… hate is an excellent motivator, but a costly one. As soon as you're free and the Nephilim are dealt with, we'll go someplace with many moons and no gods. I'm sick of gods. Except you, of course," she added with a reassuring smile.

"What about Ideth?" he asked.

She paused, a pair of large scissors in her hands, a proud smile on her faces. "She's extraordinary."

"Really?"

"Oh, yes. I've never encountered a power like hers. Once she unlocks her potential, she'll have them all twisted around her little finger. You'll see."

"If they don't kill her first."

She seemed to notice the scissors and threw them onto the discard pile. "Why would you say that?"

"You better than most know how little tolerance the Universe has for extraordinary women."

"That will change when Nyx is in power." She gave him a complicit smile. "Don't worry. Psyche has a plan. It might actually work."

Unlike most Olympians, Hermes was not prone to worrying, unless someone told him specifically not to worry. He knew well how thoroughly the plans of one god could ruin those of another, and Psyche, as instrumental as she was for their plan, had also been quite the disruption to it. The idea of the goddess of the soul having plans of her own was pretty much the very definition of worry in his book.

"What plan?" he asked seriously.

"I said, don't worry," Hecate reassured him with a kiss.

"Sorry to interrupt," said a voice from the entrance.

"Seshat?!" he croaked just in time to prevent Hecate from casting something vile. "What are you doing here?"

"I could ask you the same, Hermes." She moved gracefully down the smithy. Anubis walked at her side, both carrying a light of their own and scowling at the soot-covered walls. "Still, I'm glad we both came to the same place."

"I'm not. Keep it brief, please," Anubis said.

Hermes stood up on wobbly legs, powered by indignation. "You refused to give me Quetish, made me run all this way, and now you're *here*?" It was hard to tell what offended him more: her presence, the way she treated him or Anubis.

"I won't apologise. You behaved like a cat. I took you in, fed you, cuddled you, and the first opportunity you got, you scratched me."

Hecate's eyes narrowed dangerously at him. "Cuddled?"

"So you *punished* me?" he retorted, raising his hands and shaking his head vehemently in reply to Hecate's question. She had no objections to his activities with mortals but would not tolerate even the slightest indiscretion with a goddess.

"Spare me, Hermes. I'm not an Olympian; I don't do punishments. This is merely a fortunate coincidence."

Stars, he surely hoped Tyche wasn't involved.

"Why are you here?" he demanded.

"I need your help."

"Oh, you do, do you?"

"Yes. Unless you have better things to do than sit around making out in dark places waiting for the world to end. Do me this favour, and I'll convince Psyche to free you."

He stared at her expectantly, too sceptical to agree, too hopeful to decline.

She conjured a box from thin air and handed it to him with extreme care. "Open this box. You're the only one who can do it safely."

Hecate recoiled. "Is that what I think it is?"

"Blood of the Hydra, yes."

"Are you insane, Seshat? That turned Chiron mortal – a Titan! It will probably turn us all to cabbages!"

Hermes inspected the box. "As if Persephone would ever dare to mess with the Hydra."

"Medusa did it for her."

"Ah... right. And you want me to open it?"

"Yes. Open it, drain every drop of its contents into that forge, burn the interior, and close it again."

"Why not just burn the whole box?"

"Because Eros may come for it. I promised to keep it safe. I said nothing about its contents."

"Clever." Hermes turned the box in his hand, fascinated. There were few advantages to being a Wyrd.

Who would have thought holding the power to destroy gods would be one of them? "How can you be sure you can convince Psyche to free me?"

Seshat and Anubis exchanged glances. "She owes us one."

He glanced at Hecate for guidance, unable to Reach the details of this alleged debt. She nodded in approval, a calculating smile on her lips. "I wouldn't count on Eros' sudden appearance to claim the box back, Seshat."

"I'd rather not take any chances."

"I suppose that's reasonable," Hermes said as he moved to the furnace and cracked the lock. In all fairness, what did he have to lose?

"Wait!" Hecate said, tapping the dagger in her hand against her palm. "I have an idea."

CHAPTER 16

Reality

This must be what being in Tartarus feels like.

I'm sitting in the middle of a settlement, in broad daylight, surrounded by my faithless brothers, my enemies and a crowd of mixed breathers, most of them Narrum, one wrong word away from turning into a vicious mob.

Arianh – or Ann, as she now calls herself – chose this location. She claimed that discussing things publicly would keep everyone in line and give the population an opportunity to take part in the discussion. I think she's just hungry and wants an excuse to bask. She's not too keen on the new temple either, and no wonder. The thing is eerier than the Stump, unnaturally shiny and too large to be standing. Still, I'd rather be there than here.

Ileana is at my side. This itself should be enough to make any uncomfortable situation pleasant for me, and yet it only makes it worse. She clings to my arm as if her life depends on it, one moment begging me to look at her, the next recoiling as if scalded by my looks.

Not half as much as I am by hers, I think bitterly. She believes my coldness stems from her baldness and extensive burns. I let her... The truth is too awkward to explain. It's not just her prepubescent body that makes me cringe inwardly, it's everything about her. How she stares at me, the way she touches me, the kiss she gave me – a smooch aimed at the pleasure of an audience rather than a lover – her mean-spiritedness, petulance and wounded vanity. Try as I might, I cannot reconcile my memory of Ileana with this creature. More than the disappointment and humiliation the reunion brings, I cannot abide Psyche being right. Love can't be a curse. Of all things, love should be a blessing. Then again, now that I've met the god... saw what he did to Psyche, to *Emil...*

"What's wrong?" Ileana asks, pulling me even closer to her.

I must have groaned without realising and have to muster a considerable amount of self-control not to jerk away in reflex. "It's the sun," I lie.

Ileana sniffs in disgust. "Mother is cruel. She always has been. Only thinks of herself," she says waspishly.

There's another piece of information still burning its way through my mind. Arianh – *Ann! Her name now is Ann!* – travelled to the future, married the Suzerain and gave birth to Ileana. Why in the shadow would she do that? I thought she hated the man. And to think *we* almost married to bring peace between our peoples. Goddess, what would that have made me in relation to Ileana?

By the way she sinks her nails deeper into my arm, I'm pretty sure I groaned again...

Jonas sits on my other side, drinking copiously. I'm half tempted to ask him for a bottle myself for all the good it would do. It's not that Dharkan can't get intoxicated. We can; we just don't like it, and there's already a lot happening that I don't like.

Psyche won't even look at me. She knew. I guess she tried to tell me. I didn't listen. But burn it, she should have tried harder! The things I've endured for the sake of being reunited with Ileana. It was all pointless. She used me. Played me. Lied to me.

Sparks crackle around my fists. The queen looks at them insidiously. Does she expect me to bring light-ning down on everyone in this circle? Is that why we're gathered in the open? One more pull from Ileana, insult from Iva, glare from Oric or word from Agnar and I might actually do it!

Burning sun, I wish I could reinvent myself like she did. Like they all seem to do. I suppose I have changed since this whole nightmare started. One always does from hosting gods, even more when absorbing their talents. But I'm still me. I'll always be myself, no matter how hard I wish to change it. Or forget it…

"It's too late to move to the Gharb. The world is already breaking," Ann is saying. Which is just as well. I really don't fancy marching to the Gharb. It's getting easier to associate the queen with the new name. Her voice and demeanour are the same, even if her face, hair and Prana are not. She remains beautiful, though. Whatever she endured left no scars that I can see. *Much like a goddess,* I think acridly, glancing at Psyche's flaw-less skin as she listens intently, eyes closed. It's like her whole body is a mask and her mind a mirror.

"This temple is our only chance of survival. Not even the caves are safe this time," Agnar concludes.

"This time?" Iva asks.

"Things have changed."

"So, the world is not going to end?"

"It most certainly will. Just in a different way. You can alter consequence, not fate. Only those responsible for this world can do that. And Hel won't."

"Hel would die for Niflheim," I reply, unimpressed with Agnar's opinion of the goddess. A remnant of Odin's, for sure.

Ann turns to me. "She would. But she would die alone."

"Hades will be at her side," Psyche says.

The queen twists her mouth. "He might. But if you were in her place, Psyche. Would you compromise? Would you surrender the thing you hold most dear: yourself?"

Psyche bites her cheek in a similar facial twist. "I'm not Hel."

"She will never compromise," Iva – or more precisely, her goddess – says sternly. She's stuck inside her host – much like Loki was in me – and they are both clearly unhappy about it, making a tremendous effort to be amicable to the goddess of the soul, despite the fact they so obviously disagree with her.

"Where is Hel, by the way?" Jonas asks, his voice rising above the others. "What's the point of even having this meeting without her? You people need to stop arguing and start acting like gods."

"You mean killing or enslaving everyone for our worship?" Iva says mockingly.

He glares at her. "I mean, do something! Build more temples. Help us. Help each other for a change."

"Build temples," she echoes scornfully. "Gods don't build their own temples, and they certainly don't shy away from taking credit for their charity. Where is this benefactor god of yours? He should join us."

"Maybe he has."

Now there's a disturbing thought.

"There's only one free god here, and she's not inclined to help anyone," Pan says pointedly.

I study Psyche again: nothing. It's unlike her to let an insult go without reply, nor is she able to keep her opinions from showing on her face. It's like she's barely listening – or listening to something else.

"For frost's sake. I refuse to accept that my sanctuary will become a tomb," Jonas says.

"Did you say tomb?" asks a half-starved Narrum woman as she ventures too close to our circle to fetch a stray child.

"Keep it down!" I warn him. We really shouldn't be having this conversation in public.

"No, no. He said womb. When finished, the sanctuary will be cosy like a womb." Pan grins at her reassuringly.

"Aaah." She retreats with her charge, seemingly appeased.

"Sometimes it's easier to soothe than to scare them," Pan says sheepishly.

"Like you did with me?" Psyche asks rhetorically.

His eyes shine dreadfully. "My talent is fear, Butterfly. To both inspire it and take it away."

"It's an interesting thing, fear," Iva puts in. She and

her goddess were particularly reluctant to include the Wyrd in this discussion, either because he's fated, a satyr or an Olympian, it's hard to tell. My guess is all of the above. "The Aesir fear nothing. We teach our mortals fear is a weakness. There's no reason to fear death because their deaths have already been determined. They don't flee from their foes. Instead, they fight their way through them, unafraid, bravely and with honour."

Pan pretends to consider this. "If they don't know fear, how can they be brave?"

Iva's eyelid twitches. "You don't decide how to feel. Just how to act."

"And they choose to act like idiots, like their gods. Even animals have more sense than to dismiss fear."

Iva clears her throat, clearly not wanting to share the reply her goddess made to his comment. "Psyche, Freya has a question for you."

Psyche raises an eyebrow.

"This is a bit of a detour from the subject, but pertinent to finding potential solutions for our predicaments. How did you manage to resist Persephone's invitation to open the box intended for Aphrodite?"

"I just said no."

"Remarkable. It's such a difficult word for mortal women. They're conditioned to be amenable, to acquiesce to others' wishes. But not you." Iva pins her with a discerning gaze. "I wonder who taught you otherwise."

"I was conditioned, all right. It didn't stick."

"And yet you said yes to a dryad." Iva's smile betrays the fact that her goddess has Psyche right where she wants her. "Why was that?"

Psyche smiles knowingly. "Why, Freya, for the

usual reasons: guilt, shame, remorse. I wanted to do something right, to use my powers to help others and all that. I was obviously high on stardust to forget no good deed goes unpunished. But don't worry, it won't happen again." She glances at Ileana. Now *I'm* worried.

"She lies, Wraith. She's not like the other gods," Ileana says.

"Yes, we can see that," Iva says.

"She used me to get here to free her lover from the Underworld." Ileana says.

"Did she now? How romantic," Freya replies wickedly.

"She took everything from me. I bet she wants the world to end and all of you to die so she can take your souls and go back to the stars."

Psyche's eyes narrow slightly at Ileana, but her left eyebrow remains arched – a bad sign. "It's a dangerous game you play, young lady. Ask your mother what she saw." She turns to Ann. "After all, she was there when you entreated me to take your life so I could take you back to your father. When Prometheus tricked me to save Eternity. You accepted becoming my host because Yewlow would never allow you to travel alone. She knew your wishes too well. No one can hide their true nature from a Chronodéndron – that ability, not their link to Chronos, is the real reason they're hated. So you played the martyr instead, hoping you'd rule at your father's side using my talents – *my* soul."

"That's not true! I was deceived, misguided, like you were. I was devastated, thinking I was left behind. The gods and that stupid tree took advantage of my despair. I just wanted to leave. I'm not a bad person because I wanted more for myself and didn't care what happened to you. Why should I? You're a goddess. You already had everything, while I had nothing."

"Wow…" Psyche says.

"But I've changed. I found love." She draws everyone's attention to me as if I am indeed some precious find that they all should covet and simultaneously praise her for having.

"You found lust. Your vanity doesn't allow for more. You wouldn't even recognise love if it burned at your feet. The only thing you ever cared for is attention."

Ileana gasps in outrage, pulling at my arm. "Aedan, you let her speak to me like this?"

"I want to hear what she has to say."

Ileana lifts her chin, lips curling into a sneer. "If I wanted your talent, why did Father set you free – and destroy my body in the process – instead of putting you in the vault, huh?"

Psyche's tone and stance doesn't change. "He made a deal with Chronos. I had to be free to complete my part in his scheme. As to destroying your body, we both know you couldn't wait to get rid of it – too old, was it? – just as you can't wait to get a new one now because that one is too bald. But you know what? I think it suits you."

"How dare you!"

A profound disturbance shakes the land. *Thank the goddess!* Not the deep rumbling from beneath that has been happening with increased frequency. This sounds like an entire copse being felled at once. Our heads turn to the Stump.

A thick pluming pillar of fire and smoke reaches high into the heavens and spreads, covering the sky.

Streaks of flaming debris fly off in all directions, arching and finally falling in an incandescent rain across the land.

No one moves. Everyone's frozen in place, eyes following the trajectories of the flying debris. Most fall beyond the forest, near what's left of Relicum and the Grove. Only a few fall near us, amongst the trees. None in the actual town.

"See? I told you. We are protected! The temple is a sanctuary," Jonas cheers.

He's drunk. But I hope he's right. It would be hard to argue against him otherwise. Still, what in the flame just happened?

"Hmm." Agnar's scratching his head. "This is definitely not how it happened last time." Everyone turns to him. "The lore tells us of an explosion that consumed the Stump and Algiz – what is now Relicum – in their entirety. The Grove and the land all the way to the caves became what we know as the lava fields." He chuckles to himself. "Funny, I always imagined it'd been a volcano."

"Looks more like the tantrum of a sun god," Iva points out.

This is not what anyone wants to hear at the moment.

"A sun god," Agnar says absently, as if the possibility had never occurred to him.

The milling crowd shifts uneasily, unsure of how to react, torn between our apparent calm and the world's turmoil.

"Damn it, Yewlow, this is not good enough! I did not waste thirty years of my life paying for knowledge

I cannot use!" A flash of the old Arianh shows through her new façade as she speaks. "What do you mean those consequences don't apply to these actions? I caused what? Not in this realm?! What are you implying? Of course I want to rule! The Aossi and all the living in the land, maybe even the Dharkan. But they have to be alive for me to rule them, do they not?"

She covers her mouth, realising she's been speaking aloud.

Iva shoots a glaring look at Ann. "Rule the Dharkan, you insolent weed."

Psyche blocks her path to the queen. They exchange words I cannot hear. Iva tilts her head at her. "I want your promise."

"You have it."

An assertive glance passes between Iva and Asher.

I don't like any of this. "Psyche?"

"Stay out of it, Aedan." She walks over to the satyr. "Pan, why do you want to be free? Tell me the truth."

"My motives are selfish, always have been." He looks towards the burning Stump. "I won't submit to Zeus. We are not that different, you and I. It's just some fears are easier to overcome than others."

"Indeed." She places a hand on his forehead. They lock eyes for a moment, and suddenly there are two Pans. One is obviously a long-dead corpse; the other is a thing from nightmare.

Everyone starts screaming and running around like hens trapped in a pen surrounded by wolves.

"Thank you, Psyche," Pan says with a fiendish grin. Then his expression darkens. "What are you doing?" He grows larger; his horns, eyes and hoofs burst into flames. I shudder in horror. People are falling over, fainting, pissing themselves, clutching at their chests, cowering wherever they can hide even if it's behind each other. "Release my soul!" he thunders.

"I'm sorry, Pan. You shouldn't have told Eros where to find me. But I thank you for once again helping me become what I am." By the Shadow she sounds cold.

"My friends, lovers and followers," Iva proclaims from atop the wall. "I've promised you sustenance, land or women when we left the Shadow. I have fulfilled that promise. Now I offer what no god or living creature ever gave you: respect. Feed, brothers, and become what you were always meant to be."

The faithless close in on Pan, Asher at the lead. What comes next is both exciting and horrifying to watch.

"Go on, Aedan. Feed," Ileana urges, licking her lips as if she's the one who wants to join them. Unlike the other dryads, she's not afraid. On the contrary. She's hungry and lustful.

"No!" I tell myself I don't want to. But I do. I crave it badly.

"You must! You can't be the only one who doesn't take his talent!" she cries, as if it will make me less than the others and that would be an insult to her. I push her away with a jolt of energy, a reminder to us both that I have all the power I need.

Iva sucks down Pan's last wisp of power and laughs exultantly.

"Psyche, what have you done?" Agnar whispers. I'm fairly certain this was not in his lore either.

"I paid a debt to a friend – a friend who deserved to be free. This is what freedom does to gods. You should know." She turns a meaningful gaze to me. "The world needs monsters, for only monsters can fight other monsters. Dharkan have always been treated like villains. Well, now they are."

Ann slaps her. "They always were, you interfering bitch! You've killed us all!"

"They're yours," Psyche says evenly.

The queen blinks.

"It's what you've always wanted, isn't it? You were willing to sacrifice your youth and beauty for maturity and assertiveness. Use them wisely and you'll prevail." Psyche lifts the small pouch dangling from Ann's waist, an amused smile on her lips. "The Allfather badly miscalculated things."

"What about Iva?" Ann asks, protecting her possession from Psyche's fingers.

"I had my chance," Iva says, joining them. "Burn leadership. I've always preferred to fight my enemies personally, hands-on."

"Make sure you pick them well this time," Psyche says.

A familiar shadow passes overhead. Whoever wasn't hiding, does it now. Quetish lands in the middle of the empty square and winks at me.

"Hello again, Seshat," Psyche says, clearly expecting her.

"I see you got my message," Seshat says.

"Yes, how could I ignore it. It's not every day you have a cat scratching at your eyeballs from the inside of your own skull."

"I had to be sure to get your attention."

"You sure did. Sadly, you've just missed all the action."

"Cats." Seshat casts her gaze around the chaotic state of the town. "Whatever happened, it will be recorded in the people's minds for generations by the looks of it."

The sphinx's other passenger, a deformed dryad I had often seen with Oric, dismounts unceremoniously to stand before Psyche in a manner far too insolent for his own good.

"Are you sure about this, Seshat?"

"Yes," Seshat replies heavily. "He's my responsibility. I promise."

"Why would you help us, Hermes?" Psyche asks him.

He shrugs nonchalantly. "It's all I've been doing for the past age."

"But why?"

He turns very serious. "Because I hate bullies."

She smiles. "Good enough."

Much like Pan, his broken body falls lifelessly, and a handsome young man with blond curls and dove wings on his ankles steps forward.

The Dharkan grin at each other.

"Sorry, boys," Iva says. "This one will make one of you a very happy host, but no meal. Not today, anyway," she adds to appease the vocal disgruntlement.

Psyche walks to the sphinx, then looks at me over her shoulder. "Are you coming or not?"

"Yes!" I reply eagerly. I can't wait to be away from this place, even if it means riding through the air on the back of a highly sexual predator between Psyche and a scion of Ra.

"Aedan!" Ileana protests, pulling me back. "You can't leave me again! Not here. Not like this!"

"I have to."

"For her?!"

"No! Of course not. For you – for us. There's a cure – I mean a solution – for you. I'll find it. But I can't do what needs to be done while worrying about your safety. Stay here with your mother and your friends." That sounded reasonable enough, I think.

"I don't have friends!"

"Make some!"

I all but run to Quetish, feeling slightly ashamed of myself. By the goddess, I hope I'm telling the truth. There has to be a way to fix her.

I mount the sphinx awkwardly. There's hardly any space on her back. She looks at me askance, as if insulted by my weight.

"Here." Seshat hands me a feather. I frown at it, confused. "It will make you lighter." The frown deepens with added confusion. Seshat rolls her eyes. "It's magic, all right? You can ask Hecate how it works. Now hold tight."

"Is she there already?" Psyche asks.

"No, she's still enchanting items, and Anubis insisted on going back to the caves to study Eros' host. They'll join us afterwards."

"Study?" I ask. "You mean dissect!"

"He promised to be respectful," Seshat says.

"I don't care for his respect! The dog has no right to dissect my brother. Take us there immediately!"

"Would you rather he dissect you?"

"That's not the point!"

"No, the point is we need to get to the Stump before the next ship arrives. Now tell me – in great detail – what did I miss here?"

We take off.

I see Ileana's thin figure getting smaller, and feel relieved. Goddess, whatever happens, we never did.

CHAPTER 17

In Someone Else's Feet

The grand temple of Portum is still in sight when we land again in a patch of woodland burned clear by some of the falling debris.

Seshat motions us to dismount, pulling pen and paper from thin air. "Whenever you're ready," she says.

"For what? We already told you everything that's happened in Portum. What else do you want?" I glance at Psyche for an answer; she cocks an eyebrow at me. "No," I say.

"Yes," she says.

"You agreed," Seshat says.

"You said 'goddess'. I assumed you meant the witch, or even yourself!" I protest.

"Assumptions," Seshat tuts, obviously familiar with Loki's opinion of them but shamelessly proud of her deception.

"Anubis was right about one thing," Psyche says. "I can't risk the Nephilim taking my talent. Rest assured, I have no interest in your body apart from the protection it'll give."

"Find another way – another Dharkan to host you.

I'm sure anyone who doesn't know you will be honoured."

"I chose you. It's part of my agreement with Iva and Hel."

"*Agreement?* Have you been in touch with Hel this entire time?" I ask, still trying to get past the fact she's made an agreement with Iva – of all people – behind my back.

"No. Since we left the caves."

"Why didn't you say anything?"

"For the same reason you didn't mention your little chat with Seshat: you didn't need to know."

"Why you flaming cun –"

"Ambrosia won't affect me, if that's what you're afraid of."

"Fear is not the problem. What happened back in Portum might have been necessary, but it doesn't make it any less indecent. All my life I've felt like a monster, and now I feel I'm surrounded by monsters. I'll be damned if I'm going to become one. And I promised never to host you!"

Seshat chuckles. "Mortals really shouldn't use that word."

I throw a bolt of energy at her pages.

"Tsk. Very mature."

"Can we discuss this privately at least?"

The goddesses exchange glances. "I'll make sure to spare no details," Psyche says, to further upset me, I'm sure.

Seshat tuts again but puts her paraphernalia away, more annoyed than disappointed. "Sort yourselves out – fast. Anubis is waiting. He's insufferable when he's made to wait. I'll be with Quetish over there. She's dying to sink her claws in you, by the way. A goddess's protection wouldn't hurt, just saying."

I literally freeze all over.

"Stars, Aedan. Is my soul that repulsive to you?" Psyche asks when Seshat and her flaming pet are out of earshot.

I shake my head, unsure repulsion is the problem, either. "You deceived me," I say.

"I merely didn't share all the information."

"After everything I did for you. Everything we shared. You deceived me again!"

"Let's not forget the things you did to me as well," she says sharply, then takes a breath. "I didn't know Arianh would become Ann, or that Iva was hosting Freya. Once I learned that, I had to adjust my expectations. It still doesn't change the fact we need to return to the Stump before it's too late to help Fenrir. Or that I need your protection, for all our sakes. And in my defence, everything happened so fast! Between Seshat and Pan and" – she swallows – "everything else. I had to make decisions quickly and couldn't keep you in the loop. That won't happen if you host me. You'll know exactly what I know when I know it."

"You're worse than Loki."

"I sure hope not…"

"What about Ileana?"

Psyche crosses her arms and shrugs. "I tried to tell you. But honestly, I didn't know how you would react when you saw her. It might not have been an issue."

I scowl at her and her opinion of me. "Flaming sun, how could it not be?" I rub my eyes with my thumb and forefinger, pushing the image away. "And what was all that about Iva and the Oracle?"

She bit her lip. "You wouldn't have given it credit if I said it came from me."

I scowl at her again. "Is there anything you won't say or do to get what you want?"

"No. Not anymore."

"How can I ever trust you?"

"By hosting me. Here's a chance for you to find out anything you want about me and my intentions. My mind is yours in exchange for your body."

"I don't want it! The things I know about you are already enough to make me mad. And I already have a pretty good idea of how Ileana feels about me." I actually shiver at the memory.

"Aedan, stop being stubborn," Hel says as she appears between us.

"If you can't or won't accept the truth, then all you'll ever hear is lies," Hades chimes in, grinning at her side.

"Goddess! Where have you been? The world is –"

"Mending." She smiles. "We've taken care of it. That's what I" – she and Hades exchange glances – "*we*'ve been doing. The Merge remains intact, by the power of our wills, not Chronos'. He no longer threatens our world. The Nephilim, however, still do. We need Psyche to keep Fenrir's soul safe before we can act, so you will host her not because she wants you to but because I don't trust anyone else to do it."

"You want me to poke inside her mind," I say aloud. *Now there's a truth for both of you.*

Hel presses her lips in annoyance. "Yes, Aedan. Was I not blatantly clear?"

"As I said, my soul is yours," Psyche assures me.

Has every female in Niflheim gone mad? I wonder.

"Speaking of souls, did you just send your ex-husband to Helheim?"

"Yes, he has too many friends in Hades' realm." Psyche grins wickedly. "Besides, he hates the cold."

Hel mirrors the grin. "Does he? What else does he hate?"

"I'll give you a list." The grin fades. "Can I trust you with him, Hel?"

"Psyche, if there's one thing you can trust me with, it's the creature that made me swoon over Apollo." Hel smiles again. It's a surprisingly warm smile – a genuine smile. No wonder she rarely uses it.

"I always trusted you more than you ever did me," Psyche says. There's no judgement, resentment or even disappointment in her tone, just resignation at the fact.

"Trust is a complicated thing, Psyche. I trust your integrity and your competence. But I also trust your ambition and desire for self-preservation. As I'm sure you trust mine."

"I don't mean to be rude, but can we continue this conversation later? There's another ship approaching. And er... a situation just developed in Portum," Hades says anxiously. "We may need reinforcements."

Hel freezes. "Aedan, you'll be rewarded for everything you've done. This is the last thing I'll ever ask of you, I promise," she says before vanishing again.

Psyche looks up at me demurely, as if none of this was her doing. Hades and Hel just happened to stumble upon us in the middle of the woods. I don't need to host her to know how she thinks. She's right, I already know her well enough. And that's the problem. Still, I guess I can either do what they want or return to Portum and be what Ileana wants.

There's that shiver again…

I tell myself she can't be much worse than Loki. That hosting her will give me some control over her actions. That it's what Hel wants me to do. That it's what any Dharkan should do.

I am an idiot.

∞

'Oh, wow!' Psyche moves my arms around until the shoulders crack, flexes the muscles of my chest, one at a time in a humiliating way, then squats several times.

"Enough! Stop moving like that. Stay still, for flame's sake. You'll give me an injury. Bodies are not supposed to be used that way!" My voice falters as she jumps up and down, straining every ligament in my calves, not to mention my balls.

'This is incredible! So much mass and strength at my disposal.'

"You don't need strength – you're stronger than I am!"

'Sure, but it's not the same thing.' She grabs my forearms, my thighs, my buttocks. *'This body has substance. And vigour! How can you always be so still with all this muscle power?'*

"Stop touching me, burn you."

'Calm down. I'm just getting acquainted with my host.'

"You're molesting me."

'No. Not yet.'

"Hey! What do you think you're doing?!"

'Scratching my balls.'

"Those are *my* balls! Leave them alone."

'Oh, don't be such a child…'

"I'm the child?! You're treating me like a toy!"

Flaming sun, she's worse than Loki. At least he kept his hands to himself.

I know what she's doing. She's keeping me distracted with sensation while letting her mind wonder aimlessly, thinking about everything without focusing on anything specific so I can't tell what she really thinks or feels. That was not part of the deal, but of course, her being her, she would not make it easy for me to learn anything from this.

'I love your body!'

"Please don't say that."

'Why not?'

"It sounds wrong." It actually sounds like the truth, which makes it even wronger. "Let's not make this more uncomfortable than it needs to be, please."

'Who says it's uncomfortable?'

"It is. It really is." Goddess, I've never been this uncomfortable in my life. I'm talking to myself while peeking into my own trousers. "For flame's sake, Psyche, it's not like you haven't seen it before."

'Not from this angle.'

Goddess, give me strength. "Can we get it over with, please?"

'All right. I'll stop. A girl can't have any fun.'

"Are you done?" Seshat asks, making a considerable effort to remain serious. I bet she's loving this almost as much as Psyche.

"Yes. Very much so," I say.

"Good. Hop on again. Quick. There's a wave coming and I, for one, don't want to be caught up in it. Now, Psyche, describe everything about this experience, and please, spare no details."

CHAPTER 18

One Promise at a Time

Quetish soars through the air like wind itself. I close my eyes and almost forget where I am. It's strange being hosted by the Dharkan. Not as frustrating as being a Wyrd, but still awkward. He's animated by tremendous energy but nothing you could call life. His blood flows very slowly; each heartbeat is a conscious act to keep it going. There's no breath and no actual digestion, only a hunger for heat and Prana. I can sense it flowing through Seshat, and the palms of my hands itch to take it.

Control yourself, Aedan says, reading my thoughts.

His own thoughts are like a river running beneath a thick layer of ice. He doesn't want me to read them. I respect that, so I turn my attention to the scenery.

The world is in bad shape. The chasm we encountered earlier stretches all the way to what was once Relicum, and an ever larger one crosses the plains from the Grove to the Shadow Mountains. Several craters seem gouged out all along Aegea, some spurting molten rock.

The area around the Stump has been completely

destroyed, the Grove burned down to a few charred tree trunks sticking up from the scorched ground. Relicum is a fuming ruin, and between them a river of lava runs into the main river in a violent plume of steam. Fire and water engaging in mutual annihilation. But just as we near the Stump, there's a discernible change. It's almost as if the land is healing. Or more precisely, cooling. The fissures are knitting together, leaving only scars as a reminder of what they'd once been.

If Hades and Hel had found a way to keep their world intact, perhaps there's still hope for the Universe.

'How can I feel so differently?' Aedan asks. I can't tell if my thoughts triggered his question or if his emotions triggered my thoughts. Either way it's not like I can pretend I didn't hear the question or failed to understand it's meaning.

He's not referring to my influence on him; he's actually taking that pretty well. I'm only fifth on his list of concerns after Ileana, Emil, the Nephilim and Quetish.

The curse binds to a certain image, rather than a person. That's how those in love are able to overlook their lover's faults, and it's not unusual to fall in love with a reflection, a picture or a statue. Once that image changes, so does the feeling.

'You mean, if Eros appeared in his true form, you'd have fallen into his arms?'

No. I became immune to his talent the first time I died by his hand.

'Ileana died too. Why did that not affect her feelings towards me?'

I'm not sure. Maybe because she always fancied a Dharkan.

'Can she be fixed?'

She'll heal, I say reassuringly. *We may even find her a new body.*

'I don't care about the body!' It's a lie, but I won't call him out on it. 'It's her personality that I cannot stand.'

Now, that's true enough.

I can change her mindset, maybe… if the Nephilim's minds work similarly to ours, but is that really something you want me to do?

He rubs his face in distress. 'I don't know…'

We should agree on a few rules, I say, desperate to take his mind off the subject.

'Huh?'

Who's controlling what, for example.

'Oh, that…'

You're a better fighter and know the limits of your body better than I do, so I propose you control the fighting, running and all that fancy lightning. I'll do the thinking and talking.

'So much for a disguise then. Might as well write Psyche on my forehead if you're the one talking.'

I bite the inside of his cheek, triggering a curse.

'Do not do that again! It's a rule.'

"Humph," I say in a pretty good imitation of his favourite grunt.

'There's one thing I don't understand… Why did the Suzerain free you atop the Stump? I get why he destroyed Ileana's real body to do it, but not why he did it in plain sight. Wouldn't it have made more sense to do it inside the vault? This way he could have kept you there. It was almost as if he knew we would come, and he wanted us to attack him… Did he?'

He had a deal with Chronos. I was the payment. Alek

couldn't keep me for himself until I did what Chronos wanted me to do for him. I think most of what Alek did for the Nephilim and to the world was for that purpose. Funny, Chronos could have just asked me. I respected the God of Time enough to comply, had I known his true purpose. All this could have been avoided. As for Ileana… she always saw herself as a young girl and hated her body, thinking it was too old and damaged. The Suzerain would have destroyed it anyway, since he considered it soiled by you. Either way, it was all a show, yes. He wanted you to attack, like he wanted Fenrir to attack. We won't do what he wants this time.

Hades and Anubis are waiting next to the teleportation ring at the base of the Stump.

"Finally, Seshat. Did you take the scenic route?" Anubis asks grumpily the moment we land.

"I did. Made a few sketches too. Words won't be enough to thoroughly describe this."

"For cat's sake…"

"Seshat, welcome back to the party," Hades says jovially. "I love your mount, by the way. Where can I get one of these? Never mind, I'm more of a wyvern person myself." He turns to Aedan. "Hello again, my good man. I'd shake your hand, but you look a bit too tense. Something bothering you? Women trouble, perhaps?"

"Fuck off, Hades," I say, to his great amusement.

"Where's Hel?" Aedan asks before I have the chance to.

"Portum," Hades replies. "She had a few lose threads to tie up with the new queen and the old Aesir goddess. Not to mention that temple – it's always troublesome to see other gods interfering in your world," he says pointedly to those present. "In this case, we might have to put up with it for a while. The point is, she's not joining us on this… expedition. I am. Anubis, we're all waiting for you now."

Anubis snarls at him from behind his forearm. He'd been fiddling with his bracelet since we arrived and was growing exponentially more annoyed with it. "It's not working. Namrive wouldn't lock me out. I don't think…" he says uncertainly. "The ring must be broken."

"Do you realise how silly you look talking to your forearm?" Seshat says unhelpfully, dismissing Quetish.

He glares at her. "This is the epitome of technology."

"It's primitive."

"You'll change your mind soon enough."

'Why can't we fly up like last time?' Aedan asks.

Because we're doing things differently now.

"Speaking of changes, how are we to leave with the ship blown to pieces?" Seshat asks.

"The mother ship is still in orbit," Anubis says.

"The *mother* ship?" I ask.

"Yes, this was just a shuttle. It transports the vanguard, emissaries, supplies, that sort of thing. The time and spatial distortion around this world is too taxing on the mother ship, so we leave it in orbit."

"Like a moon?" Hades asks.

"Precisely."

"So you're telling me this mother ship can carry more ships like the ones that covered the Stump?"

"Dozens."

"Cerberus breath!"

"All right. There's another way in. Come."

We follow Anubis a fair distance around the base

of the Stump until we arrive at a crack in the bark of the huge tree. Through it, I know, lies the large room where the gliders are stored.

"I thought this could only be opened from the inside," I say.

"Manually, yes." Anubis fiddles with the bracelet again, something clicks and moments later, the door moves. "After you." He motions to us.

"Are we supposed to walk all the way up? Why can't we just fly?" Seshat mews. "There's no one up there."

"And that is precisely what worries me," he says. "This way is more discreet."

"Well, but it will not be brief," she hisses, assessing the height of the Stump.

"Er… I don't know, man," Hades says, clutching his hair. "I think I'd rather translocate up and, you know, scout the premises, keep an eye on exits, etcetera."

"You really hate it in there," I say.

"Yeah, I do. Besides, if there's another ship coming to my world. I'd rather be there to *welcome* it."

"Just get inside," Anubis says, exasperated. "The control room is not far."

"The distance is not what worries me," Hades replies darkly.

The Lord of the Underworld is highly distressed by his surroundings. Seshat too, all but hissing at the walls, ready to flare at any shadow. Only Anubis seems to be reasonably collected. I guess he's had plenty of opportunity to get used to the crippling effects of the Stump. I myself feel fine, comfortably hosted by the stoic Dharkan. They say ignorance is bliss. I'm not sure I agree, but it's certainly peace of mind.

"Aaahh!" Hades exclaims rather ungodingly when he comes face to face with a helmet on a shelf.

Anubis tuts at his side. "How can *you* rule Tartarus?"

"By not looking at it too closely," Hades sneers.

"Pathetic."

"Say that again, you traitorous canine."

The two men lock eyes with each other, puffing their chests in a silent contest of egos.

"Are you finished?" I ask in Aedan's best stentorian tone.

"It's all right, Butterfly," Hades says. "Just teaching this dog some manners."

"I didn't ask if it was all right, I asked if you were finished."

A bolt of energy crashes at their feet to reinforce the point.

"Yes," both men reply grudgingly in unison.

"Then let's go."

∞

"We're almost there," Aedan says as we approach the vault. The lights are out, but the Dharkan's vision is indeed vastly improved by darkness. Unfortunately so are his other senses. His concern has been increasing with each step in tandem with the smell of burned flesh.

"We should not have separated," Hades says, still cross that I agreed with Anubis and his decision to split the party so he and Seshat could look for clues as to Mnemosyne's whereabouts while we rescue Fenrir. Of course, he doesn't know that's what they're doing. He suspects some sort of nefarious purpose, and I'm not going to be the one to tell him otherwise.

"The place is deserted," Aedan says. He sounds almost disappointed. In truth he is very suspicious.

"Just because you can't see something doesn't mean it isn't there," Hades says as if to reinforce the suspicion. "Do you know why monsters prefer to dwell in dark places?"

"So they are left alone," Aedan replies curtly.

"Exactly! Which incidentally is why they become so angry when disturbed."

"So don't disturb them," I say in the Dharkan's deepest voice, taking great pleasure in Hades' reaction as he tries to figure out who spoke.

The corridor leading to the antechamber of the vault is black and warped with heat. Two twisted shapes lie on the floor before it.

"Flaming sun," Aedan curses, stepping back from the closest one. The corpse is badly burned but also shrivelled, dried out like a raisin.

What did this? I ask myself, unable to discern any details beyond the visual.

"Someone took his Prana – all of it," Aedan says as if it's unheard of, his mind struggling to acknowledge what he sees.

"Can Dharkan do this?" Hades asks.

"No! No Dharkan – at least no sane Dharkan, I should say – would do this."

"But they could, if they wanted to, I mean?"

"Well, yes."

"Damn..." The Underworld lord pulls at his hair, clearly seeing Hel's creations in a whole new light.

"I don't think it was a Dharkan," I say. Oreth lies further away, dead but not sucked dry. There's no time to worry or grieve for either of them. We run into the vault. A smaller shape, little more than charred bones, lies there.

"I'm not going any closer," Hades states from the threshold. I'm surprised he came this far.

I think it's safe for us to part ways now, I say to Aedan.

I feel a pang of excitement as well as apprehension. "Are you certain?"

This place is dead, deserted. I have no need of your protection.

"You – you never thought you did!" he says, reading my mind. "Why the pretence?" Ice spreads up the black walls. "Do you take that much pleasure in humiliating me?!"

You know I don't.

"Then… why?!"

So you could have your answers and tell Hel all she wants.

"I wouldn't have to spy on you had you been forthcoming from the beginning," he says defensively.

I was. But everyone already had their minds made up about me before they'd even met me. Including you. Honesty is pointless in the face of prejudice. I had to become what you expected – a liar and cold-hearted usurper – before you could actually believe me.

I leave his body and, feeling myself again, cock an eyebrow at him. "Thank you for the experience. It was quite entertaining."

"Get the wolf," he growls.

"Yes, please do," Hades stresses.

Fenrir's soul lingers inside the room, clinging to its curse like a dying man to his faith. He's unharmed and bored to tears.

'Took you long enough.'

Oh, pup, why did you stay?

'Because I'd rather be here than Helheim. Because I knew you would come. And because someone had to witness what happened here.'

You can tell Seshat all about it.

'I'd rather tell you first.'

INTERLUDE 22

Seshat

Seshat entered the control room cautiously, feeling utterly oppressed by it, much like she did inside the vault, although for very different reasons. The room was pyramidal, the walls covered in glass panels, reflecting the red light from the ceiling in a way that made it look like they were inside a red sun. Still, the most disturbing feature of the room was its very existence.

"This wasn't here before. I personally searched this level with Hel and Ideth. I crossed this corridor several times. It leads to the Suzerain's chamber."

"That is correct," Anubis said. "It's hard to find something you don't know exists. And like with most things in this place, you need the right key to access it." His fingers ran along what Seshat took for a very impractical table studded with buttons.

"Are you sure no one knows we're here?"

"Yes. The eyes are all closed. And there were none in this room to begin with. The Suzerain liked to keep certain things off the record."

"What record? Where are these records you so cunningly used to lure me here?" Seshat glowered at the empty room with dismay. Whatever records it may have contained, they were long gone.

"I told you, they're stored in their virtual realm," Anubis said, touching the buttons below a glass pane with the care one takes with thorns. "We only need to figure out how to access it…"

"What's this magical place look like anyway?"

"Look for a window."

"You're kidding, right?" If there's one thing the Stump didn't have, it was windows.

Anubis took a measured breath. "It's not a *window, window*. It's a pane, usually hidden behind the walls."

He made no sense, but Seshat did as she was told. She patted the walls, looking for oddities.

"Hmm," she said when she found a piece of stringy wire sticking out of a tiny fissure in an otherwise flat surface. "Looks like a cat trapped its tail."

"That's it!" Anubis said. "Pull it."

What folded out was indeed a window of sorts.

"Now what?"

"Look for a button."

"On the wall?"

"Anywhere close by. Something you can put your finger on."

"Why do the Nephilim have to make everything so awkward?"

"Because they were created by humans," Anubis replied. "And we all know who created those."

"Humph. Ah, found it!" Seshat stabbed at a panel vehemently, and light appeared behind the glass. She jumped back. "Cats! What's this?"

"Records," Anubis said triumphantly.

She leaned closer, hissing softly. "I don't recognise this language – if it is indeed a language." She squinted at the screen. "Looks more like equations. I wish Thoth was here. Numbers are his thing, not mine."

Anubis leaned closer. "Can you read anything? I've tried for years, but…"

"Possibly. Give me a moment," she said, scrolling her fingers down the screen. "I recognise characters from several pantheons, mostly Olympian and Aesir. But the words themselves make no sense. Still, every language follows a pattern, has a rhythm and reason. I just need to find it and extrapolate from there. What are we looking for exactly?"

"Anything."

"That's not helpful…" She pushed Anubis aside to have a closer look at the odd table. There were symbols on the buttons. The basic shapes of letters. Suddenly she realised she had to combine them in the right order to spell the word associated with the information she wanted to find.

Her hand trembled as she typed Mnemosyne.

INTERLUDE 23

Portum

Ileana watched helplessly as Aedan flew away on the back of a she monster tucked between Psyche and Seshat. Of course, the two goddesses would ally themselves against her. Gods had no respect for her kind, Father had always said so. She knew she should feel sad, heartbroken, and abandoned. But what she actually felt was furious, humiliated and, she had to admit, slightly relieved.

Aedan wasn't quite as she remembered. He was rough, colourless, tedious, cold to the touch, and he smelled of horse. His face was too angular and stern, that horrible scar more prone to inspire pity rather than fear. She'd had this image of him as the perfect male specimen: handsome, strong, and sensual. But now that she'd seen a few of his kind, she realised he wasn't the tallest, nor the strongest, and certainly not the handsomest of Dharkan. What had made her think he was so special? *Psyche…* This was all her fault, surely. The goddess of the soul had not only infected her mind with hazardous notions of altruism and empathy, but of lust as well. That's what she accused her of feeling because she'd caused that feeling. She'd used her body just like she used her identity, and she had the nerve to preach about selflessness and gratitude while doing so. Only a goddess would have such luxury. Dryads cannot afford either when everything in the world, from the elements themselves to the creatures inhabiting it, are out to eat their flesh. And love… love is an illusion. Now that Ileana was herself again, her old self – her true self – she refused to be illuded again.

"Ileana, the queen wishes to speak with you," said Asher, a much more handsome and inspiring specimen than Aedan. She was about to reply that she had nothing to say to *the queen*, when it occurred to her that perhaps there was something to gain from having a royal mother with a small army of Dharkan at her command. Father might not even come for her this time. He might just create another Ileana to keep him company. She couldn't count on him, like she couldn't count on Aedan. Right now, all she had was Mother, and Mother owed her. Why pine for one Dharkan when she could have as many as she wanted, as was her right as the queen's daughter?

"Tell her I'll join her soon," Ileana said with a coquettish smile. *She's not Father; she can wait – wait like I've waited*, Ileana thought spitefully. Asher nodded stiffly and left rather swiftly.

"Another one who couldn't wait to leave you." Oric, still tied to the wall, laughed heartily. She picked up a stone and threw it at him. He cursed at her. "They all see you for what you are: ugly."

"It's your fault I'm ugly!"

She bent to pick up another stone, and a glint caught her eye. She squinted, confused by what she saw emerging from behind the trees. It looked like a large metallic skeleton with glowing red eyes.

Oric followed her gaze and jumped to his feet. "Ileana, free me. Now!"

"What is that?"

"One of your father's faithful."

"Why does he look like that? What happened to its flesh? How did it get here?"

"None of that is important right now. Untie me. Help! Over here!" he shouted to whoever was inclined to hear. Most were still gathering inside the temple, behind its thick stone walls, while the rest had their attention on the queen.

The skeletal construct intercepted a Narrum drawn by Oric's call and ripped his heart from his chest in one precise motion before he could even scream.

"For frost's sake, girl! Don't just stay there. Do something. HELP! Jonas! Somebody!"

Ileana didn't move, delighted with the possibilities. "If they're Father's, they won't attack me."

She walked up to the faithful and pointed at Oric. "I'm Ileana Dveer. I command you to kill this man and everyone else in this settlement except the Dharkan."

She didn't need Aedan or Mother. She could have any Dharkan. More than that, she was her father's daughter. She would have a kingdom *and* a temple! She would have it all. She deserved it all.

The faithful stopped before her, the red light of his eyes running over her body in assessment. Then it lifted a metallic claw to her face, grabbed her head, and crushed it.

∞

"Help! Oric shouted again, too terrified to fully appreciate the popping crack of Ileana's demise at her own hubris. People came running to his call at first but changed their mind when they saw the Nephilim's construct. Except Jonas.

The metz came charging, emboldened by drink, broken bottle in one hand, a pickaxe in the other. He got one good swing with it, putting a dent in the machine's metal chest before being knocked aside. He hit the wall next to Oric with the sickening sound of broken bone and lay there unconscious.

The faithful pulled the pickaxe from his chest, studied it a moment, then used it on the first Dharkan who came at it and the next one with a similar result.

"They feel nothing, you idiots! Cold and Pan's talent are useless. Only force will defeat it," Oric shouted to anyone who cared.

The construct turned its attention back to him. Oric pulled at his chains with all his strength. He tore the device from his arm and flailed it at the oncoming enemy while heavy stones rained on them. The aim of the crowd was murderous. They didn't care what they hit. Oric wasn't sure if the blinding pain that bloomed on his face came from stone or fist. He fell to the ground, dazed and unable to breathe, mouth filling with blood. Someone stepped on his new arm, on his neck, on his back. He heard grunts, curses, the ringing of metal and grinding of artificial joints. There had to be a dozen Dharkan assaulting the construct. None concerned with him. The ground was covered in ice. He felt very, very cold. Then he felt nothing at all.

∞

Iva yanked out the construct's arm from its shoulder. The thing wouldn't freeze, so she had to resort to less elegant means of disabling it. Four other Dharkan took care of the other limbs. She kicked its head until it finally came off, then she kicked it a few more times for good measure and waited. The sure way to tell if something was dead was to look for movement, especially if it hadn't been alive to begin with.

"I wonder if it thinks for itself or simply follows orders," Ann said, her gaze split between it and Ileana's remains as if the question applied to both constructs.

"Does it matter? Its purpose is obvious." Agnar pulled her aside. "Ann, come away. You shouldn't punish yourself like this. That was not your Ileana."

"I am aware," she replied tautly. How would she ever explain to him how little she felt for her daughter? She'd been about to send her away, in fact. She couldn't trust her, even if she'd been the real one. She'd always been Alek's, not hers.

Have I become my mother? Ann asked Yewlow.

'No. Your mother would have drowned Ileana the moment she realised she wouldn't make a good queen.'

I'm so glad I have you to tell me these things, Ann replied sardonically.

'I live to serve.'

"Are they dead?" she asked of the two metz crumbled against the wall. There was no doubt about the two Dharkan who had attacked the construct first.

"One of them is," Asher said.

"Bring them inside the temple."

∞

'*The Nephilim are truly ingenious. To animate metal, now that's a talent,*' Freya said appreciatively.

Iva closed her eyes and allowed herself one breath. She couldn't wait to be free of the goddess. More than that, she didn't want to be in the same realm as where these things existed. One had defeated two Dharkan, and it took five to bring it down. Those were bad odds.

"Let's hope it was the only one," Iva said, the words barely spoken when screams erupted again. Dozens of the constructs were marching from the tree line. They surrounded the settlement.

"To the temple!" She did not need to repeat herself. Everyone who wasn't there already was running to it.

"Now what?" Iva asked as dozens of the constructs stalked up the hill. The walls of the temple were solid and wide, but it had no door, no means to barricade the entrance in time.

Goddess, save us.

∞

Hel was suddenly standing in front of them. "Stay back!" A dome of ice appeared around the temple.

"That's your solution?" Freya said. Iva was terrified. The Dharkan was pretty easy to control when she was scared, which was not very often. "Even if the ice holds – which it won't for long – you'll freeze the living." She smirked. "Unless that is your intention, of course."

"I'm not you, Freya."

"There's someone out there!" Agnar exclaimed.

A boy stood on the other side of the wall, facing the oncoming faithful.

"Oh, burn it, Hel. Is that who I think it is?" Freya stepped back.

"What's that noise?" Asher asked.

Ann's eyes widened. "It sounds like the ocean."

∞

An immense roar shook the ground, then a towering wave smashed over the land, washing away trees, shelters, bodies, constructs, everything but the temple and those inside it, leaving Aegea temporarily submerged in water.

Ann could swear she saw a giant snake swimming amongst the wreckage.

When the water subsided, Hel tore down the icy wall. The boy was still there, unharmed and not even wet. They stared at each other in silence, their eyes saying what they could not.

When he vanished, Hel dropped her head and whispered, "Thank you, brother."

CHAPTER 19

To Be Continued

We're rushing up the seemingly endless corridors of the Stump when a tremor rocks it to its core.

"This feels familiar," I say.

"The main teleportation ring has just been activated," Aedan confirms.

Hades pulls at his hair. "Damn it, Psyche. We shouldn't have left Seshat and Anubis out of our Reach."

"It's not them," I say, perceiving their souls just ahead and equally alarmed.

We resume our mad dash to the top and sure enough bump into the scions of Ra just short of the last flight of stairs, where we all stare at each other as if we'd done something wrong.

"Aedan," Anubis says.

"Anubis," Hades says.

"Hades," Seshat says.

"I think we all know our own fucking names," I say.

Aedan takes a step forward. "What did you do?"

"Nothing! Someone – not us! – activated the main

portal," Anubis says. His bracelet starts blinking. He curses. "And a ship is about to land."

The two men join heads to inspect the device as if they could witness the landing through its gems.

"Did you find what you were looking for?" I ask Seshat circumspectly.

"Yes, we did, thank you," Seshat replies in the same manner. "How's Fenrir?"

"Safe in Helheim. For now…" I lie.

"Good, good. Any update on Chronos?"

"He's no longer in this world," I say.

"Where is he?"

"Fuck knows." It's the truth. I can no longer sense Chronos' soul. Which makes sense since now, technically, he has none. I'm pretty certain the full ramifications of that consequence are yet to be revealed.

"Can we catch up later? There's a ship about to land on my World Tree – again. I'd like to stop it," Hades says.

Anubis chuckles. "You can't."

Hades darkens. *Can't* is not a word gods like to hear. "Then I'd rather not be stuck here when it lands."

"On that, we can both agree," Aedan says.

We climb the rest of the steps to the top, prepared for anything. What we find defies our expectations.

A tall blue-skinned woman with the wilted appearance of a candle left too long in the sun stands atop the ramp, her back to us, mumbling something about doubts and dreams.

"Namrive?" Anubis says.

She turns around, startled to see him with company.

"Don't come any closer! Either I leave this place or I destroy it. Your choice."

"It's all right. We're not here to stop you leaving," Anubis says.

"Yes we are!" Hades replies.

"No you are not," Seshat says, joining Anubis at Namrive's side.

"What's this? You're going with them, Seshat? You'd betray us?"

"I would have to have been your ally in the first place in order to betray you, Hades. I've always been and always will be neutral."

"Bullshit. Hel was right about you. What you've been and always will be is unwelcome in this world, you selfish bitch."

Seshat chuckles. "Give my regards to the goddess of the dead, Hades. May you fight happily ever after."

Her eyes meet mine. "Psyche, I guess this is for you as next of kin, of a sort." She gives me Persephone's box. "It's empty, you have my word."

"I won't have it, since your word means little. Hermes left Niflheim the moment we left Portum. He took Hecate with him."

"Yes," she sighed. "I'm aware. I still take responsibility for the cat. Not the box, though. I want no more part in this story."

"We can't let them leave," Hades says. "They'll just come back. With more ships and more constructs and stars know what else. Aedan, freeze them!"

"No we won't. I guarantee it," Namrive says.

"Frost your guarantees! You're one of them."

Namrive walks up to Hades, black eyes flickering like sparks. "I am the only ally you'll ever have amongst the Nephilim. Treat me well."

Hades is about to do the opposite.

I hold him back. "Let them go."

Namrive's gaze meets mine with something like recognition. She nods and smiles in a way that lets me know this meeting is only the beginning of our acquaintance.

∞

"Aren't you going to open the box?" Aedan asks once the Nephilim and the scions of Ra are on board the ship.

"Fuck no."

"Why not?"

"Nothing good ever came out of these boxes. I can't tell if this is a test, a gift or a warning. Likely all three," I say, holding it up for inspection.

"I'll keep it, then, shall I?" Loki says, snatching the accursed thing out of my hand.

I narrow my eyes at him. "Where the fuck have you been?"

"Here, there, everywhere. Actually, I've been here most of the time, helping Gaea prepare the tree and setting up the illusion around the world. Also had a great chat with Namrive in the interim." His expression turns from nonchalant to mischievous wonder. "Did you know artificial minds are as susceptible to illusions as real ones?"

"How convenient," I say with exaggerated delight.

He smiles wickedly. "That's what I thought."

"Prepare the tree for what?" Aedan asks suspiciously.

Loki grins. "Wait and see."

∞

Hel's gaze narrows at the departing ship. "Explain to me again why we are letting them go, Father?"

"Because we pick our fights. And this one we can't win. Not yet."

"So we hide?"

"There's no shame in being stealthy for the sake of survival."

The ship vanishes from Reach. Hel takes a deep breath. "Are you certain the illusion will hold?"

"As long as your union with Hades holds."

She glances at him. "It will."

"How was it in Portum?" I ask cautiously.

Her face twitches slightly. "Eventful. There are still a few constructs about. The damn things don't drown, but hopefully they'll rust. Overall, the kingdom of Aegea is fairly secured."

"Kingdom, huh? Going like this, it's not the Nephilim or the dead you'll have to worry about, but the actual living."

Hel narrows her eyes. "I'm done with the living. Freya was right about one thing. Taking responsibility for the living and the dead is too much. If they thrive better without my influence, then… fine. The Underworld needs souls to replace the ones you took, which were a lot more than the half we agreed, burn you."

"For the last time, Hel. I don't want souls. I guide them, not keep them."

"Well, they might want you," she grumbles.

"Didn't Aedan assure you of my intentions?"

She tsks. "Humans' intentions are contrary by nature."

"Humans may be living contradictions, but Dharkan are not," Hades points out. "If Psyche took more than we expected, it is because Gaea needed them, right?"

"She did," Gaea says, manifesting at our side. Her new aspect as the Goddess of Life and Death is intimidating, to say the least. Still exuberant, voluptuous, and beaming with life, she now has an aura of darkness around her, like a heavy cloud that promises water to a dry plain. Not a summer rain, though. A deluge.

She closes her eyes, places one hand to the ground, the other against the Stump of the World Tree.

It begins to sprout.

Moments Lost in Time

I

The New Trinity

"Hello, Chronos," Gaea said.

"Hello, dear. I've been waiting for you."

"That would be a first."

"On the contrary. I've been waiting for you since we first parted."

"Have you? And here I was thinking I never left you."

They faced each other as equals for the first time in aeons. She had no need to breathe, and he had no need to show himself. Both knew what they were and where they stood in the void.

"I'm curious, Chronos. What did you expect to accomplish with all this?"

"Peace of mind, dear."

"And have you?"

"Yes. I'm finally free from the burden of death and all obligations to life." A warning more than a statement.

"Why didn't you just ask Psyche to heal you?"

"Because thanks to your souls and their cursed free will, the only way to make gods do what we want is to convince them it's their idea."

"Mm-hmm. So this was all a game to you?"

"I don't play games, dear. Games are for minor deities. This was merely an experiment. A test of my own strength."

"That could have ended everything," Gaea said in anger.

"It could. It still can. But it won't. Not while I'm free," he replied meaningfully. "All I ever wanted was to be free to do as I wish."

"Does this mean there won't be more experiments?"

"That depends… Will you have what it takes to test yourself? There comes a time in every creator's journey when they must let go of their creations. Let them find their own paths without guidance. Which one would they choose do you think: Life or Eternity?"

"Is that a threat?"

"It's a challenge, dear. Will you accept it?"

Gaea took a deep breath, then another. Not because she needed them to remain calm but because she wanted him to believe she wasn't. The time to fight would come, for Nyx would never be truly free to rule while Chronos existed, and he would not be able to stall her full return much longer. It might take an aeon or an age, but she would become stronger than him, and then…

"What do *you* expect to accomplish, dear?" he

suddenly asked. There was no judgement, only genuine curiosity in his tone.

"I'm not sure I understand the question."

"You better than anyone know that although the future can be changed, fate can only be postponed. And change isn't always for the best, especially in the long run. Niflheim may be saved – for now – but the Suzerain will return; so will the Nephilim."

"Not if I can help it."

"Is one world really worth the sacrifice of so many others?"

"It is to me."

"Silly child." The cosmic hilarity was too much for Gaea to bear. She would not stand there to be patronised or laughed at. She would conquer the Universe from him: one victory at a time.

"Enjoy the rest of your *freedom*." The goddess of Life and Death enunciated the last word carefully. Reality shifted, and she found herself once again in Niflheim, staring at the roots of the World Tree.

Hel and Hades were already there, waiting for her.

"How did it go?" Hel asked.

"Well enough. I'm fairly confident Niflheim is no longer part of Chronos' agenda."

"Good. Let's get started, then."

II

Hide and Seek

"For the last time," Ulcan said. "Do I look like I have any money on me? I'm dead! By the looks of it, so are you! What would you do with the coins, anyway?"

"It is our policy," Kharon said.

"For death?!" He was pushed aside by a bloke getting on board the ferry. "Oh, for fuck's sake. That one only had half a copper coin."

"Which is more than you do."

"Because a fucking goddess took all my possessions before I died!"

"Is this man bothering you?" Medusa asked Kharon.

The dark ferryman gave her a noncommittal shrug. "Occupational hazard."

Ulcan stared at Medusa, dumbfounded.

"What are you looking at?" she demanded, snakes hissing. It was much harder to intimidate the dead without the power of her gaze.

"Well, fuck me sideways," he said.

"I'll do no such thing!"

He just stared harder. "I always figured my afterlife would be filled with all the snakes I've killed. But this was not what I had in mind."

"I always figured I'd be high priestess one day. A spiritual leader of an entire sect dedicated to purity and wisdom. Instead, I comfort souls in the Underworld and mediate disputes with the staff. We all bear our disappointments. But if it's a snake pit you wish to spend eternity in, I can arrange that."

Ulcan scratched his beard, not too pleased with the prospect. "So this is it, huh? The Underworld."

"A very small part of it, yes. If you want to see more, you need to pay."

He closed his eyes, straining patience. "As I've been saying: I have no money! The gods took it all. I had no burial either; my body was left to rot under rubble. Hel sent me to Relicum against my will. I shouldn't have died. I didn't choose any of this. It's not right!"

"My records indicate you should have died days ago from injuries dealt by a gryphon."

Ulcan spat, reflecting on the events that followed the attack. When he spoke, he was no longer enraged, merely resigned. "I did not ask to be spared. It would have been a more honourable way to die. Maybe I'd even have had a proper burial with coin to pay you. Seems the gods not only fucked my life, they fucked my death and afterlife as well."

Medusa sighed. "It's all right, Kharon. Hades vouched for him."

Ulcan perked up, index finger pointed at Kharon. "I told him we were friends. He refused to believe me!"

A huff came from under the ferryman's hood.

"Is there a chance I can get some booze on account of our friendship?" Ulcan asked.

"No," Medusa said.

"A cabin?"

"A private cell, more likely."

He considered this. "Sure. Privacy would be good."

They got on the boat. Kharon began to steer the ferry with his paddle.

"So tell me," Ulcan said. "What is there to do when you're dead?"

"You search for your family and loved ones," Medusa replied.

"And then what?"

"That is usually enough."

"What do you mean?"

"The Underworld is a big place. Vastly overcrowded. Well, less so now, I suppose. And the souls of your family members might have been amongst those assimilated by Gaea. But you should still search for them. You know, to stay busy."

"I'd rather hunt."

"There is no prey, I'm afraid."

"Drink?"

"There is no thirst."

Now that he thought about it, Ulcan realised that was true. Frustrated as he was, he hadn't felt the need to eat or drink since he died. Crestfallen, he said, "I have no family here. What else is there to do, then?"

She considered this, having been asking herself the same question of late, then asked, "Do you like to play hide and seek?"

Ulcan smiled at Medusa with newfound appreciation for her hair. "Yes... as a matter of fact, I do."

III

Midgharb

"That's it. That's all of them." Hades regarded the last group of Narrum forced to move to the Gharb. Most were shaking in terror with tear-streaked faces as they marched in single file like livestock to the slaughter, dragging their feet, heads down.

Jörmungandr was not impressed either. "I save them, give them a place to live, and this is their attitude? Such ungrateful creatures, are they not?"

Hades had to agree. Ungrateful and filthy. But also quite easy to empathise with. "They've been through rough times lately," the Underworld lord understated. Everything these mortals had ever known was washed away – literally. Most lost their homes, their livelihoods and one or all family members. Still, he reckoned the greatest cause of their despair was the one looming above them.

"Perhaps being greeted into your new home by a giant sea serpent is not exactly the reassurance they need. And, well, this is not exactly Midgard." Hades took in the devastated landscape, then cursed to himself for his poor choice of example.

"No, it is not," Jörmungandr hissed pointedly before he changed into Toman, his mortal guise. There was an audible relief from the crowd.

Hades forced a smile. "Midgard is still yours as we agreed. As soon as the tree is restored, we'll –"

"Discuss it again."

"Yes…" Hades was sure they would. "In the meantime, keep the ocean filled with fish and the clouds heavy with rain. The mortals should be content soon enough."

"Tzzzz."

Hades extended his hand. "May you bring us many souls."

Jörmungandr took it and held it a bit too firmly. "Our Tribute to the new mistress of the Universe. Explain it to me again. Why trade one master for another?"

Hades pulled his hair. "You know how it is: if you can't beat them, join them. There's always a greater foe, and so forth. Better the enemy you know than –"

The boy that was Jörmungandr let go of his hand with a hiss of disgust. "Just make sure you don't lose track of the souls you already have in your possession. Someone else might catch them."

"Yeah… that would be bad…" Hades mused as he watched the boy slither away.

Hel, this is the last time I deal with your brother alone. He freaks me out.

'I'll make it up to you.'

You'd better.

"Hades!"

He jumped. "Cerberus' breath! Yes, Ulla, what is it?"

"I'm not happy with this arrangement."

"No one is, honey."

"I can't work with these Narrum. All they think about is their next meal, and some look at me as if I'm it!"

"You can always return to Portum. I'm sure queen Ann would be delighted to have you back." Hades was pretty sure she wouldn't be delighted at all. The queen had hardly even mentioned Ulla since she appointed Iva as her prime escort. The two had been getting along splendidly since Psyche freed Freya from her host. Women were strange creatures.

"Frost Portum! I will never, ever live amongst Wraiths. Ann's a fool. Everyone there is already dead and doesn't even realise it."

Hades sighed. That was the fifth time he'd heard that very same sentence from five different people across both settlements. "They say the same thing about you back in Portum. I think you'll fit in here very well, Ulla, as will your baby."

"If they don't eat it," she said acridly. "Why is this division necessary if the goal is to unite us?"

"Because people can never agree on how to unite. They need to believe they have options as well as common goals with others. But for any union to take place, those goals need to be at odds with someone else's goals. All we gods can do is keep you entertained and limit the violence."

This had been Psyche's idea. Of course, the goddess of the soul, much like Hel, did not understand that goals need egos to support them, and most egos need to be fed. That's where he came in.

The Underworld lord leaned closer to Ulla. "I trust you, Ulla. And he likes you." Hades pointed at Jörmungandr, who had to everyone's horror reverted to his true form again. "You are in a position to make significant changes in their society. Think about all the things you can teach these Narrum. Ann might have the Dharkan, but you have them. And we both know who won the last time they faced off against each other." He winked.

Ulla's change in expression told him that a whole new range of possibilities had just opened in her mind.

Satisfied, Hades translocated back to Aegea. "All taken care of, my lady."

She eyed him askance. "Did you just conspire with a dryad against my Dharkan?"

"You told me to deal with the mortals. So let me deal with them as I know best."

"Hmmm."

"How are things in Helheim?" he asked, trying to dismiss the uncanny similarity of temper between Hel and her brother.

"Fine. Never better, actually. Aedan is almost too competent."

"Is Psyche still there?"

"Yes…" The word dragged with exaggerated effort.

"You have no reason to be intimidated by Psyche. So what if your souls have a crush on her? It's perfectly natural. She is, after all, the goddess of the soul. She'll always be popular amongst them. It doesn't mean they don't worship you too. You are their guardian, their home."

Hel pressed her lips. "I suppose…"

"Besides, someone has to guide the souls to Nyx – the right souls, mind. It's what she was always meant to do."

"Sure. Except, between her and Aedan, I'm practically redundant! I feel like a guest in my own realm."

"You can always help me in Tartarus. It constantly needs cooling, if nothing else…"

Hel puffed out an icy breath. "I suppose I should get acquainted with some of your monsters, for a change," she said wryly.

They shared a complicit smile. Hades extended his hand to her. "My lady."

She took it. "My lord."

IV

Old Enemies; New Friends

The first thing Zeus saw was the eye patch, then the face that had haunted his thoughts and dreams more often than any other. It grinned at him.

"Odin?"

"Welcome to Helheim, you pompous prick. Did you miss me?"

"No…" It was the truth. Missing Odin would be like missing a migraine. Zeus took in the icy walls around them and shivered. He'd finally gained access to Helheim, just not quite as he'd planned… Outrage warred with the grief and triumph flooding his soul. He really didn't know if he should laugh or cry.

Odin threw him a cloak. "Put this on. We are civilised here."

"How did I end up *here*?" That was when he remembered what Medusa and Hades did to him. He cursed.

"Cheer up. You're not the only Olympian around. Never seen an Underworld so eclectic; you should feel right at home." There was that grin again.

"So this is the sum of all our efforts? No one wins?" Zeus asked.

"I bet Hades and Hel feel pretty victorious," Odin said. "But cheer up. The board's been flipped. The Universe is a whole new game now. We will get a chance to play again soon enough. Did you bring the eye?"

"What eye?"

Odin's grin vanished. "The one I gave to your daughter, to give to you, to give to me so we can get out of here."

"You gave your eye to Athena?"

"No, you idiot! To the dryad. The queen."

"Aaah, that one. She only gave me insults. I don't have your bloody eye."

Odin's nostrils flared. "Stop playing the fool. You know perfectly well you can't use the eye. Give it to me."

"I don't have it! And you're the fool if you trusted a woman with such a thing."

There was a long moment of silence. Then the icy walls of Helheim shook to Odin's howl.

"LOOOKI!"

∞

"Much obliged." Loki tucked Odin's eye away inside Persephone's box. A golden torc suddenly appeared in his hand. "Here's Brísingamen, as promised."

Freya snatched it greedily, kissed it, and fastened it around her neck with a deep sigh of contentment.

"All is forgiven?"

She scowled at him. "Forgiven, yes; forgotten, never."

"What's so special about that necklace?" Ann asked. She wasn't one for jewellery but was willing to make an exception if it had power.

"It's mine," Freya said proudly.

"I see…"

"You will return to Asgard now?" Loki asked. The question was a mere formality. Ann knew the gods would make sure she returned and stayed there, whether or not she wanted it.

"I will. May you freeze in here – all of you."

"I think I'd rather have kept her trapped in Iva," Hel said after Freya left.

"While I'd rather keep her where she can't meddle in our affairs," Loki said. "Speaking of, why is Iva still around, daughter?"

Hel glanced at Ann. "She's been put to good use."

"We are getting along surprisingly well," Ann confirmed. "I have no heart for fights; she has no head for diplomacy. We make a good team." Especially as there was no love lost between them, no friendship, no sentiment, only a common goal and the sort of mutual respect that engendered the foundation for the strongest of alliances.

"She knows too much," he said.

"That, too, can be put to good use," Hel said.

"Mmm."

Ann cleared her throat. "Thank you for returning Freya's precious ornament and interfering on our behalf with Jörmungandr," she said to Loki.

"It's what I do," he replied, caressing the box under Hel's astute gaze.

"And you've been handsomely rewarded," she pointed out.

"I have indeed."

"So have I, thank you. I really didn't want to return

to the Gharb," Ann admitted. The memory of her time there still haunted her. "I won't stop any who do, of course. Ulla is free to recruit as many to her cause as she can, but my place is here." *Funny how things turned out*, she thought, remembering her old friend, now her greatest adversary. Occa had been right about them. Some wounds never heal.

It was worth it, though.

She looked up and breathed a soft sigh. Like pretty much everyone in Niflheim, she couldn't get enough of the sight of the luxuriant World Tree.

Loki took her hand and kissed it gallantly. "My queen. I would never force a dryad to leave the forest. May you rule in peace."

"Any sign of Ideth?" Ann asked on Yewlow's behalf.

Father and daughter shared similar expressions of dismay.

"No," Loki said. "It appears she fell through the portal along with the Suzerain. I'm afraid we haven't seen the last of him yet."

Ann clicked her tongue. "I figured as much… Is there any chance you can track them?"

Loki tilted his head side to side, seemingly reluctant to even consider the possibility. "We know where they went. And I'm in no rush to follow. We need to make sure Niflheim remains safe, and that means hidden. At least until we're ready to confront the Nephilim again."

"You won't be able to keep it hidden from him. What will you do when he returns? For it's not a matter of if with Alek Dveer. He *will* return."

"Well, as Ideth would say: one problem at a time."

∞

Psyche waited for Loki to finish his business just outside of the great tree's shade, looking up with her eyes closed, taking in the magnificent sight in all its glory.

"Psyche…" Gaea called. "Before I go. There is something I need to tell you about Loki."

Psyche opened her eyes. "Stars, why is everyone taking an interest in my personal affairs?"

Gaea pinched her face in annoyance. "Because they concern the entire Universe. What I'm about to tell you is… delicate. You'd do well to keep it to yourself."

Psyche crossed her arms and waited for Gaea to continue.

"Loki was not my creation; neither was he my creation's creation. He was – he is – a manifestation. The cosmic equivalent of blood spilled during a battle. All I did was animate it and watch as it transformed into something like a god, but not quite. In the beginning, there was so much less power in him than in those I created. And yet so much more potential. He was, in fact, the inspiration to create the other gods – but please never tell him that, his ego might explode." She smiled to herself, then pursed her lips again. "Do you understand what I'm telling you, Psyche?"

"He's a scion of Nyx. Yes. Souls are my speciality, remember? I always knew he was different. Even when I was still a mortal I could tell he was not like the other gods. When I became a goddess and was able to perceive his soul, I realised just how different. But I didn't know what I was looking at until…"

"Chronos," Gaea said.

Psyche nodded. "And you." She snorted. "Imagine my confusion. The last thing anyone sees in Loki is a god of life. He does have many children, though," Psyche added to herself.

"Life is chaos," Gaea said.

"True…" Psyche nodded again, and Gaea mirrored the movement. They discussed the implications of Loki's lineage in silence until Gaea, hand drawn to the butterfly necklace, spoke again.

"I can't say I'm happier or better than I was before, because I'm not. I miss what I was – *who* I was. And I will always resent you for taking that away."

"I understand."

"That being said, I am more powerful than ever. I am almost complete and free of Chronos' shadow. For that I thank you."

Psyche smiled. "You're welcome."

"Take care of my souls."

"I will."

The Goddess of Life and Death spared one last glance at the lush World Tree and faded into the fabric of the Universe.

V

Full Circle

"And all is right with the world once again," Loki said as soon as Gaea left.

"For now…" Psyche said.

He followed her gaze to the magnificent World Tree. "Do you wish to name it this time?"

Psyche smiled to herself. "I already have. Alma." She glanced at the box in his hand and frowned. "How did you convince the queen to give you the eye?"

"Oh, I told her it would ruin her beauty."

She chuckled. "Effective. What will you do with it?"

"I don't know. For now, it's enough that Odin knows I'm the one who has it."

Psyche shook her head in amusement as if pleased to know that no matter what happened, some things never changed.

"What will you do now, goddess of the soul?" he asked earnestly. "Return to the stars?"

She sighed. "Eventually. For now, I think I'll stay here for a while longer. There are many souls in the Underworld in need of guidance, and it's not like the Universe will run out of stars soon, right? I always thought I'd become a goddess for a reason, a purpose. I guess this is it."

Loki could well imagine the sort of guidance she would provide to souls like Zeus and Eros. He moved closer. "Hmm-mm. Is that all? Nothing to do with a brooding Dharkan to whom you might feel obliged to?"

She raised an eyebrow quizzically. "Jealous, god of mischief?"

He half shrugged. "Intrigued."

She bit her cheek to disguise a smirk. "There's no obligation. No *love*. Our relationship is uncomplicated. Besides, I found Ileana's spirit. It was hiding inside the Stump, hoping to hitch a ride with the Nephilim. Fenrir stopped her. That's why he chose to remain there instead of going straight to Helheim. Well, that and the fact he really doesn't like the Underworld. Anyway, Hel's working on a new body for her as we speak."

"Hwh… That's a bad idea."

"Agree… We haven't seen the end of Aedan and Ileana's story yet. It's another reason to stay."

Loki shook his head. "Poor Aedan. Some men never learn… Speaking of spirits, have you tracked down the Olympian twins?"

"No. It's like they fell off the Universe." Psyche glanced at him askance. "Much like Ideth."

He grimaced.

"Is there anything you wish to share about it?"

"I fucking hate sorcery," he mumbled, then he pushed the thought away and took a deep breath. Yes, he would have to deal with Ideth and the twins soon enough, and he would rather have Psyche at his side when he did, but first there was something he had to know. "So... if and when is over. The Universe survived. Eternity is saved, and we're still here. What shall we do now, goddess of the soul?"

She cocked her eyebrow suggestively. "What we do best, Trickster: we play."

Loki grinned. "Any particular game in mind?"

Psyche's eyes twinkled mischievously. She took a lock of his hair and tucked it behind his ear with a tantalising caress. "Perhaps."

"And so it begins," he whispered against her lips.

"A beginning is a great place to end," she said right before they kissed.

The End

Aknowlegements

Once again, I'd like to thank my husband, Dave, for his support, patience and ruthless feedback. Hardly any darlings made it to the final cut this time.

A huge thank you to all who helped and encouraged me through this journey.

To all who reached out with advice or a kind word.

To all who read and especially those who took the time to rate and review my work.

To all the reviewers, bloggers and YouTubers who helped bring Timelessness to the spotlight, especially Fantasy Book Nerd for his fantastic work supporting indie authors and great taste in books, Vesna S. for her earnest reviews, Tessa Hastjarjanto for the #indieApril sale, and the organizers of QuaranCon for giving me a chance to take part in one of their panels.

To Lisa Gilliam for editing another manuscript written in English but punctuated in Portuguese.

To Taylor DeVayne for her diligent proofreading of the ARC.

To Sarah Kempton for giving voice to these characters.

To Locke for always cheering me up when things got tough.

And finally, to you, for reading this series. I hope you enjoyed it much as I do. If so, please take a moment to post a review and tell your friends about it.

Until next time!